D. A. PUPA

THE MAGICIAN

A THRILLER

WingSpan Press

Published in the United States and the United Kingdom by WingSpan Press, Livermore, CA

The WingSpan name, logo and colophon are the trademarks of WingSpan Publishing.

Publisher's Cataloging-in-Publication Data

Pupa, D. A.
The magician / D. A. Pupa.
pages cm
ISBN: 978-1-59594-685-0 (hardcover)
ISBN: 978-1-59594-531-0 (pbk.)
ISBN: 978-1-59594-869-4 (e-book)
1. Serial murderers—Fiction. 2. College students—Fiction. 3. United States. Federal Bureau of Investigation—Officials and employees—Fiction.
I. Title.
PS3616.U63 M34 2014
813—dc23

2014941009

First edition 2014

Printed in the United States of America

www.wingspanpress.com

1 2 3 4 5 6 7 8 9 10

ACKNOWLEDGMENTS

To my mom, Anita, thanks for inspiring me to reach for my dreams and write this novel that I've had sitting inside my head for over twenty years. To my dad, Angelo, thanks for your never ending encouragement, wise advice and insightful editing. Most importantly I'd like to thank my parents for their support, guidance and love. Both of you are truly wonderful people and the world is a better place because of you. You've taught us all of life's important lessons, like the value of family and those you care about.

To my brother, Frank, and my sister, Lisa, thanks for all of your efforts editing and patiently listening to countless discussions regarding the book. Your feedback was invaluable and truly added to making my story better. More importantly thanks for always being there and knowing we always have each other, to laugh or find a shoulder to lean on. You are part of what makes my heart beat...your enthusiasm and never ending support is boundless. I love you both.

To my brother-in-law, Bill, and my sister-in-law, Jen, thanks for your extensive efforts in reading and then re-reading my novel. Your constant feedback was especially helpful. I love having you as part of our family.

To Olivia, my godchild, thanks for your help with showing me cover design ideas. To Lily, Danny, Julia, Sophia and Grace for always making me smile...that includes you too, Liv.

To Flora, my mother-in-law, for always making me feel at home in Arizona and of course, your stuffed cabbage. I wish you weren't so far away.

To Tessa Moeller, the talented artist who created the painted artwork, adding an extra vision to my words. To Carly, my niece, for offering to help when needed.

To Remo Strada, my friend and genius graphic artist who handled and created the book design and layout...you were invaluable.

To Emily Aronson, at Princeton University, for all of your help and being the embodiment of the esteemed university you represent.

To Lisa B, my cousin, for all of your efforts in helping to get my book recognized. Thank you for being another sister and all that means.

To Suzanne Luna, Will & Melissa Defer, CJ & Aleigh, and Varun, thank you for your generous support and special contributions.

To all my extended family (on both sides), I am blessed to have all of you in my life.

To all my friends, for making my life more fun, with a special mention to Mike Derosa and Tom Whille for helping after the book's completion in marketing my story.

To Carrie & Meg, for your help in editing and more importantly, making the commitment to be my personal assistants when we have a bestseller (lol). Your organizational skills will be greatly needed.

To my cousins, Shannon, Brunee, Jackie and Gerard for providing your legal, law enforcement and criminology expertise.

To my cousin, Brian, for helping me create a website and being like another brother to me.

To my Aunt Mary & Uncle Sam Ferretti, who have always treated me like a second son, thank you...which leads me to their actual son, my cousin, Tino and his wife, Natalie, it's great to have family like the both of you. What you've done for me is truly touching.

I'd also like to send out a prayer to those who are no longer with us, but are nevertheless here in spirit...my grandparents and Ronnie.

To my wife, Lisa, thanks for your friendship and being my inspiration. You have been with me every step of the way on this journey and those yet to come. Thanks for putting up with me, allowing me to wake you up in the middle of the night to throw out an idea and discuss it. Thanks for serving me my much needed tea in order to fuel the countless hours spent on my laptop writing. You are the love of my life.

THE MAGICIAN

CHAPTER 1

"May 26, 2016, NJ – Present Day"

THE ORANGE HUE OF THE EARLY MORNING SUN WAS CASTING ITS RAYS upon the sea shore community of Spring Lake, New Jersey. Midway down the boardwalk sat former F.B.I. agent, Frank Sorello, completely immersed in the recent number one bestseller *The Taking*. The book was a follow up to *The Blood Hunt*, by hot new novelist Gary Jones. He was just finishing the first chapter and couldn't put it down. The novel's preface could've been just a coincidence, but something didn't feel right. Every sentence he read made him more uneasy. Frank's blood pressure began to rise. Two years earlier, after finishing the author's first book he had a similar reaction and this led to a lot of people worrying about him. Frank wondered if he was losing it.

Most of the town was still asleep this brisk, spring morning and only a handful of people were at the beachfront attempting to get a jump start on their weekend. So when Frank saw Sarah jogging in his direction, he managed to force a smile. She was like clockwork, an early riser always on schedule. Frank's own routine had been altered today. Sarah was the reason he was reading and not out running. He wondered now if that had been a good idea.

The two of them first met about six months ago. It had been the day before Thanksgiving and Frank headed to the boardwalk to resume running after an unplanned hiatus. The sun had just risen on what was a particularly cold day. Frank liked it that way because the boardwalk would be desolate. Sarah had come early too, because the quiet afforded her time to think. She was questioning her current romantic relationship.

Sarah said, "Hello," as she noticed the tall, good looking man tying the shoelaces on his Nikes.

He looked up, smiled and said, "Hi, I'm Frank."

She smiled back, "Nice to meet you, Frank. I'm Sarah."

Frank couldn't help notice her long dark hair, perfect legs and big green eyes. She reminded him of Juliette, and he asked her impulsively, "Would you like to run together?"

Sarah said, "Sure," and laughed as she said, "hope you can keep up."

Frank liked her confidence and said, "I'll try, but take it easy on me."

Sarah smiled. "Only if you're nice," she said flirtatiously.

The seven mile round trip from Spring Lake to Avon flew by as they chatted. Frank learned that Sarah was a psychologist in nearby Sea Girt. He volunteered that he was retired from the F.B.I., but was guarded in sharing anything more personal. After that day, they hardly ever ran without one another. As the months went by, their friendship grew and the talks became more intimate. Frank spoke of his wife's brutal murder. This surprised him because he never discussed the tragedy. Sarah had an easiness about her that allowed him to open up. It had been cathartic. Yesterday, after finishing their daily run, Frank told her he wasn't planning on jogging today. He knew Sarah was training for the New York City Marathon, so it was really no surprise to see her running solo, or to see the smirk on her face as she continued on towards Avon.

Frank was a creature of habit. He could've started the morning as usual, meeting Sarah for their run. Instead, after his morning cup of coffee he headed out to the beach to read *The Taking*. He hoped to rid himself of the angst the first book caused. Frank shared with Sarah the details of that outburst. He had drawn a connection between Gary Jones and the lunatic who savagely killed his wife. Everyone, including his superior viewed this theory as meritless, the result of an overwrought mind. Frank was irrationally obsessed during those months. Sarah understood his response given the circumstances.

She remembered Frank mentioning that he liked to read, especially thrillers, but tended to avoid them now. During their last run, Sarah suggested that he pick up the new novel and approach it as he always had before, not as an F.B.I. investigator or even a grieving spouse, but as an avid reader. She clearly knew Juliette's death was the root of his inability to move forward. Frank had been stripped of his sense of control.

He decided to read Jones' second novel at the prodding of his running mate to address that very issue. Frank secretly feared it might incite the same reaction previously induced by *The Blood Hunt*. The fixation over his wife's murder made him search for answers, even when none were there. When he hadn't responded to her suggestion, Sarah let it go. In fact, she worried that she overstepped her bounds, because Frank mentioned he wasn't going to run with her the following day. Sarah recognized she was his friend and not his therapist. So when he didn't meet her at the usual spot for their morning ritual and later noticed him reading further down the boardwalk, she felt satisfaction and smiled. Frank had taken her advice.

It had been a little less than three years since his retirement from the Federal Bureau of Investigations Violent Criminal Apprehension Program (ViCap). This unit was responsible for analyzing information about homicides, sexual assaults, missing persons and often serial murder. The horrors he witnessed had fractured the man he once was and though the healing process had begun, it was far from complete.

Following the murder of his wife, Juliette, Frank went through a deep depression. During this time he withdrew from his normal patterns and became reclusive. His anger and pain pushed him toward self destruction and he couldn't find his way. With no emotional support system to lean on, Frank crumbled. Juliette had always provided him with a reservoir of strength and now she was gone. There was no one else left to pick up the pieces. His parents died when he was young and he had been their only child. It was all too much for him to handle and this culminated in a three month long drinking binge.

Frank's free fall didn't slow down until his long time martial arts teacher, Grand Master Daniel, intervened. The sensei didn't do this right away, because he wanted to respect his student's need to grieve. Although there had been a sudden withdrawal from instruction, it was understandable. Juliette's loss was brutal and unexpected. Healing would take time. However, when another student mentioned having seen Frank during lunchtime completely drunk, Master Daniel recognized the man had lost his center. His student had always exhibited an inimitable willpower to focus his energy and overcome any obstacle. Frank's mental acuity surpassed even his physical gifts, so this recent behavior was very troubling. The sensei saw Frank as a younger version of himself and could no longer watch his most prized student fall apart. Grand Master Daniel reached out and made contact.

"Frank, you loved Juliette and she loved you. Your loss was unimaginable and pain can lead someone down a road from which they don't return. Is this what your wife would have wanted? Honor her memory and live."

"I just feel so lost...I don't know if..." Frank began to cry.

The sensei held his student and allowed him to weep. As a grandmaster, the lifetime of training brought much wisdom. The martial arts were grounded in respecting life, family and tradition.

"Thank you, Sensei."

Grandmaster Daniel let go of his student and bowed. This had been his most important lesson.

Before the murder Frank was an affable guy who liked being around people. He was now more sullen and socially isolated. He came back to the Dojo for training, but the physical regime still didn't erase his emotional trauma, even though Master Daniel had always preached the connection between body and mind. So Frank stopped drinking and a gradual resiliency surfaced. He began to focus not only on his physical well-being, but also his mental health.

The months away had not affected Frank's physique; the muscle memory came back quickly. At six foot five, the former agent was still an imposing presence. Being a third degree black belt and all it entailed kept his body chiseled. It wasn't quite as easy to return to his previous emotional state, but the serendipitous connection he made with Sarah, began the more difficult process of healing his heart. Slowly, the old Frank started to resurface.

Normally, he would have been somewhere far from this serene shore town engrossed in capturing some psychopathic monster. After all, Frank was the most decorated and high profile investigator at The Bureau over the last two decades, having caught three of the most notorious serial killers in history. At twenty-seven, he caught Arthur Montrell, who had been responsible for the murders of nine young women. At twenty-nine, he almost died apprehending Derek Hernandez, who killed four families in nine months. Then at thirty-two, he took down the "Tinseltown Strangler" the most infamous and nationally publicized case of his career. Yet, now sitting on the bench, each page read, brought him further and further from where he wanted to go.

Frank couldn't shake his past. The knot in his stomach was real, stemming from an instinctive sixth sense. He knew where this was headed. Frank retired at forty-three, emotionally shattered by the pursuit of the only killer that had escaped him. This psychopath left eleven people dead in a span of one year and then completely vanished. Eight months after the murder of his wife he quit the Bureau.

It had been a new experience for Frank, a case that led to no resolution. Juliette was dead, along with many others. He had not been able to find justice for the bereaved families. Their haunted looks reminded him of his personal torture. Every day he had flashbacks of finding Juliette's bloody body. Two years ago, those vivid images sent him over the edge while professing Gary Jones was a serial killer. The murders drained Frank of his desire to continue working for the ViCap unit and pursuing other violent killers. In fact, it led to his retirement. His boss urged him to reconsider, telling him to take a leave of absence and leave the door open, but Frank was done.

During this timeframe, the media had jumped all over a story written by a small town reporter about the first murder in the chain. The writer, Brian Webster, grew up in an area close to where the initial killing took place. Consequently, he possessed a strong familiarity with the town's history and its more accomplished residents. The ambitious, young scribe recognized there was a possible storyline that might draw attention. In 2004, he had attended a heavily promoted magic festival honoring Appleton's most famous former resident, Harry Houdini.

Brian vaguely recalled that several historical facts might match up with the recent murder. He decided to explore the possibility. According to his research, there were several coincidences tied to the deceased magician. The killer's first victim had been a Jewish rabbi murdered in Appleton, Wisconsin on the thirty-first of October. A pamphlet had been found near the body from Wahl Organ builders. It was located at 320 North Durkee Street. The owners and employees of the store were all questioned about the homicide. Eventually, they were all cleared as suspects. The flier from the shop created yet another connection. The family-run business was the original wooden structure of the former Temple Zion. It had been built in 1884. Ironically, Appleton's first Rabbi was Mayer Samuel Weiss. He had led the Jewish congregation since 1878, but was dismissed just prior to the Temple's opening. The community was in the process of embracing the Reform Temple's practice of worshipping in English. The former Rabbi only spoke German. The man was Houdini's father. Even after his dad was replaced, his son still considered the town his home. Although Harry Houdini's actual birthplace was Budapest, during his rise to fame he claimed to have been born in Appleton. The final connection was that Houdini had died on the same day as this initial killing, the thirty-first of October.

A few months later, when it was apparent a serial killer was at work, the Associated Press reprinted Webster's story. The unusual facts surrounding the Rabbi, which strangely connected to Harry Houdini, coupled with the killer's penchant to vanish without ever leaving a trace of evidence, led to a national newspaper following up on this story and branding the serial killer, "The Magician."

When the murders suddenly stopped it left Frank feeling lost. His wife Juliette had been the last brutal act of the madman and he hadn't been able to prevent it. The guilt stayed with him for a long time and just recently he began to let it go. It seemed impossible before he met Sarah. She tapped into his desire to feel alive again, to relax and enjoy simple pleasures once more; like reading a novel. Now as Frank sat alone on the bench, he knew that could not be the case. Yes, he knew that "The Magician" had written *The Taking*. Sweat broke out on his forehead and Frank dropped the book to the ground.

It was half past six in the morning when the Director of the F.B.I., Rob Sullivan, looked at the number on his private cell phone to see who was calling. He was surprised, realizing it had been two years since he and Frank had spoken. At that time Frank had been drinking heavily and was despondent over the loss of his wife. Rob had listened to Frank talk of an outlandish theory regarding the "Magician Case" involving a fictional bestseller. Being aware of his agent's pain, he wanted to be sympathetic, but had to let Frank know there was absolutely no evidence...aside from pure conjecture. Since Frank was fragile, Rob tried not to sound harsh and advised him to begin rebuilding his life. That was the last they had spoken, until now.

Rob wanted to reach out numerous times to Frank after his retirement. But once the pursuit of the "Magician" became a cold case, he felt it forced Frank to confront the loss of Juliette. Her murder had nearly destroyed him and Rob knew contact would not allow the open wounds to heal. The Director fought his desire to convince Frank to come back and work again. It had been a big loss for the bureau to lose their best man at hunting these predators. Frank often found connections where others simply missed them. His insight into the minds of these psychopaths was a blessing for the bureau, but a curse for Frank. So when Rob answered the phone, he wondered what could have precipitated this early morning call.

"Rob, it's Frank. He's alive! The Magician is alive!" The tone of his voice was urgent and desperate, bringing a sense of déjà vu to the Director of The F.B.I.

"Hey, Frank, settle down, this sounds awfully familiar. I thought we settled this last time, when I suggested you get it together." Rob paused and said, "I don't mean to sound like an ass, but have you been drinking?"

Frank tried to respond calmly. "No, I haven't had a drink in almost two years and I know how this comes across. I've got to come down to D.C., I'm one hundred percent certain this psycho's back."

"Frank, are you sure this has nothing to do with you not being able to let go, well you know, because of...Juliette. It's been years since his last known kill. This guy always loved the spotlight. If he were back, I wouldn't need you to tell me. It'd be all over the headlines. He had the taste, you said it yourself when everything just stopped. We both agreed he either died, left the country or was already in prison."

"You're right, I did say that and I know where you're coming from, but it's been two years since I fell apart and have you heard from me even once on this matter? I've gotten my shit together since then. I understand your skepticism, but in the past when I told you I was sure about something, was I ever wrong? Five minutes ago I broke into a cold sweat and knew I had to call! We need to talk."

"Okay. What's changed, Frank?"

"This has to be face to face. Maybe I'm asking a lot, Rob, but what if you ignore this and I'm right?" Frank didn't want to talk about the book on the phone because he felt Rob would cut him off at the first mention of Gary Jones."

"Frank, what murders have gotten your attention?"

"Listen, I chased this psychopath for years and I deserve your time. It's him. Once you see the evidence you'll agree. Rob, last year I flew off the handle and told everyone involved what I was thinking. I haven't spoken a word about this, because I know how the media would have a field day with it. I'm not looking to embarrass you or the Bureau."

"Okay, Frank, I'll arrange a flight for you this afternoon. My assistant will contact you with the details. Let's hope for everyone's sake you're wrong."

"I wish that were the case, but it's not. He's still out there. I'll brief you when I arrive in D.C., Rob, thanks for agreeing to meet me," as he hung up the phone.

The F.B.I.'s Director felt a sickness sweep over him. "Dear God, for everyone's sake I pray he's wrong," Rob muttered.

CHAPTER 2

ON THE FLIGHT FROM NEWARK, FRANK ATTEMPTED TO COMPOSE himself. In order to catch this abomination he had to be focused. So he spent his time on the plane ride acclimating himself to what he was about to undertake and went back to reading the book. Frank landed at Dulles Airport in the early afternoon and was met at the gate by a recent graduate of the Academy. When he saw the young agent at the gate he felt a sense of déjà vu. He remembered when he started at the F.B.I. and was once given basic tasks such as these driving assignments. Before long, he was spearheading major investigations. Frank wondered with a sense of melancholy, if he had only done something else, would Juliette still be here.

"Agent Sorello. Hi, I'm Agent Tucker. It's an honor to meet you, sir. We spent so much time at Quantico studying your cases. You're a legend at the Academy."

Frank shook his hand, smiled, and said, "Hi."

I've been instructed to take you right to Director Sullivan. Do you have any luggage, sir?" the recent Bureau graduate asked.

"No luggage, I came in a hurry. As for the compliments, thanks... though I'm sure some of what you heard was exaggerated. Hey, I just gave every assignment all I had. If you do the same, someday they may be discussing you at the Academy," Frank stated graciously.

It was difficult for him to make small talk given the circumstances, but Frank didn't want to seem rude to the eager agent. So during the forty minute ride over to F.B.I. headquarters on Pennsylvania Avenue, the two agents talked about training at Quantico and how things changed since Frank attended. Electronic surveillance and

9

the sheer speed at which information could be accessed were obviously advanced from twenty plus years ago. But in whatever ways the methodology had changed, one thing remained the same; everyone who went through the rigors of training was expected to do so with a commitment to excellence.

Upon arrival at headquarters, Frank felt the excitement begin to rush through his veins. He was here to finish what the "Magician" had started and smiled knowing there would be no escape for the maniac. Not this time.

When Sorello entered the office of Director Sullivan, it felt like he'd never left. Every fiber in his body was energized. Rob, he noticed, hadn't changed. His eyes still showed that fiery resolve. It was this very commitment which led him to the top of the hierarchy at the Bureau. Rob possessed an uncanny ability to recognize talent in people and get the best out of them. He was a master at seeing the big picture and understanding when to delegate and when to lead. Frank had some of these same characteristics, but more often than not, took over as the alpha dog and ended up ruffling feathers in the process.

Rob stood up and shook his former agent's hand.

"Frank, it's been a long time," he said while assessing his former agent.

He noticed the clarity in Frank's eyes; it appeared he had stopped drinking.

"You look to be in much better shape than the last time I saw you. I'm sorry you had to go through all of that. Anyhow, I hope you're wrong about things. Sit down and tell me what makes you believe he's back."

Before he sat down in the chair across from the Director, he dropped the copy of *The Taking* on Rob's desk. Immediately, he saw the hint of disappointment in his former boss's eyes.

"Frank, I thought you were past this," Rob said with sadness. "I believed you uncovered something serious and based in reality, not the same bullshit."

"Hey, Rob, I get it. I understand your doubt, but humor me for a minute. You'll change your opinion pretty quickly. Start with reading the preface."

CHAPTER 3

Preface from "The Taking"

I WANT TO ACKNOWLEDGE IN THIS BOOK THE MANY PEOPLE WHO HELPED inspire me throughout this journey, but since there are too many to name and you know who you are...

I will just say thanks to the man who led me to this place in time, without you so many of the individuals that drove me would not have been there to stimulate my creative process...

Here's to my compass and the man who challenges me to strive for greater heights...Frank S.

CHAPTER 4

ROB PICKED UP THE BOOK AND READ THE PREFACE. THE DOUBT DIDN'T dissipate from his eyes. He placed the novel back down.

"Frank, you're better than this. Back then, I understood what was happening with you. Finding Juliette the way you did, well, that would have fucked anyone up. So when you reacted the way you did, after reading that novel of his…I knew you hadn't healed. But Frank, it's almost four years since her death. I'd hoped you were getting better," Rob paused and said with frustration, "How many Franks are there in the country? In fact, let me grab the Washington, D.C., white pages or call four-one-one and ask how many Franks there are with the last name beginning in S., it'd be too many to count. That's just in this city. C'mon Frank, you know this is paper thin!"

"Rob, I expected that. Shit, if you didn't respond that way I'd of thought you'd lost it too. I wanted you to read that first, in order to piece it with what follows. In investigations, when coincidences begin to pile up, they're not coincidence! Read chapter two and then tell me what you think. I didn't come here half-assed crazy… this is without doubt 'The Magician.'"

Frank reflected for a moment, as Rob listened.

"It's not like *The Blood Hunt*, events loosely connected to one another. Take a look and tell me you disagree. If you still think I've lost it, then I'll walk out of this office forever. I will, however, track down and kill that motherfucker with or without your help."

Rob met Frank's gaze, as he picked up the novel and began to read.

CHAPTER 5

"Chapter 2 of The Taking"

"THE TAKER" SAT ALONE IN THE GARAGE AS THE LAST LIGHT OF DAY began to fade, waiting patiently to quench his blood thirst. Yet, as he heard the wind whip into a frenzy it fed his lust. Hurricane Sandy had been predicted as the storm of the century, the Jersey Coast was its targeted epicenter. The fury of the night was coming.

Two days earlier he had left a young woman dismembered in Pittsburgh as bait. The famous hunter of madmen would go there and leave his own home unprotected. The Taker was always one step ahead. As the famous detective pursued leads in western Pennsylvania, the taker of lives had driven directly to the affluent seaside community of his nemesis. On the day before the storm, he observed families pack their luggage and leave their homes. The predator then watched the home of his adversary to see whether or not the beautiful wife moving about inside would seek refuge from the storm too. He had a perfect vantage point to observe her as he sat in an abandoned home across the street. The family who lived there had chosen to heed the advice of the authorities and sought refuge elsewhere. If they had ignored the storm warnings, they would have suffered the same fate as what he coveted. Emily apparently chose to ride it out and stay, not knowing the terror that lie waiting. Her husband would not be able to save her, just as he had failed to save the others, in his endless pursuit of this monster. Before the winds became too violent, he crossed the street and entered the garage of the home. The outside door had not been locked. He placed the bag he

13

had been carrying on the floor. It was the day of the storm. The time was near and he savored the craving.

Night fell and still the madman waited. As the hours passed the storm grew. Electricity was lost and the town was gripped in darkness. Howling winds ripped trees from the ground the way he had ripped limbs from unsuspecting prey. About midnight, he rose and left the garage wearing his night vision goggles. Casually grabbing a large branch that lay on the ground, the taker threw it into the picture window. Shattered glass let the wind and rain in, along with death. Quickly he entered a nearby room on the first floor, noticing it was a home library. His wet footprints were immediately disguised by the rain pouring inside.

He heard the footsteps come down the stairs to investigate the loud crash, followed by cries of exasperation. Emily set down her flashlight and quickly attempted to cover the broken window with a large blanket, but realized it was hopeless. So she did the next best thing by placing several blankets on the floor to try to absorb some of the water. Emily needed some help, knowing she couldn't handle the situation alone. But what could she do? The power had been out for hours and there would be no way to reach anyone. Emily now wished she had listened to her husband and stayed with family members out of town. Crossing a street with the eighty mile an hour gusts outside would be impossible. Clearly it was too late to leave her home; the danger was too great outside. There would be no help from the neighbors or anyone else. Not knowing what else to do, Emily went back up the stairs.

When she entered her bedroom she tried not to worry about the damage downstairs and told herself that when her husband got back he would take care of everything. She changed into her pajamas and took a valium to help fall asleep. After all, she could do nothing to change the situation. The intensity of this hurricane scared her and sleep would be her refuge. At least that is what she thought, not realizing the danger lurking below.

The Taker had noticed the countless books lining the walls of the room. There were volumes of professional books related to forensic evidence, psychopathology, and investigative techniques. Additionally, there were many novels on the shelves by James Patterson, Thomas

Harris and John Sandford. His photographic mind took it all in, tonight was going to be special. He exited the room and began to explore the first floor. The pictures on the wall captured the couple's life. The smiles on their faces he could not comprehend for he now only understood rage. Over the next hour he did what he had always done, attempted to take in the minutiae of humanity. He walked back in the library where he had placed his bag and opened it. Reaching in, and surveying his tools, tonight he chose the serrated knife and needle nose pliers.

Silently he began to move up the stairs. The storm was in full force and any noises would be masked by the hurricane. All power in the town was out and it was pitch black. He loved the darkness, quietly he entered the bedroom. Emily lay in a restless sleep unaware of his presence. The Taker looked down at her and watched her breathe. He was excited by the thought of her last moments of peace, for soon there would be fear, and he loved fear.

Emily's long brown hair was strewn across her pillow leaving her neck exposed. Now he thought, as he leaned close and licked her neck. She purred thinking her husband had somehow made it home, but as her mind cleared she thought how could that have been possible. Seconds later her eyes opened wide expressing horror. Her scream was drowned by the storm's ferocity.

The Taker placed the chloroform cloth over Emily's mouth and allowed its vapors to depress her central nervous system until she was unconscious. Next he walked to the closet where four ties were selected to bind her hands and feet together. He picked out three formal business ties and one with a picture of John Lennon on it. He liked the idea of using something of the hunter's to help exterminate his prey and this tie seemed to especially suit his purpose. Now he would wait until the effects of the chemical began to wear off so he could observe her and the visceral responses to the pain he would inflict upon her.

Emily reopened her eyes and tears began to form. She lay naked and tied up staring at the man looking down at her, expecting him to rape her. She whimpered because she could not cry out for her mouth had been gagged. The Taker had no intention of performing this act; he had other things in store.

He picked up the knife that he used to cut off her clothes and ran the flat side of the blade across her breasts, careful not to cut her. There would be plenty of time for that. He loved to see the terror build almost more than when he would hurt her, but not quite as much. Emily began to shake and then he moved the knife down across her belly and lower across her thighs. Emily's muffled cries could not be heard even if she had been yelling from the top of her lungs. Frenzied winds and driving rain were flexing their power. Sandy was doing its damage and The Taker was about to unleash his wrath.

Emily began to pray as she watched the lunatic raise the knife above his head. Suddenly he plunged it down directly into the pillow next to her head. Urine spread onto the bed sheets and the madman smiled. The Taker loved the game. Now he pulled the blade up again and slowly ran the serrated edge with just the right amount of force to slice into Emily's skin down the length of her right arm. He made sure the cut was only on the surface of the flesh and avoided her veins and arteries. The Taker did not want his prey to bleed out. Emily's tears poured down her face as she realized she would never see her husband again. This thought hurt more than the physical agony she felt, as the psycho repeated this procedure down her other arm. The Taker applied slightly more pressure cutting down the length of her legs because he expected his victim to go into shock like the others eventually did.

Blood covered the bed and The Taker ran his fingertip inside the slice he had made on her thigh and brought it to his lips. Her blood's metallic taste was an elixir to him. Next he placed the knife down and reached for the needle nose pliers. It would all be over soon.

Emily passed out from the pain of having her nails snapped off. The Taker placed down the pliers and picked the knife back up. He was about to plunge the knife into her and changed his mind. He thought he would make this special; he had never performed the taking with his bare hands. So he placed the knife back down and put his hands around her neck and began to squeeze. Emily's eyes opened and she began to buck wildly as he applied more pressure. He watched the panic in her eyes turn to resignation and the life drain from her. Emily had been taken.

Calmly he walked to the master bathroom and removed his blood drenched clothes. Utilizing Emily's flashlight to see, he showered and then changed into the clean clothes from his bag. Next, he placed the soiled garments he had been wearing inside a plastic bag and put that into his travel bag. The Taker did not worry about leaving forensic evidence. He had never been fingerprinted and would not be in any law enforcement database. DNA evidence did not matter to him because he was too smart to be caught. Evidence collected by the forensics team would only matter in a trial and that would never happen. The forensic material gathered by the police and F.B.I. had led them nowhere. They were his minions. They served his need to be feared.

In the morning, the storm had released its grip and The Taker left the house wearing a hooded jacket. He was careful not to be seen as he disappeared. The community was too concerned with its own damage to be aware of his presence. The killer vanished in plain sight, how appropriate he thought to himself.

CHAPTER 6

AS THE DIRECTOR BEGAN READING THE CHAPTER, DOUBTS STILL remained. Gary Jones certainly utilized some poetic license, not everything written was factually accurate to the case. Certainly there seemed to be more direct correlations than in the first novel. Yet the author could have heard the rumors circulating at the time of Juliette's death. After the murder, locals in Spring Lake were likely to have gotten wind of some scuttlebutt. Gossip would spread and if Gary Jones had done any research then this could be easily explained. At the time, the Director had instructed everyone involved to not release any specific information regarding Juliette. Rob felt this would serve two purposes, control the media circus and pay deference to Frank's feelings.

Rob set down the book and said, "Frank, I'll assemble a task force, because I do agree it's worth checking out. But I'm sure you know I can't have you lead this investigation because of Juliette. I'll still want you involved because you may have more insight into the case than anyone and you've always had great instincts. So I'll bring you in as a consultant with access to whatever you need. I'm going to want us to act quickly, but at the same time cautiously. Understand me, I'll pull you off the minute I think you can't handle it."

"I appreciate that, Rob. I agree with the sense of urgency, in fact if this were two years ago, I would have already found where this fucker lived and taken his heart out. But now I know I need to avenge my wife's death the way she would have wanted. Juliette always believed in doing things the right way and I want to honor that. But as for me being cautious, it's not like Gary Jones didn't just say come and get me! He's now the one that needs to watch his back."

"Frank, I agree with you, but the reason for circumspection is twofold. I didn't rise to my position at the Bureau without looking at the big picture. First, we don't need the media all over this until we've established more evidence of his guilt and have him in custody. Second, and here is the part you may not want to hear, what if Gary Jones isn't 'The Magician'?"

"Rob, are you kidding me? This psychopath laid out a road map of my wife's killing and for whatever sick reasoning he has, I'm sure he's already expecting me to come after him!"

"That might be true and if I were sitting in your shoes that would be my thought process. I know you want him, I do too. The deductions you drew after the first novel were without any real merit, other than your gut instinct. That gut instinct may now turn out to be right. But I have to ask myself, why is Gary Jones just announcing to us that he is a murdering sociopath? If it is him, every psychological profile we have of 'The Magician' is wrong. It's not like he has a need for repentance."

"Alright Rob, what other explanations do we have for a book coming out which details information only the killer could have known about?"

"Only the killer?" Robert said inquisitively.

"Yeah, like I told him," Frank said sarcastically.

"I didn't say you told him. But there were a number of people on your task force who were aware of the specific circumstances regarding Juliette. Gary Jones is a novelist. He has written two bestsellers about serial killers. Is it possible, that he has done research about you, in order to help aid him in his process? Is it also possible, that particular someone, decided to share information with him about the specifics of her death? Frank, I'm not saying that's the case, but that's why we need to proceed with caution."

"I never even considered that when I read about Juliette. I was so filled with rage I didn't consider any other possibilities. I just wanted to get this psychopath. Even on my way here from Jersey, all I thought of was fighting my urge to kill him," Frank stated begrudgingly.

"That's my concern. I have to know you'll be able to keep your emotions in check. Now if this turns out to be leaked information that helped some guy sell a goddamn book, I'll have that agent out on his ass. In fact, they'll be prosecuted for divulging classified information. I'm sorry, Frank, if that turns out to be the case; I know how much you want this bastard. But logically, that makes more sense than a killer who carefully evaded us during an entire murder spree and then just divulges his identity in a book. Yet, I'll admit from experience that logic doesn't always dictate the facts. Maybe Gary Jones is "The Magician," and just wants to bask in the glory of his infamy. Maybe he wants the fame and notoriety the media will give him. I can imagine the storyline, The F.B.I. were so inept in tracking him that he had to write a bestseller for us to catch him. That could be motivation for a psychopath."

Sorello knew he needed to stay in control and responded in a measured tone, "Either way, I want to meet Gary Jones. The monster who murdered my wife or the guy who profited from the way she died."

"Frank, if it turns out to be the latter, I'll make sure you don't get prosecuted for breaking his fucking nose. If it's the former, then we make sure this maniac gets what he deserves."

"Rob, what if Gary Jones has another idea? What if he's a serial killer that just loves games and wants us to arrest him? Next, he proclaims innocence stating all the evidence is circumstantial. He then hires a defense team claiming he was given off the record information about a murder that was never reported and just wrote about it in the novel."

Rob pondered that for a moment and said, "Interesting thought, Frank. What if he believes a judge wouldn't issue a warrant because everything we've got is purely circumstantial. He just states that he's an author protecting a source of information. That certainly could be a worthy defense. Plus, we don't have much in the way of forensics. All DNA, fingerprints and blood samples were singular to their own murder site...indicating anything we've collected was more than likely, left by house visitors. Nothing can be tied to any other murder scene. Even if we're lucky and something was left by our guy, we currently have nothing from Gary Jones to match against our own forensics. Hell, without any hard evidence, this might not even get past a grand jury."

"Rob, there are other ways to lift a fingerprint or collect a hair follicle. If that's all that stands in our way, I'll find a way around that little problem. However this plays out, I'll need to meet with your task force so we can get things moving and determine who the fuck this guy really is."

"That sounds like a good plan. Go to your hotel and get some sleep, because once this begins you may not be getting much rest. I'll have everyone briefed by tomorrow."

"What time do you want me here?"

"Given the nature of what we're potentially dealing with, how about seven?"

"See you then," Frank said as he got up and shook the Director's hand.

He contemplated getting some sleep, but not before going over *The Taking* with a fine tooth comb. Rest would come later.

Rob picked up the phone as soon as Frank left the office and began making the necessary phone calls. He knew this required his immediate attention.

CHAPTER 7

"1998 – Los Angeles"

SAM CARLSON WAS ONE OF THE MOST SUCCESSFUL MOVIE PRODUCERS in Hollywood. His wife Amy was gorgeous and a well known writer. She had written several top selling novels and her most recent book was a number one bestseller. They lived together in a twenty-eight room mansion in Malibu with their only child. Their son James was eight years old and possessed an I.Q. that was off the charts. Everyone considered their life to be charmed.

Yet below the surface, their storybook life had its own set of troubles. Their son since birth always seemed a bit different. When James was five, Amy caught her husband having an affair with a young aspiring actress, named Sophia Nero. Prior to catching him in the act, Amy had suspected Sam of being unfaithful, but didn't want to believe it. The fledgling actress had been cast opposite one of Hollywood's top leading men in a huge budget film. Amy loved Sam deeply, but distrust crept into her head upon learning of this decision. Sophia was twenty-two years old and had only been in three low budget movies before this part.

Amy knew her husband wasn't a risk taker and always stuck with his formula when putting together big budget pictures. She knew Sam like the back of her hand and this casting was so unlike him. Her husband had always chosen top box office draws as his leads in major films. Amy loved her husband deeply and wanted so much for her fears not to be true.

They had met on a beautiful summer day, at a local coffee shop in Malibu. She was only twenty-four at the time and an unknown, aspiring author. The ocean she romanticized was her muse, so Amy made sure to find a table with a view. She was entrenched in writing her first book when Sam swept her off her feet.

All Amy remembered when she heard the words, "What are you working on?" were the bluest eyes she had ever seen.

The rest was history.

Once Sam and Amy began dating, she became aware of his power in Hollywood. They would attend parties with famous celebrities and go out to dinner with movie stars. It was all very intoxicating. Even with the deference paid to him by the rich and famous; Sam remained unassuming whenever they were together. His magnetism was impossible for her to resist. Not a day went by without Amy reminiscing about how lucky she'd been.

Therefore, it had been devastating when she decided to come home early from a book tour and found Sam in bed with this actress. Amy screamed like a wounded animal and smashed a window while throwing whatever she could find at her husband. Still in a fit of rage, she practically dragged the actress out of her home. Afterwards, Amy wept inconsolably.

The next day, she tried to find some measure of solace and focused all her thoughts on her son. She didn't want to think about Sam. Amy kept telling herself, over and over, how lucky it was that James hadn't seen the outburst. She would try to hide her pain and hysteria. After all, her little boy had never been good at controlling his own emotions. With all the luxuries in the world, James still seemed unhappy. Amy wanted to protect him from potential worries and further sadness.

Despite this effort, the images of betrayal were too much to handle. The purity of her marriage was now tainted. Conflicted feelings tore Amy up inside. They argued constantly. Still, she couldn't find the resolve to leave and ended up giving her husband another chance. Sam cried, promising never to hurt her again.

For months they slept in separate bedrooms and eventually began couples' therapy. Their once perfect marriage was marred with distrust and pain. As the bickering became more contentious, their son began to act out beyond his regular tantrums. He started breaking things in the house on a daily basis. James became uncontrollable. This led to further stress on the marriage and their fighting intensified. The vicious circle continued.

Their marital therapist, Mary, eventually helped them recognize the cycle of discord. Sam and Amy consciously began to address each other's feelings and the marriage began to improve. Sam became more attentive and Amy less vitriolic. The constant tension gradually dissipated. Their relationship moved closer to what it had been prior to the indiscretion, but some residual impact remained.

Two years after the affair, Amy's lingering distrust led to her firing the couple's nanny. Lily was young and beautiful. She had been working for the Carlsons since the birth of their child and was like a second mother to James. Amy felt Sam had been acting friendlier than usual to Lily and this raised her insecurity by triggering memories of Sophia Nero. The jealousy was baseless because there had been no affair. Regardless, the decision to let her go was upsetting to everyone. Lily had always been like a part of the family, especially for the young boy.

During this time, James became more difficult than ever. In school, his perfect grades slipped and detention became the norm. Teachers began sending him down to the principal for bullying other children. This behavior escalated to fighting and James was suspended three times. The last of which, almost led to expulsion. He took a stapler from a teacher's desk and smashed it into a boy's face, resulting in fourteen stitches.

The Carlsons made a very large donation to the school and paid for a premier plastic surgeon. The injured boy ended up without any noticeable scarring. Finally, the family received a very substantial check to help quiet down the uproar. Yet even after this incident, the suspensions continued. James started skipping classes and disobeying all authority.

Sam and Amy began taking their son to a prominent child psychologist; Olivia Hart. James was extremely resistant to the idea. The sessions ended up being verbal chess matches. James seemed to take pleasure in his attempts to frustrate Olivia. Though he participated in talking about his behavior, a lack of remorse for his actions was apparent. Dr. Hart had an I.Q. of 147, which is considered to be in the highly gifted range of "genius". Yet at times she felt he was toying with her. This led to the therapist testing his intelligence quotient. She had never seen anyone handle the test so easily. Several sessions later, Doctor Hart informed his parents that James had an I.Q. of 200, which is often referred to as "unmeasurable genius." Sam and Amy knew their son was extremely intelligent, but didn't realize the extent of his intellect. Unfortunately, they were also told that their son had Conduct Disorder of the Childhood-Onset type.

Sam asked, "What exactly does that mean?"

Dr. Hart knew this was a difficult diagnosis for parents to hear about and tried to phrase things in a way that didn't scare them too much.

"Mr. & Mrs. Carlson, the simplest way to put it is, James isn't exhibiting age appropriate behavior in respecting the rights of others. Also, there seems to be little, if any, remorse in his actions."

Amy worriedly asked, "Will James grow out of this?"

"That's a good question; the course of this can be variable. Often it remits by adulthood."

"Is that likely?" Amy asked.

"James presents with both positives and negatives, as far as predictive factors go. Mild conduct problems are better and severe ones are obviously worse. Those presenting with extreme behaviors at an early age have a worse prognosis. This increased risk isn't a steadfast predictor, but rather a statistical commentary. I don't mean to scare you, but I'm just making you aware of the research," Dr. Hart said sympathetically.

"Are James' behaviors considered mild or severe?" Sam asked this because he was concerned about hearing younger kids have a worse prognosis.

"I'm most concerned with James striking a student with a stapler and his apparent lack of remorse. Immaturity and impulsivity could explain the action itself, but not the lack of guilt. The good news is there have been no more altercations and his incredible I.Q. is atypical of the disorder."

The statement shook them up. It was hard for them to imagine their son felt no guilt over his actions.

"I'd like to ask you a few questions. Have you noticed whether or not James has ever been cruel to animals?" Dr. Hart asked.

Sam and Amy answered simultaneously, "No."

Amy then added, "We don't have any pets."

"Why do you ask?" said Sam.

"I'm just exploring for extreme dysfunction. What about setting fires?" Olivia continued.

"Of course not," Sam said defiantly.

Clearly the questions were making the Carlsons feel uncomfortable.

"I don't mean for these questions to offend you, but I'm trying to get a better picture of what we're dealing with. It's good that James hasn't done any of those things. Of course, you'll keep me abreast of how things are going," Dr. Hart replied.

Amy said, "We will. So where do we go from here?"

"I'd like to see James twice a week, at least until we feel there's improvement. As for the both of you, be as loving and supportive as you can with him."

Amy fought back tears, "Is this our fault, Doctor Hart?"

Olivia smiled and said, "Stop worrying about blame and focus on our goal of helping James. Isn't that what we really want?"

"Thank you," the parents said as they left the office.

It was a Friday night, so they stopped for dinner at one of their favorite restaurants. While eating, they promised James things would get better. He didn't respond and was quiet the entire time. Sam and Amy hoped their pledge would come true. After the meal they headed straight home. When they arrived at their Malibu mansion, Amy and Sam hugged James, even though he tried to break from their embrace. Both parents said, "I love you," and expressed sorrow for not being better parents. James immediately went upstairs to his room.

Amy and Sam kissed and held each other in the large foyer. They desperately longed for what they once had together. The crisis with James sparked a need to connect and forgive. They both realized their family was in danger of falling apart.

Sam said to Amy, "Do you want to go to bed?"

She looked into his eyes and said, "Yes."

26

Walking hand in hand up the grand staircase they held renewed hope. Their faith would go unanswered.

Sam and Amy made love. They were unaware of the man in the ski mask watching them from inside their walk in closet. When they fell asleep, the trespasser quietly moved toward the bed. He took the paper weight from his pocket and casually smashed it into the head of Sam. Amy began to stir as her husband was knocked unconscious. The man quickly placed the gag into her mouth, muffling her screams. Amy struggled fiercely as he climbed on top of her, but he was too powerful. The man placed his hands around her neck and slowly squeezed the life from her body. In his frenzy he failed to notice the young boy standing frozen in the doorway behind him. After Amy was dead, the man moved over to Sam and strangled him.

James fearfully ran back toward his room. Tears streamed down his face as he opened his closet door. He moved to the rear and entered numbers on a keypad, opening the steel safe room that was installed in the back of his closet. He entered and shut the door, just like he'd practiced in the event of an intruder. James trembled.

The room had been part of the architecture of the mansion when it was built. It was virtually impenetrable from the outside and only the code could open it. Whenever the proper sequence was entered, it would send a signal to a security firm assigned to the household. No alarm would reach them. The interloper was an expert in security systems and disabled the alarms before the family returned home.

After Sam stopped breathing, the intruder casually left the bedroom and walked down the hallway. He enjoyed the sense of power that killing stirred in him. He was prepared to take his final victim; knowing only three people lived in the house after Lily's dismissal.

He had formed a delusional relationship with the nanny while observing her for months prior to tonight. The obsession started when Lily smiled at him as they passed each other in a local grocery store. He waited in his car for her to exit and followed her back to the Carlsons' mansion. When she drove into the gated estate he headed back into town. The next day, he waited in a park directly off the roadway, not far from the house. Lily's car never passed by that day, but it did the next afternoon. He began noting her hangouts whenever she left the estate. Then several weeks later, Lily surprisingly rented an apartment. This made it easier for him to track her. One day when Lily left for her new job, he couldn't resist the urge to know more about her. He broke into her home. Lily's secret admirer looked at photographs, smelled her clothing and read her e-mail. The password was written down on a piece of paper, inside of her desk drawer. One of the messages was from her sister Taylor in Arizona. The tone of the note was very consoling. Lily was apparently devastated from having been summarily dismissed from her longtime employer, the Carlsons. It wasn't the false accusation of sleeping with Sam that upset her, but rather having to sever her relationship with James. Lily cared deeply for the little boy.

The nanny's delusional suitor swore, then and there, that he would avenge her. The Carlsons' callousness would not be ignored. He would make them pay for hurting her. Tonight he reveled in his success.

When the man walked into the boy's room he wasn't asleep in bed. He noticed the closet door was slightly open. Checking to see if the child was hiding he saw the steel door at the other end of the large walk in closet. This infuriated him. He placed his hand on the door handle and as expected the door didn't open. The safe room was designed to be a last measure of defense that couldn't be breached. The man walked out of the closet and glanced under the bed. He then walked through each room in the mansion and made sure the boy was not anyplace else. The killer took valuables and cash as an afterthought in his search. He smiled thinking that these murders provided an added bonus, aside from the thrill.

After doing so, the madman left the grounds of the estate. On Monday, with the family unreachable, the L.A.P.D. was contacted by concerned friends. When the police arrived and found the bodies in the bedroom, they searched for James. Upon discovering the safe room they contacted the security firm for the code to open the door. When they punched in the numbers and entered the room,

James sat catatonic in the corner. Childhood Protective Services were immediately contacted to help with the traumatized boy.

The homicide department suspected the murders were a robbery that had gone wrong. But the detectives also checked to see if there was any family or friends that might benefit from the slayings. With this type of extreme wealth the possibility existed that someone stood to inherit a lot of money. These motives sent the initial investigation in the wrong direction. Four prostitutes had already been strangled by the same individual and a connection had not yet been made.

The man in the ski mask targeted the rich and famous after murdering Sam and Amy. Their killing spurred a new delusion, the little people didn't matter. Lily had been one such example, discarded like the trash. Now he craved retribution. His own dream of being a star was laughed at when he'd first come to town. The power players would pay with their lives. So once prominent members of Hollywood started turning up dead, the media dubbed him the "Tinseltown Strangler."

Frank Sorello would eventually follow the trail and apprehend the murderer. But that wouldn't change what had happened on this night, Sam and Amy Carlson were dead.

The case would gain national attention. The murders at this palatial Malibu estate would lead to Frank's fame as a slayer of monsters. His insight into their minds was a cursed gift. A movie would later be made, loosely based on his life. Yet the wealth Frank gained from the film would never compensate for what was taken away in the process.

The eight-year-old boy who survived that evening was also lost...but James would eventually find his own calling.

CHAPTER 8

"Present Day"

As Frank left his hotel the next morning to meet with the Director and the task force that was assembled, he felt that familiar exhaustion. He had spent most of the night reading and then re-reading Gary Jones' novel. It left him believing his initial gut reaction to be correct. This author was sending him a message, one that he would follow incessantly. Frank just had no idea where it led.

When Sorello entered the Director's office he was surprised to see just one person sitting across from Rob. It was a woman dressed in standard Bureau attire. She was strikingly beautiful, with dark hair, green eyes and a slim athletic figure. Both stood to rise as Frank approached the desk. The female agent's piercing eyes locked on to his gaze, as she put out her hand to greet him. Frank responded in turn and they shook hands.

"Hi, I'm Frank."

"No need to introduce yourself, your reputation precedes you. I'm Beth."

Rob interjected, "Frank, I'm sure you're wondering why Agent Gregg is the only person here this morning."

"That certainly crossed my mind," he said back.

"Until we have a better feel for what's going on, I want a tight circle. Beth's an outstanding agent and I believe she'll complement you perfectly. She's worked several high profile cases and proved to be invaluable. Beth is going to lead our task force. If the situation warrants, she has an entire team ready and waiting."

"Rob, I've always respected your judgment, so I'm sure Beth will be perfect."

This surprised the agent. Beth had expected Frank to be a bit resistant not running lead on a task force.

"Beth has a law degree from Harvard and I think she can cut through any blockades or red tape we might face in getting Gary Jones to talk to us. Also, her investigative mind is exceptional."

Beth smiled at the compliment, "Thanks, Rob."

She turned and looked at Frank. Beth knew that she could learn a lot from the former agent and wanted his respect.

She also wanted him to like her, so she said, "Frank, I want you to know I'll provide access to whatever you need. Do what you do best, solve the puzzle and catch him."

This response seemed to appease Frank's apprehension. Acting as a consultant with access to resources would be the best of both worlds. He could focus on the task at hand, while not worrying about stepping on anyone's toes. Leading a task force, could sometimes be tricky. You needed to get the best out of everyone, yet issue directives. Agents sometimes wanted to standout and break a case on their own initiative. Following orders were often at odds with this type of agenda. Frank didn't need the unnecessary conflict.

"Beth, I'm already beginning to like you," flashing a smile.

She was glad to see he responded the way she'd hoped.

"Frank..., Beth and I, both read *The Taking* last night and would like to compare our thoughts with yours. I'm sure you ignored my order for rest and spent the night poring over every word in Jones' book."

"Damn right and whatever doubt that surfaced yesterday in our meeting is gone. Rob, it's him. Not that there's much in the remaining chapters to suggest it, but it's in the small little pieces, that he's daring me to find. He's clever, but maybe too smart for his own good. His little game is going to end badly. I don't like being played with."

Rob replied, "Beth and I had time to talk this morning. We agreed there was nothing beyond the details concerning Juliette to suggest it's him. It's likely Gary Jones gained access to classified information to help write his novel."

Beth responded, "Rob, that's true, but I'm still bothered by something. The preface on its own would be inconsequential, but combining it with the details of Juliette is troubling. Jones thanking Frank S., might tip the scales in favor of him being the guy."

"Beth, I had this conversation yesterday. Let's get real for a minute, what are there, a million, two million people with that name? I'm not saying you're wrong, but the rest of the novel is about three more killings that aren't remotely linkable to 'The Magician.' In fact, no murder I am aware of matches them at all. It's pure fiction."

Frank listened to Rob and stared directly at him, "What if there was another coincidence? Would that change your mind?"

Beth and Rob looked at him with curiosity after that question.

"At the very end of the chapter where he described killing Juliette, he finished with the words, '*The killer vanished in plain sight, how appropriate he thought to himself.*' That seemed odd to me, almost unnecessary. So I thought about it some more and kept thinking why would it be appropriate? He could have just said that he vanished or disappeared. Instead, he added...'*how appropriate he thought to himself.*' Almost as if he were commenting on what comes naturally, like for instance, a magician vanishing. Magicians vanish in plain sight, Rob! Add that to him thanking me in the preface and aspiring to greater heights, well that assures me I'm right."

Beth and Rob sat transfixed, because in that moment, they realized what made Frank special. He picked up on imperceptible details and connected them. His sixth sense, his gut feelings, was nothing more than an innate ability to see what others couldn't.

"If this information wasn't leaked, then this asshole, is taunting you, Frank," Rob said incredulously.

"If it's true, he's showing his arrogance," Beth added.

"That's his fucking mistake," Frank whispered.

They still realized this theory would have to be proven, but deep down inside, they felt something was here.

CHAPTER 9

"2006"

I<small>T HAD BEEN EIGHT YEARS SINCE</small> J<small>AMES' PARENTS WERE MURDERED.</small> At that time he had been placed in the foster care system. Sam and Amy Carlson had no living relatives. Additionally, they had no friends that would be considered truly close. The power couple had done what was necessary to rise to Hollywood elite. This meant at times being calculating and sometimes ruthless in their business dealings. Their friendships were really nothing more than a wealth of acquaintances looking to gain entry into their rarified air. Accordingly, Sam and Amy's will designated all of their assets would go to their son, but the money was placed in a trust fund that couldn't be accessed until his eighteenth birthday, at which time he would be notified. James would inherit approximately two hundred million dollars. The will also stated that a five thousand dollar monthly stipend would be given to whoever eventually raised their son, right up until the time of his inheritance. Sam and Amy were advised by their attorneys to limit the amount provided. The legal experts also suggested that this remuneration not be given, until after a period of one year. Like the inheritance itself, this would be kept secret, until the time the stipend would be released. After all, they had no way of knowing, with certainty, if the money would actually be used for James. These precautions were instituted as a way to limit someone taking care of their son for the wrong reasons. Besides, Sam and Amy never really thought James would be left parentless at such a young age.

Nine families had sent James back to Child Welfare over the course of eight years. Most of these foster parents had the best of intentions and genuinely wanted to raise him. Sadly, some just wanted the money they received from the state. In either case, the selfless or the greedy, couldn't handle the troubled young boy.

James' initial foster care parents, Jeff and Samara Collins, were a young couple incapable of having children. They decided to give their love and support to a needy child and felt that if everything worked out they would adopt. During their interview the couple was given information about James's sad history. The case worker, Jen, told them he would require a lot of patience given his behavioral issues. The story broke Samara's heart, although Jeff was a little concerned that it might be more than they could handle. Samara begged Jeff to overcome his trepidation and he acquiesced. Money wasn't a factor in the decision since they were set financially. When Jen completed the interviews of all prospective parents, she chose them.

The relationship lasted two years, longer than any that followed. As much as they tried to show love, James met them with resistance. He stole money, constantly skipped out on school and his temper sometimes scared them. Samara and Jeff mutually agreed to return him to the Child Welfare Department after James lit a family photo album on fire. Luckily, Jeff smelled the smoke and put it out before it spread and burned the house down. It had been their breaking point. What they received from the state and the unexpected stipend that was paid out after the first year didn't matter. It had never been about the money with them and so it hurt all the more knowing that it hadn't worked out the way she and Jeff hoped. Samara cried, thinking they had failed.

James had pushed them away, but contrarily hoped to be held tighter. He wanted Jeff and Samara's unconditional love. To James this just proved his belief; humanity sucked and couldn't be trusted. This self fulfilling prophecy continued to be reaffirmed, as disappointment snowballed.

Each family thereafter was met with similar, if not worse behavior by James. Everyone failed to get through to the brilliant, but troublesome boy.

It was on his sixteenth birthday, the eighth of September that James was placed with Karen and Paul Cortland, his final foster care parents. The Cortlands fell into the group of unsavory people taking advantage of the system. They manipulated interviews presenting themselves as loving and caring individuals that wanted to help parentless children, but all they wanted was the money. They really poured on the charm in hopes of gaining an additional income stream. Karen and Paul held hands as they talked of the fulfillment this would bring to their lives. The caseworker assigned to the boy thought they were a godsend, since there were no other real options, after the previous difficulties involving James. Everyone else upon hearing of the boy's age and behavioral problems backed away from the placement. Typically prospective parents wanted to raise younger kids, thinking it would be easier to bond and shape values.

Paul was a thirty-six year old struggling magician and his wife Karen was his assistant. They had no children, but had a pit bull named Max. Their house was in a low rent area where most families kept to themselves. The dog served primarily as an anti-theft measure. Paul was narcissistic and incapable of really caring about anyone. Karen was subservient, needy and lacked confidence; she did whatever she could to keep Paul happy.

When the Cortlands arrived to pick up their foster son, James was silent. His new parents tried to engage him in conversation and were ignored. James didn't speak a word in the car. This frustrated Paul since he expected to be revered. Karen told the boy they were taking him to Applebee's for his birthday.

James snarled, "What a fucking joke."

Karen kept quiet. But Paul decided to show his dominance and said in a menacing voice, "Listen, you disrespectful prick, now you're going straight home."

"Suck my dick, asshole. You're just some pathetic loser taking me for the cash the state gives you. It's not my home." James replied.

Paul was enraged. He was looking for praise and instead received abuse. At that moment, he decided to show James who was in charge. Paul didn't say another word until they pulled up to their run down old home.

"Just like I thought, you're a loser," James said looking at the house.

"Alright, I'll show you who the loser is now," Paul retorted. "Come here, Max, let me introduce you to your new housemate," as he led the boy to the cellar doorway.

James assessed the situation and realized the dog could harm him, so he followed Paul downstairs.

"This will be where you'll stay, until I decide otherwise."

James was shown to a small, dark room in the unfinished basement. The room was bare except for a sheetless cot, which had a dirty blanket and pillow on it. Paul said this was to be his bedroom. The only other thing downstairs was a toilet and shower. This was not the nicely decorated room upstairs that the Child Welfare worker had been shown during their house visit.

The planned birthday celebration that the foster care caseworker was told about turned out to be quite a bit different too. Paul instructed Karen to prepare a special meal as per his command. If the boy wasn't going to show him gratitude then he wouldn't even bother keeping up the pretense of being nice. Paul smirked as he handed James a bologna sandwich on some stale bread and a coke. Paul enjoyed the display of being master.

He took pleasure in sarcastically saying, "How's that for your special meal?"

James finally responded, "Like I said before, thanks for my birthday, loser."

He noticed how the term had struck a nerve with Paul earlier and gained his own measure of satisfaction by repeating it. When he mouthed off about the meal, James didn't expect the retaliation to be physical. Paul slapped him hard across the face. The young man was now about six foot tall and in naturally good shape. James was about to strike back, but the pit bull bared his teeth and growled. The fire in the boy's eyes quickly shifted to an eerie calm. He turned from Paul and looked directly at Karen. She felt uncomfortable when James suddenly smiled at her. The couple went upstairs for the night and locked the door at the top of the stairs.

James lay on the cot in the cold, musty room and fantasized. His thoughts were growing darker.

Paul lay in bed with Karen falsely believing that he established control over James. He saw the anger flash in the boy when he hit him and how he backed down. Max served his purpose. Paul felt himself getting hard and climbed on top of his ever compliant wife. Karen lay there and allowed him to enter her; she knew better than to deny Paul when he was excited.

Karen felt trapped in her marriage. She was twenty-four when she met Paul at a local mall. He had just performed a magic act at a local bar during talent night. When he approached her and asked her on a date, she immediately said yes. He had impressed her during his show.

The first few weeks of dating they really hit it off. Karen thought Paul was interesting because of the unique career path he had chosen. He was good looking in a rugged sort of way. Karen had only dated blue collar type guys in the past. She herself worked in the local Walmart. Each was struggling to escape the memories of their home life and forge a better future. Karen had a physically abusive dad who regularly hit her mom and on occasion beat her as well. Paul had alcoholic parents and was severely neglected while growing up. Both families had lived in near poverty. Eventually this family history would repeat itself.

Karen loved it when Paul asked her to be his assistant. She hated her menial job and would do anything to find a way out. She didn't mind the skimpy costumes he had her wear during the performances. The men in the local bars would often yell crude remarks to her. Karen knew she had a great body and liked the attention. Paul didn't mind because he hoped it would advance his career.

Paul's ambition had always been to become a famous magician. This desire started when he was a little boy and he saw a film about Harry Houdini. Magic became an escape for him, he dreamed of disappearing from his family life. He read books on Houdini at the library and collected whatever he could that pertained to the famous illusionist. Paul still stored all of the memorabilia in boxes in the basement.

Paul and Karen married after about a year of dating. They moved into their current house and were convinced it would only be temporary. Paul assured her wealth and fame would soon follow. As the years went by, their dreams became hazy. Paul continued working in bars, doing birthday parties and grand openings. He began drinking as his frustrations grew, not understanding why he hadn't been discovered. Paul became a functioning alcoholic and this addiction would progress to other substances.

Karen eventually accepted her fate in life. Visions of a mansion on the beach were replaced with finding ways to pay the bills. She eventually returned to part time work at Walmart. Paul would never look for other work and he certainly didn't complain about her taking on the extra job. This was just the beginning of Karen's frustration. She still remembered the first time Paul hit her. He had gotten drunk after another birthday party show and blamed her for not bringing enough to their act. Paul asked her to be topless during their next local bar performance. Karen said no. The next week she wore pasties on her breasts at an old tavern called "Joe's Pub" while Paul performed. The men in the audience appreciated the addition to the magic show. This led to Paul getting a weekly slot on Friday nights. This helped a bit with their money issues, but not enough.

Several weeks later, Paul and Karen ended up having drinks with a regular at "Joe's". Neil was a lowlife who was always searching for an angle to a better life. The couple and he commiserated about financial problems. Neil ended up telling them about how his family received money every month from the state for foster parenting. The next day Paul and Karen looked into the application process and requirements expected of the applicants.

It was no wonder things all led here. Their lives were re-enactments of what they wanted to leave behind. The bitterness inside them needed a release and James would suffer the aftermath. Paul decided he needed to manage his temper. Though he enjoyed striking James, he recognized this couldn't be an everyday habit. Bruises could be documented and he might lose the income stream or worse be prosecuted. Forcing the boy to stay in the barren room in the basement sated his cruelty and could easily be denied if questioned. Paul knew the extra money was too important to let slip away. Cash was needed to support his now burgeoning, cocaine usage. He needn't worry about a witness to contradict his side of things. Karen would never say anything that would displease him, she was afraid to do otherwise.

So the next morning before waking the boy up for school, Paul resolved to apologize. He unlocked the basement door and called down for James to get ready for school. He was surprised to see him dressed and ready to go. James walked up the stairs and smiled. Paul was caught off guard; he certainly didn't expect this response after last night. Paul thought maybe the boy was already fearful and ready to comply with his wishes. He was pleased thinking James would be like Karen. Paul couldn't have been further from the truth.

James from the moment he was born observed every life detail. His mind logged facial expressions, tones and the responses they precipitated in others. His mind was like a super computer storing information and processing it. James' heightened awareness made him hyper sensitive to everything happening around him, during his parent's marital problems his anger commenced. If he hurt, then so would everyone else. When Lily left, this need inside of James intensified. Lily was always so sweet and kind to him. Then while watching his parent's murder, it was like something in his mind short circuited. The pain he felt was incomprehensible. James emotionally shut down to protect himself from the trauma. The fear he felt that night only exacerbated his lone emotion; anger had now turned to rage.

The only people that were truly kind to him after the murders were his initial foster parents, Samara and Jeff. Unfortunately, James' capacity to accept love was vanquished. His mind no longer trusted anyone and his actions kept everyone at bay. The inner rage he felt created a protective shell. James burned their family pictures in an attempt to stop re-forming feelings he no longer understood. The subconscious dread of allowing himself to feel was too great. Upon being returned to Child Welfare, bouncing from family to family only exacerbated his fury. The walls surrounding him grew higher.

So when Paul struck him across the face and the dog snarled, it triggered a visceral turning point, the physical assault topped off his long list of perceived wrongs. He would no longer be the only one suffering. James had wanted everyone around him to feel his emotional pain, now the thoughts were more physical in nature. The images conjured in his mind were of brutality. Yet he had no desire to be imprisoned, acting impulsively would be his demise. James' brilliant mind began to plan, if things were to change, so would he. He saw it all play out before him and what he needed to do. James would erase his previous record of ignoring societal norms and mimic the actions of a model citizen. There would be no trail of a troubled child, only that of a young man who recovered and defeated his demons. Of course, James knew this act would allow him to make his dark fantasy a reality.

James' first step in that direction was when he smiled at his foster father upon coming up the stairs. He noticed last night the way Paul's eyes lit up when he backed down after the near altercation. James also logged into his memory how Karen just watched in silence. Paul fed off admiration and Karen was subservient, so he would satisfy their needs, until his own desires took over.

"Paul, I'm so sorry for being disrespectful last night. I should've been thankful for you taking me into your home," he said with just the right amount of sincerity.

"Thanks for admitting you were wrong. As long as you remember who the boss of this house is, we'll get along just fine," Paul said with a touch of arrogance.

"I'll do that, and really, if I appeared unappreciative it won't happen again. I don't want to start things out on the wrong foot. So I don't make the same mistake with my new school, when does the bus arrive?"

"I was told seven o' clock and it stops right outside the house. I'm glad to see your attitude seems to be in the right place. Have a good day at school; I'm going back to bed."

"Okay, but can you do me a favor and apologize to Karen for me."

Paul nodded as he turned and headed toward the bedroom.

"See you later," James said.

He knew Paul would never pass on the apology to Karen. The man never did say a word to his wife, he was too self absorbed. Paul just stroked his ego believing everyone was there to meet his needs. Either way, it didn't matter to James; his vision involved appeasing his foster parent. James understood what needed to be done to achieve this transformation. He would take the next step.

James entered the doors of the high school knowing the administration had probably been notified of his background. It was the beginning of his junior year and the game would have to be played here too. He would meet all of their academic expectations and none of the disciplinary ones. In order for his desires to be met, he would have to become someone everyone admired. James would need to become a chameleon.

CHAPTER 10

"Present Day"

BETH AND FRANKS' TOP PRIORITY AFTER LEAVING THE DIRECTOR'S office was locating Gary Jones. They decided to start their search through his publisher. *The Blood Hunt* and *The Taking* had been published by Artista and its corporate headquarters was located in New York City. Beth had a member of the task force contact Gary Jones' editor for a meeting. The purpose of the engagement was not stated, only that the Bureau had some questions regarding some information in one of his novels. The editor, Sonny Thompson, set the meeting for 3:00 p.m. the next day.

Beth informed Frank of the appointment time with Jones' editor. He decided to head back home to New Jersey for the night and said he would meet her at Artista. On his way to the airport, Frank noticed there was a message from Sarah on his cell. She wanted to know if everything was alright because he hadn't met her again today, nor even called. Frank felt guilty for having not touched base with her. He realized she might be worried about him since they hadn't gone a day without talking in months. Frank figured he'd call and ask her to dinner. He didn't want to lie to her, so he decided to share some pertinent details as to what had transpired. Once things started moving he might not see Sarah for some time. Frank got her voicemail and left a message that he was on his way back home from out of town. Sarah had been out running errands and when she heard the message, she immediately called back. She was happy to hear his voice and agreed to meet for dinner. Frank didn't share any details during the brief conversation stating he was rushing to make his flight.

Frank and Sarah met at Brando's in Asbury Park. Sarah had mentioned to Frank on the phone that all her friends raved about the restaurant. She hoped her hint would have the desired effect and it did. They made eight o' clock reservations. She was excited because everyone told her the food and atmosphere was fabulous. She wanted the evening to be special.

Sarah had ended the relationship with her boyfriend one month earlier. She felt things with Nick had run their course and he wasn't the right guy for her. When she arrived, Frank was waiting outside and held the door for her as she entered. He then took her coat and hung it on the rack. The Maitre D' led them to a nice corner table and Frank pulled out Sarah's chair. She smiled.

"Thank you, Frank," she said while mentally noting his manners.

"You're welcome, I'm glad you could make it. By the way you look beautiful," Frank responded, appreciating that Sarah had worn a sexy dress.

"Thanks. I was hoping to impress you."

"Mission accomplished," he replied while looking into her eyes.

"So tell me, Frank, why did you have to leave town?"

Frank paused before answering. "Let's talk about that after we order. I don't know about you, but I'm starving."

He realized this was going to be more difficult than he thought.

"Sounds like a good idea," as Sarah picked up her menu.

After the waiter took their order, Frank said, "I had to go to D.C., to meet with my old boss."

"You mean the Director of the F.B.I.," Sarah said emphatically.

Frank smirked and said, "That would be the guy."

Sarah sounded concerned, "What about?"

"Please don't worry when I say this, but my trip had to do with Gary Jones' new book. The Director agrees with me this time, there is classified information in the book concerning Juliette."

"Oh God, I never dreamt something like this would happen when I suggested you read it. Frank, I was trying to help, I'm so sorry."

"Sarah, you have no reason to feel sorry. This has nothing to do with you. If anything, this will still help me find a resolution. We both know I need that, so thanks for caring."

During the rest of dinner the two of them discussed what he'd found in *The Taking*. After they were finished Frank paid the bill. Sarah was still shocked by what she heard and hugged him as they left. Frank was surprised by the embrace, but it touched him. He hadn't felt these emotions toward another woman since Juliette died. Yet he realized now wasn't the time to move the relationship beyond friendship.

"Sarah, I don't want you to worry. Everything's going to work out. I promise. I wish we had more time together, but I really need to get some rest before tomorrow. Hopefully we'll be able to do this again soon. I'll call when I can," Frank said as he kissed her on the cheek.

"Please be careful and if you can't call I understand. I'll see you when you get back."

The two of them hugged one more time before going their separate ways. The night ended with both of them feeling their connection growing stronger. Sarah went to sleep worried. Frank lay in bed with a single minded purpose, to find The Magician.

CHAPTER 11

"2008"

James was two months from graduating as class valedictorian. His girlfriend Carly was head cheerleader and they had been dating since the day after he threw the game winning touchdown in this past season's conference championship game. Everyone in the high school viewed James as the all American boy. He was tall and athletic with blond hair and blue eyes. James was the object of girl's desires, boys wanted to be like him, and teachers felt he was a once in a lifetime student. If they could have seen what was below the surface they would certainly have felt differently. James' ability to mimic behavior was a simple application of his computer like mind and it served him well in his transformation. Had they looked any closer, perhaps they would have noticed his charming smile never reached his lifeless eyes.

During his junior year, James never missed a class and attained a perfect, one hundred average in all honors classes. He was extremely popular and got along with everyone, never having a single altercation with another student. The administration couldn't understand the negative reports they received from his previous schools. James was picture perfect. The acclimation to his new environment was completed when he formed a friendship with the most popular boy in the school, Tom Derosa. The two of them were inseparable and did everything together. Tom was the football team's star receiver and he inadvertently played a part in James joining the squad.

Before practices started senior year, Charlie McNeil noticed the boy's arm as he zipped the ball through the air while having a catch with Tom outside of school. The coach asked him to come out for the team because his star quarterback graduated the previous year. James put on a smile and agreed to play. This turned out to exceed the void left by the coach's departed starter. In all his years of coaching Charlie never saw someone master a playbook and the nuances of reading defenses as quickly as James. It amazed him all the more since the boy had never played before. The fact that the boy was now an athletic six foot four and had a rifle for an arm didn't hurt his rise to stardom. Coupling this with his grades and a perfect SAT score had every university in the country courting James.

The first half of his senior year passed quickly as he began applying to universities. James turned down all the football scholarships, which were offered by everyone from L.S.U. to Alabama. Instead, he narrowed his choices to three of the finest academic universities in the nation, Harvard, M.I.T. and Princeton.

One afternoon in late February, James was down in the basement of his home staring at his acceptance letter from Princeton. Harvard and M.I.T. had already offered theirs the previous week. It was cold and he decided to go upstairs where it was warmer. James knew he wouldn't have this opportunity in a little while because of the house curfew. Paul let him know the first week in their home he was expected to follow the rules. He was only allowed to spend time upstairs until dinner time, which was at 5:30 every day. James' ability to go out was limited to weekends and he had to be back in his dungeon like room by 10:00 p.m.

Even though his foster son never challenged this order, Paul still liked to have Max sit beside him during dinner; it inflated his sense of power. Paul maintained his self made pledge of avoiding physical cruelty, but fed his sadistic side, psychologically. Karen as always never objected to this subtle torture, which was made easier because James had never complained or shown any defiance. She thought he was a loner who liked the isolation, not a burgeoning psychopath. During his first few weeks in the basement, James perused the Harry Houdini memorabilia that Paul worshiped. Everyone thought he spent his time alone in the empty basement studying, due to his academic proficiency. James didn't need to spend much time with books; he scanned information into his photographic memory instantly. His brain would take learned information and utilize its building blocks to conceptualize future theory. When James finished exploring Paul's boxes, his mind returned to Max. He hated the pit bull almost as much as his foster parents.

As he was approaching the door at the top of the stairs he heard Paul enter the house and excitedly tell Karen to sit down. James removed his hand from the doorknob and silently listened to his foster parent's conversation.

"Karen, is James downstairs in the basement?"

"Yes, he's been down there since he came home from school."

"Okay, we need to talk quietly. I just came back from having a beer with Neil. The two of us were talking about the money we get from foster care. Anyhow, Neil practically flipped out when I mentioned the extra cash we get from that attorney's office. I told him how shocked we were to get the additional five grand a month after the first year. He said the parent's must have been loaded and maybe there's an inheritance. Maybe the little shit is keeping it a secret," Paul said in a hushed tone.

"What are you talking about? We were never told about an inheritance," Karen replied.

"I know that's what I told Neil and he said the attorney's wouldn't tell us because we're not the beneficiaries, the kid is!"

Paul couldn't contain his excitement.

"We need to figure out a way to get that money," he continued.

"Paul, we don't even know if that's true. Even if it is, it's not like he's going to give it to us. You haven't exactly treated him like a son."

This was the first time Karen ever made a derogatory statement toward her husband. She became frightened when he glared at her. Paul wanted to strike her, but didn't want to cause a commotion. James was downstairs and it might draw attention to their conversation.

"Well, maybe we need to change that. I'm going to talk to a lawyer and see if we're entitled to anything. If that doesn't pan out, I'll think of something that will," Paul said ominously.

"We don't have money for a lawyer and what if there's no inheritance? That could be Neil's imagination. I don't want to see you get upset," Karen said attempting to placate Paul.

"Neil knows a guy that turned him on to the whole foster parenting thing. He's some shady attorney that works downtown. His name's Eddie Renneker, I'll see if he can help."

"Okay, Paul, if you think that's best."

As James listened to the possibility of an inheritance, there was no excitement, no greed; no remembrance of the deceased... those feelings no longer existed. His brain simply calculated the information. Money would provide resources to aid him in killing and avoid being caught. James saw the events before they were to happen, the story in his head had already played itself out. Only the actual execution was to follow.

He waited a few minutes after they stopped talking and opened the basement door.

"Is dinner ready?" James asked.

Paul worried if he'd been overheard, but relaxed when James asked about eating supper.

He tried to hide his anxiety and yelled out, "Karen, is it almost time to eat? James is hungry."

"It'll be about twenty more minutes. Sorry," she called from the kitchen.

During dinner, Paul decided to work on taking down the walls he built up between them. He would pretend to be the concerned father. He began by apologizing for being rough on James, but said it was to build discipline and character. Paul reinforced this theme by stating that it was because of James' previous disciplinary problems. Then Paul patted himself on the back, saying the tough love worked. He complimented James for turning his life around, while Karen parroted the praise. Paul pointed out his foster son's perfect grades; his athletic achievement and social acceptance. James didn't speak, but conveyed to Karen and Paul, that the relationship was not beyond repair. The chameleon softened his facial expressions as his foster parents spoke and appeared genuinely moved, as if starved for love. However, this was not what James hungered for.

The rest of senior year James played his role for the outside world, as if it were a theater audience on Broadway. Karen and Paul believed the walls they constructed had fallen because of the way James responded to their feigned affection. They were consumed by this thought, because the attorney Eddie Renneker had already informed them that they had no legal right to any possible inheritance. They both imagined sharing a possible fortune with James. Paul and Karen decided to keep up the act until the time came when the money dried up. Since James was turning eighteen in a few months, the state would stop the foster care payments. As for the five thousand dollar stipend, the attorneys stated they were not at privilege to indicate when that would cease. Karen and Paul figured they would know relatively soon and would wait it out. If both sources of income ended on his upcoming birthday, they would cut him loose.

James followed his own agenda. At school, he was named class valedictorian and chose Princeton University as his next endeavor. Outwardly he pretended to struggle with the decision, but this was preordained before ever beginning the application process. James had every intention of attending the Ivy League School. Princeton was not far from Spring Lake, New Jersey. This allowed him to be closer to the home of Frank Sorello. James' obsession with the man began as happenstance.

It sprouted as a result of his classmates asking him to attend a movie the beginning of his junior year in high school. The blockbuster film was loosely based on Frank's life. It highlighted his ability to get inside the mind of a serial killer, create a profile and catch them. Since the original screenplay was developed shortly after the "Tinseltown Murder" spree, it played a large role in the movie.

James sat in the darkened theater, watching on the screen a little boy cower in fear as his parents were strangled. He remembered his former life, but still couldn't connect with any feelings associated with those thoughts. It felt like an out of body experience. The memories were there, but the emotions had been blunted. It was strange watching the reactions of his classmates as they cheered on the main character. James didn't see him as a hero.

When the audience gasped, as the producer and his wife were murdered, James had been silent. To him it was far more personal. He remembered his mother and father being treated like royalty. After all, his dad was a star maker and his mom an adored author. Yet even with a legion of people wanting to gain access to this world, their family was isolated from true friendship. Everyone was always looking to gain a piece of this affluence and power. James' photographic memory recalled conversations his parents had about these perceived parasites. Therefore, they kept everyone at an arm's length away. No one, other than Lily, had ever really gotten close to them emotionally. Sam and Amy had loved their son and each other, but their busy lives kept them from ever having a healthy family dynamic. Those long forgotten feelings had been gradually washed away. Distrust of humanity was all that was left.

Finally, as the credits began to roll, everyone clapped and praised the film. Since the characters names were fictional, it didn't evoke questions. But reviews of the hugely successful movie mentioned it was based on real life events. In the past when anyone ever mentioned the Carlson name, he said he wasn't related.

James walked out of the theater in a zombie like state focused on revenge. The film caused him to relive that fateful night and the events preceding it. His mind saw things that no one else did. His parents could have been saved...should have been saved. Letters had been sent to the Bureau providing hints as to the killer's identity. Any correlations to the previously strangled hookers were ignored. The serial murderer engaged in a cat and mouse game for months. Yet these connections between the Los Angeles underbelly and its glitterati were initially seen as two separate investigations.

It tormented him that Frank was idolized, unable to see clues until it was too late. James' psychotic hatred revolved around this fact. The necessary information to piece it all together had been out there. The renowned F.B.I. agent had been too slow. His parents' murder could have been prevented if only the killer had been stopped earlier. Sorello became the center of his lunacy, the eye of his storm. James set out to destroy the man's reputation and make him suffer. All would soon realize there was only one true master, and inflicting immeasurable pain would be the process in which he would show his superiority. His future victims were just unfortunate souls that crossed the path of a hurricane.

CHAPTER 12

"Present Day"

FRANK WAITED FOR BETH TO ARRIVE AS HE STOOD OUTSIDE THE MAIN entrance to Artista Publishing House on Broadway. He arrived an hour early after taking the train in from Metro Park. Frank felt this was the quickest way into Manhattan from the Jersey Shore, after previously trying every other method of transportation. New York City had been the site of many of his previous investigations. Beth showed up at two thirty and after exchanging pleasantries, they walked into the building.

As they entered the elevator to go up to the fifty-second floor to Mr. Thompson's office, Frank asked, "Beth, how do you want to handle this? Since you're F.B.I. and I'm now a consultant, I don't want to step on your toes. Do you want me to sit back as you question this guy?"

"Frank, I'm a big girl, so don't worry about hurting my feelings. Like I told you before, we're in this together."

"Okay, don't forget that I asked," Frank said with a smirk.

"I won't. Now let's see where this takes us," she replied as the elevator doors opened into a large waiting area.

Beth and Frank approached the pretty receptionist, informing her of their scheduled meeting with Mr. Thompson. She let the editor know his guests had arrived and was instructed to send them in. They followed her to a set of large double doors and were led into an opulent room. The two men inside were sitting in chairs talking and when the visitors entered they rose to greet them.

The distinguished man in the grey Armani suit spoke first, "Hello, I'm Sonny Thompson, but please call me Sonny. This is Jack Harrison, head of our legal department."

After everyone introduced themselves, they sat down in the large antique chairs overlooking the Manhattan skyline. The presence of the attorney signaled to Frank and Beth this might be more contentious than they hoped.

"So what can we do for you regarding Mr. Jones?" asked Sonny.

Beth replied, "Did anyone at Artista assist him in any capacity regarding his recent novel, perhaps brainstorming in building the storyline?"

"Not that I'm aware of. We just provided standard editing before publishing his work. Why do you ask?"

"We're in the middle of an ongoing investigation and we're exploring every lead, big or small...any asset that may help us. Mr. Jones seems to have a knack about writing stories that fit the mold of what our profilers compile about sociopaths. So we're hoping if we provide a broad narrative of the case we're working on, maybe his insights could give us something we might have missed. You know, out of the box thinking. Mr. Thompson, perhaps you can provide us with his contact information?"

"Well, we protect the privacy of all our authors. Perhaps I can pass on your cards, allowing him to contact you," Sonny responded.

Frank countered with, "We certainly can understand your hesitancy, but I feel he might be more inclined to help if we contact him directly. Once we provide him with the background information, I think he'll want to get involved. Unfortunately we're only able to divulge the specifics of that with Mr. Jones. So if you can just give us his contact information, it would really be appreciated."

"Mr. Sorrello, thank you for being so understanding, but I really can't oblige," Sonny replied.

Beth replied with a bit more force, "Mr. Thompson, you do realize you're talking to the Federal Bureau of Investigation, not some crazy fans or someone looking to profit from your client. This is a sensitive matter in which we need to speak with Mr. Jones."

"Jack, can you take over?" Sonny asked his legal counsel.

"I'm sure Mr. Thompson would love to help, but he really doesn't have a legal right to do so. Neither he nor any employee of Artista is looking to obstruct justice, but regarding Mr. Jones, we're legally bound to protect our client's privacy," the attorney stated.

"And why is that?" Beth asked confrontationally.

"The contract that Artista entered into with Mr. Jones explicitly states, under no circumstances, are we or any other party to contact him directly. If we provide you the information you're requesting without a federal warrant, we would expose the firm to a rather large lawsuit."

Frank asked, "Who then can you contact?"

"His literary agent, Jill Santos, but I'm sure that won't help. Miss Santos presented the original manuscript for *The Blood Hunt* to Artista. Once we decided to publish it, we requested to meet the author, and she informed us that they'd never met. The manuscript was delivered to her by his attorney. The second manuscript, *The Taking*, was sent to her via mail and once again, they never met."

"This guy really likes his anonymity, doesn't he? Can we have the attorney's contact information?" Frank queried.

"I'm sure you won't like this either, but Artista is legally bound via the contract to keep Mr. Jones' legal representative confidential."

Beth asked, "Doesn't this strike you as odd, that your client poses for his book jackets and then goes to these extremes to protect his privacy?"

"I'm afraid I can't answer that," Jack said.

Sonny chimed in, "Sometimes creative types are unusual; we just thought he was another J.D. Salinger. Whatever the case may be, we wanted the rights to publish his novels and met his rather unique requests contractually. His books are brilliant works of fiction."

Beth noticed Frank look her way after the editor's last statement. This certainly was circumstantially supportive of Frank's supposition, Gary Jones' guilt.

"I guess for the moment we're at a standstill. Thank you for your time," Beth said.

They all stood and shook hands, feeling the palpable tension in the room. Frank and Beth left the building with the same thought; it was time to request a federal warrant.

CHAPTER 13

"September 1, 2008"

IT WAS ONE WEEK BEFORE JAMES' EIGHTEENTH BIRTHDAY AND HE was preparing to leave for Princeton in a few days. Most of his clothing and his few personal possessions were already packed. Instead, he was getting ready for the beginning of something else. Tonight he would take advantage of his freedom; both of his foster parents were working.

Earlier, Paul and Karen left the house feeling excited and not because they were proud of their foster son's achievement. While getting dressed in their bedroom they discussed how life would change with a possible inheritance. For months, the foster parents continued their efforts to salvage the relationship with James. Their attempts seemed to be making headway, just last week James told them "he would miss them and Max" and asked for a photograph of everyone together. Paul took some snapshots and James kept one framed in his new room upstairs. The smile on his face appeared so real, with his arms wrapped around Karen and Paul. Driving to their scheduled show, the magician and his assistant fantasized how life might change; unaware their foster son's vision was frightfully dissimilar to their own.

At that moment, James was grinding a sedative into powder form. A classmate had given him prescription sleeping pills after complaining of not being able to sleep. In actuality, he had no trouble with insomnia, but the sleep aid would help in another manner. It had been easy to manipulate the girl into giving him the drug. Now he would take advantage of his alone time. When he finished crushing the pills, he walked to the kitchen and began cooking hamburger meat. Max stood next to James, staring eagerly up at the frying pan. The pit bull was salivating.

James looked at the dog, "Max, do you want some food?"

The animal began to whimper. When James finished cooking the hamburger meat, he mixed in the powdered drug and placed the bowl back on the floor. The dog ravenously swallowed his last meal, as James' demons surfaced, beyond those repressed in his imagination.

When Max was unconscious, James picked up the dog and hid it inside a blanket taken from his bed. He proceeded to carry the pit bull outside and placed the animal into the trunk of Karen's rusted out old Honda Civic. James then drove the car to the desolate parking lot of an abandoned factory not far from his house. With the headlights out, he parked the car in the back and walked over to a dumpster. James reached in and took out a large plastic tarp that he stored there the previous week. He then took Max out of the trunk, removed the blanket and rolled him up inside the canvas, placing him on the ground. James got back in the car.

Turning on the ignition, he put the automobile in reverse and backed the car over the pit bull's head. After hearing the loud crunch, he parked the Honda a few feet from where Max lay dead. James stepped back outside and attached a rope to Max's collar. He then took the other end of the rope and tied it to the car's undercarriage. James wanted this to look like an accident and needed to get the dog to the road. In this area of town, the police rarely patrolled, but as an extra precaution he killed the lights upon starting the car. Making sure he saw no headlights, James drove to the edge of the dark parking lot and stopped the vehicle. Quickly he got out and removed the rope from Max's collar and dragged him into the street. James then drove the Honda back behind the deserted manufacturing plant, untied the rope and carried it along with the tarp, into the woods behind the vacant complex. Upon finding the small hole that was dug the other day; he buried the tarp and rope. James prepared all of this in advance in order to minimize time spent in his kill zone, thus limiting unexpected complications.

When James got back home he checked to make sure no blood

was on the tires. Realizing the tarp had served its purpose, James put the shovel back in Paul's shed. He then went back inside the house and climbed into bed. James wrapped himself in the blanket that only an hour ago had covered Max and fell sound asleep.

The next morning he got up and made a bowl of cereal while Paul and Karen slept. After he finished eating, James filled Max's bowl with his dog food. He placed it back down in its usual spot, next to the doggy door.

James yelled out, "Max, are you outside? C'mon back in boy, it's time to eat. Max...Max..." he continued to cry out.

Paul shouted from the bedroom, "James, he'll come back like he always does, we're trying to sleep."

"Dad, I'm just worried because he always comes in when it's time to eat," James replied in a panicked tone.

Paul and Karen couldn't believe what they just heard; it was the first time James ever said the word "dad." They looked at each other and smiled, they had won. Each imagined how a possible inheritance would forever change their lives. Their premonition would have a significantly different ending.

That same morning a police officer noticed the dead dog on the road. He was a pet lover and hated seeing animals left to be obliterated. The officer removed the partially crushed pet off to the side of the street and called the animal control center. He removed the name tag from Max and drove to the address listed.

Paul saw the police car park outside their home and wondered why the officer was at their house. He was visibly upset when informed of Max's death; the dog had always been loyal and provided him with a sense of power. James came over to his foster dad and placed his hand on his shoulder, expressing mutual grief. Karen attempted to console them both over the next several days before James left for college. She seized the opportunity to further create the appearance of bonding.

It was the day of James' departure, two days before his birthday and everyone seemed happy. Karen and Paul drove their foster son to the airport from East L.A.; he sat silent replaying in his head the details of killing Max, knowing it had begun. His smile was barely perceptible.

CHAPTER 14

"Present Day"

BETH WAS HEADING BACK TO F.B.I. HEADQUARTERS TO INFORM THE Director of what transpired at Artista, while Frank returned to his home in Spring Lake. The retired agent knew a search warrant would have to be approved by the federal magistrate court in Manhattan and since he was only a consultant to the Bureau, all he could do was wait.

A strategy was formulated as to how to proceed with the investigation after leaving the publishing house. They discussed how to employ the task force and assign responsibilities. During this conversation Beth spoke of the team members' strengths and weaknesses, which triggered an image in Frank's brain. He remembered being a young task force leader and how he delegated duties. Agent Tucker suddenly flashed through his mind, something about the eager young agent innately impressed him during the initial ride over to see the Director.

Frank asked, "Beth, is there any chance you know Agent Tucker? He picked me up at Dulles when I first came to meet Rob."

"No, why do you ask?"

"I really can't say, when I met him I just liked his enthusiasm. I'd like you to give this kid an opportunity; can you put him on the team?"

"Frank, I trust your instincts, I'll let Rob know you'd like to have him join the task force."

"Thanks, I appreciate it."

"Not half as much as Agent Tucker will," Beth replied.

Frank smiled, "That's true. Hopefully he'll be an asset. Anyhow, I have to run and catch my train. Call me when we have something new. Take it easy, Beth."

"You too, Frank."

On the train ride home, he focused his thoughts on what else could be done at the moment. Frank realized everything was now in motion, so he began to relax. His eyes started to close and he drifted off, his body needed sleep. Frank dreamt of Juliette walking on the beach. He ran to catch her but for some reason, couldn't gain any ground. He could see her profile from behind as she talked to another woman. Their features were very similar, suddenly they turned and smiled. Frank recognized Sarah as they both waved. Finally he started getting closer and a huge wave came out of nowhere, sweeping both women into the ocean. He tried to swim in and rescue them, but his feet were stuck in the sand. All he could hear were their cries and the roar of the sea...

Frank shivered and woke up in a cold sweat. He didn't recollect his dream, but after taking a few seconds to regain his composure, he felt an overwhelming urge to call Sarah.

When she answered, Frank said, "Hey, I was just thinking about you. I'm sitting on the train and we're just passing Rahway. I was wondering if you haven't eaten yet, maybe we could have dinner again tonight?"

"I'd love that, but instead of going out, why don't I cook you a meal?"

Frank had never been to her house in the evening. He only stopped by in the past to pick her up for breakfast or lunch, usually after one of their long runs. His feelings were conflicted, torn between wanting her and the fear of what a relationship might mean, especially given the current circumstances. Frank wasn't sure if he could resist being alone with Sarah, without it impacting his decision.

He ignored the cognitive dissonance before responding, "That would be nice. I should be home in about forty-five minutes. What time should I come by?"

"If you don't mind waiting while I cook, as soon as you'd like. I'm going to make you my world famous Veal Marsala."

"Sounds perfect, I'm gonna grab a quick shower as soon as I get home. I'll be over in about an hour and a half, is that okay?"

"Can't wait," Sarah replied.

When she hung up, the smile on her face wouldn't go away. Sarah quickly took a shower and picked out her favorite black dress. After putting on her makeup and some perfume, she got dressed. Seconds later, she unzipped the dress and took off her plain underwear. Sarah went to her dresser drawer and took out her black Victoria Secret's g-string and matching bra. After getting dressed again, she looked in the mirror one more time, before heading to the kitchen.

The doorbell rang as she was setting the table and called out for Frank to come inside. He was dressed in jeans, a nice white linen shirt and black shoes. Sarah thought he looked fantastic, noticing the way the clothes hung perfectly on his body. He walked over to her holding two bottles of wine and set them down on the table.

"Wow, you look incredible!" Frank exclaimed.

Sarah blushed and said, "Thanks, you look pretty great yourself."

"You're just being nice, but thanks for the compliment and for going through all the trouble of making me dinner. I wasn't sure what goes with veal so I brought over red and white wine. The guy at the liquor store recommended the Duckhorn Merlot and I'm guessing we should listen to his advice. When I showed him the bottle I picked out, his disdain was hard to ignore. I'm thinking a career as a sommelier isn't in the cards."

Sarah laughed at his self deprecating sense of humor. She thought to herself how he always put her at ease, as if they knew each other their entire lives. Sarah asked him to sit down and relax while she took the food out of the oven.

"Is there anything you can't do? That smells delicious."

"Frank, you haven't tasted it yet, so maybe you'll want to hold back on the praise. I'm not known for my cooking."

"I thought you said I was going to have your world famous Marsala," he said playfully.

"I did say that, didn't I? You have to stop listening to everything I say."

"Now why would I ever do that, Sarah, when all you do is make me smile," as Frank looked up at her from the table.

Sarah couldn't help notice his green eyes and how they complemented his wavy dark hair and strong jaw line. Noticing his gaze made her feel warm all over, like a teenager's first crush. Frank found Sarah equally enticing and it was if he were transported back in time. Whenever she spoke, he found himself enveloped in her words. As she moved, his eyes couldn't help but follow. Juliette had been the only other woman ever to make him feel this way. The trepidation of moving the relationship beyond friendship was fading, but Frank still struggled with the timing. He didn't want to draw danger to Sarah; the thought of another loss would be too much to overcome.

During the meal, they talked about growing up at the Jersey Shore, family histories and what happened at Artista. Even with the seriousness of the investigation surrounding them, they laughed and enjoyed the wine; the chemistry between them was unmistakable. When they finished eating, Frank got up to help clean off the table and Sarah said she'd take care of it later. She asked if he was interested in watching a movie in the other room. Frank said "sure" and complimented her on the food as they walked into the den together. As he sat on the couch, Sarah snuggled up against him. Reflexively he wrapped his arm around her and she felt the tautness of his muscle. Sarah leaned into him and they kissed. Frank wanted to resist but couldn't, her lips were so soft and a long suppressed desire was resurrected. Intimacy had been too long dormant. His large hands gently touched her face and moved down to her body. Sarah loved the way he felt.

She looked into his eyes and said, "It might be more comfortable upstairs."

Her proposal was intoxicating, but it also snapped him from that moment of reflexive passion. Frank tapped into his intellectual side and made a decision. It took all of his willpower.

"Sarah, there isn't anything in the world I'd rather do right now. I want you so much, but I'm afraid of drawing you into this nightmare."

"I understand how you feel, but I'm already involved; I worry about you and can't exclude you from my life."

"I can't risk placing you in his crosshairs. Sarah, for us to have a normal start to things, we can't always be looking over our shoulders. I have to know the threat is gone, I just can't deal with the thought of you being hurt."

Sarah wrapped her arms around him and said with a smile, "I'm not crazy about you rejecting my advances, but I get it. I don't want anything else hanging over your head. I worry about you too, but this isn't how I imagined our evening ending."

"Don't worry about me, I'll be fine. But before I change my mind and tear your clothes off, I really have to go. If you need me for anything, make sure you call."

Frank got up from the couch and Sarah walked him to the door. They kissed goodnight and she locked the door when he left. As Frank walked down her porch stairs he noticed a car move slowly in his direction. He was just about to get into his BMW as the approaching vehicle suddenly stopped.

The young man in the blue Acura rolled down his window, "Hey man, can you tell me how to get to Bar Anticipation?"

The former F.B.I. agent's warning signals were heightened as he cautiously approached the car. The guy inside looked to be in his mid-twenties. This was probably nothing but Frank always paid attention to his gut and for some reason, he sensed danger. The muscles in his body were on high alert and prepared to react. Frank controlled his physical tension as he talked to the guy in the car, informing him how to get to the popular shore nightspot. He memorized the license number as the vehicle drove away and took note of the guy's blond hair and blue eyes, making sure to store his facial features in memory. Frank imagined he was probably just being paranoid, but better safe than sorry, especially when his body reacted as if a predator was near.

The following morning Frank gave Beth a call and told her about the incident with the man in the Acura. He asked if she could get someone to run the plate as a precaution. Beth said she'd pass it on to Agent Tucker and then updated Frank on the current status of the investigation.

Rob had been briefed the moment she returned to headquarters and was onboard with their investigative plan. A member of the task force was working on getting a warrant issued from a federal magistrate judge in Manhattan, which would force Artista to comply with their request regarding contact information. Everyone else on the team was cross referencing law enforcement databases for possible leads. Sorello would be kept abreast of developments.

An hour later, Frank's cell phone rang. He didn't recognize the number, but it had a D.C. area code.

"Hello, this is Frank," as he picked up the call.

"Agent Sorello, this is Agent Tucker. I have information on that plate you requested."

"Great, but since we're now working together, please call me Frank."

"Alright, but only if you call me Rich, and thanks for recommending that I be put on the task force," Tucker replied enthusiastically.

"My pleasure, so what do you have for me, Rich?

"The car belongs to a Bill Dames. He's twenty-six years old and lives in Edison, New Jersey. He has no priors and just to make sure it was the same person that asked you for directions, I checked out his DMV photo. Blond hair, blue eyes...does that sound like your guy? Oh and by the way, the car isn't listed as stolen."

"Nice work, probably nothing, but let's keep him on our radar. Thanks again, Rich."

After the call ended, Frank relaxed a bit thinking Sarah was safe. The information on the guy in the Acura seemed okay. The car wasn't stolen and the man had no criminal history. It was probably an overprotective response. Frank realized he might have to stay away from Sarah for awhile. He was having trouble distinguishing between his usually infallible instinct and what might now just be a trauma related overreaction.

What Frank hadn't seen was the man in the leather jacket and hoodie casually strolling by Sarah's sidewalk five minutes after he left her house. The observer had watched from the shadows, fascinated by the subtle tension in Frank's body language as the Acura unexpectedly pulled up. It was like watching a Lion move toward prey, ready to pounce. He could see why the hunter was formidable; the transformation from average citizen to lethal warrior was almost imperceptible. Yet to the trained eye it had been obvious. Frank hadn't seen him, but felt his presence. The psychopath's adversary was a worthy opponent, which would make his game all the more invigorating. The killer loved a challenge. Standing perfectly still, he watched the lights go out in the upstairs bedroom.

Sarah had trouble sleeping that night, it was especially windy outside. She remembered Hurricane Sandy and the fear she felt that evening. The noises tonight were far less intense, but she still felt nervous. Sarah realized the hyperawareness had something to do with Frank. She had fallen in love with him. His concerns were now hers as well.

Several miles away in Spring Lake, Frank lay awake in his bed thinking of Sarah; she had somehow broken through his heavily walled exterior and managed to find her way into his heart. The connection was undeniable, it was the feeling Juliette had brought to him, a sense of being truly alive.

CHAPTER 15

"September 8th, 2008"

ON THE MORNING OF JAMES' EIGHTEENTH BIRTHDAY, THE PHONE RANG at his foster parents. Karen answered as her husband continued to sleep. An attorney from the firm of Gerard, Crake & Carroll asked her if James was available to speak regarding a legal matter. Karen nudged Paul as she gave the lawyer his number at school. The couple was ecstatic as they began thinking of what they would do with the money. There was no doubt in their minds that anything other than fortune lie ahead.

James had arrived at Princeton University two days earlier and moved into his assigned dormitory, Holder Hall. This was part of Rockefeller College. "Rocky" as it's affectionately known by students and faculty, is one of six residential colleges on Princeton's campus. These were created to provide a sense of community to those attending, each having their own dining halls, living space and social settings. Students are randomly selected as freshmen to live in one of these "Princeton Communities," and the diverse makeup provides a distinct learning environment. James instantly was drawn to its atmosphere. It had a living and breathing presence that seeped into the troubled genius.

Throughout his childhood and adolescent years, James' brilliant mind had never truly been stimulated. Although his parents had bright artistic minds, their intellect was far beneath his own. The various families and the communities James had lived in thereafter, also provided little in the way of mental arousal. In fact, the only person that remotely challenged James had been Dr. Hart. As a young boy he found the whole process amusing, he remembered the psychologist attempting to probe his thoughts. James gave her responses that contained partial truths to watch the Doctor attempt to psychoanalyze him. He was filled with anger stemming from his mother and father's issues, but still he toyed with the psychologist. James acted as if he felt no remorse or emotional attachment to his actions, but at that time, there was still a human element inside. His mind needed to find ways to provide a challenge, and instead of addressing his guilt, it sought something more interesting. James' irrational behavior was tied to the underlying conflict and his craving for stimulation. Misleading Dr. Hart was just a game to appease this need.

The horrific trauma caused by his parents' murder began to dissolve James' humanity like battery acid. The anger shifted more toward real rage, and without any mental stimulus, his mind's purity became tainted. His many foster parents and their acquaintances had provided no creative spark to allow his brain to engage and prosper. The school systems and the academic programs in these communities were leagues beneath his capabilities. His mind was then consumed by the only thing it knew, instability, disappointment and pain. This bleak landscape fed and fanned James' psychotic thought process because it allowed his brain to find an outlet, like a channel going out to a vast, open cold sea. His dark mental obsession served as a pressure release, but also served to suppress the thing that made him human, his feelings.

Sadly there had been no counter balance to help prevent this breakdown. Very little love and emotional support were present after Sam and Amy were murdered. Only James' original foster parents, Jeff and Samara, provided this necessary elixir, but this came too close to his parents' tragic deaths. His feelings were stunted and the fear of opening up was too great to counterattack this distortion of innocence. Each step toward growth or healing had been thwarted with another obstacle, and finally when James was placed with Paul and Karen, his ominous fantasies began to emerge.

Something about the historic and hallowed grounds of Princeton shifted James' single minded purpose of inflicting pain on the world. The genius had another outlet. Brilliance was everywhere.

He had just entered his dorm room after hours of wandering about the campus, mesmerized by the gothic architecture offsetting the natural beauty of the grounds. His brain was fueled with the energy of the university. Synapses were firing, igniting his genius to learn, absorb and create. James' constant need for retribution no longer occupied his every thought; his mind needed more than just cataclysmic purpose. Princeton University had only been a means to an end, part of his imagined design, but that was before he actually had the opportunity to be in its midst. The map James envisioned, guiding his every action, had found a new direction, inspiration sans horror.

James decided to lie in his bed and take advantage of the quiet. Silence enhanced his creative process, and for the first time in two years, it had a different focal point. The possibilities of his new habitat were endless, so many things to ponder. His assigned roommate still hadn't arrived on campus, with classes not beginning until the following week. Contemplating the dynamic of living with another student was one of the countless new stimuli. The phone rang interrupting his solitude. James answered the call and didn't recognize the voice. A lawyer informed him of the two hundred thirty-eight million dollar inheritance that was bequeathed to him by his parents.

James flashed back to his past upon hearing the news and the competing demons struggled to regain control. The newly wealthy young man gave instructions as to what to do with the money as he fit this new piece of information into his plan. The attorney offered the firm's services in helping manage his affairs. James accepted their proposal, if his initial request was handled properly. The interloping evil inside of his damaged brain didn't want to disappear without a fight. As if angels sensed these intruders, his door opened at that exact moment.

"Hey what's up, you must be James. I'm your roommate, Marty."

CHAPTER 16

"Present Day"

FRANK WOKE UP AT 5:00 A.M. AND WAS GETTING READY FOR HIS DAILY run with Sarah. The struggle with his emotions was ubiquitous. Frank didn't want the bull's-eye on Sarah's back to get any larger. He just didn't know how to avoid it. Their relationship had reached a critical crossroads. Neither of them was capable of pretending what they felt wasn't real. But further involvement would only complicate matters. Even their morning jog might bring the danger closer. There appeared to be no good choice. Losing Sarah would be more than he could stand.

Frank suddenly felt nauseous. A flashback of Juliette's blood stained body overtook him. His heart started to race and he recognized the onset of a panic attack. Frank focused on slow, controlled deep breathing. After reducing the physical sensations tied to his anxiety, he accessed the memory of his therapy sessions. He needed to live his life and not be afraid of it. The past couldn't be reversed, but today and tomorrow still lie ahead.

Just as Frank was putting on his running shoes and getting ready to leave the house, the phone rang. He picked it up. Beth was on the line and asked if he could catch the next train into Manhattan. The federal warrant had been approved and she was now boarding a flight to Newark. Frank arranged a meeting time with her and quickly changed his clothes. On his way to the train station he tried calling Sarah, but only got her voicemail. After leaving a message explaining why he didn't show up, he felt guilty drawing her into this lifestyle.

Frank assumed Sarah was already waiting at the boardwalk. There had been many times Juliette was left in similar situations, wondering if her husband was merely late or not showing up at all. Being called away at a moment's notice was part of his job and something his wife had learned to accept. Frank reasoned, this was another factor holding him back with Sarah, guilt. He tried to find some solace in knowing she would run without him. There had been a standing agreement between them, if either was late more than fifteen minutes, to go on ahead. But since this had never actually happened, Frank hoped Sarah wouldn't kill too much time, ignoring his instructions.

"Hopefully, she's halfway down the boardwalk already," Frank muttered to himself.

He hated that Sarah was being forced to deal with the tribulations of a Bureau agent. The irony of him being retired didn't help matters. Frank swore, once this case was put to rest, the F.B.I. would never impact his life again. Before Juliette's death, it had been about solving cases and protecting law abiding citizens. After her brutal loss, it became about revenge. Now it was about finding a way to have a normal life and hopefully growing old with someone you love. He wondered if that person might be Sarah.

Frank exited Penn Station and hailed a cab outside. Normally, he would have walked to get his blood pumping. But walking approximately twenty city blocks would have taken too much time. The ride only took a few minutes and as he paid the cabbie, Frank saw Beth talking on her cell phone. She was standing near the entrance to Artista. Frank got out of the car and waved. Beth nodded, while communicating orders to one of her agents. She put the cell phone away as Frank approached.

"Ready to get this party started," Frank said with a touch of sarcasm.

"Absolutely. Nothing's turned up so far. The team's been searching through NCIC (National Crime Information Center Database) and all of the state law enforcement databases, including DMV records. Plus Tony Hillmann, our computer expert, has been combing through the new Data Integration and Visualization System. Unfortunately, Gary Jones is such a common name it's yielding too many results."

The Data Integration and Visualization System (DIVS) was a new tool developed for the F.B.I. to ease the massive burden of searching manually through hundreds of databases, all with their own passwords and providing a single search capability. It accessed the most used databases and allowed searches by name, phone number and identifiers to other case requests. Millions of documents could be processed and links could be established much quicker. This was implemented after Frank's retirement from the Bureau.

"I read about DIVS, does it measure up to its expectations?"

"Frank, it's invaluable. It sifts through mountains of data looking for missing links to find the needle in the haystack. Plans are being made to make it available to other intelligence agencies so we can share and analyze information as efficiently as possible."

"Beth, have you had Tony cross reference against income tax records? Gary Jones has made an awful lot of money from these books, which should narrow the search quite a bit."

"He's already on it, a few millionaires with that name have turned up, but none with the income I would expect a bestselling author to have, plus none listed their occupation as a writer. Additionally, the license photos don't match the picture on his book jacket."

When they reached the receptionist's desk, Beth asked to see Mr. Thompson. Liz was his long time assistant and acted as his gatekeeper. She said there was no scheduled meeting and inquired as to the nature of their business.

Beth replied, "We have a federal warrant requiring Artista to provide us with information in an ongoing investigation."

"I'll get him right away," as she walked into the editor's office.

Liz informed her boss of the situation. The editor instructed her to get Jack Harrison to his office immediately and to bring the Bureau representatives inside. Liz brought Beth and Frank back to Mr. Thompson's office and left.

"Good morning, Agent Gregg and Agent Sorello."

Frank nodded in acknowledgment, "I'm just a consultant these days, so call me Frank."

Beth said in an official tone, "Mr. Thompson, we have a warrant requiring you to provide us with all contact information related to Gary Jones."

"Agent Gregg, I'm sure you remember our legal counsel, Jack Harrison. He's on his way up to my office. As soon as he looks it over and says everything is okay, you'll be given whatever you need. In the meantime, can I offer either of you something to eat or drink?"

Both Beth and Frank declined and waited for the firm's lead attorney to arrive. Sonny Thompson appeared uncomfortable with the silence.

"I thought you just wanted Mr. Jones to provide insight into whatever it is you're investigating. This certainly seems a bit more serious. You suddenly show up unannounced with a federal warrant. What's this really about?"

"The nature of our investigation is confidential and highly sensitive in nature," Beth stated.

"Sonny, we don't need rumors spreading to the media, so I'm asking you to keep this matter between yourself and Jack Harrison," Frank added.

"Of course," the editor replied.

Seconds later, Jack entered the office.

"I suspected your previous visit wasn't quite so innocuous. May I see the warrant?" the lawyer asked.

Beth handed it to him and the attorney looked over the legal document.

"Sonny, everything's in order. We'll provide whatever you need regarding Mr. Jones," the lawyer said as he handed the federal warrant back to Beth.

The attorney made sure Beth was given everything pertaining to the author. All contact information for both his lawyer and literary agent was handed to the F.B.I. agent. Jack Harrison also informed them all royalties generated from Jones' book sales and any other forms of payment had been wired directly to Chase Manhattan Bank. This had been stipulated as per instructions in the initial contract with Artista. The depository's location and phone number were also given to the agent.

In order to expedite matters, Beth decided she would meet with

Gary Jones' attorney and Frank would go see the literary agent, Jill Santos. He believed in leaving no stone unturned and wanted to make sure she had never met with the author. Agent Gregg figured that her background as an attorney might come in handy when dealing with Jones' lawyer.

Since Miss Santos was only four blocks from their current location, Frank chose to walk over unannounced. Meanwhile, Beth ran into an immediate snag. When she called Fred Kimmel's work number, she was informed the lawyer's phone had been disconnected. Beth called Tony back in D.C. and asked him to look into where the attorney currently was located.

She instructed him to check with the phone company for possible forwarding numbers. Beth also asked him to contact the State Bar Association to find out where he was currently practicing. Tony said he would get right on it and call her back. Beth decided to grab a cab downtown to check out the location to see if anyone knew where the attorney might have gone.

She called Frank from the taxi and let him know of the unfortunate circumstance regarding Fred Kimmel. Frank told her he just arrived at Jill Santos' office and would get back to her as soon as he was done. He introduced himself to Miss Santos' assistant and let her know that Sonny Thompson from Artista had been his conduit regarding Gary Jones. Frank was sent right in.

"Hi, thanks for not making me wait. I'm Frank Sorello, a consultant for the Federal Bureau of Investigation. I understand you're Gary Jones' literary agent, is that correct?"

"Yes, I am. What can I help you with?"

"We need to speak with him regarding an investigation and we're having trouble locating him."

"Mr. Sorello, do you have any identification? I'm not trying to be difficult, it's just not every day the F.B.I. walks into my office," Jill said guardedly.

Frank pulled out his former badge and said, "That's perfectly understandable. I'm currently retired, but like I just said, I'm acting in an unofficial capacity for them. I can give you the number to the Director of the F.B.I. or you can call Sonny Thompson to further verify my credentials."

"That's unnecessary. It seems that you're legitimate. Unfortunately, I won't be able to help you locate him. I've never met Gary Jones directly. I was given his manuscripts through a legal representative. I'm also legally bound to not divulge his name. I'm so sorry. Is Mr. Jones okay?" she said in a concerned tone.

"He's not listed as a missing person, if that's what you're asking. But we really need to speak with him. Can I ask if you know anything about the photograph on his books?"

"His attorney gave them to me when I decided to represent him. There was a signed document approving the photo's release by Mr. Jones."

"Can you tell me anything about his lawyer, Fred Kimmel? His phone number has been disconnected. Has he been in touch lately?"

"Not since the original contract was signed, making me Gary Jones' literary agent. I shopped his first book and like I expected, was met with many offers to publish. After I negotiated a deal with Artista, I met one last time with Mr. Kimmel. We went over the contract with the publisher, specifying the terms of the deal. It dealt with not only his first novel but also any future books. I was then asked to sign numerous confidentiality agreements protecting the author's identity, which included his attorney. It was a bit strange, but I assumed his privacy was extremely important, and he didn't want to lose his anonymity."

"I understand that his second manuscript was mailed to you. Was there any return address?"

"No, it arrived regular mail with no special markings. I remember being surprised when I opened up the package and realized it was Gary Jones' second novel. I really wish I had something to share that might be valuable, but your best bet would be finding his attorney. I'm really sorry."

"You do understand that if we find you withheld any information, then that would make you an accessory to a crime, Miss Santos?"

"I would never do that because I have nothing to hide, and I really wish I could help."

"Well, thanks for your time. If anything new turns up, here's my number."

"I'll do that, and good luck with your investigation.

73

Frank left her office and called Beth to see if anything was happening on her end.

"Hi, Frank, any luck?" she asked.

"None at all. What about you?"

"I spoke to several business owners that were near his old office. Apparently he was a one man operation and struggling. I was told he didn't have many clients and had a drinking problem. They said he was always very erratic with his patterns, but came in two or three times a week. Then suddenly, he just stopped showing up altogether. As far as anyone remembers it was approximately two years ago. After his mail began piling up, the shop owners figured he was ill or went out of business."

"That would have been right around the time of the release of Gary Jones' *The Blood Hunt*, his first novel," replied Frank.

"Hmmm, that's something to think about. It sounds like this guy, wasn't the most ambitious individual. I'm sure the money he received for handling Gary Jones' affairs was significant. Maybe he just packed in his regular business and lives off his milk cow. Given his apparent alcohol problem, that might explain all of this," Beth surmised.

"Or he could be deceased. Why not have someone check the Social Security Administration's Death Index, to see if Fred Kimmel's name shows up and fits his general profile."

"Good idea. I'll check back with Tony and see if anything turned up with the phone company or State Bar Association, and if not, I'll have him look into it."

"Sounds good. Why don't I catch a flight back to D.C. with you and we'll discuss this some more?"

"Okay, let's meet at Penn Station. We'll catch a train over to the airport and I'll arrange the flight for us."

"Thanks, Beth; I'll see you in about ten minutes."

CHAPTER 17

"James' Freshmen Year, Princeton University"

WHEN JAMES WAS INFORMED OF HIS INHERITANCE, HE INSTRUCTED the attorney to locate a realtor in Monmouth County, New Jersey and buy a home costing no more than a half of a million dollars. Power of attorney documents were signed to handle this purchase. James had no intention of sharing the true nature of his immense wealth. He planned on telling his foster parents that he inherited a little over two million dollars. He was going to surprise them with the house, which would continue the illusion he wanted to perpetuate. Bringing them closer in proximity would further create an image of a tight knit family. James would also be seen as a generous and well adjusted son. If they were to disappear, he would be an unlikely suspect. It would also make them a quicker target if anything unexpected happened and he needed to act quickly.

However, something unforeseen did occur that hadn't been accounted for in James' master plan. His diabolical vision was somehow sidetracked by his new environment and the impossible possibility of an altogether different ending suddenly existed. Princeton University began to catalyze a healing process and became an opposing force to this maniacal alternate destiny.

James' fragile metamorphosis continued to gain momentum his first few weeks at Princeton. This change was no longer a charade; his actions weren't guided by malice and deceit. The entire academic ecosystem slowly funneled its way into his being. Each day that went by, the laurels of this esteemed learning environment exerted its willpower, as if it were alive. James' fury had found a more constructive escape mechanism in which it could be diffused.

Everything was new and exciting. The five hundred acre campus was filled with positive stimuli. Being the fourth oldest college in the country had given this Ivy League institution plenty of time to perfect a setting that promoted personal growth. James was captivated by the genius all around him, the architectural wonder, the brilliance of his peers, and the revered faculty interaction. The design of Princeton's educational process was all encompassing. James' monsters were kept at bay by the constant stroking of this critical learning process.

It was like the tides were slipping back and uncovering the soul that had been buried. James' latest transformation was only in its infancy, but whatever goodness lying dormant within was being given the chance to escape its tortured shackles. He was thrown into the absorption of knowledge.

James decided he wasn't going to play football for the Tigers during his freshman year. The coach of the team implored him to reconsider, but the student was adamant in his stance. James stated he wanted to concentrate on academics, but would reconsider playing the following season. Coach Pete Rosetti was practically heartbroken, but tried to find solace in the possibility of him returning to football next season. James had been recruited by every powerhouse team in the NCAA and he selected Princeton University to be his alma mater. Unfortunately, since there were no athletic scholarships to be given at the university, the coach had no leverage. All students at Princeton were accepted on their merits, without regard for their ability to pay. Upon acceptance, a no loan aid package would be determined based upon need. Princeton prided itself on its alumni walking away with no student debt. Pete Rosetti prayed that the potential college football superstar would ultimately change his mind.

James had been given his financial package prior to learning of his inheritance. He would need to reapply the following year and of course, his aid would likely not be renewed at that point because each year's application was considered independent. Before the unforeseen alteration in his grand design, college football had not been part of his plan. He now felt swept away, like a leaf in the wind. There was no predetermined landing spot; his mind was floating in a new direction. Inspiration had found a new home.

James had been given advanced placement standing and was on a path to a three and a half year graduation rate. As he approached the examination period of his first term, the inner recesses of his genius had awoken. Whenever he wasn't in his actual classes, he sat in on lectures that were not even part of his academic course load. James spent hours reading in the library or meandering around the quaint, academic community. He started to believe maybe there was more to this world than suffering and brutality.

In high school, when James played the part of the chameleon he established the façade of relationships. His ex-girlfriend, Carly, had been fooled by his ability to mimic an emotionally healthy person, as had Tom Derosa, his teammate and friend. They did all the things that kids their age were wrapped up in, like going to parties, drinking and having sex. The laughter and joy had been real for Carly and Tom, but James' behaviors were devoid of the feelings connected to these human actions. During this time there hadn't been a compelling distraction for his inherent distrust and hatred of everything surrounding him. Therefore, James never connected to the emotional underpinnings of these interpersonal interactions. They were just deflected off his hardened exterior, absorbed in playing a role. One in which only a shell existed.

For the first time since his parent's murder, he was no longer guided by a single minded purpose. James' famished soul was now being fed and sated his emptiness. There was something positive living inside of him, a competing energy counterbalancing the negative entity which craved destruction. James started to look at people as not just husks or pieces to be moved around a chessboard. He contemplated the notion that decency actually existed in the universe. Each day that went by this notion grew ever stronger.

The day he received the phone call about his inheritance, like everything at Princeton, had been somewhat fortuitous. James was intertwined in the atmosphere of Princeton the moment he arrived, and small inroads had already been paved for his path to redemption. Compulsively replaying the images of killing Max subsided, and the quest to live out his preordained murder spree was interrupted.

Yet, the attorney's call almost reignited the fire burning inside of James, waiting to torch whatever crossed his path. The brief discussion informing him of the money bequeathed to him by his parents, acted like oxygen supplied to dying embers. It resurrected painful memories. But just as fuel was being added to the fire, Marty, his roommate, fortunately had walked into their dorm room and served as an extinguisher. The toxic memories that had been flooding back were reduced to evaporating fumes.

The two new roommates learned that there were commonalities existing between them. These shared traits led to the first real bond that James ever experienced as an adult. It also reinforced the factors supporting his mental rehabilitation and retarded the evil that had long been festering.

Marty Fogel was an only child. Both his parents were killed in the Twin Towers on 9/11. He had been in the foster care system and unlike James, was eventually adopted. The third family he was placed with developed a shining to the extremely intelligent and quiet boy. Marty was a mathematical genius and carried with him the values of his adoptive parents. He was a caring and hard working young man that believed in trying to make the world a better place.

Marty's parents were slightly older when they decided to be foster parents. They had married later in life and had no children. Both were successful in their careers and lived in Rumson, New Jersey. This was an extremely affluent area of the Central Jersey shore. Among its residents were Bruce Springsteen and not too far away, Jon Bon Jovi. The couple believed their lives to have been blessed and wanted to help someone less fortunate. When they met Marty it was only a matter of time till they fell truly in love with his gentle soul. They filed for adoption when he was fifteen years old. The family was as loving as any with biological ties. Marty was as good for his parents, Chris and Susan, as they were for him. Their lives were enriched by each other.

This hope and love emanated from Marty and the slight breakdown in James' outer walls allowed some access to his humanity. The fortuitous pairing generated a genuine affinity, and although the connection was not without a fragile foundation, it accomplished a miracle. James felt an indisputable attachment and something other than venomous intent. An antidote had been prescribed at the ideal time, when James' receptors were open to new information. Promise existed for healing, if only fate hadn't carried with it more harm. This last straw would not be drawn at Princeton for some time.

Their first semester was drawing to a close and the two roommates were at the Seely G. Mudd Manuscript Library. Most of the students at Princeton were wrapped up in their course loads and preparing for final examinations. James and Marty didn't have the normal anxiety associated with this time of year since they knew their exam material inside and out. They were there just to read whatever sparked their interest. This particular library housed a huge collection of public and foreign policy papers, along with a record of the senior theses written by generations of alumni. James liked perusing these historic documents because it showcased the brilliant minds that had once walked among its walls. Marty had a similar attachment to these rare books and manuscripts.

As they sat reading, James noticed an attractive girl approach the table. She was a petite, blue eyed blond. The freshman girl's name was Grace and she walked right up to them. She had gotten to know Marty at a preceptorial the previous week. Princeton students often referred to these as precepts, which were in essence, small discussion groups. They centered on the social sciences and humanities. The precepts were not lectures and were merely designed to facilitate intellectual discussion and insight among those attending the weekly sessions. James watched as she whispered into Marty's ear and invited both of them to attend a party at "the sticks" the following weekend. This was one of the nicknames that students of Princeton's Butler College fondly called the area. Marty enthusiastically responded this would be a great way to celebrate after exams ended and accepted the invitation.

On the day of the party, James found himself reluctant to attend. The thought of surrounding himself with people he didn't know made him nervous. He kept his relationships at Princeton cursory in nature and was slowly learning to trust people. Marty was his first real friendship and he didn't want to disappoint him by not going. James searched for a reason that would assuage his guilt. He rationalized that Marty carried an innate ability to fit into any social situation. His personality was just so open and devoid of any self serving traits. This lack of selfishness is what made it difficult for James to listen to his own internal needs.

It was Marty's intelligence that initially fascinated James. His intellect was vast, not on par with James, but stimulating nonetheless. His friend was able to hold his interest with his intellectual insights when they debated various academic topics. But it was the purity of Marty's being that allowed James to let down his previously impenetrable walls. This innocence was so foreign to James that it left him perplexed as to how he would handle the situation.

Marty noticed his friend seemed to be lost in his thoughts and said, "Hey, bud, what's up? Is anything wrong, you're just staring off into space?"

"I'm alright, but I don't think I'm going to this party tonight."

"Are you kidding me, you have to go. Grace said there'll be a lot of hot girls. Besides you know my policy, no man left behind."

"You've been watching too many war movies. I won't die if I stay in tonight," James replied.

"But I will, if you don't come with me. We just kicked ass on our exams and deserve some fun. Listen pal, if you aren't enjoying yourself after an hour, we'll hit the pavement. Deal?"

"Marty, if you don't follow through with your plans to be an astrophysicist, you might consider a career in politics or hostage negotiation. Okay, I'll give it a shot," James replied reluctantly.

"That's my man! Now let's grab some lunch. Grace has worked up my appetite," Marty said with a huge smile.

The two friends decided to walk to Olive's Deli over on Witherspoon Street. After eating, they checked out the University Store and then headed back to their dorm room at Rockefeller. For the next few hours they killed time watching *A Few Good Men*. It was the second time they watched the movie on DVD together.

Marty loved that film, and James had unwittingly memorized every line in the classic movie.

After the flick was over they went down to Rockefeller's Dining Room and briefly chatted with some other students about the party. Marty did most of the talking as they sat next to the fireplace on the comfortable leather couch behind the long dining room tables. The room itself had a medieval feel to it, consistent with the traditional gothic style of the university. Marty and James then sat down and ate with Walter Chiang, the Master of Rocky College. He was extremely popular with the students and was always available to offer advice or just provide a daily intellectual discussion. Today they conversed about everything from exams and the party, to genetic mapping and the possibility of extending life spans by preventing telomerase breakdown. Princeton University encouraged the creative mind to explore possibilities. This guiding principle was what made it such a revered institution of higher learning.

Upon finishing their meal, Marty and James headed over to the party. When they got to Grace's dormitory at Butler College, they just followed the incessant beat of loud music. James wasn't quite prepared for the sheer size of the bash. A DJ was blasting the Black Eyed Peas "Boom Boom Pow," as girls gyrated in outfits designed to attract the guys watching them. Marty headed over with his roommate to a group of fellow "Rocky" residents. This put James more at ease, since he already knew most of them. At the beginning of the term, Marty pulled them all into his circle by creating a corn hole tournament outside of their dormitory. Everyone commiserated about the classes they just finished. As they were chatting, Grace came rushing over with a friend. The girl accompanying her had long jet black hair, olive skin and was an exotic beauty. Grace tapped Marty on the shoulder and smiled.

"Hi guys, I'm so glad you made it. This is my roommate and best friend, Maria."

"Hey, Maria, I'm Marty and the shy guy standing next to me is my partner in crime, James. Hopefully Grace told you what great guys we are because nothing could have stopped us from coming," Marty said as he made eye contact with Grace.

"I've heard nothing but good things about you and James," she said with a slight Italian accent.

James nodded to the girls and then stared down at the floor. Although he felt uncomfortable getting to know new people, he usually was able to engage in perfunctory conversation. He remained tongue tied as he glanced back up at the pretty young girl standing before him. Marty sensed his friend's attraction and tried to force a conversation between them.

"Grace, why don't we go grab some drinks. You can tell me about your plans for break. Besides, my friend seems to be entranced by Maria," Marty said as he reached out for Grace's hand.

Grace grasped Marty's hand and smiled, "You two have fun."

"It looks like you're stuck with me," Maria said demurely.

"I'd say it's the other way around, I don't have Marty's way with words. I'm just really shy meeting new people, especially beautiful girls."

"I promise I won't bite, besides I like the strong silent type."

"Then it must be my lucky day," James responded, unable to meet her flirtatious stare.

This was the beginning of James' first legitimate romantic relationship. In high school, his girlfriend Carly had been more of a prop than a real emotional connection. Maria became the only person aside from Marty to gain entry into his very fragile psyche. His other friendships at Princeton were purely superficial. James still struggled with forming attachments since letting people get close allowed for the possibility of disappointment and loss. It took a special softness of spirit to move past James' protective barrier. Maria and Marty possessed this inimitable trait.

James' first term at Princeton ended as it had begun. Serendipity was overflowing. He met Marty at exactly the right moment and now Maria followed suit. The demon inside of him was disappearing. It was as if life itself recognized that James' humanity suffered enough damage and the scales needed to be balanced. The scarcity of mental stimulation was now bountiful, fortune replaced tragedy and most importantly, love now trumped the cruelty previously entrenched in James' life.

The second half of his freshmen year became a mirror image

of the first. James was beginning to remember what it was like to be happy. This was a feeling he hadn't felt since he was a little boy. Even the sporadic contact he maintained with Karen and Paul was not having the usual impact of stoking his now sleeping fury. James knew his foster parents didn't care about him and that their only concern was the income stream he provided. Now when he spoke with them his anger had been replaced with apathy. This emotional disconnect acted as a buffer suppressing the monster wanting to tear them apart. James' interests were now elsewhere. He was picturing a new life, a rebirth of sorts.

James impulsively purchased a home on Mercer Street in Princeton. He bought it because it was only a few houses down from where Albert Einstein had once lived. James had developed a fascination with the deceased genius. Einstein had fallen in love with Princeton University and the surrounding community. James imagined himself to be his kindred spirit. His friends were shocked to hear the news since they had been unaware of his massive wealth until now. James explained the inheritance but left out any of the details about his parents. He just told them he didn't like talking about it because the memory hurt too much. Each of them respected his request and didn't press him on the issue.

He still planned on living at Rockefeller with Marty, but this afforded him the opportunity to stay in Princeton during the summer months and after his eventual graduation. It also allowed him to spend time alone with Maria. The two of them were now inseparable. The first time they had sex, James finally understood why they called it making love. The only other person he ever had intercourse with was his high school girlfriend Carly. This had been a strictly carnal act with no sense of actual intimacy. It hadn't been Carly's fault because she cared deeply for James. Her feelings were unrequited, as everything at that time had been a mere stage act for the broken soul. James' dormant goodness was awakening to love, something that had been gone since early childhood.

At the end of the second term of their freshmen year, James and Marty maintained their perfect grade point averages. The two friends were now joined at the hip. They did virtually everything together; Grace and Maria, of course were their cohorts. The four of them had just finished helping each other pack up their stuff for summer break. They were all saddened by the prospect of not being together for the next several months. Marty was heading back home to his parent's house in Rumson, while Grace was leaving for Arizona. Maria was travelling back to Italy where she was born and raised. She was the only member of her large family to leave the Amalfi Coast. James was the only one that was remaining in Princeton. All of them were saying their goodbyes at the house James purchased on Mercer Street.

"Hey, we're going to hit the road now, I have to get Grace to the airport so she doesn't miss her flight. Take care guys; I'm going to miss you. Maria, have a nice time with your family and James, you'd better visit me this summer," Marty said while giving his friend a hug.

Grace gave Maria and James a kiss, "I already can't wait to see you both, and I haven't even left yet. Call, text, stay in touch."

"I have an idea, why doesn't everyone come to Italy and we'll backpack Europe this summer?" Maria said spontaneously.

"I'd love too, but I'm not sure my parents will pay for a summer abroad," Grace replied.

"I couldn't go without my babe. It just wouldn't be the same," Marty said as he put an arm around Grace.

"I'll pay for everybody if you want to go. I was already planning on surprising Maria this summer with a visit. She asked me to come with her and I pretended I couldn't make it. But the thought of us all hanging out in Europe is worth ruining my little surprise. So what do you say?" James said excitedly.

"Are you serious? That's incredibly generous and if you mean it, count me in. Of course, that's only if Marty comes along," Grace said.

"You're awesome bud. I'm in, but I'll need to go home for a few weeks to spend some time with my family before I visit," Marty replied.

"Me too," Grace interjected.

"Well then it's settled. This makes me very happy, since you're my real family and everyone was heading home to someone, except me," James responded with a sense of melancholy.

The three friends were aware of James having been raised by foster parents, but nothing beyond that fact. He hadn't been able to share the more horrific details that were walled up inside. His contact with Paul and Karen had become more and more infrequent. The connection waned the moment they believed there wasn't any more money to be exploited. Since James never spoke of Paul and Karen, his friends inferred there was not much of a bond. James simply let them disappear from his life rather than pursue his original plan. His new existence eschewed this need. Love had entered his life and it was something he could never live without, inconsolable to even imagine. Grace and Marty gave him one more hug before they left. They agreed to call and make arrangements for their trip to Europe in the next several days.

After their friends left, James and Maria spent their remaining time in bed. Later that evening he drove her to Newark Airport. He parked his newly acquired Porsche in short term parking and carried her luggage to the gate. Her flight on Alitalia was due to board in fifteen minutes. The couple hugged as they waited for her departure.

"I love you, James," Maria said. She then kissed him passionately.

It was the first time anyone spoke those words to him since he was a boy. Teardrops formed in his eyes. This was another emotional breakthrough, James hadn't cried since the night his parents were strangled. Locked away in that safe room were memories too dreadful to access.

"I love you too. Thank you for making me understand what that means. If you only knew what my life was like before I came to Princeton. I never trusted anyone since my parents died. Marty helped me, then I met Grace and ultimately you. I never want to be like that again," James spoke with his resurrected emotions.

"I'm so sorry for whatever you suffered, but as long as I'm here, I won't allow that to happen. I promise," Maria replied.

They kissed once more before she walked through the checkpoint to catch her flight. James felt like there was a chance for happiness as long as he had Maria and his friends. They couldn't erase his past, but they could support his ability to cope with the overwhelming pain he shut away.

As he drove back to his new home and his beloved Princeton University, he wept. Life had finally given him something other than tragedy. James visualized a new future, one which held hope and promise.

CHAPTER 18

"Present Day"

BETH AND FRANK WERE FRUSTRATED WITH THE DEAD ENDS THEY both encountered and hoped Tony would provide them with a better lead. When they got back to F.B.I. headquarters more disappointment was waiting.

"Beth, I'm sorry but it seems that Fred Kimmel has disappeared. The phone company disconnected his number for non-payment and no new number was established. The State Bar also suspended his license because he didn't pay his biennial registration fees. As far as Social Security's Death Index, there are no records matching his profile. He's actually been listed as a missing person for almost two years. No tax records, no credit card usage, unreturned mail, nobody that I've contacted has seen or spoken with him during that timeframe. He just up and vanished," stated Tony.

"It appears the mystery of Gary Jones just keeps getting bigger and bigger. This disappearance just reinforces our suspicions; yet the shroud of secrecy around him isn't going to last forever. It's time to trace the money trail from his publishing royalties," Frank responded.

"That's exactly my thoughts. Tony, find out where Chase wired any payments," Beth instructed her subordinate.

"I'll get right on it," Tony replied.

After filling Rob in on where they currently stood on the investigation, everyone agreed that the money trail was the appropriate path to follow. Beth and Frank decided to grab some food at Morton's Steakhouse to run ideas by one another and generally get to know each other better.

The two of them learned they came from similar backgrounds and were alike in many ways. Although Beth's parents were still alive, Frank and she had been the sole child of their respective families. They both were raised in strong Catholic households and grew up with a love for the beach. Beth's family had lived near the Outer Banks of North Carolina and Frank's on the Jersey Shore. Each joined the F.B.I. straight out of college.

Eventually they discussed the impact their careers had on personal relationships. Beth mentioned she broke up with her boyfriend about a year earlier. He hadn't been able to handle the demands placed on her by the FBI. This led to Frank talking about how excruciating it had been to lose Juliette and relating it to the fear he now had for Sarah. Over several more drinks, they continued to commiserate about the lifestyle and agreed that although the demands were steep, someone needed to protect the innocent from predators. Each knew they were born to do what they did for a living. Frank just felt that it was his cross to bear. He would sacrifice himself if it meant catching "The Magician".

Just as they ordered dessert, Beth received a text from Tony saying he had been able to trace the funds. The two of them decided to cut the meal short and head back to headquarters. Each felt excited to hear the details of where the money trail led and rushed back.

The instant Beth walked into Tony's office she asked "What have you got for us?"

"The payments made by Artista into Gary Jone's Chase Account were apparently just a stepping stone. Every last cent instantly transferred out. All the money was rewired to four different out of state banks. I assumed you'd want federal subpoenas requiring those banks to provide us with the relevant account information and I've already gotten that process started."

"Great work. I'm guessing we won't be able to do anything more until tomorrow. So let's all head home and get some rest. At least we can get some sleep knowing we actually have something tangible to follow."

"That's true, Beth. I can't wait to see where this leads. But based upon everything I've seen so far, I'm not expecting this to be a slam dunk."

"Let's hope you're wrong about that, Frank. But either way, the money has to take us somewhere. Gary Jones' anonymity won't hold up forever and then we can start looking for answers," Beth responded.

That night Frank woke out of a deep sleep with the same dream he had about Sarah and Juliette on the beach. The vivid nightmare made him uncomfortable. He wanted to call Sarah, but realized it was only 3:00 a.m. and didn't want to wake her. Frank checked his cell and noticed there were no texts or messages, so he attempted to calm his nerves by looking at things logically. It was only this past morning that he missed their scheduled run. He assumed she probably had a busy day and didn't get the chance to respond to his earlier message. This had happened in the past and sometimes they didn't get a hold of one another till the next day. If he still didn't hear from her by tomorrow morning, he would make it a priority to contact Sarah.

CHAPTER 19

"James' Sophomore Year, Princeton University"

JAMES RETURNED TO PRINCETON IN AUGUST, SEVERAL WEEKS BEFORE classes were scheduled to begin. He decided to play football after the constant prodding of coach, Pete Rosetti. The "two a days" of summer practice would begin tomorrow. James actually found himself looking forward to the physical grind that the morning and afternoon practices would demand. His need for a challenge was ever present. Lacking an immediate test he did the next best thing. James had the ability of total recall and visualized a chess match he had while in Europe. Every move from start to finish was replayed in his head. All the sights, sounds and smells of the day came to life. When he tapped into this part of his brain, he actually relived the event. He was temporarily transported back to Italy.

Marty and Grace were holding hands while looking inside of a jewelry shop. The four friends had just crossed over the Ponte Vecchio, an ancient stone arched bridge sitting above the Arno River in Florence. The smell of fresh baked goods was in the air, as Maria smiled at him. James had stumbled across a chess grand master giving an exhibition. She shuffled her hands in the direction of the crowd, as if giving him permission to play.

Several months earlier, he'd developed a fascination with the game after watching a documentary on Bobby Fischer. James was hooked. The following day he went down to Firestone Library at Princeton and read a book on advanced tactics. While he sat in its atrium he was enthralled by the intricacies of the age old game. He had never actually played after reading about chess strategy, but was excited to take his learned knowledge and apply it. Maria knew he would love to take advantage of this opportunity.

Grand Master Giovanni Luca was playing twenty separate games all at the same time. James took one of the spots available and as player after player was beaten, he alone remained. He found himself engaged in a one on one battle with the former international champion. He recognized that Luca was playing a variation of the Sicilian Defense and James countered with a Wing Gambit. He continued to strike with aggressive variations which led to his opponent's resignation. The inevitable checkmate would have followed seven moves later. James reveled in the image of the grand master tipping over his king.

This thrill of competition is what led him back to playing football. That very day, James texted his coach from Florence stating he was going to play for the Tigers and would be at the first scheduled practice. Although he was blessed with superior athleticism, he didn't stand alone. The gridiron held a unique appeal since intellectually he had no peer. On the field it was different; he was faced with a contest where the end result wasn't guaranteed. James loved the uncertainty because it stirred his desire to be the best of the best and he had to work at it. This focused effort acted as another sentinel over what lie underneath. Everything that was happening drove him away from where he'd almost gone. The madness that wanted to swallow him up disappeared.

So after replaying that moment in Florence, James' mind drifted toward his true source of emotional sustenance. He sat alone in his dorm room at Rockefeller College and closed his eyes; he was once again with Maria, Marty and Grace. They wouldn't be returning for several weeks and he missed them. James concentrated on one of his favorite mental pictures from the past summer. All four friends, stood in front of the Roman Coliseum with their arms draped over each other's shoulders while another tourist snapped their photo. A content smile spread across his face, as he realized what it felt like to have a family.

James continued to reminisce about his trip to Europe. He had travelled to Italy with Marty and Grace during the third week of June. Everyone stayed with Maria at her parent's villa on the Amalfi Coast. Mr. & Mrs. Grazia were extremely hospitable to their daughter's American friends and the rest of the large family was equally welcoming. They doted on James and at first this made him feel nervous, but eventually he grew to like it.

While he was there he learned to speak fluent Italian. His photographic memory absorbed the language as if he were learning the alphabet. Marty and Grace learned basic phrases. By the end of the trip they wanted to take classes in Italian back at Princeton.

But before returning home, the four friends also visited France, England and Germany. They hit all the tourist attractions, but also spent time just hanging out in pubs and cafes. Getting to know some of the locals added flavor to their experience. James loved the long history of these countries. He envisioned the days of Michelangelo, Shakespeare and DaVinci and how they once walked on these same streets.

His own past no longer revolved around his aggrieved existence. James wondered what contributions he would make and how he would be remembered. James left the virtual tour in his mind feeling energized.

The next day at practice he was introduced to his teammates and began working with the second stringers. James memorized the playbook the night before. While many of the newcomers struggled with the calls, he executed everything to perfection. It was apparent to everyone, coaches and players alike that he possessed rare talent. His arm was both strong and accurate, in addition to possessing above average speed for a quarterback. Yet the attribute that truly made him special was his ability to analyze a defense and visualize their weaknesses on any given play. Pete Rosetti already knew by the afternoon practice that James would win the starting job. He just wanted it to appear that the competition was real and not offend his current varsity starter.

The week before his classmates were scheduled to arrive back at school, James was officially named the starting quarterback for the Tigers. He was excited to have the opportunity to lead his teammates and face the challenge of the upcoming season. He felt proud of the accomplishment, but was euphoric about the impending return of his friends, most importantly Maria.

The exhilaration James was feeling carried over to the practice field and this quickly spread to his teammates. Coach Rosetti envisioned a special season for the Tigers. Everyone expected Harvard to win the Ivy League this year, but an extraordinary quarterback was about to be unveiled. The coach just watched his quarterback scramble to avoid an all out blitz and throw a perfect spiral on the run sixty yards downfield, only to see his starting wide receiver lay himself out to make a diving catch in the end zone. Inspiration had the ability to be contagious and James always brought a focused intensity to whatever path he followed.

The relationships he forged only became stronger his sophomore year. Marty was now like a brother, Grace a sister and Maria the love of his life. James did everything with complete passion. His grades continued to be perfect and his quest to learn never ceased its hold. James read book after book on any topic that peaked his interest. His capacity to store information was without bound. Aside from his intellectual cravings, his athletic goals were also a driving force. James was named Ivy League player of the year and earned the prestigious Bushnell Cup. This annual award was established in 1970 and given to the most outstanding player as voted on by the eight Ivy football coaches. Since James led Princeton to an undefeated season and an unexpected championship over Harvard, the choice to honor him was unanimous.

At the end of the school year, the four friends once again went to Europe. James insisted on paying for the excursion after meeting some initial resistance. Marty and Grace felt they were taking advantage of James since he covered all their expenses the previous summer. However, he convinced them to come along. They graciously accepted his offer after he practically begged them to accept.

Maria was thrilled to see James act so carefree. He appeared far removed from the overly serious and shy individual she'd first met. That first impression hadn't mattered to her because the attraction was electric. She remembered feeling drawn to him from the moment Grace introduced them. The reason she was pleased to see him behave happy-go-lucky was tied to some of their more intimate conversations. In the past, whenever she'd asked about his family background, James clammed up. Apparently it had been too awful to discuss. He would shut down whenever she pushed him on the matter. Eventually, Maria chose to leave it alone. If ever a time came that he was ready to open up, she would be there to listen and offer comfort. She had fallen madly in love with James. His passion to throw himself completely into whatever he undertook was enthralling. Maria was his heart and soul. James was hers.

CHAPTER 20

"Present Day"

FEDERAL WARRANTS HAD BEEN GRANTED ALLOWING ACCESS INTO the bank accounts in which Chase had wired funds. Before Frank headed over to F.B.I. headquarters he once again checked to see if Sarah had attempted to contact him. He didn't expect any messages this early since it coincided with their usual running time on the boardwalk. The supposition was correct because she hadn't responded as of yet. He planned on calling her around lunchtime. In the meantime, he was looking forward to the possibility of finally tracking down Gary Jones.

When Frank arrived at the Bureau he was told to head over to Beth's office. She had all the information regarding the accounts and wanted to fill him in on the details. Frank could barely contain his excitement as he felt they were getting closer to something useful in the investigation.

"Good morning, Beth," he said as he entered her office.

"It's not as good as I hoped; it seems we still don't have a direct trace to our suspect. None of the accounts are listed as Gary Jones. This is getting to be an annoying habit; we seem to face a different maze every time we dig deeper. There are four different account holders we're going to have to investigate and hopefully we can start figuring this out."

"It would stand to reason that Gary Jones is just a pseudonym at this point. Nothing appears as it seems, the guy really is a magician. Obviously he's doing all he can to create uncertainty. One of these people must be him...assuming all of the money is tied to the account holders? We'll have to check if anything's been siphoned off. Maybe they're all red herrings," Frank responded.

"I'll have Tony make sure all proceeds were fully transferred into these accounts and that no money was rewired anywhere else. We'll also need to decide who's going to meet with each account holder. Each location is in a different state and of course, none are close to each other," Beth said with minor frustration.

"Lucky we have the full resources of the F.B.I. behind us. Does any one of the account holders stand out for any reason?" Frank asked.

"All four names are males, but beyond that we just gained access to the accounts a little while ago. Tony is actually researching their backgrounds as we speak," Beth answered.

"Good. If anything is unusual with any of them, I'd like to be given that specific directive. If that's alright with you?"

"I'd have expected nothing less. Why don't we go and fill Rob in on what's happening while we wait for Tony to provide us with some more details."

"Sounds like a plan, Beth."

Rob was intrigued by the continued subterfuge. He was coming around to the idea that there was something more to this than an author using classified information for his book. The odds had swung in favor of "The Magician" actually being at the center of this quagmire. Rob granted full authority to Beth to utilize any resources needed in the course of the investigation. He was afraid of the potential for a new murder spree and wanted to prevent that at all costs. Inwardly, Rob hoped it wasn't a return of the madman, but that likelihood was diminishing by the minute.

After they filled the Director in on the full status of things they returned to Tony's office to see what other details he uncovered. All of the royalty money paid by Artista had been split equally among the four individuals. There had been no rewiring of the funds, at least not directly from any of those accounts. The possibility still existed that any money withdrawn could have been sent or given to anyone. This prospect would have to considered and checked. Yet one name on the list did stand out. The others would have to be vetted, but they would be deemed a lower priority.

Tim Richardson was the person that had drawn the most attention. He had served a little more than a year in prison for grand theft auto. It had been a first offense and he was let out early on parole. Tim had been involved in a high speed car chase with the police after an officer attempted to pull him over for a broken taillight. Once he was apprehended it became apparent that the Corvette he was driving had been stolen. It had not yet been reported and Mr. Richardson claimed he took the vehicle on a joyride. He said he planned on just leaving the vehicle nearby, but panicked when he saw the lights flash on the police car before he had the chance to do so. The biggest red flag was that this incident happened in Manasquan, New Jersey just two weeks after Hurricane Sandy.

The timing and location of the crime caused Frank to insist on being part of the questioning of this suspect in regards to the current investigation. The proximity to Spring Lake and his time served fit the puzzle. Beth decided that the two of them would travel together to Dallas, Pennsylvania where Mr. Richardson resided. She also strategized with Frank and together they laid out a game plan for the rest of their task force.

Agent Tucker was assigned to interview Eric Duritz. He lived in Los Gatos, California and was twenty-five years old. Mr. Duritz was married and had two small children. He currently owned a local restaurant. Prior to this he was the owner of a failed small business. Nothing seemed too out of the ordinary at first glance, other than whatever ties he had with Gary Jones.

The third suspect was Nolan Russeck. He was a divorced English Professor living in Scottsdale, Arizona. He worked at a small community college in the Phoenix area. Nolan was thirty-two years old and worked two days a week for the school. Mr. Russeck had also published two novels that were commercially unsuccessful. Beth instructed the senior member of the team, Agent Julia Thorn to question the writer. The fact that he was an author stirred some interest, but not quite as much as Tim Richardson.

Justin Logan was the final account holder that needed to be questioned. He was a thirty-nine year old former airline pilot that stopped working shortly after Gary Jones' first novel was published. He was currently unemployed and living in Chicago. The two remaining team members, Agent Bucko and Agent Gelaszus had been given this assignment. They would attempt to feel him out and ascertain his connection to the writer.

All team members were instructed to be cautious due to the possibility that any of these individuals could be the Magician or have some type of relationship with the killer. Obviously they could be harmless pawns in his game or just simply further barriers for an eccentric writer to hide behind. The agents all wondered if they would come face to face with a psychopath, a reclusive writer or the author's benefactors.

Travel arrangements were made by ancillary staff. The task force would be on the road tomorrow. The recent activity had everyone hyped up and ready to go. The investigation was a possible career maker, but for Sorello it was about closing a chapter. He needed closure.

The intensity surrounding the case had picked up and Frank lost track of time. It was two thirty in the afternoon when he happened to glance at his watch. Suddenly, Sarah flooded all his thoughts. The uncomfortable feeling he had the previous night still hadn't subsided. He desperately wanted to hear her voice so that he could satisfy his need to know that she was alright. Frank called, hoping she'd pick up.

CHAPTER 21

"James' Junior Year, Princeton University"

JAMES' JUNIOR YEAR WOULD HAVE BEEN DESCRIBED BY AN OUTSIDE observer as a fairy tale existence. It was like he was royalty and Camelot awaited his command. Everything that could be desired was within reach. James was rich beyond anyone's wildest dreams. He had an inner circle that was loyal and true, without jealousy or avarice. Maria, his stunning girlfriend, loved him to no end. James possessed model good looks and intelligence on par with DaVinci, Hawking, and his beloved Einstein.

If that were not enough, fame seemed to be creeping in his direction. James just led the Tigers to its first bowl appearance in over fifty years. Princeton beat Stanford in a thriller 45-42. James threw five touchdowns and passed for over four hundred yards in the victory. The team had once again won the Ivy League and gone undefeated. The Tigers were expected to be nationally ranked in preseason prognostications for the following year. James had his second Bushnell Award and was considered to be a Heisman Trophy candidate. Agents were attempting to convince him to go professional and forego his senior year. Of course, he rebuffed any of these requests. Princeton University had saved his life and he wanted to remain at his kingdom as long as he lived.

If this were Greek mythology, the lore would be that the gods were now smiling down upon him, as a favored son. Yet, like Achilles, fate often swung both ways.

James had just written and signed the statement, "I pledge

my honor that I have not violated the Honor Code during this examination." It was his final test of the first term's culmination. This provision was a requisite of all students at the university. As incoming freshman everyone was notified of this requirement and expected to abide by its covenant throughout their time at Princeton. All work on tests or written exams was to be completed without cheating or plagiarism. This agreement was instituted in 1893 and required the first year students to sign their name pledging to uphold the code. If anyone noticed anyone violating this doctrine then they would be required to inform faculty. James had never witnessed an infraction. This time honored tradition worked hand in hand with all the other aspects of his college experiences, to overcome his learned disdain for the capacity of people to be good. Honor and faith in grander beliefs; striving to be the best of your capabilities were at Princeton's center. If only the outside world managed to meet this same lofty ideal, then perhaps James would have found his perch on Olympus. Perhaps one day, another Greek tragedy would be written about his story.

James carried his perfect grade point average into the year's second semester. He loved all of his classes but was majoring in Computer Science with a systems concentration. Of course, he read everything he could about his field of study. The other areas of concentration he didn't ignore. Computer theory and architecture, programming, networking, security and artificial intelligence were all integrated into his outside study. His desire to be stimulated caused him to sit in on classes he wasn't even signed up for and this applied to other fields as well. James would just pop into an art class, human biology or whatever appeased his appetite at that moment in time. His capacity to absorb information was endless. Marty sometimes joined him on these ventures but to a much lesser extent. Maria and Grace just laughed when they discussed their men's zealousness, but also admired the drive for knowledge.

All the positive changes that had surfaced in James since coming to Princeton were amazing. The relationships forged here had done wonders. He was passionate and happy, experiencing emotions that were nearly lost forever. The goodness inside of him was bursting at the seams, constantly searching for new outlets. Pure chance seemingly led the way.

Maria was sitting in her dorm room preparing to watch her favorite program. It was mid-afternoon and James had just finished class. He was about to go to the library as he did every day at this time, when his cell phone rang.

"James, will you be a sweetheart and pick up a sandwich and a Coke for me. I'm starving. I'd do it myself, but Ivy is about to come on and I don't want to miss it."

"Sure, if you don't mind telling me who's Ivy?"

"Ivy...from *The Ivy Whille Show*, you dummy. Why don't you watch it with me?"

"I'm not really a fan of tv, besides this is my library time."

"I'll make it worth your while," Maria said seductively.

"How do you propose to do that?"

"Just get over here and after the show ends, let's just say that you'll be very happy."

"I'll be over in a few minutes," James replied enthusiastically.

Maria was addicted to the show. The very first time she watched it, her smile was endless, as she saw Ivy dance to "Moves Like Jagger." The talk show host gyrated among the audience, completely lacking inhibition, as DJ Joey pumped up the crowd. Ivy was a fun escape from the rigors of classes. Maria was hooked.

James too, became a fan. Maria was happy that they'd found another interest together. Everything between the two of them was symbiotic. Maria practically ripped James' clothes off the second the show was over. Later that night, Marty and Grace stopped by to hang out with their friends.

James and Maria were giddy and laughed with innocence only youth can provide. Marty and Grace stared in bewilderment as if they were standing on the outside of an inside joke. Yet as always the couples fed off of one another and before long they just joined in the moment, telling stories and sharing each other's joy. The spirit of that evening held true throughout their relationship.

The four of them continued to be inseparable. They discussed the future in ways that incorporated one another, as if they would never be apart. A rare connection existed as each person made the other better. It was as if they were the embodiment of Princeton's spirit.

James and Marty were sitting in on a lecture about Ancient Rome and were fascinated by the technological advances of the civilization. They marveled at the Roman Aqueduct system which transported water throughout the city. Each conferred as to how ingenious it was for the time period. James savored these interactions with his friend.

It was at that moment he decided to share his plans with Marty. He wasn't going to tell anyone what he had been thinking about, but realized he wanted his best friend to know. James had been contemplating this for awhile.

After the lecture they headed over to Rockefeller to have lunch in its dining hall. James was so excited he couldn't wait any longer.

In mid-step he just blurted out, "I'm going to ask Maria to marry me."

Marty stopped dead in his tracks and hugged his friend, "That's fucking fantastic. Congratulations, man, the two of you are perfect together. Eventually I plan on doing the same with Grace, just not yet. Do you have a ring?"

James replied, "I'm planning on going into the city on Saturday morning. Maria is going to be working on a paper that's due soon, so it'll give me the perfect opportunity. Do you want to come, we can check out different jewelers?"

"I'd love to. Manhattan is always a blast and besides I want to be remembered as being a part of this epic event."

"Great, we'll catch an early morning train Saturday."

That weekend, Marty and James visited numerous jewelers on Fifth Avenue. Finally, after an exhaustive search a ring was chosen. James purchased a 2.5 carat, emerald cut diamond in a platinum setting. It was flawless and exorbitantly priced. CEO's and celebrities would be envious of such a ring. James decided he would give it to Maria on her birthday which was right before the end of the semester in May.

The next several weeks couldn't go by fast enough for James. His excitement was tough to control, but he managed. His former self had practiced the fine art of mimicking facial expressions and his poker face showed no tells. What was once so easy had become difficult because now he actually connected to the feelings he had once imitated.

Maria's birthday finally arrived after what seemed to be an eternity for James. That morning he told her of his plans to take her to a special dinner in Hamilton, New Jersey. James researched online romantic and unique restaurants in the Metropolitan area. He chose to make reservations at Rat's. This charming restaurant was on the former site of the New Jersey State Fairgrounds. Aside from having a reputation for fine dining, artistic sculptures were strewn throughout the forty-two acre grounds. Patrons were allowed to walk among the whimsical creations and James felt it would be the perfect place to ask Maria to be his wife.

That night the two of them dressed up and jumped into James' red Porsche for what was to be a memorable evening. Maria had no idea of the intended proposal. She was just happy to be spending her birthday with the young man she loved so dearly. Dinner was delicious and the grounds were incredible to survey. James wanted the evening to be perfect. So when they came across a sculpture of a man passionately kissing a woman hidden among the bushes, he knew he'd found the right moment.

James dropped to one knee, looked up and said, "Maria, will you please do me the honor of spending the rest of your life with me?"

She burst into tears and practically screamed out, "Yes, yes, yes. I love you, James."

The two of them shared in an embrace not too dissimilar from the lifelike statue standing right beside them. It was a storybook memory. A couple standing not too far away had witnessed the proposal and snapped pictures. They waited until James and Maria finished kissing. Then they offered their congratulations, along with the photographs that commemorated the blessed event. Since the pictures were taken on a smart phone, they immediately sent them to Maria's email address. The newly engaged couple thanked them profusely for capturing the moment. Maria was so thrilled she hugged the couple before saying goodbye.

On the ride home, Maria called her family in Italy informing them of the engagement. Her mom, dad and siblings all got on the phone expressing their joy. Maria was elated. She then followed with another call to Grace who was almost as excited as the bride to be. At that same moment, James was asking Marty to be his best man and he gladly accepted. To cap off a perfect day, later that night Maria and James made love as if it had been their first time.

The following day classmates and faculty alike shared in the newly engaged couple's bliss. They decided on a summer wedding at the Amalfi Coast. Maria didn't want to wait until graduation to marry. She still had another full year left, whereas James was on pace to graduate early with an Engineering Degree. Due to advance standing he would meet and exceed the required thirty-two course minimum load of the program by the end of his senior year's first term. Although he was close to finishing his undergraduate curriculum it was tough to concentrate on anything other than Maria.

The examination period of the second term flew by as thoughts of marriage filled his head. It was a testament to his intelligence that James still managed a perfect grade point average while working to complete his senior thesis in advance. This academic dissertation was required of every senior at Princeton and James worked diligently with his department faculty adviser to complete it early. His innovative research centered on artificial intelligence. He was looking to expand on IBM's ground breaking Watson. This super computer was programmed by Big Blue to understand natural language and in essence predict outcomes through evidence based learning. Massive amounts of data are rapidly filtered in its circuitry to generate logical hypotheses. Watson then seeks the best answer to problems that require establishing connections, just the way humans do through a lifetime of experience.

James was working to build upon this by developing an algorithm which would accelerate the movement toward true artificial intelligence. In essence computers could improve on their own source codes through true analytical thinking. This would eventually lead to machines being capable of processing information like the human brain, but at exponentially faster rates. As computer chips inevitably increase in power and store information on infinitely smaller materials through advances in nanotechnology, the science fiction of movies like "The Terminator" could eventually become a reality. Robots could merge into society as human replicants or people themselves could be engineered with cells containing A.I. (artificial intelligence). James saw a future where this could lead to curing all diseases and a potentially infinite life span. This idea was born the day he met Maria at Grace's dormitory party when he and Marty discussed telomerase implications with Walter Chiang in the dining hall at Rocky. This conversation served as creative inspiration triggering his genius. James wanted to impact future generations and be forever remembered. He was very close to achieving this endeavor, but his path was not yet set in stone.

Unforeseen events would lead James elsewhere, just like the day he met Marty at Mudd Library. It was funny how the simplest event could trigger a whole series of consequences. It was there he met Grace and through her Maria. Inadvertently this led to the subsequent dinner conversation with Marty and the college master, Walter Chiang about the potential for immortality. Had they not gone, Grace might never have invited them to the party. Maria may never have entered his life and all that was to follow would have taken an entirely different course, but that was not to be the case. This series of chance encounters was already set in motion. It was like the so called Butterfly Effect where a small but subtle change in a system could lead to a much larger change in a later state. This certainly would hold true for James, those close to him and others far from this serene, academic paradise. Life's unpredictable patterns had a strange way of forming a connected web. The vibrations tethered through James' past, present and future interactions would soon bring on a spider's descent; not the beauty of a butterfly flapping its exquisite wings.

Fates shadows were not far off in the distance, but still remained out of sight. The last day of the term was a perfect spring day. A cloudless sky allowed the sun to shine brightly down on Princeton's residents. James felt its warmth as he walked toward his home on Mercer. All he could think about was Maria and how she created a similar sensation, but one that was infinitely stronger. James couldn't contain his happiness and wanted this same feeling for the two other people he loved in life.

Marty planned on proposing to Grace in Italy the day after James and Maria's wedding. His best man wanted to wait until then, so that he didn't steal their spotlight. James loved his friend's selflessness and how this changed his view of mankind. It made him want to give back what he received. This instinctive response would rear itself in another manner soon, but for now altruism reigned.

Every fiber of James' being was focused on his fiancée's happiness. Actions, guided by benevolence and generosity, provided an additional reward. They helped to ease the discomfort, he felt from having killed Max. James was in the early stages of building emotional maturity. Like a child, he feared disappointing those he loved, in this case, Maria. He knew how much she loved animals, so it gnawed at him that he had killed the dog. More complicated feelings, such as guilt and empathy, were still developing as was the concept of unconditional love. Anger was being replaced with acts of kindness, mostly directed at Maria, Marty and Grace. Retribution was no longer his guiding force. Instead, life was showing him another path. Maria's belief that you reap what you sow now compelled him to do good things. At this point, the drive stemmed from a will to please her rather than any deeply felt personal belief. James wanted to surprise Maria with something that would further accomplish this task.

Her family always had a host of animals living on their property in Italy, which led to Maria developing a deep seeded passion. She always talked to James about her desire to have pets become a part of their eventual home once they were married. A few weeks back, they were watching Ivy, in what had become their newest shared ritual. A segment of the show was dedicated to a sanctuary for abused animals called The Happy Farm. A woman named Lisa ran it with her husband in Mesa, California. A clip of the refuge was being shown. Afterwards, the host and guests discussed additional ways in which this wonderful place helped children. Inner city kids, troubled children and those in foster care often were brought to visit. This acted as a rehabilitative process in restoring happiness not only to the children, but also to the animals. At the end of the piece, Ivy asked for charitable donations to help aid in more animals gaining care.

Maria cried, "That's beautiful, we should visit there sometime."

"We will, I promise."

Later that same day, James made arrangements to visit The Happy Farm following their honeymoon. He also felt a strong desire to help their cause because it hit home on multiple levels. James made a one million dollar donation to the place in hopes of furthering the sanctuary's goals. His plan of keeping it a secret was thwarted when he received an unexpected phone call a few days later.

"Hello, am I speaking to James Carlson?"

"Yes, that'd be me."

"Hi. This is Ivy Whille and I wanted to personally call you for your generosity. I was so touched by your donation that I'd like to have you on my show."

"Are you kidding me? I'd love that, but I think you should be thanking my fiancée instead. Maria loves you and shares your passion. To be honest I never really watched television until she introduced me to your show. Don't get me wrong, you're awesome, I'm now one of your legion of fans. As for the donation, I'm glad I could help such a worthy cause and I'd like to thank you as well for introducing me to it."

"You're too kind. Why don't you invite your fiancée along, so I can thank her as well?"

"Really? She's going to lose her mind."

"I don't want that to happen. Then I wouldn't be able to thank her."

James laughed.

"I'll have a member of my staff call you later today to make the arrangements, if that'd be okay?"

"Absolutely, and thank you again."

"I really should be thanking you, James, not the other way around."

Later that night, when James told Maria she was ecstatic. They were scheduled to be on the show two weeks prior to leaving for Italy and their wedding. Everyone was thrilled by the news.

The day of the show, Maria could hardly contain her excitement. Sitting in their dressing room was surreal. James held her hand as they were told they were about to go on by one of Ivy's staff. When they heard their introduction, Maria squeezed his hand all the tighter. As they walked on stage, the two of them danced to the music blasting from Joey's speakers.

"James and Maria, thank you for coming."

"Oh my God, can I give you a hug," Maria blurted out.

Ivy smiled, stood up and embraced Maria like an old friend.

"If you don't mind, someone else wants to get in on the action," Ivy said waving on the guest waiting in the wings.

Lisa from The Happy Farm walked out, grabbed James by the hand and had him join in on the group hug. When they all sat down, Ivy praised James for his large charitable gift, talked about the sanctuary, the upcoming marriage and James' notoriety as the star quarterback for the Princeton Tigers. After the show, she graciously thanked Maria and James once again. The experience had been exhilarating and was an excellent precursor for what was to be their greatest memory.

James purchased first class tickets and booked a deluxe suite for Marty and Grace at the Santa Caterina. This was considered by many to be the premier hotel in the area and it sat directly on the rocky Amalfi coastline. The breath taking view of the Mediterranean Sea was only part of its magnetism. Fruit orchards, olive groves and lush flower gardens surrounded the luxurious property enhancing its elegant, old world charm. The wedding was scheduled for the middle of July and James booked the suite for the entire month. He wanted his friends to enjoy their stay before and after the impending nuptial and for their engagement to be as memorable as his own had been.

James and Maria were to stay at her family's large seaside home, where the marriage ceremony and reception was to be held. The property was both beautiful and expansive with its own spectacular vista. Maria's family owned a large vineyard in the Campania wine region in Southern Italy and this was where their wealth was derived. The Grazia's were well known in this exclusive community, winemaking was in their blood. Maria's father Angelo, built the business into a multimillion dollar enterprise after taking the reins from his father. Her mother, Anita stayed at home and provided the loving foundation in which the entire family thrived. Their home was always open to anyone who showed up at their doorstep and this hospitality was well known. Over four hundred people in the village were to attend the celebration and the wedding was the focal point of the summer.

Maria wanted her special day to be perfect, so she flew to Italy hours after completing her last test. Her sisters and mother were sure to be immersed in planning for the occasion and she felt the excitement welling up inside. Everyone was elated to have her home as the upcoming marriage was right around the corner. Maria was the first of her siblings to be wed and this was sacrosanct since it was the epitome of what they were all about, family. Maria was the happiest she had ever been and wanted James to come as soon as possible. They had been virtually inseparable since the engagement and she missed him terribly.

Across the ocean, James sat equally lost without Maria. She inspired him the way the aura of the university had done. Now all he could think about was joining her at the Amalfi Coast. Just two weeks prior he was engrossed in tracing modern computing capabilities all the way back to Alan Turing. This former Princeton Alum was considered to be the father of computer science. His doctorate degree in mathematics at Princeton in 1938 precipitated the first digital computer and the development of artificial intelligence. Every day until the moment she left he inched closer to finding the answer to his senior thesis and finishing the algorithm in his brain. This work consumed him, but without Maria he was paralyzed. She had overtaken Princeton and became the vessel which fed his soul.

Realizing this James picked up the phone and dialed Maria. At that same moment as if connected, she reached for her phone. Seconds later, the phone rang and she smiled seeing her fiancee's number on the digital display. Their love for one another was truly special.

"Were you reading my mind? I was just about to call you. Please get on a plane so I can see you," Maria said exuberantly.

"As soon as I hang up I'm catching the next available flight. This place isn't the same without you," James replied.

"Then put the damn phone down and get over to the airport. I miss you so much."

James smiled and said, "Thanks babe, me too. Alright, I'm going to call Alitalia now. Ciao bella."

"Ti amo."Maria told him she loved him in Italian.

James dreamt that night of a long and wonderful life with Maria. On the rainy ride to the airport he continued to fantasize about what the future held for them. Even throughout the turbulent flight his thoughts centered only on the tranquility she brought to his existence. The thunder and lightning which bounced the plane around didn't have any effect on his peaceful state. All James saw in front of him were bright skies and Maria.

CHAPTER 22

"Present Day"

"Hello," Sarah said as she picked up her phone.

"I'm so glad you answered, my head was getting the best of me," Frank replied.

"I'm sorry, I didn't mean for you to worry. I was swamped today with appointments and I was going to call you tonight. Besides, I figured you were just as busy, if not more. How are you?"

"Things are moving along, a little slower than I'd like, but we have some leads to follow. So overall, alright, I guess."

"I have an idea how I can improve your mood. Oops, maybe I shouldn't have said that, given our last conversation. I just can't help myself around you; the bad girl just seems to creep out in me."

"Sarah, when this is all over, I hope that bad girl still wants to come out and play. Just right now, I need to be focused and even as things stand right now, I couldn't sleep the other night, praying you were okay."

"That's sweet, but like I keep telling you. I'm fine. So stop stressing out over nothing. Just get this job finished and we'll pick up where we left off. How's that sound?"

"Like a great plan. You always know what to say to me. Anyhow, I'm gonna have to get going. So I'll see you when I see you."

"Can't wait. Bye, Frank."

Sarah sighed as she hung up, thinking how she wished they didn't have to hold back on their very obvious feelings for one another. She kept telling herself everything would work out fine to help compensate for the frustration mounting. Frank locked out his own emotions by wrapping himself into the task at hand.

He was meeting Beth at the gate in fifteen minutes to catch their connecting flight from Philadelphia to Wilkes-Barre Airport in Pennsylvania. She wanted to grab a quick cup of coffee from Starbucks. Beth said she needed it to function properly. Their next stop in the investigation would require their attention, so he asked her to get him a cup also. Frank was wondering if this lead was in fact the Magician, when Beth tapped him on the shoulder.

"Here you go. Black, no sugar."

"Thanks, this was a good idea. They just announced our flight will be boarding soon," Frank said.

"Okay, let's head over. So what were you thinking, you seemed lost in thought just now?"

"If this is going to be our guy?"

"Me too. What's that famous instinct of yours telling you?"

"That I'm just not sure. Everything about him seems to be just a mirage."

Beth wondered to herself if his intuition meant this was going to be another dead end. She really believed in gut feelings, especially those of the F.B.I. legend standing next to her.

As they boarded Beth said, "Either way we're going to find him."

CHAPTER 23

"James' & Maria's Wedding"

JAMES STARED INTO MARIA'S EYES AND SAID "I DO."

His dream was becoming a reality. The girl who taught him love and how to live again, stood before him. She was radiant in her flowing white wedding gown. Her eyes lit up with joy and the smile on her face would make the Mona Lisa pale in comparison. When she said "I do," James couldn't believe that this woman was his and would be forever. Their vows till death do us part would never be broken by their own hands. James kissed his bride with a lifetimes worth of longing as Maria filled his aching heart with a newly found faith.

Life wasn't an exercise in cruelty as he once believed. Instead, an elusive peacefulness settled around the young man who had suffered through disappointment and tragedy. This twist of fate felt almost surreal to James.

His best man and the maid of honor, Marty and Grace, stood at their sides. Each beamed with joy while watching the newlyweds laugh as rice rained down from the sky. The looks on their faces were not lost on James. Even while immersed in what seemed to him like a fairytale, their love was apparent. Marty and Grace represented his only family at the ceremony, which stood in stark contrast to his bride. Maria's large family and friends seemed to be everywhere offering up congratulations. The sheer number of people that knew and loved her was without bounty, but James felt no jealousy. The connection between the four friends was one of total fulfillment.

It was more than enough for James, because the love he received from them was more than he could ever have imagined. The groom almost couldn't believe the blessings now bestowed upon him. James felt that his moment in the sun had arrived.

The reception that followed was filled with revelry and carried on into the night. Even the brief and unexpected thunderstorm that drenched the guests didn't slow the party. People rushed under the tents that were set up in the event of just such an occurrence. James and Maria danced in the rain like all the others sharing their special day. Angelo and Anita were thrilled to see the ecstasy in their daughter's eyes as she waltzed with their new son-in-law. It was a night to be remembered.

Following the reception the bride and groom's storybook affair continued in a private jet ride to Paris. They were taken by a stretch limo directly to the Shangri-La Hotel. Maria and James' suite was the crown jewel of the five-star establishment. The opulent room was over two thousand square feet and had a separate terrace with sweeping views. The newlyweds drank champagne while staring at the most spectacular sight of the Eiffel Tower. After absorbing the romance of the Paris skyline the bride and groom spent the rest of the night making love.

In the morning, the couple wandered outside to the Trocadero, walking hand in hand while gazing at the garden's beauty. James and Maria felt there wasn't a care in the world as the Seine and treasures of Paris were all around them. The serenity of the moment caused James to think of Marty's planned proposal today and he smiled.

"Is that for me?" she asked while noticing his large grin.

"Who else would it be for, I love you, Maria."

"Kiss me."

James was happy to oblige, not only for the passion she stirred in him, but also to steer the conversation away from the reason of his smile. He wanted to keep the promise he made to Marty. His friend was the brother he never had and keeping the pledge intact was important. Marty wanted Maria to hear the news directly from Grace so the surprise would be genuine. Even though James wanted to tell Maria of the upcoming proposal, he honored the request, knowing the excitement would soon be shared.

Later that evening, Maria heard the news and was elated. She invited the newly engaged couple over to the Shangri-La. The wedding celebration continued together on the terrace of the newlywed's suite. They laughed and told stories of their initial meeting and of memories that followed. The name of the hotel was very apropos, because it appeared that James, Maria, Marty and Grace had found paradise while rejoicing among the city of lights.

Vintage bottles of Dom Perignon were ordered up to their room. James loved being able to lavish his friends with whatever he possessed. They were all that was important to him in the world. Of course, Maria was the center of his universe.

James raised a glass of champagne while standing on the terrace, with Paris painting a canvas around their intimate circle.

"Congratulations to Marty and Grace on their engagement. I'm sure that their marriage will hold nothing but happiness and love. I'd also like to thank them for leading me to the woman I could never live without, my exquisite bride, Maria. So let's toast to a lifetime of future memories and the days ahead of us. I love you all."

"Here, here," Marty chanted.

With their flutes raised, they tapped glasses, drank champagne and hugged. Each believed that James' words would forever hold true. That night they held on to their youthful spirit and like Napoleon once imagined while wandering Paris, the world lay at their feet.

CHAPTER 24

"Present Day"

TIM RICHARDSON WAS SITTING ON HIS COUCH WATCHING THE METS and Phillies battle it out on his state of the art Samsung OLED when his doorbell rang. The tall, bearded man had hoped to relax undisturbed and watch the game alone. He debated on whether or not he should get up to see who had arrived. Tim was a loner and rarely had visitors so he decided to answer the door. When he saw the two strangers standing on his front porch, one male and one female, he assumed it might be Jehovah's Witnesses. Tim grumbled to himself wishing he pretended not to have been home. He opened the door with a beer still in his hand.

"What can I do for you?" he asked.

Beth and Frank were surprised by his size, not his height, but his muscle mass. Tim Richardson with his bodybuilder physique certainly had the capacity to overpower his victims, if in fact, he was the perpetrator. He looked quite intimidating as he approached the door with a scowl on his face.

"Are you, Tim Richardson?" Beth inquired.

"Who's asking?

"I'm Special Agent Gregg, with the F.B.I. and this is former Agent Sorello," she replied while flashing her badge. "May we come in and ask you a few questions?"

"I've got nothin to hide, so whatever this is about, come inside and I'll answer anything you like."

"Thank you," she said, as they entered the suspect's home. Frank remained quiet and kept his eyes on Richardson. They were in a fairly large foyer and could hear a television on in another room.

"Why don't we talk in my kitchen, because I'm ready for another beer. Do you want one?"

"No thanks, we don't drink on the job," Beth answered.

"Suit yourself," Richardson said as he turned around and walked down the hall.

The agents warily followed the hulking presence as he headed toward another room. As they passed the room with the ballgame playing on the large flat screen, Frank subtly nudged Beth and pointed into the den. On the wall was a glass enclosed hunting case with various rifles and knives inside. Since Richardson had his back to them, he hadn't noticed.

"Who's winning the game?" Frank asked off the cuff.

"The Phillies, 3-1 in the seventh. Are you a baseball fan?"

"Yeah, die hard Yankees fanatic," replied Frank.

"Now I really don't like you," Richardson said in a tone that was tough to read.

He certainly carried a degree of arrogance and displayed a lack of deference toward the law enforcement agents. Beth and Frank weren't sure if he was joking or just attempting to rattle their cage, usually it worked the other way around. Tim Richardson sat down at his kitchen table and slugged down the can of Budweiser, while pointing at the open chairs. Beth and Frank sat down opposite the large man.

"So...," the suspect asked in an inquisitive and directive manner, dragging out the word sarcastically.

"Mr. Richardson, we'd like to know what connection you have to Gary Jones," Beth asked.

"Who the fuck is Gary Jones?"

"Are you saying you don't know him?" Beth queried.

"If this is a former cellmate, I knew a lot of guys, but it's not like I've kept in touch. I figure this has something to do with me serving time; otherwise I have no idea why you're here. So to answer your question, I have no goddamn clue who you're talking about and if that's all, I'd like to get back to my ballgame."

Frank just watched the interaction, observing the whole

dialogue and Tim Richardson's demeanor toward the questions. He was going to let Beth take control of the interrogation, allowing his instincts to be free of distraction. So far, he felt that the lack of respect shown by Richardson was just an act to appear carefree. That could have been for a multitude of reasons, but the knives in the gun rack had caught his attention. The other thing that Frank noted was the large home's isolation. It sat on the outskirts of the town in a heavily wooded area. The weapons, location and timing of Tim's arrest were certainly worthy of suspicion. Still, Frank wasn't feeling the tingling sensation that usually overcame him when he was upon a true predator. This guy seemed to be playing the part, probably due to survival instincts learned from having been locked up. Yet, he thought to himself that also might be part of the charade itself.

Frank took the suspect's last statement as an opportunity and said, "We appreciate your cooperation, but we do have a few more questions. But as a huge baseball fan myself, I understand. Maybe you'd like to take this into the other room, so we can kill two birds with one stone. Besides I wouldn't mind checking out that sweet set you have. Is that a new OLED?"

"Yeah, I just picked it up yesterday."

"That must have set you back a few paychecks," Frank said.

"Alright, let's take this in the other room. The sooner I answer your questions, the sooner I can enjoy my peace and quiet."

As they entered the den, Frank noticed there were no pictures of family or friends anywhere. He also casually drifted toward the hunting case and glanced at the two large serrated hunting knives. The pieces were certainly here, but he wondered why the alarm signals were not sounding.

"What do you hunt?" Frank asked.

"Mainly deer, that's why I moved out here, when I was younger my uncle took me and I liked it. After my arrest, I wanted the solitude and the woods met my needs, on both counts."

Beth interjected, "Mr. Richardson, you said you don't know Gary Jones and yet you're receiving a portion of the proceeds from his novels, can you explain that?"

"What the hell are you talking about?" Tim responded quizzically.

"Listen, we might as well cut through the pretense. We've traced wire transfers from his bank account and know you're receiving significant amounts of money from him. So I'd like to ask you again, how do you know him?" Beth asked forcibly.

"I don't know anything about this author you keep talking about, but I can explain the money. About a year after my prison release, I was approached by a lawyer who said he was representing a rich guy who was aware of my situation. He said the guy liked to help people who had suffered through unfortunate stuff and I wasn't about to turn his offer down. I was working for a shit wage for a local landscaper, living in a crappy little apartment and out of nowhere a miracle happens. An ex-con doesn't exactly have a lot of opportunities, especially one without any real education. What would you do, turn it down? Give me a fucking break."

At exactly the same instant, both Frank and Beth blurted out, "Can you tell me the name of this attorney?"

"Yeah, Fred Kimmel." Richardson noticed the look on their faces as he said the lawyer's name. "By your expressions I'm guessing you know who I'm talking about."

"When was the last time you saw Mr. Kimmel," Beth asked?

"Oh, I guess about three weeks after we first met. I really sweated it out. After introducing himself the first time, he said I was only being considered for his charity and then he asked about my background. After giving him my life story and the stolen car ordeal, he left and said he'd get back to me. After a week or two, I thought I lost my golden ticket. Then just when I gave up hope, he shows up on my doorstep, has me sign some forms and before you know it, the cash started flowing in. I was like holy shit, jackpot, never expecting that amount of dough, I remembered what my grandpa once told me, never look a gift horse in the mouth. Anyhow you can verify this with Kimmel, he's somewhere in New York City."

"Can you give us a bullet point version of the story you told Mr. Kimmel?" Frank asked.

"Yeah, it goes something like this...born at Wilkes-Barre General Hospital, which isn't far from here. Got an older brother. My mother and father moved to the Jersey Shore when I was nine. School was never my thing. I was just a wild ass teen. My dad always thought I was a screw up, him being a doctor and all. So when I got drunk the night of my twenty-third birthday and decided to go for a joy ride, I proved him right. My mom and him split up shortly after their embarrassment. The only person that I have any contact with is my mom. Freddie my big bro, is a big time attorney and well, he's pops' pride and joy...the golden child. We don't speak since I ruined the family name. To make a long story short I wanted to escape and came back here. How's that for a bullet point?"

"Thank you, Mr. Richardson. We'll probably be getting back to you if this story doesn't check out," Beth said.

As they were exiting the household, Frank turned and said, "Do you mind if I ask you one more question before we go?"

"Might as well, if it keeps you from coming back."

"When you lived out in Jersey, did you ever leave the state at any time?" Frank asked.

"Never alone, but I went on vacation with my family a few times, Disney and the Bahamas, that's about it."

"Thanks, Mr. Richardson, have a nice day," Beth said as they walked toward their car.

"Should I be calling my attorney?" Tim said as they were leaving.

"That depends, did you do anything that would require legal representation?" Frank said.

Richardson smirked, as the agents drove away. Beth and Frank had conflicted opinions as to the viability of him being the Magician. There were obvious reasons to like him as the perpetrator, but other things reduced that likelihood. The former inmate had been forthcoming with answering their questions and his demeanor albeit arrogant, seemed relaxed and honest.

"What do you think?" Beth asked Frank.

"There were a lot of red flags waving all over the place, but my heart's not racing and it usually does when the noose is tightening. How do you feel about him?"

"He's a loner that lives in relative isolation in a wooded area. The knives in that case appeared serrated."

"They were, but that's not unusual for hunting knives. Although their presence certainly ratcheted up my attention; it's like the pieces fit, but something's just not right."

"That's just it. Is it a coincidence that right after he gets locked up the killing abruptly stopped and that Manasquan, is near your home in Spring Lake? Then factor in, his tie to the book sales and Gary Jones. That fills in a lot of the puzzle. But what doesn't fit, are his carefree responses and how genuine they appear. Richardson definitely seemed surprised when we mentioned Gary Jones and the story about Kimmel came off as authentic. Plus, his intellect didn't support that of a brilliant novelist," Beth responded.

"That could be part of an act. He could be manipulative and hiding his intelligence. Also, the arrogance that we perceive could support a sociopath's lack of fear and present itself in that manner. If it were him, his alibi would be well rehearsed and provide a reasonable doubt."

"But you said your heart wasn't racing."

"It wasn't which means we've got a lot of work to do. We'll have to check with his family and see if the story matches up, especially his claims regarding leaving the state. Have someone on the team check cell phone records as to their location during the timing of the murders. Then we need to hear what the rest of the team has to say regarding their investigations."

"I have a feeling we're going to be hearing Mr. Kimmel's name come up again. Don't you?"

"You read my mind, Beth."

"Let me see if I can do it again. You're dying for some wings and a beer before we head back to D.C.," she said while pulling into a parking lot on the side of the highway.

"Wow, you're really good. Now I can see why Rob put you in charge, you're clairvoyant. "

As they got out of the car, Frank noticed the small sign with *all you can eat chicken wings* printed on it. He quickly added, "Or maybe it's your eagle eyes; nothing gets by you either way."

Beth smiled and commented on the row of motorcycles parked near the front door, "Nice Harleys."

"Seems like my kind of place," Frank replied with a grin.

Upon entering the local tavern, it was apparent that it was a biker bar. The smell of wings filled the air, while ZZ Top played "Tush" on the jukebox in the dimly lit establishment. Beth and

Frank made their way past two large guys shooting pool and found an empty table. The men eyed Beth up and down, flexing their tattooed biceps as she walked on by. Everyone in the bar, aside from the staff, wore leather jackets with dragon emblems on the backs. Nobody paid much attention to Frank.

While waiting for someone to take their order, the leers continued from the drunken patronage. It felt like high school where someone sat at the wrong table in the lunchroom. Clearly Beth and Frank were viewed as outsiders.

"Hey, we could leave if you'd like?"

"I'm used to guys checking me out, besides those wings have my name on them. Why, are you scared?" Beth said teasingly.

"Just trying to be a gentleman. But since you're comfortable in a den of wolves; I might as well enjoy myself."

The bartender made his way over to the table and took their order, all the while focusing his attention on Beth.

She appeared as comfortable as ever and said, "We'll have whatever you have on draft and a couple of dozen wings, hot."

The bartender replied, "I like it hot, too."

"I'll keep that in mind."

After he walked away, Frank smiled and said, "All kidding aside, I can see why Rob has so much faith in you."

"As a woman, I've learned I can't let someone think I'm intimidated, much less, by a bunch of local yokels. At the Bureau, being in charge of a task force means I have to keep my composure at all times, so this is me just following that motto."

"I'm impressed. With your looks I'd imagine that's even more important, because a lot of guys at the Bureau, probably see you as just another pretty face. If they do, then shame on them."

"Hmmm, it's nice to know you think I have a pretty face."

"You're much more than that."

"Are you flirting with me, Frank?"

"I'm just saying you're a force to be reckoned with."

"That didn't answer my question."

"Beth, unfortunately for me, I'm a one woman kind of guy and I'm still figuring things out with Sarah. I just want you to know I really do admire you as a person."

"Thanks, that means a lot to me and if things don't work out with Sarah, well…I'm just putting it out there."

Frank couldn't help but smile, "I'll keep that in mind."

The bartender walked over with their order and said lecherously, "Hot, just the way you want it and I hope the head on the beer isn't too big for you."

Frank was about to say something and Beth cut him off, "By the looks of it, your head is a lot smaller than I'm used to."

The bartender flashed an angry look and walked away in irritation. The two Bureau agents smiled at one another and began to eat their meal.

After finishing up the wings and beer, Frank excused himself to go to the men's room. He thought to himself as he walked away that Beth was an extraordinary woman and if he weren't emotionally involved with Sarah he would have responded to her advances. Frank wanted to piss as quickly as possible because he didn't want to leave Beth alone for too long. Even though she had shown the ability to handle herself, he still felt uncomfortable leaving her alone with the unruly bunch in the bar.

As soon as Frank left for the bathroom, the guys playing pool walked over to Beth. Both of the men were well over six feet tall and looked to be on steroids. The rest of the gang immediately followed, creating a circle around Beth. The largest man approaching Beth waved two guys over toward the restroom. Each one looked like a professional linebacker with deadly intent.

The leader said "I'm Mace and I was told you like it real, real hot. So we're going to give it to you just like you asked for it."

Beth pulled her jacket aside, making sure that her badge and gun were visible. She was hoping to diffuse the situation before it got out of hand. Mace took notice of the display and Beth gave him a look as if to back off. It had been a mistake, since it only served to enflame the drunken ringleader. He was used to being the one giving orders and Mace liked to intimidate people.

"Is that supposed to turn me on, cause that pussy just got a little sweeter."

Beth decided she was going to show a little more force, but before she had a chance to reach for her gun, two men grabbed

123

her by the arms. Mace placed his hands on her breasts, and smiled showing her that he was in control. Suddenly he heard a loud crash behind him and everyone turned as a gang member went flying into a nearby table. In the next instant, Frank pointed the sight of his gun at Mace's head.

When he had exited the men's room and started to push the door open, he caught a glimpse of a biker standing off to the side. Frank's instincts kicked into immediate gear and as the man attempted to grab a hold of him, he drove a lightning fast jab directly into his nose, breaking it. He quickly followed this with a vicious uppercut to the jaw sending his quarry sprawling to the ground. While that was happening the other threat came at him from behind, so Frank swirled and hit him with a roundhouse to the chest and combined it with a jumping hook kick to the head. This is how the man had been forcefully knocked across the room into the shattered table. Both men were rendered unconscious in seconds.

One was lying at Frank's feet bleeding profusely from the nose and the other likely suffered from broken ribs and a concussion. Before they even hit the ground, Frank had drawn his gun and focused it directly on the apparent person in charge of the hooligans.

"Okay, guys the fun's over. So let go of my friend, before heads start exploding like firecrackers. By the way, yours will be the first to go boom," Frank said menacingly while looking directly into the eyes of Mace.

"No need for that," as he motioned for Beth to be released.

The biker's fury was clearly visible, but his eyes recognized that his opponent needed to be taken deadly serious. Mace had never seen anyone handle his men with such expert efficiency, besides the sight of the revolver was trained right at him. He had no doubt that the man would carry out his threat if further provoked. Mace wondered how he had underestimated this man so completely. Frank had not shown any signs of dominance and appeared docile when the woman had interacted with the bartender. Mace would never again mistake quiet calm as a lack of power, because Frank had proven this to be fool's gold.

Beth had now drawn her gun while backing away from the group. She ordered everyone to raise their hands slowly and to place them behind their heads. Each man reluctantly did so, while Frank had them turn around facing up against the wall. Beth then called local law enforcement to have them arrested for assaulting a federal officer. Minutes later, a host of squad cars arrived and took them all down to police headquarters.

On the ride back to Washington, D.C., Beth replayed the event over and over in her head. It had been the first time she had ever been face to face with real danger. Even though she directed hazardous operations, it always remained outside of her immediate peril. Beth felt scared knowing that just exhibiting control and being prepared wasn't always enough. She hoped this fear would bring about an increased awareness and make her a better agent. Yet she knew she'd never be like Frank; she had been amazed at the speed of his movements and how quickly he gained control of the chaos. His reputation for being able to get inside the mind of a killer was not his only skill. Frank was a force of nature, possessing all of its power and she thought to herself luckily he's on our side. The whole ride back she made small talk, avoiding discussing what had almost happened and Frank seemed to understand. He never once brought up the topic, but instead focused on interests outside of the job, like his deep rooted love for the New York Jets. Beth found it all to be comforting and by the time they were back she felt more relaxed.

As Beth was dropping Frank off at his hotel, she leaned over and kissed him on the cheek. She couldn't help herself, wishing that he wasn't such a good guy and felt a flush of jealousy toward Sarah. Although they had never met, Frank had spoken of her many times. Beth usually was the one fighting off men, not the other way around.

She said, "That was for rescuing the damsel in distress and to let you know, I admire you too. Like I said earlier, if your situation changes, you know where to find me."

Frank gave her a sympathetic smile and said, "I was just lucky and glad I was able to help. Beth, don't let what happened get to you. It was a random event that turned out alright. We have a better chance of being struck by lightning than anything like that happening again. You're still a great agent and you have no need to thank me. You would have done the same for me, I wasn't the one surrounded by a bunch of guys."

"That would have been a sight to see. Although, I suspect there would have been more than two of them going to the hospital."

"That only happens in the movies."

"From what I saw, Jason Statham has got nothing on you."

"That'd be an ass kicking I hope never happens. Goodnight, Beth," he said while getting out of the car.

"Whose ass are we talking about?"

"Certainly not his. See you tomorrow."

CHAPTER 25

"James' Final Term at Princeton"

JAMES HAD JUST FINISHED FOOTBALL PRACTICE AND WAS HEADING over to the library to pick up a book on theoretical physics. He loved reading anything pertaining to Einstein, whom he always found to be a source of inspiration, and was looking to find some sort of edge. James was close to completing the algorithm which he had been working on in his head for almost nine months. The final term of his senior year had arrived and this problem needed an answer since it was the key to his artificial intelligence thesis. James was on course to complete his undergraduate degree a semester early and wanted to provide his theoretical framework with an actual proven foundation. Even though he planned on continuing his education through his doctorate at Princeton, he obsessed with completing his task as an undergraduate. This single mindedness stirred his creativity. Regardless, he wanted to remain a resident just as Albert did long ago, to search for other intellectual pursuits. James needed to always have something directing his energy.

There had been so much good fortune the last three years that it helped channel his quest for stimuli into something grand. Everything seemed to be coalescing into a special moment in time. Maria and he were now married, with Marty and Grace planning to follow in their footsteps next summer. The Tigers were nationally ranked for the first time since the 1950's due to James' play at quarterback. Heisman Trophy talks were in full force; with the first game two weeks away, the chatter would only get stronger.

To top it all off, James was about to complete a senior thesis that would secure his place in the academic annals, alongside his hero, Einstein.

He was becoming somewhat of a legend among the campus community. Everyone was well aware of his athletic and intellectual prowess. This led to people placing him on a pedestal. It was no wonder he was driven toward meeting their lofty expectations. Still nothing was more important than Maria, and his friendship with Grace and Marty. Without them in his life, James would be a shell with nothing inside. He finally reached a place where he managed to accept the horrors of his past and stored them away. Like a rebirth of innocence it helped provide refuge from the trauma that had been on the verge of sending him on a path toward destruction and vengeance.

Maria knew her husband had suffered a painful past, as he always shut down whenever the subject was broached. Sensing his aversion to the topic, she never pressed him on the matter, but wished he would take comfort in her emotional support. Maria was majoring in Psychology and just the other day she spoke to the head of the department about bottling up trauma. She didn't divulge that James was at the center of her inquiry, but casually mentioned she was considering making this the focus of her own senior thesis. The esteemed faculty doctor impressed on her the importance of dealing with unresolved issues.

So that night, while lying in bed she asked James what he was like as a little boy and much to her surprise, he answered. Since this was not a direct assault on his walled up history, but rather his traits, he began to talk. Maria was shocked though when he filled in more details of his tragic background in the conversation. Upon hearing that his parents were murdered and that his foster care memories provided little relief, tears formed in her eyes and she hugged him tightly. James still didn't get into the specific details, not even mentioning their names, but she felt this was a start. The trust issues were something that would need to be repaired over time, with patience, empathy and unwavering support. Maria swore to herself she would give this to him until the day she died.

As brilliant as James was in his capacity to think outside of what most of us could even imagine, his emotional reservoir was only now reaching that of a young adolescent. Concepts of trust, love, anger, jealousy and compassion were not fully developed after being stunted for so long. All of his emotions were closer to that of an innocent. James was learning how to process and manage his emotional state, since there were many years that he felt nothing at all. Now just like a child, his need for love and attention was endless, guileless in nature. He found what had been taken away from him so forcefully and therefore, the grasp he held on to it was exponentially tighter.

Maria's inherent desire to nurture this love and reinforce it led to an idea. She knew James' twenty-first birthday was close at hand. It was only a few days away and she decided to make it special. Maria hoped to eradicate any negative lingering effects tied to James' recent revelations. She wanted to make every new day together a healing memory. With this in mind, she secretly arranged for Marty and Grace to join them in celebrating in New York City, which was just one of her planned surprises. They would go out for a night of revelry. Dinner would be followed by dancing until the wee hours. Since James' birthday fell on a Thursday, he wouldn't suspect anything. Skipping a day of classes would never enter his mind and yet that is exactly what needed to be done.

Maria wanted the night to be memorable. James certainly would never forget it.

CHAPTER 26

"October 2011 – Frank & James"

THE BLOND HAIRED MAN SAT IN FRONT OF HIS TELEVISION. HIS COLD blue eyes seemed lost in the distance while watching the evening news. It was the 1st of October, but the days, weeks or months didn't matter anymore, since all he cared about was gone. His world had once again been turned upside down. Insurmountable pain ripped at his insides. It was like the last four years were torn away and all memories of goodness had been shut down forever. Death seemed to follow him wherever he went. Now instead of it coming to his doorstep, he would become its messenger.

The six o' clock news was reporting on a breaking story involving the resolution of a major case involving two Russian brothers, Dimitri and Vlad Aleksandrov, who were responsible for a five month murder spree. The case was big news because the killings had drawn a lot of attention. All the victims were well connected citizens with deep pockets. This created significant pressure to apprehend the killers. Initially, local law enforcement had taken the brunt of the uproar. Elected representatives of where the crimes were committed were also under siege. As the murders crossed state lines, the Bureau claimed jurisdiction over the case. Pressure mounted and the best agents were assembled to bring the perpetrators to justice.

A close up of the lead F.B.I. agent drew increased attention from the man watching the screen. As the figurehead spoke, all the suppressed memories of the transfixed viewer surfaced. Frank

Sorello, the special agent in charge of the investigation had failed him once again. If one happened to look closely, they would see the psychotic rage hidden behind James' faraway eyes.

It was a television network's dream; FBI legend, Frank Sorello had once again ridden to the rescue. He was answering a horde of questions regarding the two, sibling immigrants responsible for these recent murders.

Throughout the night, back stories of this so called "hero" popped up on every station. It was like a highlight reel of his achievements. James listened to every detail, all the while envisioning retribution. He wanted to show that Frank Sorello was unworthy of praise and instead deserved contempt. As far as he was concerned, his life was now left in ruins and the F.B.I. agent had done nothing to alter that course. Once again Sorello hadn't been quick enough and now blame would be placed atop his shoulders. James would let Frank experience, what it felt like to lose everything you have ever loved.

The murder of his parents and subsequent trauma had almost sent him over to the edge of madness, yet that thin line had not been breached. This time there was nothing to slow the descent into lunacy, as his warped thought process focused solely on savage retribution. He believed if worship was placed on a hero without merit, then society would have to be taught a lesson. This would be James' mission.

Frank Sorello, if left alone, would allow the current paradigm to flourish. This grand delusion led James to imagine his part was to destroy the worship of false deities. He now believed everything had been preordained. He saw himself as the hand of God, guiding poor souls to a higher stream of consciousness. James envisioned what needed to be done; his mind played out every move, like that long ago victory over the chess grandmaster. However, this game would have far greater repercussions. James foresaw using fear as the method, in which he would redefine, the societal perception of hero worship. Frank would be his sacrificial lamb.

This distortive reality, ignored all of the good that actually did exist in the world, banished from his mind, like all that Princeton once represented. His memories of Grace, Marty and Maria were exiled from his being. James couldn't withstand the agony of remembering their former existence. Those traces of what had been taken away from him needed to be erased completely. Everything had now become black and white, good and evil, right and wrong. James suffered a psychotic split, leaving himself to believe he was a messenger of God that needed to punish the sinners all around him; mankind itself.

His delusion interwove Vlad and Dimitri Aleksandrov, as merely opponent's pawns, forcing him to undertake his own counter offensive. Inherent to James' warped sense of reality, God created the brothers to be part of his fated path, while the media served as a carrier of tablets down from the mountaintop. With the delivery of this message, James saw the two brother's lives, as being interconnected with his own destiny. In his mind this was all set in stone, long ago.

Everyone played their role, so that it would all come together. The past in James' mind was predestined, helping to guide what followed. Just like his own history now shaped him, so did the story of the Russian siblings.

Dimitri and Vlad's father, Viktor, worked hard to put food on the table. He was a laborer that took whatever jobs came his way. Viktor remained proud of his working class heritage and never kept his head down even when his wife, Anna, died of leukemia. His sons were seven at the time of her death, leaving them with very little parental supervision or guidance. Viktor's long hours often dragged late into the night. While he was working, his brother Vasily, would check in on Vlad and Dimitri. He recognized the boys were not like his brother, Viktor, but instead took after him. Their uncle taught them at a young age how to work as pickpockets and then as they got older, burglary. The three of them were building a minor criminal enterprise when Vasily made the sudden decision to go to the United States.

During that time, Vasily was afraid that he would be connected to a robbery gone wrong, leaving a senior citizen critically injured in the process. The man had been smacked in the head with a flashlight during an attempt to stop the theft and was left in a coma. If he awoke he would be able to identify Vasily. Upon exiting Russia he informed Vlad and Dimitri of his plans. His nephews continued with a string of robberies and when their father found stolen goods in their room, he threw them out. They decided to contact their uncle and see what things were like in America.

Since Vasily had left eight months prior, he was more than happy to hear from his family. This had more to do with a scheme he was working on, than any real emotional connection. Vlad and Dimitri would be perfect instruments to carry out his plan.

Vasily was working at a regional car service as a dispatcher. The company was family owned and growing. It provided high end limousines to wealthy clientele in the tri-state area. The business model catered to the very rich and tried to accommodate all requests. If a specific vehicle was unavailable, they would subcontract out to other luxury limousine providers, which might fill the specific demand. Vasily talked the owners into hiring him, stating he was willing to work below minimum wage. He saw an opportunity, not with career advancement, but with the client base as potential targets. Vasily contacted virtually every limousine company in the market demographic, hoping to expand the company's partner network. He then entered each fleet's specific car specifications and driver information into a database. It appeared to the owners that he was a hard working immigrant looking to impress his superiors. In actuality, Vasily was searching for sole proprietors that owned a high end limousine. These car services would be the tool to help carry out his plot. Since there wouldn't be a dispatcher in these owner operated companies, it would lessen the likelihood of an immediate trace back to where he worked and more specifically himself. Vasily knew his nephews liked to dispose of eye witnesses.

Dimitri and Vlad were only too glad to be involved in their uncle's plot. They possessed an inherent hatred for the rich Americans, holding more than their fair share of wealth. So the brothers were ruthless in their execution. Vasily's original plan was to arrange two or three robberies using subcontracted vehicles in various states and then get out before anyone put the pieces together. He didn't count on his nephew's greed and their threat to kill him if he quit. Vasily knew his brother's sons were vicious and crazy, so he hoped he would escape before things totally unraveled.

After the first three jobs netted almost twenty-five thousand dollars in cash and jewelry, Vlad and Dimitri thought that life was going to be easy. All they saw was unlimited opportunity and not the corresponding risk of being caught. The brothers lacked the intelligence of their uncle. Their sense of invincibility lay in the fact that they never left witnesses alive. If someone happened to be in the wrong place at the wrong time, Vlad and Dimitri took perverse pleasure in knowing it would be their end.

So when they called their Uncle Vasily at his office and were told he no longer worked there, the brothers decided his betrayal would have repercussions. They immediately went to his house and caught him preparing to leave. Just as Vasily began to plead for their forgiveness, Vlad told him there was no need for an apology and then smashed him in the side of the head with the butt of his gun. Dimitri got some rope from the garage and tied his uncle up while he was still unconscious. The brothers planned on waiting for nightfall to kill him. They didn't want to run the risk of someone hearing the gunshot. Their plan was to dispose of the body, by dumping him in an alley, not far from a known drug den. A single shot to the back of the head would create an image of an execution. Dimitri and Vlad dragged Vasily into the garage and placed him inside the trunk of his car. Then they placed a gag in his mouth, just in case he woke up before they killed him.

After that, the brothers began to search the house for any records or notes connected to clientele of the car service. Dimitri came across files on a flash drive that was filled with scheduled pickups for the rest of the month. Their uncle had planned on taking it with him in order to buy time and disappear. Vasily's ruse was to inform his nephews that the company needed him to meet with some potential partners out of town. While he was away, he would supply them with a list of future jobs. This would effectively keep them occupied. It was just bad luck that Dimitri and Vlad called his office before he actually had the opportunity to flee.

Around 3:00 a.m. they decided it was time to take care of Vasily. In the middle of the night it was less likely for someone to witness the execution. When the brothers got to the alley they surveyed the area and didn't see anyone. They pulled the still unconscious Vasily out of the trunk and without emotion, shot him point blank in the back of his head.

After their uncle was dead, Vlad and Dimitri, left for Atlantic City. The brothers booked a suite at the Borgata and planned to gamble for a few days before their next job. The high roller they targeted from Vasily's list was scheduled to stay at the casino. The man was supposed to be picked up on Sunday evening, in a super stretch luxury limousine, with multiple high definition flat screens. Apparently, the individual loved betting on sports and the satellite feed in the vehicle allowed him to enjoy the ride while feeding his addiction.

The sole proprietor that owned the specially outfitted limousine had established a contract with Vasily when available. This was to be his first subcontracted job. He fit the profile of an owner operator and this would be his last such service. Vlad and Dimitri would kill him the day of the scheduled pickup. Afterwards, one of them would pose as the driver at the arranged meeting time. The other brother would wait at a predetermined location to help in the robbery and subsequent murder. This was always their pattern and so far, it had gone off without a hitch.

However, this time Frank Sorello was in charge. His task force was instructed to go over all the information provided to him by each law enforcement agency. Every robbery involved in the previous murders was scrutinized from the moment they took control of the investigation. The resources of the F.B.I. were far greater than that of individual police departments and everything was gone over with a fine tooth comb. Initially it appeared that the car owners were all unrelated and somehow the perpetrator was selecting extremely wealthy victims. The link had evaded detection just as Vasily had calculated, but he knew eventually someone would put two and two together.

By having his nephews eliminate the sole proprietor, there was no dispatcher or company representative to question. Previously all they had found in the books were the name and time of pickup of the clientele. Since each robbery and murder occurred in a different state, it took a while to make the connective pattern. The lead detectives on the first case focused most of their attention on individuals that knew of the victim's travel plans. They really didn't have any other leads, with no witnesses left alive. The second set of murders followed a similar path on the investigative end. Finally, after the third such event, a connection was made. A diligent homicide detective in Pennsylvania scoured through the JNET Database and discovered the previous out of state crimes. The Bureau was notified of the interstate nature of the criminal activities and this led to Agent Frank Sorello becoming involved in the manhunt.

With their combined resources, the scope of the investigation took on a wider lens. The pieces of the puzzle that were previously spread all over the place were now coming together. Frank struggled with the idea that these were just random robberies that lead to murder. If they were, then what were the odds that every victim, in all three states, were extremely affluent? Frank surmised that not everyone renting a limousine was rich and since the driver was murdered the same day as the passengers, it would be unlikely that anyone would be able to pinpoint these people with such precision. Without the driver giving away his passengers background information, there had to be something missing. Frank's instincts told him this wasn't random; there had to be a connective tie. He had his task force pour through the back records and files of each limousine owner. Shortly thereafter, the subcontracting agreements were found and this quickly led to Vasily. The Russian immigrant's employer informed the Bureau that he no longer worked for the company.

This led to Frank checking into the Russian's background and the Aleksandrov name popped up once again. Vlad and Dimitri were drawn into the web of suspects, as their immigration status, listed them as living with their uncle. Once Frank was informed that the crimes began shortly after the brothers' arrival from the Soviet Union, his radar definitely pinged. A warrant was issued to search Vasily's residence and a piece of paper was found with a name and date circled in red ink.

Stanley Flora was the person listed and the date was for Sunday, which was the following morning. Underneath the name was written "CEO – LFD Capital. Frank's alarm bells were firing and he quickly had a member of his team pull up information pertaining to those names. A member of the task force said that LFD Capital was a large hedge fund in New York City. Frank was quickly given contact information and called Mr. Flora's private home number. The CEO's spouse answered and Frank asked to speak to the woman's husband. She informed him that Stan was away for a few days and Frank urgently explained the reason for his call. When Mrs. Flora realized her husband was in possible danger, she divulged he was in Atlantic City at the Borgata.

Frank thanked her and quickly added, "more than likely it would turn out to be a false alarm."

Immediately after hanging up, he called the Borgata. When Frank rang Mr. Flora's hotel room there was no answer, so he followed up with hotel security, asking if they could locate their guest. He left his satellite phone number with the security team and instructed them to call the minute any information could be provided, as to Mr. Flora's whereabouts. While this was happening, a task force member was arranging for a helicopter to take Frank directly to Atlantic City. About a half hour later his phone rang while he was in the chopper.

"Hello, this is Agent Sorello."

"Hi. This is Stan Flora, can you please tell me what's happening?"

"There's a possibility you may be in danger, Mr. Flora, and I'm contacting you as a precautionary measure. I'd like you to stay with the security team at the hotel. Once I get there I'll explain the situation further. I'm currently on a Federal helicopter and we'll be there in less than two hours."

"What makes you think I'm at risk?"

"Are you aware of the robbery and murders tied to limousine rides over the last few months?"

"No."

"Are you scheduled to have a limo pick you up tomorrow?

"Yeah, as a matter a fact, I do."

"Don't take that ride. I have to make a few calls, but I'll explain more when I see you."

"Wow! This is pretty unbelievable. Let's hope it turns out to be nothing. Thanks for the heads up."

"Well, I'm actually hoping it does. I plan on being you."

"What exactly does that mean?"

"Mr. Flora will be picked up by that limousine, he just won't be you."

After arriving at the Borgata, Frank explained in more detail why there was such urgency to the situation. Mr. Flora realized that he was lucky to have been reached in time, because the situation certainly seemed to be serious. He gave Frank all the information regarding the scheduled pick up and thanked him once again. Sorello passed this information on to his team, so that they could tail him in the event of a problem.

The following evening at 8:00 p.m. Frank waited in the lobby. He was dressed in an Armani suit and wore Salvatore Ferragamo loafers. To top off the look of a high roller he had a solid gold Rolex on his wrist and a Hermes Travel Bag at his side. When the chauffeur showed up inside the lobby Frank recognized the pictures he'd seen of Vlad Aleksandrov on his passport. Even though the Russian wore a hat and sunglasses to shelter his identity, it didn't fool Frank. The F.B.I. agent kept his face emotionless as he walked over to the man, holding the sign, with the CEO's name written in bold letters.

"Mr. Flora?" Vlad asked with a Russian accent.

"Yes."

"May I take your bag, sir?"

"That's okay I prefer to keep it with me."

Frank noticed the glimmer in the man's eyes when he said he would hold on to his valuables.

Vlad thought to himself, "This fucking rich American is going to give me a lot more than that in a little while."

Frank was looking forward to surprising this piece of garbage. He anticipated that at some point Vlad would make an excuse to pull over somewhere and the man's sibling, Dimitri, would be waiting to pounce. If he was right, Sorello had his own plans.

He wore a hidden mike and GPS tracking device, so that an F.B.I. support team could follow undetected. Two members of his task force would be in a car trailing behind, while an F.B.I. helicopter would track them through the air.

Frank kept quiet once he was in the limousine and ignored the chauffeur's attempts to make small talk, knowing the driver's goal was to relax his prey. This infuriated Vlad because it reminded him of how the wealthy politburo of his homeland treated the less fortunate citizens of his country. He thought he would take extra pleasure in killing this rich prick and taking his money and jewelry. Perhaps he would drive with Dimitri to the man's home and kill his wife and family. Vlad smiled after that particular thought entered his head; that would be fun.

About a half hour into the ride, the moment Frank had been expecting occurred. They were on the Garden State Parkway heading north when the Russian instituted his plan.

"I'm so sorry, but I must pull over, my temperature light just came on. I have a water container in my trunk. It will only take a moment and we will be back on our way."

"Just make it quick," Frank said with an authoritative tone.

Vlad wanted to take a knife and slit the passenger's throat. Dimitri would be told to keep his gun trained on the man until he murdered the arrogant businessman in the back of the limo. Vlad pulled into an especially dark and deserted, rest area on the side of the road. When the Russian exited the vehicle, Frank pulled out his Glock 23 and prepared for the impending assault. A minute later, the back door of the limousine suddenly opened and Dimitri cocked the hammer on his gun. As if in tandem, the opposing door started to open. Frank knew they would have him trapped if he didn't react immediately, so he shot Dimitri right through the heart. All in the same instant, Frank noticed out of the corner of his eye, Vlad's knife being brought down toward his neck. The F.B.I. agent's martial arts training took over, as he raised his non gun hand upward, to thwart the killing motion of his attacker. Although Frank deflected the blow from ending his life, it still cut into his shoulder blade. He dropped his gun with his right hand and drove a knife hand fist, straight into the larynx of Vlad, crushing his windpipe and snapping it like a bamboo twig. The man died instantly.

Seconds later, the support team showed up. Frank was transported by the F.B.I. chopper to a waiting, medical facility near his home. The bodies and crime scene analysis were handled by the arriving task force.

The legend of Frank Sorello continued to grow. The media ate up all the details of the capture with the correspondent killing of the savage brothers. The newspapers the next day showed pictures of Frank arriving at Jersey Shore Hospital in an ambulance. The blond haired man thought to himself how the life of this unsuspecting, so called hero, would soon be forever altered.

James booked a flight to Wisconsin.

CHAPTER 27

"September 8th, 2011 – James' Birthday"

MARIA WAS SO EXCITED; HER HUSBAND'S BIRTHDAY HAD FINALLY arrived. She had been counting the days till his big surprise. Her life had taken such a wonderful and unexpected turn. In no way did she ever imagine getting married before starting her career. Yet, that's exactly what happened.

When she had come over from Italy to pursue an education at Princeton, it was done with the intent of returning home with a degree from the Ivy League institution. As far as she had been concerned, a serious relationship was out of the question. Yet life with all of its intricate twists and turns had chosen to intervene. Maria met her best friend Grace, which then led her to James through Marty. It hadn't been her chosen path, but now it was the only road she would ever follow. James was what made her heart beat and she in turn had the same effect on him. The blood that flowed through their veins was forever interconnected. It was a once in a lifetime love and Maria wanted to share her joy by announcing to everyone tonight what she had been keeping secret until now. Yet she needed to be sure and had gone to her gynecologist earlier in the morning to confirm what she already suspected, she was pregnant.

The night ahead was already shaping up to be perfect. James was clueless about the planned festivity, but most importantly he seemed to have no inkling about the impending news of fatherhood. The evening was going to be memorable. Maria imagined the Big Apple as being the ideal backdrop to announce life's next big turn and she wanted to have Marty and Grace along to complete the evening.

Everything was working out the way she had hoped. Maria previously arranged for Marty to take James out for a few beers until 4:00 p.m. and he agreed without hesitation. Her husband believed they were all going to have a quiet dinner together later that night. It was all a distraction for her bigger plans. A full blown bash was to be held on Saturday and that helped disguise her true intentions for the evening. Since it was a Thursday, it led further credence to James' perception that everything was going to be low key.

Grace arrived at 3:30, dressed elegantly in a short black dress with a strand of pearls draped around her neck. These had been purchased at Tiffany's as a birthday gift from James and Maria. She looked beautiful and was thrilled to be part of the celebration. She hugged her best friend in the world, as if they were never going to see one another again. The two young women looked like models in a magazine. Yet Maria would have been on its cover. It wasn't so much her natural beauty, or the elegant ensemble she wore, but rather the glow emanating from inside of her. The radiance she emitted was unmistakable; her boundless happiness was like a tiara being placed upon a storybook princess.

Marty and James returned from their afternoon out together and walked into the house on Mercer Street. The girls came down the stairs to greet them and smiled.

"The two of you look incredible, should I assume we're not staying in tonight?" James asked.

"Wow, is this a photo shoot?" Marty added.

"Good guess. We have reservations at Sparks, in Manhattan. I know you both love a great steak and the place is supposed to be phenomenal," Maria replied.

"The two of you should change because our ride will be here any minute. Marty, I brought over some clothes and left them upstairs for you," Grace added.

"A ride," James asked?

"You'll see, I wanted your birthday to be special," Maria said lovingly.

"We're all together and that's all that matters. I'm sure I'll never forget it. Thanks, sweetheart."

As the two best friends were upstairs changing into more formal attire, the doorbell rang. Grace walked over to answer it and saw the chauffeur standing at the door. In the driveway was a super stretch limousine; it looked like something you'd see at the Oscars.

As she opened the door Grace said, "Hi. I guess you're our driver for the night?"

"Yes, I'm sorry if I'm a bit early," he responded.

Grace replied, "That's fine. We'll be ready to go shortly. Are you from the Soviet Union? I've taken several foreign languages and I recognized your accent."

"Yes, my brother and I came here together, to live a better life... the American dream."

Vlad noticed the expensive looking jewelry on the woman standing before him and couldn't help but smile. He thought the necklace alone would fetch far more money than the first two robberies combined.

"Is there anything I can help you with? Otherwise, I'll wait outside near the car?"

"No thank you. We'll be out shortly."

"Take your time. I'll be right here if you need me."

When James and Marty came downstairs, the two couples headed straight outside to the limousine. Vlad stood near the vehicle, waiting to open their car doors. Once inside the plush vehicle they opened the high end champagne from the top shelf liquor cabinet. On the way to the restaurant they finished off the bottles of Dom Perignon and Cristal. Maria excused herself from drinking; claiming she had two glasses of wine before anyone arrived and needed to slow down. As the car pulled up to the restaurant, the celebration was already in full force.

"A toast...to a long life filled with health, happiness and love. Thanks for being the fabric of my life," James said with pure emotion, while everyone downed the last of their alcohol.

During dinner, the four of them enjoyed the spectacular food and first class service. They reminisced and at the same time talked about the days ahead. The conversation was a perfect setup to the wonderful news that followed. While everyone was having dessert, Maria, shared her joyous secret. James embraced his wife, with Marty and Grace joining in the hug. If time had stopped in that moment; the past, present and future were all bonded together. Memories flowed into new memories and tomorrow promised to hold more of the same.

Upon leaving the restaurant, they headed to a club where they would dance until the wee hours, reveling in their youth, filled with visions of possibility. Marty, Grace and James continued drinking as the night went on; while Maria remained content watching those she loved, live life to the fullest. The night was meeting all of her hopeful expectations.

Maria's smile stretched for what seemed to be a mile long.

When they informed Vlad they were ready to leave, he asked if he could quickly use the bathroom in the club, before beginning the return trip home. While in the restroom, he texted his brother and instructed him to meet at their predetermined location. Dimitri could barely control himself. Vlad had mentioned the expensive jewelry worn by the women, along with the men's Rolexes. Any cash would be considered a bonus. Yet, Vlad was more driven by a growing blood lust. Killing the driver had only wet his expanding appetite and he almost couldn't contain the thoughts of ending their lives.

It was almost 3:00 a.m. and the passengers were falling asleep in the back of the car. Vlad was approaching the area selected by Dimitri. Just like on the previous robberies, his brother had scouted for desolate locations, in which to avoid unnecessary interference.

"My temperature light just came on, I'll need to pull over and check it out. I have a water container in my trunk."

Maria was the only one awake and she said, "Alright."

A premonition of sadness swept over her unexpectedly and she wondered if her hormones were at fault. The chill in her body made her embrace her husband and James awoke from his slumber.

"I love you so much. Thanks for my birthday," he said.

Suddenly the doors opened on both sides of the limousine and this startled Marty and Grace awake. All they saw were the gun barrels being pointed at them by the crouching men on either side. Grace screamed as the silenced pistols began to fire. She saw the blood suddenly begin to stream from her fiancée's head and seconds later, she saw no more. James' athleticism automatically took over, as he instinctively lunged in front of his wife. A bullet creased the side of his head, knocking him out, as blood oozed from the wound. The next shot immediately killed Maria and their unborn baby. Vlad and Dimitri removed the jewelry and cash from the dead bodies and calmly drove off in a car with stolen plates, leaving no trail behind. They were unaware that James survived the carnage, as he lay unconscious in a pool of crimson.

When he next awoke he was in a hospital bed. Physically he would recover, but nothing would ever be the same again. All that mattered to him was gone, taken away in the blink of an eye. James was granted a leave of absence from Princeton University. Its faculty and fellow students sent him get well cards, the football team a signed football with notes of condolences attached. They would all go unread.

Media stories were plentiful and continued on into the football season. The Tigers finished with a losing record and there would be no championship, no national ranking and no Heisman Trophy for its former star player. James would never again return to Princeton. All the promise it had instilled was for naught. If only he could have remained in its protective cocoon, perhaps the world would have reaped the benefits of his wondrous mind. As time moved on, focus as always waned, as other stories shifted attention to other news of the day.

A serial killer eventually took over the public's imagination. Einstein and Joe Montana's successor faded from memory, since there hadn't been anymore great accomplishments to place in the spotlight. His hand was now guided by pure vengeance...his blue eyes bereft of any glimmer of light.

He was no longer James, but the Magician.

CHAPTER 28

"Present Day"

FRANK MET BETH AT F.B. I. HEADQUARTERS THE FOLLOWING MORNING and the two of them brought Director Sullivan up to speed on the recent turn of events in Pennsylvania. When they got to the part about the biker gang Rob smiled.

"I see you're back in rare form. Do you think the two guys you busted up are going to be suing us for hospital bills and claiming overuse of force?

"Rob, I don't think they'd be that stupid. Besides they're lucky I didn't know their plans for Beth while I was in the bathroom, otherwise they might be someplace other than the hospital."

"That's true; the morgue is too crowded already."

"It sounds like this kind of thing has happened before," Beth added.

"You could say that," as Rob glanced over at Frank.

"Hey, I'm a sucker for a damsel in distress. What can I say?"

"How about let's keep the body count down. So what's next?" asked Rob.

The three of them discussed the various options until more information came forth. The other agents were still not back from their own investigations regarding Gary Jones' ever expanding spider web. Frank decided he would head back home to New Jersey where he would be able to follow up on Tim Richardson by questioning the man's friends and family. Beth said she would call him once she received reports back about the other three possible suspects.

Frank called Sarah while returning to Spring Lake and she immediately asked him to have dinner at her house. At first he declined, but she ignored him and said all they were doing was pretending the feelings they had for one another didn't exist. Frank knew she was right, but tried in vain to resist.

"Sarah, I'm not saying you're wrong, but that still doesn't change the fact that more attention is drawn to you every time we're together."

"We can't control everything in life, Frank. I know that's hard for you, but I don't want to live like something bad is going to happen. Besides, we've spent an awful lot of time running together every morning. If anyone paid attention to us I'm sure by our body language they'd figure there's something between us. Spending the night together is not going to change that fucking fact. I'm sorry, I'm just really frustrated. I don't want to wait anymore."

"I'm assuming you're not talking about dinner anymore?"

"This isn't funny to me; I need to know that I'm not going to become the type of person who is afraid of tomorrow. I understand what you do for a living carries with it a certain amount of danger and I'm alright with it. Can you do the same?"

"Okay, I'll try. See you in a few hours."

Sarah smiled at the other end of the phone.

"Just so you know, when you get here we're skipping dinner and heading straight to bed. So if you're hungry I suggest you eat something before you arrive."

The ride home seemed like an eternity as Frank realized he was beginning to let go of his past and move on. It excited and scared him at the same time. Juliette would always remain with him, but Sarah gave him a reason for wanting a future, something that had seemed impossible after his wife's death. It was intoxicating to desire someone like this once again.

Frank's craving became uncontrollable once he arrived, as Sarah answered the door completely naked. Her body was as beautiful as he imagined. Sarah turned and walked up the stairs, as Frank followed behind, looking at her perfectly shaped ass.

The night was filled with frenzied sex, yet their passion went beyond just a wild physical encounter, as their bodies seemed to ignite all the pent up emotional underpinnings of their relationship. Sarah seemed to possess all that he was feeling, as she rode him with wild abandon, but afterwards caressed him with such tenderness that it seemed like they had been together forever.

The following morning when Sarah got up to make her man breakfast; she felt the intensity of his stare upon her body. It made her wet once again.

"If you don't take your eyes off of me, I'm not going to make it into the kitchen. I was planning on surprising you with breakfast in bed. After all, we never got to eat last night."

"Maybe you didn't."

She smiled and walked sexily back to the bed. Frank laughed in such a way, that he hadn't laughed in years. It was carefree and was completely devoid of his painful past. He wrapped his powerful arms around her and pulled her close.

"There's plenty of time for breakfast later."

CHAPTER 29

"Appleton, Wisconsin – October 2011"

"THANK YOU, YOUNG MAN," THE ELDERLY WOMAN SAID AS SHE LEFT the coffee shop.

James said, "Anytime," as he held the door open for the woman approaching.

She smiled appreciatively at the tall man. He reminded her of an old time movie star, striking in appearance and charming. Yet for some reason she found herself surprised at the next words that came from her mouth.

"Cheer up, things can only get better."

She noticed the beautiful smile he flashed while exiting the store, but his eyes seemed to lack a spark. Normally she wouldn't have said anything over such a simple observation, but it felt like she crossed paths with a lost soul.

James had mastered the ability to mimic behavior in high school while he was on the verge of losing his humanity. At Princeton, he had found those emotions, but now they were a lost relic. So he felt confused by her response, not realizing that his inability to feel, translated to flatness in his blue eyes.

"I'm sorry, ma'am, but everything's okay."

"Well I'm happy to hear that, but if they're not, God works in mysterious ways and like I always say, there's light at the end of the tunnel, if you look for it."

"Thanks for the advice."

James walked down the road and past the synagogue. The rabbi still hadn't come out the front door, so he continued walking two more blocks on to the side street where his black Honda Accord was parked. He got into the car and drove toward Rabbi Ari Goldberg's home. For the last week he blended into the city and its inhabitants, all the while watching to see his target's daily patterns. If the rabbi followed his daily ritual he wouldn't be home for at least two more hours. This would leave James plenty of time to prepare.

It was the thirty-first of October and the time had come to begin God's work. James believed selecting his first victim was preordained. Magical images, like the parting of the "Red Sea" and turning water into wine, were integrated into his past memories, feeding his psychotic delusions. James saw his background as another sign from the heavens. Paul, his foster father chose magic as a profession and Harry Houdini had been his idol. This man represented everything evil about false worship and his treatment of James was only God's way of leading him down a divine path.

He needed to be bigger than life and achieve notoriety on a mass scale to help the world reform, like the plague of locusts that delivered its message on Egypt long ago. The killers etched in infamy carried memorable nicknames, like the "Boston Strangler" or "The Night Stalker"; while others were remembered simply for the horror they instilled like Ted Bundy. If James was a messenger of God's will, as his delusion led him to believe, then his legend would have to reach biblical proportions and his name needed to be spoken in fear.

James' visions placed Frank Sorello as an adversary that needed to be defeated. The more memorable the foe, the greater the legend and James wanted it to be epic. The clues he left behind would help gauge the ability of his enemy and also to establish a link to his elusive ability to escape anyone that stood in his way. If need be, James planned to leave as big a trail as necessary to achieve those ends. He would be like magic itself, something to behold.

The city of Appleton was about thirty miles southwest of Green Bay and had one of the lowest crime rates in America. Although approximately 70,000 people lived in the community, murders were practically non-existent, but not this coming night. James sat patiently, waiting in the empty house.

Ari Goldberg, left his home early that morning and headed to his place of worship. Like his father before him, he was a well respected rabbi in the community, even though the interpretation of his beliefs were grounded more in the modern world. Ari devoted his life to spreading the word of God and promoting the Jewish faith in a less traditional manner. As the leader of a reformed temple, he reflected the newer generation and was very connected to its members. Today, he was meeting with a young couple that had lost their child in a car accident and was hoping to help them find the strength to cope with this tragic loss. He related to their pain because his own brother died at seven years old from Leukemia. Rabbi Goldberg had seen the impact this had on his own family and knew all he could provide at this point was empathy. After the couple left he spent the rest of the day praying.

While Ari was at the synagogue, James wandered through the home observing the things that helped define the rabbi; the pictures, books and the general feel of the home itself. On a shelf near the fireplace, was a photo that made him think of how fate placed him here. Rabbi Goldberg was standing next to another man who had come perilously close to being his initial victim. The rabbi in the picture was the first person James stalked upon his arrival. He had browsed through lists of names in Appleton synagogues and chose Rabbi Smallowitz. Shortly after following the man to his home from a prayer service, James noticed the area presented several potential risks. The homes were close together with lots of activity and the traffic lights in the neighborhood had cameras attached to them. James didn't want to leave tracks and selected the next man on his list, Rabbi Goldberg. Apparently God had chosen him to be a sacrificial lamb, because his home was more isolated and the surrounding streets were without the security risks he previously observed.

The sun had just set and James knew the rabbi would be home soon. He stood in the pantry room dressed all in black. Like a spider he knew where to place his web. The man would eventually get hungry and be unprepared for what lie in wait. Thirty minutes later he heard the key in the front door turning the lock. James had the chloroform rag ready as he heard footsteps move in his direction.

Next the sound of a television came on and the footsteps receded. James was completely alert, listening to every sound. The news was apparently discussing the Green Bay Packers being 7-0 and their upcoming bye.

The rabbi had gone into his bedroom to change his clothes. He felt excited by the thought of unwinding and listening to the local sports networks talk about his beloved Packers. All of the earlier talk dealing with death and loss had taken a toll. Ari decided he needed a drink and would cook up some dinner.

The sound of footsteps returned to the kitchen and next James heard the refrigerator door open. While he stood in utter silence, the sound of a bottle being opened came next. James sensed the moment was close at hand. Seconds later, the door handle began to turn. James knew his prey would be stunned by his presence and the rabbi's eyes conveyed both shock and fear as he recoiled from the man reaching toward him. It all happened so quickly, that Ari momentarily felt this couldn't be happening. But then he was asleep and when he awoke it was all too real.

The rabbi only gained consciousness briefly and the pain quickly led his nervous system to shut down causing him to pass out once again. James watched the blood flow from the cuts he made on his victim's four limbs. The man would soon bleed out, so he raised the blade in his hands and plunged it straight into the man's heart.

It was the first human life that he had ever taken and he felt nothing. James picked up the finger nails that he had removed from the man's right hand and placed them in a plastic bag. He placed the pliers and knife back inside his travel bag and walked in to take a shower.

When he was finished he got dressed in unsoiled clothing and placed the blood stained garments in the plastic bag that he had taken with him. In the middle of the night he left as silently as he had come.

All that was left was his first victim and the plastic bag containing the nails of the rabbi. When the police eventually found the body, they bagged as evidence, the nails in the baggie. Written on the outside of the bag in permanent black ink, was the letter "M."

James saw himself as a messenger of God and wanted to create a signature that would let Frank know that the murders were his work. It became a satisfying twist that a small town reporter later branded him with the nickname "The Magician." The killing of the rabbi had been a clue planted for Sorello. James wanted to show that his nemesis was incapable of seeing what was placed right in front of him. The clues he had left were subtle, but if he had been the one in pursuit, then he would have seen them as clear as day. The signs pointed to his identity and also as to where he would go. James thought it was ironic that someone other than the "great" F.B.I. hunter found the first clue.

"Perhaps, I should visit Brian Webster," James said out loud.

CHAPTER 30

"Present Day"

FRANK AND SARAH WERE STILL IN BED, WHEN HIS CELL PHONE RANG. He glanced over to read the display; it was Beth. As much as he wanted to ignore the call, Frank also knew he needed to finish this case once and for all.

He reached across Sarah's naked body and answered the phone.

"Hey, Beth."

"Hi, Frank, I just got the initial reports back from the other agents and as expected, everyone interviewed claims to not know what we're talking about. All the suspects gave us the same story as Tim Richardson did regarding the money. Any progress on him by the way?"

"I haven't met with anyone yet, that's on my agenda for today."

Beth replied, "That's not like you. I figured you'd be all over it as soon as you got back."

"I had some other stuff to take care of."

"Oh?" Beth said with a hint of curiosity.

"I'll call you later this afternoon when I have some more information regarding Richardson."

"Okay, umm…I'll let you go," she said with an unexpected twinge of jealousy, thinking he was with Sarah.

"Bye, Beth."

"Is she pretty?" Sarah asked.

"I'm not going to lie, yes she is, but you're in a league all your own."

"That's good to know, just don't you forget it."

"I won't," Frank replied.

"By the look on your face, I'm guessing you have to go?"

"Am I that any easy to read? That's not good in my profession. But yeah, I have to check out some background information on one of our suspects. So I'd better get moving or I'll never leave."

"I'm going to miss you, sweetheart."

"I know how you feel."

After leaving Sarah's house, Frank went over to talk with Tim Richardson's family. They verified that their son hadn't gone anywhere out of state, other than the family vacations mentioned during his interrogation. This still wasn't enough for Sorello because parents would often lie to protect their children, but employers would have no such loyalty. Mr. Richardson informed Frank that Tim had worked for a local roofer since he was twenty-one and rarely missed any time. Later that day, Frank met with the roofer at his office and was shown payroll stubs proving that Tim was working when the Magician was committing out of state murders. He crossed his name off the list, so Frank decided he'd head back to Washington and begin the process of evaluating the other suspects.

He called Beth to let her know he was coming back to D.C.

"Hey, just thought I'd let you know that Richardson is in the clear, with a water tight alibi, anyhow I'm on my way back to Washington so we can work on where to go next."

"When will you be here?"

"Later tonight. I'll call when I'm in town."

"Great, we need to decide on our next step."

"Anybody else stand out?"

"That's just it; each person has some things worth exploring, but nothing that leaps out at you like Richardson. I think it would be best to sit down with the team and lay out a game plan."

"Alright, I'll see you soon."

CHAPTER 31

"May 2012 – The Magician"

"MICHELLE, DO YOU FEEL LIKE STOPPING BY THE MALL WHEN WE leave the beach?"

"Sure. When do you want to head out?"

"Well I'm pretty baked, how about another fifteen minutes?"

"Sounds good to me, Mandy."

The two girls had been friends since they were seven years old, but became inseparable in high school. Although they lived all of their lives in Charleston, South Carolina they chose to attend the University of Colorado together. Now they were home for summer break enjoying the beach that carried with it so many memories.

"Do you think Ian might come and visit before school starts up again?"

"I hope so; I really miss him, Michelle. What about you and Kevin?"

"He said he's planning to come down in July. I promised I'd teach him to surf, since he and Ian taught us both to ski."

"I'm sure you'll have him riding more than the waves."

"Mandy, you're so bad. You know I haven't slept with him yet."

"Hmmmm, you just said yet."

The two girls laughed and Mandy said, "Ready to go?"

"Yeah, let's head out."

At that moment, not far from where Michelle & Mandy were, James stopped at a gas station to fill up his white Camry. He had no set destination; the only thing that mattered to him was that he be in this approximate area. "The Magician" believed in establishing no patterns, because random events were impossible to predict.

While pumping gas, James overheard a woman tell her children they would stop at the mall before heading back home.

"Excuse me, but can you tell me how to get to the mall?"

"It's about four miles up the road on the right."

"Thanks a lot."

The woman and her family drove away, and thirty seconds later James followed. He could see their blue minivan ahead in the distance. Shortly thereafter, James saw the vehicle's turn signal come on. He trailed behind and ended up parking his car on the uppermost level of the mall's garage. This section had more spaces, since the other levels were completely full. James parked the Camry in the row across from the minivan. He observed the mother and her children enter an elevator for the shopping center. James sat in his car, waiting.

About ten minutes later, a tan BMW convertible drove past James' car and parked several spaces away. Two college age girls got out of the vehicle and were oblivious to his presence. James' sole concern was to be like a ghost, unseen by anyone, yet still there. He thought to himself, "Who'll be chosen." For the next hour, James remained in a trancelike state, neither moving nor thinking, yet all the while his eyes were that of a hawk's. His surroundings were full of prey and he would strike when the opportunity arose.

The lights on the elevator lit up, indicating movement. The door opened and out came the mother that led him to this place. She appeared distracted by her kids running past. James started to open his car door, and just at that instant another car pulled into the lot. The man inside the Acura parked his car right next to the minivan and James pulled his door shut. James said to himself, "God's will." A minute later, the family drove away unaware of their brush with doom.

James watched as others continued to exit, but fate seemed to save them as well. Dusk began to settle in and only a few cars remained, including the convertible that the girls parked nearby.

"Would you like another drink?" the waitress asked the two young women.

"No thanks. How about you, Michelle?" Mandy asked.

"Me neither, we'll just take the check."

As the server walked away, Mandy said, "These fake I.D.'s are amazing. I can't believe we've never been shot down. Jill told me when we were in Abercrombie that they took away her I.D. at this place."

"Thanks for not telling me till now, what if the same thing happened to us?"

"You know me, I like taking chances. Besides, we could always get another one."

"You know Mandy, one of these days you are going to get us into trouble."

"Maybe, but not today," Mandy said mischievously.

The two friends paid the bill and decided they were ready to head home for the night. So they grabbed their shopping bags and walked toward the elevator leading to the parking garage.

Just as Mandy pressed the button on the wall, Michelle said, "Oh crap, I think I left my cell phone on the table. I'm going to go back and get it."

"Don't worry. I'll get the car and you can meet me at the mall exit right near the restaurant."

"Okay, I'll see you in a few."

As soon as the waitress saw Michelle walk back inside the establishment, she smiled and raised the cell phone up in the air. After thanking the server, she went outside and looked for Mandy's car. Five minutes later she tried calling her friend, but only received a busy signal. Another fifteen minutes passed, and Michelle became impatient.

Michelle mumbled to herself, "I'm going to kill her if she's flirting with someone."

At that moment, Mandy was in the trunk of James' car and would never be seen again. If she had only stayed with her friend, perhaps things would have turned out differently. Instead, a plastic bag containing her nails arrived at F.B.I. Headquarters two weeks later. The letter "M" was once again scrawled on its' outside.

Frank Sorello swore he would hunt down the owner of the black sharpie. This had become personal for him; yet it would become far, far more personal. This had been the sixth bag collected by the F.B.I., starting with the rabbi.

While Frank held his wife Juliette in his arms, he couldn't shake the idea that this killer was just getting started. He had come home from D.C., for the weekend to decompress and all he could think about was stopping this psychopath. Far away in Charleston, South Carolina sat Michelle. She was staring out her window, looking out at the moon, and wondered what would have happened if she hadn't forgotten her phone. Tears streamed down her face, realizing the innocence of her youth was gone forever.

CHAPTER 32

"Present Day"

FRANK CHECKED IN AT THE FOUR SEASONS IN D.C., AT AROUND NINE in the evening. It was one of his favorite hotels and close to F.B.I. headquarters. As soon as he settled in, he called Sarah to let her know he arrived.

"Hey, I just figured I'd let you know I'm here. I didn't want you to worry."

"Thanks, so how was your trip?"

"Not bad, the worst part was leaving you."

"That's cute, the rough and tough, Frank Sorello, acting all girlie. You do know that you already have me?"

"I do, but I figure it never hurts to pour on the charm."

"That's for sure, and by the way, I miss you just as much."

"I hope to make it back to Jersey in a few days, but I'm not sure how that's going to work out. This investigation seems to be just getting started."

"Just do what you have to and I'll be ready for you the moment you get back."

"I hope that's a promise!"

"So, should I tell you what I'm wearing?" Sarah said seductively.

"Not if you want me to be able to think clearly?"

"Alright, I'll save that for when you come home. I'm sure you're worn out, so I'll let you get some rest."

"Actually, when we hang up, I have to contact Beth; this case isn't going to get solved by itself."

160

"I think I'm a little bit jealous, she has you all to herself."

"I can't help being so irresistible."

"Well, I can't blame her for that. Just remember what's waiting for you at the good old Jersey Shore."

"Goodnight, Sarah..., maybe I'll listen to some Bruce on my ipod, a little "Jersey Girl.""

"Good idea. Goodnight, Frank."

"Have a nice night."

As soon as the conversation was over, Frank sent Beth a text letting her know he was at his hotel. She responded by letting him know, she'd be at headquarters by eight in the morning. Just as Frank was about to get ready for bed, another text message arrived, asking if he'd like to meet beforehand for breakfast. They eventually decided it'd be easiest if she picked him up at the Four Seasons around 7:00 a.m. and eat in the hotel restaurant, and then Frank could catch a ride with her to the Bureau.

The following morning, Frank met Beth in "Seasons," which was considered a power breakfast spot of Washington's movers and shakers. The Four Seasons' restaurant was already packed as the two of them sat down. After exchanging pleasantries, they both ordered the renowned lemon ricotta pancakes, at which point they began to discuss their game plan going forward.

"I've arranged for our entire team to meet us at headquarters later this morning. I'd like for everyone to be on the same page, as to where we stand, in regard to the current suspects. This way it'll be easier to coordinate things and effectively delegate our resources. Plus, we can all provide feedback together and maybe gain some additional insight."

"Like I said before, I like the way you operate."

"Frank, you ain't seen nothin yet," she said with a wry smile and a little wink.

He smiled back at the beautiful F.B.I. agent sitting across from him and swiftly moved away from the momentary flirtation back to the investigation.

"I know you told me on the phone that all the suspects, more or less, had the same story regarding Gary Jones. Was there anyone or anything that might seem out of the ordinary?"

"I don't want to influence your opinion, that's why I arranged things this way. We can all sit down together and feel this thing out."

After finishing their breakfast, the two of them headed to the Bureau.

CHAPTER 33

"July 2012 – The Magician"

JAMES SAT ALL ALONE ON THE WRAPAROUND PORCH OF HIS MONTANA Home. Elk were drinking from a small, natural lake situated near the wood line, and their presence caused the nearby geese to fly away. The solitary man appeared to be surveying his expansive property and the picturesque beauty of its surroundings. Even though there wasn't a cloud in the sky, the wildlife might as well have been invisible, as the team of geese flew directly overhead. James was so immersed with the images in his head that the world happening all around him had gone completely unnoticed.

Rocking on the porch swing, he contemplated his next maneuver. Everything he had done so far was calculated and had been mentally rehearsed well in advance of any subsequent action. Each decision was made with a measure of anticipatory cautiousness, which included a corresponding analysis of all the logical, expected responses to those choices. Those hunting him would follow specific protocols of crime scene investigation, carefully collecting any forensic evidence left behind. DNA, fingerprints and blood spatter analysis would be documented. Everything would be stored in the case file. James knew this would be immaterial, unless he was caught. He had never been fingerprinted, nor had any DNA samples been taken from him and it was doubtful that he accidentally left anything at one of the crime scenes. Therefore, the biggest risk of apprehension would be if he became careless or predictable. Good investigators would look to find a modus operandi. Frank Sorello was especially adept in this area. All the articles, along with the movie based on his life, illustrated his uncanny ability to get inside the mind of a psychopath and eventually put together the puzzle.

James continued thinking, "Whatever pattern he sees, will be the one I want him to see."

Every consideration was held to the same level of circumspection, weaving together the past, present and future to help create an appearance of random selection. At that moment, James shifted back to the here and now, and the retired teacher, Matt, shackled inside the basement of his house. His time was at hand.

As James entered the house he reflected on how fate played a part in this man's impending death. After his last kill in Arizona, James drove back to Montana. About twenty miles short of Billings, a car was broken down on the side of the road. Since there were no other vehicles in sight, James pulled over and offered assistance.

"Hey, can I help?" he said while getting out of his black pickup truck.

"Oh man, you're a godsend. My car died about five minutes ago, plus my cell phone is out of charge. I guess it's just my unlucky day."

James smiled and said, "I've had worse...besides, this allows me to play the Good Samaritan. Can I give you a ride to the nearest service station so you can arrange to have your car towed? I'm sorry, since I don't have a phone...it's the best I can do."

"That's awfully kind of you, thanks a million."

"Is that an offer, I can sure use the cash?"

The man laughed and got into the vehicle. While the man was completely at ease and just sitting down inside of the pickup, James immediately reached over and forced the chloroform rag over his face. He attempted to fight him off, but James was too fast and too strong. The struggle ended quickly.

James drove the truck with his passenger out cold, right in the seat beside him. If anyone were to glance inside the vehicle he would appear to be fast asleep. James drove for about two miles and then turned off on a gravel road. It appeared to be a long driveway, but no house could be seen from where he was at that moment. James parked and then quickly removed the man from his pickup. He lifted him up and placed him into its cab. He bound the man's hands and legs and placed a gag in his mouth. Then James secured the tarp cover over the cab area. It was unlikely the man would awake before he got to his destination, but James was precautionary. If someone had come along, then that person would have been handled accordingly. The handgun in his glove compartment was for just such an occasion. James had never used it, other than at a firing range.

He got back into the pickup and continued onward. There were no security cameras on this particular road, which is why James chose it. He always made trips up and down various roads leading to and from the houses he purchased. His photographic memory logged every potential threat, knowing that law enforcement would seek pictures of vehicles in the area of a crime. James avoided such threats at all costs. Everything he did was carefully orchestrated. Once he was several miles away from an abduction or killing, the cameras would be useless. It would be impractical to investigate that many vehicles outside of the immediate location of his work. Having a place that was secure from prying eyes was paramount to accomplishing his task. That's why James had purchased several other workstations scattered in various parts of the country with the same profile, isolated privacy. These properties did not hold any emotional ties or a sense of belonging; rather they served as a tool for his new passion.

James knew that by controlling his environment he could work without exposure. Hotels, motels or public places had too many risks. There were cameras, unintended witnesses or worse yet, law enforcement in public places. If he abducted or killed someone, it was only done after observing the area for any such potential problems. His selection process always took this in to account. James knew to be patient and allow fate to guide him. His delusion of being God's messenger was strengthened every time someone was chosen, if opportunity and the conditions weren't exactly right, he would wait until someone else walked into his sights.

Matt had just been in the wrong place at the wrong time. When he heard the footsteps coming down the stairs, he cried. At first, he tried to connect with his abductor by providing him details of his life, but that had been to no avail. He knew that there would be no escape, and that his wife and children would suffer from his loss. On the first day he was taken, the blond haired man informed him that he was God's messenger and that his creator selected him for a higher purpose.

Up until that point, James had always killed the same day of his attack. His previous victims either died in their own home or at one of his workstations that very night. James decided he would alter any perceived methodology that might be a help in profiling him. He would further change things as he went along, leaving an impossible trail to follow. James never used the same car twice when working and always used models that were popular for the area. Every garage had several vehicles to choose among.

James had in his hand a serrated knife and Matt knew it would all soon be over. His screams would not matter; no one would be there to help. Every day he had yelled at the top of his lungs and each day there was no rescuer. The forty-three acre property was surrounded by woods and the nearest neighbor was miles away, not that they would ever visit, for this was not a home.

His house on Mercer Street in Princeton had been a home, but he never returned there after the trauma. That person had been destroyed. Family, friends and a sense of belonging were long gone. All that remained was a structural façade, just like these houses were an illusion to cover up their real purpose.

James had truly become a magician, in that, people were meant to be fooled, mesmerized by observing what really wasn't there. No stone was left unturned, everything was considered. Even his property in Princeton became part of the deception, as he hired a staff to maintain it. The surrounding memories had disappeared; James had completely disassociated from the community that brought him the only happiness he had ever known. It was like that person had never existed, like some forgotten face on a photograph from long ago, unable to connect with the life that slipped away. But no detail escaped his mind. If the house was kept in good condition, unwanted attention would not surface. Besides, it would appear that its owner would eventually return, thus creating an illusion that he still belonged. People found comfort in stability and maintaining relationships. Change could be scary to the average person, and James wanted to appear as if he were still there. The last memory of those he once knew would be of the brilliant and affable young man, who held the world in his hands.

Now instead he held a blade meant to scare and he achieved just that objective. Matt was petrified as he begged for his life. The pain of being cut was unimaginable and his will soon faded, along with the endless cries.

The bag with the letter "M" would soon arrive at F.B.I. Headquarters and thereafter, a number of other unexpected surprises. The killing would stop before anyone knew what was happening and the next chapter would begin.

CHAPTER 34

"Present Day"

BETH ADDRESSED THE TASK FORCE, "SINCE WE'VE NOW RULED OUT Tim Richardson as a suspect, we need to determine whether or not, the remaining persons of interest have any involvement in the Magician Case. I want everyone to provide feedback in case we might be overlooking something."

Frank added, "No supposition is off the table, I've learned over the years to consider everything as a possibility. Sometimes as investigators we have a tendency to hone in on the most obvious candidate, and dismiss the bread crumbs forming another trail. What I'm saying is, let's evaluate every idea as being the right idea, and sort it all out later. The trail is here, we just need to find which one and follow it."

Beth asked, "Tuck, can you give us all you have on Eric Duritz, including your own feelings regarding the man?"

"He's married, twenty-five years old, lives in Los Gatos, California and has two kids. He's lived there for about three years, and the residents of the community describe him as a great guy. Eric was a high school football star and the prom king. He married his wife, Tania, shortly after she graduated from UCLA. They have two boys, Luke, aged three, and Jackson, aged two. By anyone's account, they're the picture perfect couple; she was her high school's head cheerleader and prom queen. They met at the beach one day and apparently fell in love.

Agent Tucker continued, "During his senior year of high school, he said that he blew out his knee. Apparently he wasn't a great student and as a result, when the athletic scholarships disappeared, he decided not to attend college. He had a part time job the latter part of high school, working as a cook in a local pizzeria. This ultimately led to him opening his own restaurant. His parents helped fund the initial investment, along with some bank loans, and when the economy took a downturn the place eventually went belly up. I don't know why, but it seemed to me that there might have been more to the story about the business folding, but I'm not sure."

"What makes you say that?" Frank asked.

"Just the looks between him and his wife when they told me about the restaurant going under...I sensed a lot of discomfort."

"Maybe they were just embarrassed," added Agent Bucko.

"That's certainly possible, it just felt like there was something more to it."

"Okay, go on," Beth interjected.

"This all happened about a year before he claims to have met the attorney setting up his charitable trust. He said he never heard of Gary Jones. Mr. Duritz was on the verge of filing for bankruptcy when he was approached by Fred Kimmel and was told a wealthy philanthropist selected his family for charitable assistance. At first he said he was skeptical, wondering if this were some kind of a con. But he quickly figured that he had nothing to lose, and since there wasn't much a grifter could get from him, he didn't want his family left in financial ruins. So he agreed to accept the offer. When the money started rolling in, he used the income stream to open another restaurant. Mr. Duritz said that he wasn't sure how long the charity would last and wanted to ensure that he could still provide for his family. In my opinion, he appears to be a really nice guy who ran into trouble and was approached with an offer that he really couldn't refuse. If I had been in his shoes, I can't say I would have done anything different. Bottom line, I think he's legit."

"Anyone have questions or an alternate viewpoint?" Beth asked.

Frank kept quiet and just wanted to hear what the other members of the team had to say. He knew that just because someone seemed like a model citizen, the appearance could be a well crafted disguise. Frank had seen too many sociopaths that had learned to blend seamlessly into their environment. Although this particular back story had a ring of truth to it, Frank wasn't ready to completely rule Mr. Duritz out.

Julia Thorn responded, "Was he ever out of state during the year the murders were committed?

"He and his wife don't recall taking any special vacations around that time. Besides the whole line of questioning, starting with Gary Jones caused them to be...from all appearances, surprised."

"Being that the restaurant was failing around the time of the murders and also that he was the owner, payroll records won't help us much, if he still kept them. Employees would have a near impossible time remembering if he took any time off, certainly leaves us wondering," chimed Agent Bucko.

"How does the guy come across? I know you said that you feel he's legit, but is that strictly based on his story?" Frank finally added.

"Like I said before, he comes across exactly like you'd imagine a high school football star, slash, prom king would...an all American guy, you know the type, blond hair, blue eyes...beautiful wife. He was engaging and appeared to be sincere."

"You noticed discomfort when he was asked about the bankruptcy, if he's hiding something regarding that, then maybe he's keeping other things secret. See if you can find anything else, look more into his family and friends. We don't have much beyond the Gary Jones' connection, but that doesn't mean it's not there," Beth responded.

"I'll get back on it as soon as this meeting's over," Agent Tucker replied.

"Good work, Rich, keep it up. Any other questions for Tuck?

Everyone shook their heads and seemed ready to move on to the next suspect. Beth looked over at Frank.

"I'm ready to hear what else we've got."

"Julia, why don't you fill us all in on Nolan Russeck?" Beth asked Agent Thorn.

"First off, he seemed completely perplexed when I introduced myself as an F.B.I. agent. If he was acting, then we have a potential

Sir Laurence Olivier on our hands. Then at the first mention of Gary Jones he was equally shocked. He knew of the author, but not of any connection to him. He was forthcoming during the whole interview and gave me a detailed history of his life. He was born in Montana and has a twin brother, Keith who lives in Wisconsin. Certainly that information raised red flags for me, given that those states were murder locations of "The Magician." Add to that he lives in Arizona, another state our killer has visited and I became extra alert. However, there wasn't even the slightest hint of anxiety when he mentioned the information. Mr. Russeck held eye contact the entire time, no inordinate blinking or signs of nervousness."

Frank interjected, "Sociopaths can have a predatory stare and thus no discomfort in prolonged eye contact the way the average person does. Since they have an absence of nervousness, remorse or shame...their actions can come across as very sincere. Life can be like a game to them, to play their part with a single minded purpose, in this specific case, to show their superiority or dominance and kill without being caught."

Beth added, "Frank just made a point that might be helpful in how we view our killer, which can be beneficial in catching "The Magician". Let's make sure we understand the critical differences in behavior. If someone is psychotic, that just means they've exhibited delusions or hallucinations and that does not make them a killer. A person can be psychotic for a host of reasons. A psychopath differs from a sociopath, with the sociopath being the more difficult person to identify. Each type is considered to have anti-social personality disorders. A psychopath is congenitally based and a sociopath environmentally rooted. Sociopaths usually have experienced severe abuse, neglect or trauma which impacted their ability to feel. They can understand human interactions and patterns, and often mimic them to a tee, they just can't actually experience the emotion itself. Therefore, they learn how to fit in among us. Psychopaths are usually more reckless and live on the outskirts of normal society, ala Ted Kazinsky, the Unibomber. They have a tougher time maintaining normal relationships. Bottom line, a sociopath makes our work a lot more difficult."

"Beth just made a great point. I know we tend to use a lot of these terms interchangeably when talking about monsters, myself included, and that's a societal influence. Sometimes we can let these subtleties lower our guard, it's human nature. But unless we understand the difference, we tend to morph the two together and this can alter our analysis when hunting these predators. Not every sociopath, nor every psychopath is a killer...although the chances of violent behavior is greater with a psychopath. They're more impulsive which is why they're easier to catch. Sociopath's behaviors are varied and their motivations can be different. A person can be driven by greed and have no empathy for another person's loss...Bernie Madoff comes to mind. Our serial killer is driven by something else, his actions are varied, controlled and calculated. Remember he's the guy that you might not notice sitting next to you on a train or park bench, so keep your senses heightened, we're dealing with a very dangerous and cunning individual."

"That's why we can't rule out Mr. Duritz, Russeck or Logan until we have definitive proof of their innocence. A sociopath can come across as quite charming; remember that in your investigations. Anyhow, Agent Thorn, please continue," Beth stated.

"His parents split up when he was nine years old and both are now deceased. Mr. Russeck stated his father was an alcoholic and physically abusive. He and his brother lived with their mother who gained full custody of the children. Shortly after both boys graduated from college their mom died and they followed their chosen career paths. Mr. Russeck took a job as an English Professor, where he still currently resides at a community college in Scottsdale, Arizona. It was here that he met his now ex-wife, Roz. She was a fellow faculty member at the time they met. They divorced after four years when she couldn't get over two miscarriages, ultimately pulling her away from him. During this time he focused on his bigger goal of becoming a novelist. He wrote two novels that were published. He said both were works of fiction that just couldn't find an audience."

"What genre were the books?" asked Agent Gelaszus.

"Thrillers."

"Obviously not that thrilling, since they ended up in the dustbin," joked Agent Bucko, "but in all seriousness, the writer component is intriguing, especially with him having a connection to three states where killings took place."

"The way this is shaping up, it just might be too obvious," Agent Bucko chimed in, "it appears that Gary Jones or whoever he is, loves creating a maze. You think you're headed in the right direction and suddenly realize it's a dead end."

"Maybe that's another misdirection, thinking we went right for the bait with Tim Richardson only to realize it was a waste of time. So maybe, we stop looking at the logical choice this time and look at the less evident. We could go on and on, so let's not over think this and just rule out each option until we locate the correct one. This is what "The Magician" wants, to have us see what's not there," Frank replied.

"Frank's right, we need to be methodical, explore every nook and cranny until we catch this bastard," Beth said emphatically.

"Shall I continue?" asked Agent Thorn.

"Yes, what more do you have for us," Beth answered.

"He's currently working on another novel and is continuing to teach two days a week at the college. He could have retired once the money flow started streaming in after meeting Fred Kimmel, but he said he wanted to continue with his passion."

"What reason was given as to why he was selected by Mr. Kimmel?" Beth asked.

"He was informed by the attorney that a wealthy philanthropist supporting the arts chose to support his work. The client's name wasn't given, but that he really enjoyed Mr. Russeck's novels and wanted to provide financial incentive to keep on writing. He never expected the amount of money to be so extreme or for it to continue, but just like everyone else, he wasn't going to turn it away either. Mr. Russeck assumed his benefactor was an upper crust eccentric with boat loads of cash. Besides it helped to erase his doubts concerning his proficiency as an author or at least that's what he said to me."

"Has Mr. Russeck been involved in any serious relationships since his divorce, it might be a way to find out more, like for instance, does he travel much with such a light work load?" asked Julia Thorn.

"He said there hasn't been anyone serious in his life since his marriage ended and that he has no real desire to get tied down again."

"What's he look like?" asked Julia.

"Good looking guy, tall, blonde and in shape."

"Hey, did Tim Richardson have blonde hair?" Julia asked while looking in the direction of Beth and Frank.

"No. Dark hair and brown eyes. Why do you ask?" replied Beth.

"Just looking for patterns, I know none of these guys matched the photo on Gary Jones' book jackets."

"Frank and I believe that Gary Jones is likely a pseudonym and that the photograph is some other person altogether. In any case, keep being inquisitive. That's exactly what I meant when I said explore every nook and cranny."

"Just for the record, Justin Logan is about six foot tall, dark hair and brown eyes," added Agent Gelaszus.

"A perfect split, I'm surprised we didn't have a red head in the mix," said Agent Tucker.

"Maybe we still will, when we locate Gary Jones. It certainly appears the man is hiding in a labyrinth worthy of Sherlock Holmes," Agent Tucker responded.

"...or Frank Sorello. Any doubts this was just some author using classified information are gone. I believe "The Magician" is directly tied to Gary Jones in some capacity. There are too many quirky connections and oddities tied to the money trail. Even a hermit protecting his anonymity wouldn't have this many layers of misdirection," Beth said while glancing at Frank.

"Beth, I appreciate the level of confidence you have in me, but I want everyone to know that without a talented task force, I'd be nowhere on this. What I'm saying is, I need all of your help. From what I've seen so far, this group more than meets that standard. Trust me when I say, we're going to catch his scent, hunt him down and make him pay!"

"Julia, put together surveillance on our author and continue looking into his background for possible ties to the murders. Agents Bucko and Gelaszus, you're up."

"Joe, you have seniority, so why don't you take this?" Agent Bucko asked while addressing his partner Agent Gelaszus.

"Thanks, John. Jump right in if you want to add anything."

"Sure."

"Mr. Logan is certainly worth a strong look. There's nothing concrete, but his background gained our attention. He's an only child and both parents live in Arizona...he's thirty-nine years old, a former pilot for United Airlines, single and never married. He went to the Air Force Academy and flew fighter jets during the Iraqi War from 2003 to 2006. His best friend, another pilot, was shot down and killed in 2005, while they were out on the same mission. This pushed him toward wanting to exit the Air Force. When Justin left the military after fulfilling his service contract he got a job in the private sector with United. This is where things get interesting. His hub of operation was at O'Hare in Chicago and according to him he flew virtually every domestic route from the airport. Mr. Logan said he had no idea what specific cities he traveled to from the end of 2011, through 2012. In fact, his demeanor was somewhat nasty during this line of questioning. He also admitted to having a drinking problem that developed during the inception of symptoms related to PTSD. Mr. Logan stopped working right around the time that the first novel was published. Did I miss anything, John?"

Agent Bucko replied, "Not much, but I'd like to add a couple of details. Logan said he saw a psychologist due to post traumatic stress after leaving the military. He claimed to have flashbacks, heightened startle response, nightmares and depression. His drinking at the time was described as somewhat excessive, but he denied ever flying drunk. He further stated he would usually be inebriated during his layovers, which often lasted several days. During these benders, Logan said he would just hole up in his hotel. He would begin sobering up the day before the next leg of his route. The toll it was taking on him was becoming too much to handle and once Mr. Kimmel provided another source of income, he gave up flying completely. Logan said this allowed for some emotional healing and put him on the road to recovery."

"John, is he still seeing the therapist and can we talk to this person?" Beth asked.

"He discontinued therapy after several years once he got things under control, including his drinking. The name of his former psychologist is Dr. Cathy Howlett. Her practice is in Chicago and since Mr. Logan wouldn't sign an information release form, we'll need a search warrant forcing her to break client confidentiality. If we just hit her with a subpoena, it's likely she'd fight it tooth and nail"

"Given that we have nothing more than circumstantial evidence, mainly his accessibility to all of the murder sites in a very general sense; it'll be tough to get a federal judge to grant a warrant forcing a therapist to break privilege. I agree that a subpoena would be stonewalled. Ethically, the psychologist would likely hold her ground, citing the potential for harm to her client," Frank stated, "so we'll need to have a judge's order. Therefore, we need the circumstantial evidence to be much stronger. Let's not forget that this man served our country in the military, and a judge is not going to take that lightly. Can you check with the airlines to see if Mr. Logan was somewhere close to each murder location during the time they occurred? That would strengthen our argument significantly since we can show a direct connection to the money trail."

"We'll look into it," replied Agent Gelaszus.

"Anything else as to why we should place a high priority on Logan?" asked Beth.

"Obviously his ability to move around the country is worth noting. Since the murders occurred in six different states in a period of one year, it's tough for the average person to explain that kind of movement, unless they're retired or their job entails a lot of travel. Now let's add in his agitated state during questioning, his refusing to sign a release providing access to his psychologist and maybe PTSD isn't the only thing we need to consider. What if he's had psychotic episodes or violent thoughts, perhaps brought on by the trauma he experienced?" Gelaszus responded.

"Also, let's not forget him being only one of four people connected to the money from Gary Jones' novels," added Bucko.

"Speaking of that, what was his reaction to the author's name?" asked Agent Tucker.

"Same as everyone else, bewilderment," replied Bucko.

"Those are all good reasons, but they still could be explained. Any pilot flying for a major airline would have the same accessibility to those routes. Also, the man served his country and might be irritated that he is being considered a suspect, thus explaining his agitation. As for not wanting to provide access to his psychological records, I'm guessing a lot of people would want to protect that information. Do you see the problems we might have with getting a warrant issued?" Frank replied.

"That's true, but Logan is directly connected to Gary Jones, while other pilots or people protecting their privacy are not," replied Bucko.

"I'm not debating the merits of that argument, just the reality of getting a judge to sign off on the matter," Frank stated.

"I agree, let's see if we can match the murder dates with his locations during those times. I'm not requesting a federal warrant until we have more to go on," Beth added.

"Do you think we might be able to check old cell phone records as to what towers his calls pinged, as another way to establish his whereabouts at the time of the killings?" Frank added.

"Great idea, I want everyone to get on that regarding each of our suspects, not just Logan," Beth ordered.

"What about text messages?" asked Agent Tucker.

"Text messages will be useless, since the carriers never maintain that data more than a few days time."

"It looks like we still have a lot more digging to do," Frank said with a hint of frustration.

"Alright, let's get back to work. Great job everybody, the next time anything pertinent surfaces we'll all sit back down. Frank, let's go back to my office and decide where else we need to deploy our resources."

"Let's do it."

CHAPTER 35

"August 2012 – James"

JAMES WALKED BACK UPSTAIRS AFTER FINISHING HIS WORK. THE blood still needed to be washed from his body. He would clean up and then sit outside on the porch of his Montana home. The body of the girl left downstairs would need to be buried later in the day. James liked to process after every killing, evaluating what had been done and what was still to come.

Approximately eighteen hundred miles away, a picture frame sat collecting dust on a mantle in an uninhabited home. It was a brutal reminder of how quickly things had deteriorated. The photograph showed James beaming with pride as Maria stood lovingly in the background. Marty had wanted Grace to capture the moment of his friend shaking the hand of the defeated chess grand master, so she quickly snapped the picture. The Palazzo Vecchio had provided them many memories and that had been one of its highlights. The four friends spent hours that day marveling at the centuries old palace, taking in the sights, especially the copy of Michelangelo's David, but the joy of their experience had been timelessly captured on James' face. That young man brimming with promise had been replaced by a ruthlessly efficient killing machine.

Those images were relics of the past, impossible to summon. That photograph would forever remain sitting atop the fireplace of his Mercer Street home, along with all the other forgotten mementos detailing a life lost. James' psyche was shattered so completely, leaving him so disconnected, models in a drug store picture frame would carry the same emotional response; none.

Violence had become nothing more than moving pawns around a chess board. The female that bled out only an hour ago was the next to last move in "The Magician's" grand opening. James and Frank Sorello were engaged in a match of life and death. Each decision was made to outmaneuver the opponent, and in order to be the best, everything had to be calculated in advance. James saw the end game during his very first move, but still chose to evaluate every possible permutation, including the unexpected. His distorted mind still worked on a different plane, able to see beyond that of normal brilliance.

Maggie Donnelly had been his tenth victim. He would kill one more, before entering what he considered to be his mid-game. Fate once again played a part in the deceased girl's demise. On her twenty-fourth birthday she broke up with her long time boyfriend and on a whimsy, changed her Facebook status to single at the exact moment James was surfing for a suitable victim. She fit the requirements for what he was planning; she was a resident of the state of Montana like his previous victim, Matt. If the broken down vehicle had possessed an out-of-state license plate, the retired teacher would still be alive. However, each of the last two casualties was perfect for the vision in James' head. He knew that his adversary would look for patterns and they would be laid out for him to follow. "The Magician" knew that the best laid traps were those that were not easily seen.

The plan's evolution was hidden in a maze full of misdirection, but like everything else it needed a starting point. The initial seed was planted in James' subconscious by his foster father's sadism. This cruelty helped in formulating a denouement, while simultaneously providing an opening gambit. The time spent in that dark basement filled with reams of Houdini memorabilia ignited an idea. The rabbi from Appleton, Wisconsin, became the first speck on a trail ultimately leading to a predetermined destination. The link had been so subtle, it surprised James that a reporter found the connection to the famous magician and escape artist so quickly. Initially this had been a clue for Frank Sorello to discover, but it still held a purpose. Any single event was designed for confusion, but taken as a whole the picture would become clearer, with each action unraveling a mystery. Yet the ending was designed by a master of illusion.

CHAPTER 36

"Present Day"

IT WAS 7:00 A.M. AND AGENT THORN WAS ANXIOUS TO SPEAK WITH Beth. New information had been uncovered that still needed to be disseminated to the task force leader. Over the last week, Julia had been digging deeper into the background of Nolan Russeck. His colleagues, family and friends were contacted in the hope of discovering something pertinent to the investigation. Agent Hillmann was also helping to review any financial transactions made by Mr. Russeck around the times of the actual murders. He perused the suspect's credit card purchases and ATM usage, along with phone records in an effort to establish his whereabouts during these dates. The efforts proved to be valuable and this is why Julia knocked on her supervisor's door.

"Come in," Beth said.

"I hope I'm not disturbing you, but I think we have definitive proof that eliminates Nolan Russeck as a potential suspect."

"Okay, what do you have?"

"Since our team meeting last week, I've been busy questioning everyone surrounding Mr. Russeck and getting nowhere. Yesterday, Tony came across financial records pointing to his innocence. Apparently at the time of the third murder, our suspect was thousands of miles away. Mr. Russeck used his American Express Card several times in Atlanta. There was also a cash withdrawal made from an ATM minutes before the victim died and to top it off, cell phone records show that towers in that area were pinged by his phone."

"What if someone else used his cards and phone?"

"I considered that, so I contacted Mr. Russeck and asked him what he was doing in Atlanta. He was at a funeral. A friend of his died of a heart attack. Nolan apologized for not mentioning this before and said it was too personal to share. Anyhow, the family of the deceased corroborated his story. So it seems another name comes off our list."

"Good work, Julia. I'll pass this on to the team. In the meantime, ask the other members of our task force if you can help out in any capacity."

"I will."

Beth contemplated this recent bit of news and knew the circle was getting smaller. She wondered if better luck would be coming.

She thought to herself, "When are we going to catch a break."

CHAPTER 37

"October 2012 – James and Frank"

THE STORM OF THE CENTURY WAS COMING, AT LEAST THAT'S WHAT the news called the hurricane working its way toward the eastern seaboard of the United States. It was expected to turn directly inland near Monmouth County, New Jersey. James took this to be a divine message, since the focal point of his lunacy, Frank Sorello, lived there. James originally intended to visit during the holidays, but not as a welcomed guest. Now he would come sooner, unannounced and bring death with him. The ferocity of Hurricane Sandy would create the perfect backdrop. If Juliette didn't heed the warnings and evacuate, she would die, but not from gale force winds.

Everyone would be preoccupied in preparation for nature's onslaught, affording James a cloak of invisibility. The only threat to this cover would be the trained eyes of Frank Sorello. He would notice things that were out of place, such as a stranger milling about for too long. James envisioned a solution to deal with this threat. He would lead the hunter away, making him believe his quarry lay elsewhere.

James booked a flight to Philadelphia. The city was close enough to Spring Lake, that if the bait was taken, he could remain ahead of the hurricane that was rapidly approaching. If the lure went untouched, then James would adapt. Even though everything was choreographed in his mind, flexibility came in handy.

For example, when James decided to purchase isolated homes, the only motive had been to find killing stations. But since he had no specific locations in mind it led to an idea. James would formulate a sequence for his enemy to follow and selected homes according to the pattern he would develop.

During his time at Princeton, James once read, Max Tegmark's "theory of everything," which proposed that our external physical reality is a mathematical structure. It fascinated him to think that equations were tied to the mysteries of the universe and found it fitting to incorporate patterns into the riddle he was creating.

The decision to kill in specific locales had been derived shortly after murdering the rabbi, but James knew that predictability meant danger. So in selecting his victims, he altered methods. The retired teacher, Matt had been a spur of the moment opportunity, while others were carefully chosen. In either case, they had to match the pattern he was establishing. Eventually he would change this protocol, but not until it served his ultimate purpose.

James realized his every move would be analyzed, so he needed to always stay one step ahead by leading Frank in a hundred directions. Let him think a certain mode of behavior existed and then change it. Everything James did was designed to bait and confuse. With calculated precision, nothing stayed the same for very long.

The Rabbi from Appleton, and Juliette were anchor points, before a long pause was planned. The nine victims taken in between were less significant. Killing the Jewish holy man had been an offshoot tied to his hatred of Paul. The specific rabbi chosen didn't matter, only that he hail from Appleton, Wisconsin. James wanted to establish a link between his first bloodletting and his loathed foster father. Houdini and his birthplace served that purpose nicely. Whereas his brilliance may have once led to linking otherwise random facts into transformative good, his burgeoning madness now ran the show. It was only through the ambition of an astute reporter that a connection was made to the seemingly senseless death of the good rabbi and Houdini. The link to Paul would come much later. Ultimately, Juliette's death would serve to personalize the battle with Frank, leaving both of them with losses that the famed F.B.I. agent had been too late to stop. Everyone that died served a purpose, as would those, yet to die. Insanity guided James toward what lie ahead.

The crazed genius arrived in Philadelphia two days before Sandy was expected to hit the Northeast. He left from Chicago where he had been researching another part of his plan. After getting off the plane he took a shuttle to long term parking and pretended to be looking for his car. Within minutes he saw what he was hoping to find, a couple parked their SUV and wheeled two large suitcases toward the shuttle area. James casually walked over to the vehicle, making sure there were no cameras or anyone in the immediate area. He quickly removed the license plates and placed them in his carry bag. A few minutes later he took the next shuttle back to the terminal where he rented a car, selecting the most popular model. James didn't drive directly to Philadelphia, instead he stopped in Norristown, a small suburb not far from the City of Brotherly Love. He drove around until he found an isolated area and changed the plates on the car he was driving. James was being extra careful because he didn't have the usual time to scout the area for possible risks. Normally he operated in locations that he knew inside and out, mentally taking the time to mark potential hazards. His photographic mind took everything in as he scouted territories, but now he had to use more expediency. He didn't have the luxury to map out everything in advance. Changing plates would serve as a precaution against a camera or an unforeseen witness taking down a license number. James wore a cap to cover his hair and sunglasses to hide his deep blue eyes in an effort to limit anyone from getting a good description of him. These measures were superficial, so vigilance and the right opportunity needed to be found.

He quickly passed through the heavily populated shopping districts and the more affluent sections of Norristown, careful to not travel the same road or to circle back. James wanted to appear if he was headed somewhere specific if cameras traced his movement. It would appear as if he were a resident and therefore wouldn't stand out. James then came across something that held promise. He noticed a small pawn shop with an "out to lunch" sign on the door. James reasoned that the store was likely run by a single employee. Since this section of town appeared to be impoverished, there were far fewer pedestrians walking on the street and more importantly, no security cameras. The setup of the small business was also ideal. Directly to its left was nothing but trees and on the other side was an abandoned dry cleaning shop. A narrow driveway led directly between the two buildings.

He parked his car down the street and walked back toward the driveway, avoiding direct contact with anyone. Only one person passed by across the street, seemingly oblivious to the killer nearby. In this neighborhood, people minded their own business. James casually strolled down the driveway with his head down and saw the empty parking spot at the back entrance of the shop. There was a dumpster a few feet away, directly opposite from the closed down dry cleaning store. James sat down behind it and waited. He assumed that the store owner wouldn't be long. If his assumption was wrong or anything felt uncomfortable then he would seek out another target.

Approximately twenty minutes later, he heard a car enter the driveway and readied himself. James gripped the revolver that was tucked inside the front of his pants. He figured from the moment he heard the car door open it would take less than a half a minute before the proprietor would unlock the back entrance. James knew he would be much quicker than that and listened for the jangle of keys. At that instant, before the elderly man had time to turn and see who belonged to the rapidly approaching set of footsteps, the blow to his head knocked him unconscious. James made sure not to use too much force as he hit the man with the butt of his gun. He wanted the store owner alive.

James bent down, picked up the set of keys and opened the door to the pawn shop. He walked inside and found himself in a small back office. From there he entered the store itself and strolled toward the door, flipping the sign from "out to lunch" to "closed." Immediately thereafter he went back outside and dragged the man into the back office. James used rope to secure the store owner, gagging and blindfolding him as well.

About three hours later, he was ready to set the wheels in motion. He took out of his travel bag, a disposable cell phone and a portable voice changing device. He knew everything would be recorded and wanted to digitally alter the sound of his speech. These measures were taken as extra precautions. The items themselves had been purchased months earlier with cash. Each had been acquired separately from different locations.

James thought of every detail. He made the call from a diner's parking lot several miles away from the pawn shop. He wanted to ensure a local cell tower was pinged to establish his whereabouts as being in the area. He delayed placing the call until this moment in order to shorten the time that law enforcement would have in their subsequent search. Yet not long enough to stop him from his primary goal.

"Norristown Police Department, how can I help you?" answered the desk officer.

"A resident of your town is being held hostage. I am the "The Magician." I've left a small package between two row houses on the five hundred block of Arch Street. Frank Sorello of the F.B.I. will know by its contents that this is not a joke. The clock begins now... blood will flow before the week is up."

James hung up and left no time to start a trace.

The officer that had answered the call rushed into his commander's office and had him listen to the recorded phone call. The digitized voice created a sense of foreboding and the message was taken very seriously. Within minutes the F.B.I. had been contacted and several squad cars headed out to locate the package on Arch.

Once it was found, the bomb squad was called to check for explosives. When all was cleared, the box was opened. Inside were three bloody fingernails, each attached to a golden ball.

At the bottom of the box was a note covered in crimson.

This is for Frank. Fingernails from one hand, not 2. Not in their usual bag. Giving you a chance to save someone. I doubt you can do it. They say you are smart. You are famous. FBI. Ha, you can't catch me and I'm just someone nobody ever notices. I will be here for seven days. One per day. Tick Tock. Maybe you will stop me from taking the other nails. Either way, I will take another. Unless you are as good as they say you are. M.

James knew every word would be analyzed. Therefore, he

avoided scholarly phrasing. He also implied in the note resentment toward success and fame, hoping to create an image of being part of the struggling working class or unemployed. It was all misdirection, just like the abduction itself.

The three artificial golden balls though held specific purpose. James noticed them prominently displayed on the owner's desk and recognized their significance. The story behind these trinkets would aid the police or F.B.I. in locating the missing pawn shop owner. The only drawback would be if they inferred from the symbolization that his intellect was genius. But James reasoned the logical assumption would be that he hadn't known what the balls represented; instead, that they were just a personal possession of the owner which helped lead to his rescue.

James never planned on killing the pawn shop owner because it would change the pattern he was establishing. The man was strictly a clever diversion. Since everyone called him "The Magician"...a grand illusion was in store. Frank Sorello would initially believe he saved the man's life, when in fact it caused the death of another, his beloved Juliette.

Later that evening, James drove to Philadelphia where he stayed the night. He changed the plates back to their originals out of sight from prying eyes. He wanted to appear as if his visit had a purpose, so he went shopping and saw a play. At 6:00 a.m., he checked out, going back to the airport where he returned his rental car. From there he took a cab to Cherry Hill, New Jersey. James was dropped off not far from several car dealerships. He walked to the closest one and purchased an Acura, which wouldn't stand out where he was headed. After all, he was a resident of the state. James didn't waste any time because the storm would make travel conditions impossible later in the day.

Minutes later he was on the Jersey Turnpike, heading toward his destination of Spring Lake. Everything was going perfectly as planned. The afternoon before, one of the residents of this affluent shore community took a chopper from Wall Airport to Philly. The arrangements had been made minutes after Norristown's police chief made a call to the Bureau. Frank Sorello had taken the bait.

The F.B.I. agent was energized with the possibility of catching this elusive killer. A note and the chance to stop another senseless death fueled his fire. While Frank was in the air he arranged for members of his team to meet him at the Norristown Police Headquarters. He would ask for full cooperation between the police and the F.B.I. Task Force upon his arrival. When the chopper landed he was taken by a squad car to the police department. The officer led him directly to his superior's office.

"Hi, I'm Special Agent Frank Sorello. I'd like to thank you, Chief, for contacting me so quickly."

"You can skip the formalities, I'm Guff Strada. As for the help, no problem, I'll make sure we do everything we can to help you catch this fucker!

"Thanks, Guff. That's what I was hoping to hear. I know how sometimes local police departments take offense to us claiming jurisdiction over their cases. I told my guys that this will be a total joint operation. Can we set up a command post somewhere?"

"It's already done. Every available man is on notice and I've green lighted all overtime. When do you expect the rest of your team?"

"They're in flight and should be here shortly," Frank responded as he entered the command center.

Introductions were quickly made and Frank was shown the box and its contents. The lab had dusted it for fingerprints and it had come up clean. The chief took the time to bring the F.B.I. agent up to speed on all the pertinent details. Shortly thereafter, Frank's fellow team members arrived.

"Okay, now that everyone's here, I'd like to get started. For those who don't know me, I'm Frank Sorello with the F.B.I. My task force has been working on The Magician case since last November and this abduction appears to be related. The little present he left is his calling card. I want to stress the importance of keeping that information in this room. The finger nails have been kept out of the papers as a way of weeding out false information, copycats and your general nut jobs. The additional contents of the gift box deviate from what we've received in the past."

One of the Norristown detectives interrupted, "In what way?"

Frank paused before answering and decided to leave out the

information that the nails previously arrived in a plastic bag, with the letter "M" scrawled in black indelible ink. He thought it would be prudent in case one of the local law enforcement officers slipped up and revealed the finger nail information to a reporter. Agent Sorello wanted to maintain some level of control over this classified information.

"First off, there's never been a note attached or any items delivered other than fingernails. So the golden balls are certainly new. Also, going back to the fingernails, they've always come post mortem. It seems our guy is becoming bolder and challenging us to stop him. He specifically addressed me in the note."

"Any ideas as to why?"

"In the note there's a tone of anger and narcissism. He mentions fame with disdain, showing a sense of superiority. My reputation or something else I've done has apparently pissed him off. I think he wants to show off, but that gives us an opportunity. If his message is legit then we have seven days to prevent a killing and hopefully catch this maniac. Maybe he's spiraling out of control and will start making mistakes."

"Where do we start?"

"Well, let's begin by going over what we know. The three finger nails appear to be male, but the crime lab is testing them along with the blood. I'm pretty sure that'll confirm our current viewpoint. So we'll begin by looking to see if any males have been reported missing in the last few days. That doesn't mean to put less emphasis on a missing report for a female, there might be others coming."

"Do we have anything else that might help us? A description of possible suspects? Does he kill a specific type?" asked an eager member of the force.

"Unfortunately, we've been chasing the wind. Nobody has ever seen him. Any crime scene evidence found at the murder scenes was singular to that specific location, meaning no prints, DNA samples, or blood...has ever been found at more than one location. So it's likely that none of it belongs to him. There's been nothing in what we've collected as evidence that matches anything in our criminal databases. His kills appear to be indiscriminate. Even the first murder from which he got his nickname appears to have been random. There have been no other religious figures murdered since then, so the reporter that coined him 'The Magician' due to the Houdini tie, likely was coincidence. Yet his nickname certainly fits, because he disappears after every kill."

"He didn't this time."

"That's why this is our first real chance at finding him; assuming he's telling the truth. So let's work together and end this here and now!"

"Frank, what are your thoughts about the balls? Guff asked."

"Maybe you two should discuss that in private," a detective yelled out.

Everyone in the room laughed, including Frank and Guff. The joke cut through the tension that had been building in the room. It was going to be a long stretch before they'd be able to relax; a citizen's life was in their hands.

"Frank, I've come across something on the Internet that might be of interest. These goddamn phones are amazing, I just entered three golden balls in the search engine and..." said Agent Len Newton.

"Let's hear it."

"Hey it might be nothing, but here goes. Apparently, during the late middle ages, three golden balls represented the House of Lombard. They acted as a lending institution comprised of a group of pawn shops. The golden balls acted as a symbol associated with the pawn industry."

"Okay, we've got nothing else. Get on that, Len. Check on all the pawn shops in the Norristown area. See if anyone has gone missing."

"Alright, boss. I'll get right to it."

"Guff, let's get some men back out on the street. Maybe they'll get lucky and come across something. I'll have some of my guys look through the reports of any people recently reported missing. I'm going to start checking out some of these pawn shops, if you want to tag along. As crazy as it seems this wack job seems to like his riddles."

"Sounds good to me, Frank. We really need to get our asses in gear because once the storm hits tomorrow we might have to hole up inside."

Approximately ninety miles away, on the following morning, James stood not far from Frank's house. He was looking to see if any homes appeared to be evacuated. Since the house was near the ocean, he blended in on the boardwalk appearing to be just a storm watcher. The winds were picking up as the waves were growing ever larger. Rain was coming down heavily in advance of the huge weather system approaching. James wore rain gear to protect himself from the elements but to also provide cover. If someone approached he walked away with his head down and returned when they were gone.

James had just seen Juliette pass in front of her large picture window. Lightning shot like tentacles through the sky as her neighbors across the street came outside. Everything was falling into place. It was another sign. The family was carrying luggage which they packed into the back of their Cadillac Escalade. They were fortunate to heed the warnings for the promise of terror was coming soon.

Back in Norristown, a detective for the police force had just received a phone call about a possible missing person. The previous twenty-four hours had presented no breaks in the case. Nobody had been reported missing from a pawn shop or otherwise. There had been no signs of forcible entry anywhere. The only thing that had changed was the weather, which was becoming increasingly more violent. After the phone call ended, the detective rushed into his chief's office.

"Guff, I think we've got something! I just got a call from a guy named Terry Calhoun. He said he's been trying to reach his brother Lou since late last night. Nobody's heard from him since yesterday. He owns a fucking pawn shop!"

"Holy shit!"

Within the half hour, a search warrant was issued to search Calhoun's home and the pawn shop. Squad cars sped to both locations hoping to not be too late. The search of the man's home came up empty, but his place of business did not. As soon as they broke down the front door of the pawn shop, a muffled grunt was heard from a back room.

Frank ran toward the sound with his gun drawn. Lying on

the floor was Calhoun completely bound and gagged. Blood was everywhere from the fingernails ripped from his hand. The man sobbed as he told what had happened. Frank called the Norristown Police Chief and told them they located Mr. Calhoun and that he was alive, but there was no luck with "The Magician." The task force leader refused to give up hope.

Frank barked out, "Listen up; I want someone to get him to a hospital right away. Then let's see if we can get that door back on its hinges quickly. I know it's not going to be perfect, but maybe it'll look like storm damage. That note said 'one per day', there are seven fingernails left on Mr. Calhoun's hands. If he thinks we haven't found his victim, he might return to tear another one off. 'One per day'...that's what he fucking said!"

That night Frank waited along with his men to no avail. Hurricane Sandy passed through leaving catastrophic damage up and down the seaboard. Yet it was the following morning in which Frank felt its true aftermath.

The Magician left his calling card covered in the blood of his wife.

CHAPTER 38

"Present Day"

IT HAD BEEN ONE WEEK SINCE THE TASK FORCE LAST ASSEMBLED TO discuss the progress of the investigation. At that time, the details surrounding Nolan Russeck, Eric Duritz and Justin Logan were evaluated and each agent had been instructed to dig deeper into their backgrounds. So far nothing had turned up regarding the serial killer they were chasing, but yesterday morning Russeck had been removed as a person of interest due to an air tight alibi. His name, along with Tim Richardson's, was crossed off the list of potential suspects.

Beth and Frank were anxious to hear about the remaining two people still on their radar. Therefore, a meeting had been scheduled with Agent Tucker regarding Eric Duritz, though not much was expected to come from it. The night before leaving the west coast, Rich called Beth and informed her he'd run into a dead end. The task force leader still wanted to assess her agent's report first hand. Beth's nature was to be extremely thorough in every facet of an investigation. Besides it would help her to determine whether further resources should be allocated toward the restaurant owner or redeployed elsewhere.

Beth could sense the frustration building in Sorello, as they waited for Rich Tucker. She'd already given Frank a status update and since nothing had gotten them any closer to Gary Jones, the tension was palpable. Both of them were getting frustrated with the lack of progress.

"Frank, let's think outside the box for a minute. Richardson and Russeck, both have an alibi. They couldn't have been at certain murder locations. But they're still tied to the money trail...what if we stop looking at each suspect individually, but instead, the group as a whole?"

"I've been considering that myself, but my instinct keeps telling me it's one guy. The knife patterns were so consistent in each murder that I don't think it's a group of psychopaths working together. Yet there was a deviation with my wife...the fucking maniac strangled Juliette, but not before cutting her like the others. So maybe I'm wrong, but I don't think so."

"I'm sorry, Frank, that memory must be unbearable."

"I've learned to live with it...but I still want to tear that cocksucker apart."

At that moment, Agent Rich Tucker walked into the office and said, "I hope you're not talking about me."

"That depends," Frank replied to the young agent.

"Frank, it's good to see you too," he said with a smirk, "I wish I had something more, but I've got nothing on Duritz, other than his tie to the money."

"Well then I guess I'm going to have to kill you," Frank followed with a slight grin.

"Rich, fill us in on every detail. Frank and I don't want to discount any possibility, including the idea that the four suspects could be working together in some capacity."

As the three of them discussed his history they all felt it was unlikely that Duritz was involved. Everything in his background supported that of a man beyond reproach. Nothing seemed inconsistent or out of place and after about an hour, they decided he was no longer a person of interest.

"Three down and one to go, the group theory I just don't buy. If Logan doesn't pan out, then we've got nothing."

"Frank, I didn't want to say anything earlier because nothing's concrete, but there might be something there."

Agent Bucko and Agent Gelaszus informed her earlier in the morning, that some of Logan's more frequent routes, had him travel into areas where various murders had occurred. They were checking with the F.A.A. and United Airlines, as to the specific flight records. If it could be established that he was in the general location of each murder, it would make him the primary focus of the investigation. Since the records were older and specific dates needed to be cross referenced, it was taking some time, but they expected to have the information soon.

The task force's very existence hinged on this report, because if there were no more impending leads, it would only be a matter of time before things were shut down. The Magician would have effectively escaped, once again.

CHAPTER 39

"November 2012 – James"

Now that the opening moves had been made and the early game was over, James felt satisfied. His mind continued to visualize this as he would a master level chess match. The midgame would require patience because this was the point that would dictate what followed. So he analyzed the board, looking at all the pieces and where to set his traps. Since his enemy was skilled, this game would require an elaborate design and so far, that had been achieved.

Yet, James pushed for perfection and without a full emotional spectrum to cloud his thinking, he was like a computer running calculations. The only thing that guided him was vengeance and a total maniacal disconnect from humanity. Viewing people as nothing more than game pieces effectively allowed him to proceed with his mad delusion. The only time he felt anything was when he killed. The guttural responses of his victims' stirred deeply buried emotions and during those brief moments, he felt alive.

In vein with this irrational state, James saw the vanquishing of queens as an uneven trade. Sorello hadn't seen what he himself had witnessed. James wondered that perhaps he should have filmed the "taking," and left the clip on their nightstand covered in Juliette's blood.

Frank would never forget her loss, yet that was not enough for him. The F.B.I. Agent had been spared witnessing his wife's last seconds, unlike himself. James took solace in having watched Juliette's eyes shift from terror to resignation and that had been exhilarating. He thought of Sorello imagining that very moment and being left inconsolable.

James' endgame would seek utter destruction, not with the opposing king resigning, but being left totally decimated. To do this, he would prolong the pain and utilize all of his many gifts.

During his time at Princeton, he learned that he possessed his mother's talent for writing. This inherent ability would be applied in toying with the man he hated. By disappearing he would leave the man without a sense of closure, and after a period of time without finality, he planned on resurrecting hope, only to take it away once more. James wanted to lead Frank to the gates of Hell over and over again.

During the night of the hurricane, he found a portal. Every facet of the household was mentally absorbed in an effort to find something useful. He stared at pictures, touched mementos, gaining insight into his hunter's passions. In the library, he noticed Frank loved books, especially thrillers and crime novels. The bookshelves were filled with them and a seed was planted.

James reasoned that if he were to write a story worthy of attention then his enemy would read it. His very actions had already created a brilliant outline and he was sure he held the inspiration to fill the pages with words worthy of notice. This would be the torment he sought for Sorello and although the story in his head was complex, it would all tie together. He would tell the tale through multiple books.

James wanted the story to be read, as if written solely for Frank's eyes. The novels from start to finish, were to be guided by that principle. The author would take on the mind of Sorello and if he were in fact truly brilliant, he would see what others would not. The patterns and hints woven into the piece of "fiction" wouldn't escape him. He sat inside the thoughts of the hunter and what he would do from that perspective. The connections would be made and the trail followed.

If this presumption proved to be false, then the revered agent wasn't really worthy of praise. In that case, he would deliver more obvious clues. But at first, until he was sure of his adversary's intelligence, the trail would be almost imperceptible. The details would eventually be more clear, especially to those looking with heightened focus. Yet, everything would be written with the purpose of manipulating the pieces into a grand finish.

James recognized in order to do this, he would have to ensure that Sorello, would eventually read his words. The novel would have to be a masterpiece to attract publishers. If it were anything less, he would utilize whatever resources necessary to accomplish this end. Money placed in the right hands could help bring it to market. Those who came into contact with him would need to be dealt with as necessary.

If all of this failed, then he was prepared to alter his plan, perhaps by delivering an unprinted manuscript to the Sorello residence. In any case, he would adapt if necessary and follow through with an alternative solution.

But his genius would ultimately prove prophetic, as the books would become bestsellers and have the public clamoring for his novels. Yet the mass audience was never his target, although the income stream would create another opportunity.

As fate would have it, the eyes of Frank Sorello would ultimately read the story written solely for him.

CHAPTER 40

"Present Day"

"Beth, the flight records all match. He was in the area of every murder during the time they occurred, not in the air, but on the ground, leaving plenty of time to kill his victims. That can't be a coincidence!"

"I agree with you, especially with his tie to the money. I think we found Gary Jones."

"What's next?" asked Agent Bucko.

"You and Joe, stay put in Chicago. I'm going to call Frank with the news and then work on a warrant."

"Alright, we're here if you need us."

"Thanks, John. Great work."

The second she hung up with her agent, Beth was speed dialing Frank. She could feel the excitement as the phone began to ring.

"Hello."

"Logan was at every location, Frank. It's all circumstantial, but we have the motherfucker in our sights."

"Can you have someone book me on the first flight back to D.C.?"

"Already done. Check your messages for the flight information."

After they ended their phone call, Frank's demeanor quickly shifted from relaxed and carefree...to resolute. He had come home for a few days to see Sarah, while the investigation had hit a standstill. The two of them had spent every free minute together and it reinforced his desire to be with her all the time. She felt the same way about him. Life was complete when they were around one another, and Frank's state of being, was as healthy as it had been in a long time. Sarah had become so in tune with her man, that she noticed the very subtle change in his eyes, within seconds of ending his conversation with Beth.

"What's going on?"

"We may have a real break in the case. There seems to be some pretty strong circumstantial evidence, regarding one of our suspects, and I need to head back to Washington."

"That's great news. Hopefully this will all be over soon."

"My flight's in four hours, so I'm going to have to get a move on it."

"I'll drive you to the airport. I didn't schedule any patients today."

"That would be great."

On their ride to Newark, they jokingly argued over what station to play on satellite radio. Frank turned the channel when a popular new song came on which he hated.

"What are you doing? I love Lady GaGa."

"This new stuff just doesn't hold up," as Frank turned up the volume, while "Whole Lotta Love," by Led Zeppelin played.

"What are you still in high school?"

Frank smiled, while looking at Sarah, and he sang out the lyrics alongside Robert Plant's famous wail.

"Apparently you are," and then Sarah laughed. She agreed to leave the classic rock station on for Frank, because she enjoyed watching him like this and imagined what he was like as a young man. At the airport, she kissed him goodbye and said, "stay safe."

On the way back to the Jersey Shore, she continued to listen to the station because it kept Frank close to her. But when a song by the Doors began to play, she became uncomfortable...listening to the lyrics about a killer, hitchhiking out on the highway. Sarah turned it off, as a tingling sensation ran down her spine.

CHAPTER 41

"January 2014 – James"

JAMES' FIRST NOVEL, *THE BLOOD HUNT,* WAS FINISHED AND THE manuscript still sat on his desk. It had been there for almost two months, completely untouched. He had spent the last two years writing and laying the groundwork for his return. *The Taking*, was almost done as well, but James had no plans to release the novels in tandem. The sequel would be released when the time was right and everything was in order.

James' hibernation period had been spent preparing for what was to come, by creating mental flow charts. He evaluated decision paths and the likely responses to those choices. Therefore, since everything was predicated on Frank Sorello taking his bait, he needed the lure to be strong. James felt *The Blood Hunt* would act as his worm, while *The Taking* would be his hook. Either way, they would be useless without reaching their target.

So everything hinged on them being read by the right people. James knew the novels were brilliantly written and contained the necessary "scare factor." After all, they were written by an actual killer. James knew if the books were not mainstream successes, then he would be forced to follow an alternative path; but the genre always had a very large audience waiting in the wings. If placed in the proper hands, his work stood a chance of achieving "overnight success."

As a result, over the last eight weeks, James researched power players in the publishing world, with hopes of establishing the right representation. Writing a great novel was only half the battle, the other and equally challenging task was what he now faced. He had learned from his days at Princeton, that marketing was sometimes more important than the product itself.

James believed he had found a solution to that very issue, literary agent, Jill Santos. She had a stellar reputation for turning first time authors into household names and carried a lot of weight in the industry. If she represented his book, then there was a great chance of it being published by a major house. This in turn, would provide the publicity he needed to increase the odds of it reaching the only person that mattered to him, Frank Sorello. From that point on, it would only be a matter of time until his dream, would take the form of reality.

The subtleties that had been placed into *The Blood Hunt,* were designed to rouse his foe. James juxtaposed events with miniscule touches tied to some of the murder scenes, such as, the color of a wall, or the way a home was decorated. Furthermore, he laced the novel with psychological triggers, hoping to tap into Frank's need for closure. Yet nothing in the book held a direct correlation to any of the murders, but taken as a whole, eerie similarities might poke a highly trained eye. All of this was done simply to heighten the pain and suffering of Sorello.

James wanted Frank to lose sleep, stuck replaying each horrible moment, just like he had when Maria was killed. His failed attempts at making sense of the tragedy eventually drove him to utter madness, leaving a hole that was bottomless. He wanted the same emptiness to consume the man he held responsible.

James planned on eviscerating the former F.B.I. agent, piece by piece. He would begin by dangling the hope of catching his tormentor and then taking it away. Torture would lie in his inability to relax. Frank Sorello, as far as James was concerned, would never rest again. Wounds that had begun to heal would be reopened and once restored back to health, James would slice them back open, even wider. He hadn't videotaped Juliette's murder, but he would do the next best thing. *The Taking* would be the weapon used to cut deeper, gnawing the inside of Sorello, till nothing remained.

Beyond that, James had his sights set on destroying the man's reputation. The F.B.I. and their most legendary member would be humiliated in a forum of public embarrassment. He would lead them on a wild goose chase and once all the connections were made, it would once again bring "The Magician," front and center to the national media. Illusions within illusions would captivate their attention.

While everyone was preoccupied, death would come to many more.

James knew he needed to remain in the shadows by finding an intermediary. Meeting with Jill Santos would create too many unnecessary risks. Yet, she might decide to pass on being his agent without a face to face meeting. Her stable of authors were always promoted, as she stood by their side in very public arenas. This would have to be accounted for through a well designed story.

James' mind scrutinized every detail the way only a true genius could, and saw how all the pieces came together. Nothing escaped the creation in his mind's eye. Over several months, James trolled the Internet for the perfect middleman. He wanted to find a smalltime lawyer that worked alone, someone that would be hungry. The biggest factor though in his selection, would be finding someone he could manipulate without questioning his story.

James knew he'd found the right person in Fred Kimmel. The search had been time consuming. But patience was a virtue of James, and he never rushed things. He wanted to find someone with money issues, which would make the person far more malleable.

Attorneys had been weeded out, one by one, until finally coming across Mr. Kimmel. The primary focus of his search had been to find out their secrets and this was done by illegally hacking into their personal computers. This had been relative child's play since he knew how to hack into the most secure systems on the planet.

This effort basically consisted of him sending out e-mails and requesting an appointment. Once he received a response, it was a relatively quick process before he gained access into their personal laptops. When someone responded to his phishing effort, he traced the IP address until he found a backdoor. Rudimentary firewall protection was no challenge for him. James knew that any system could be hacked if you understood how the system was built and where the weaknesses were inherent. James' computer expertise was unparalleled, as his genius was honed in every aspect of computing at Princeton. Software, hardware, system architecture, and security design were all hardwired into his photographic memory.

He'd also worked on cryptography which was rooted in mathematics so that he could write programs that could decipher complicated computer code and find design flaws. "Black hats" as they were known in computer circles looked to exploit systems through these weaknesses. Some of the most secure and highly protected governmental systems had been breached in the past, by people like Kevin Poulsen and Jonathan James. None of them were intellectually in the same league as "The Magician."

If you understood everything from the ground up, then there would always be vulnerabilities to exploit. Internet protocols, and the security filters built to examine packet headers for communication permission could be tricked into allowing acceptance if you knew what you were doing.

Yet equally important, in the hack, was leaving no traceability. James hid his digital tracks by hiding in an immense digital network by using proxies and remote servers. Connecting the dots through the global trail he established, would be like finding a needle, among a thousand haystacks. Even with this knowledge, he still protected himself further by destroying any computers he directly used. He never allowed himself to stay too long where a trace could be executed.

Even with that level of cautiousness he took things even further. Once he had "root," which provided him access to the highest level of the machine after finding the sysop's password, he erased all his tracks. By creating legitimate looking user accounts, he masked himself from attracting attention, by deleting system logs that might point to him ever having been there.

So after each and every search he erased his tracks. James never took an unnecessary risk and even with the hack of a personal laptop, he followed the same measures. After he wiped all traces of himself off of Fred Kimmel's computer, he was ready to arrange an appointment with the attorney. The man was ideal for what he had in mind.

James previously discovered that Fred Kimmel owed large amounts of money to a bookie with ties to organized crime. Most of his savings and virtually all of his investments had been wiped out. Over the last year, he exhausted all of his personal resources in paying off debts. This had all been spelled out in e-mails, wherein he pleaded with friends and family for assistance. The people in his life were aware of his problems and began to cut him off. They all decided they were no longer going to enable his destructive habit. In fact, his brother had recently staged an intervention aimed at confronting the addiction. Fred Kimmel was desperate and James was prepared to take advantage of this, by appearing to be a godsend.

The following morning, a call was made to the lawyer's office. James used a disposable phone with pre-purchased minutes. If an answering machine or service picked up, he was prepared to hang up and try again later. James had no intention of leaving his voice on a recording.

"Hello, this is Fred Kimmel."

"Hi, Mr. Kimmel, my name is Gary Jones and I'm in need of legal services."

"How can I help?"

"Hopefully you can, I saw your website and it states you handle contract law. So I'm pretty sure your legal expertise is sufficient, but I'm going to be honest with you, I have some special needs that can be...well, somewhat odd. I'm prepared to pay a very substantial cash retainer to address those requests."

"May I ask Mr. Jones, what those special needs are exactly?"

"I'm agoraphobic, but I've been seeing someone to help mitigate my problem. I don't like being around more than one person at a time and even that is really difficult for me. It's worse when I don't know the person. I also don't like being in public places, but I've been working on that. Before I met my therapist I hadn't left my house for over two years. If you think you can work around these problems, I am prepared to offer you a twenty-five thousand dollar initial retainer, and if this turns out to be a good fit, I would like you to become my personal attorney. Money is not a problem. So, are you interested in taking this further?"

Fred Kimmel, attempted to contain his excitement and answered as calmly as possible, "Well, I'm not promising anything, but I'm willing to listen to your legal needs and as you just said, if it's a good fit, then we can discuss this further."

"You sound like a wise man, and that's exactly what I'm looking for Mr. Kimmel."

"Call me Fred."

"Okay, Fred, I'll do that."

"Mr. Jones, can you tell me what contract work you'd like me to handle?"

"I'd prefer we discuss everything in person."

"Alright, when would you like to meet?"

"How does Friday sound?"

"I assume you'd like me to come to you, given your condition?"

"Actually, that's kind of you to offer, but I am trying to follow my therapist's advice and take baby steps. I'd like to meet you, but here is what I mean by meeting my special needs. I'd like to meet you late in the evening, I know it's a Friday, but that's exactly why I chose that day. Everyone likes to head out and get ready for their weekend. What time do most of the businesses around you close shop? I know this is New York City, so if there are any bars or restaurants right next to you, we may have to figure something else out."

"I'd say by eight o' clock we should be okay."

James wanted to test Kimmel's willingness to please and responded, "I'm sorry that's just too early, how does 11:00 p.m. sound?"

"Mr. Jones that's a bit extreme, but given your situation I'm willing to agree to that."

"You just passed my first test, Fred. I'll see you Friday night."

"Do you need directions?"

"No, thank you. I'll be fine."

"Alright, Friday evening at eleven."

"Bye, Fred."

James was pleased because he knew that his choice was the

right one. Fred Kimmel didn't even put up a fight and as long as money was being dangled in front of him, then he would follow orders. Since that wouldn't ever be a problem, cash would flow until he was no longer needed and then...blood would flow in its place.

CHAPTER 42

"Present Day"

THE F.B.I. TEAM SHOWED UP UNANNOUNCED AT JUSTIN LOGAN'S HOME with a search warrant. The former pilot wasn't home and the agents knocked down his door to gain entry. Every room was thoroughly searched and nothing out of the ordinary was turning up inside of the home, until Rich Tucker began rummaging through the garage. After going through boxes and anything else stored inside of it and finding nothing, he pulled on the cord leading up to its attic. He turned on the light switch in order to see in the darkness. At first glance, the area seemed to be completely empty, but Rich noticed in a far corner that the fiberglass insulation seemed to be somewhat out of place relative to the rest of the attic. It was raised a bit higher than everything else, so he carefully walked on the beams making sure to not fall through. When he got closer, it was clear the insulation was raised several inches higher than anything around it, so he lifted it up. Agent Tucker felt his heart race as he saw the serrated knife and a small decorative box next to it. He looked inside and found various items, it was mostly jewelry, but what really got his blood pumping, was when he counted everything. There were eleven items in total and that matched the number of victims of "The Magician."

Rich Tucker hurried back into the house and yelled out, "Beth... Frank, come quickly I've got something."

The two of them came down the stairs in a rush and when they saw the knife and box in the evidence bag that Agent Tucker was holding, Beth asked, "What's in the box?"

"I think you should take a look," Tucker replied with a hint of excitement.

Beth took the evidence bag and opened it up with gloved hands. Frank peered inside and for a few seconds he couldn't breathe.

"What's wrong, Frank?"

"That heart shaped silver locket, I'm pretty sure it's Juliette's. Can you open it?"

Beth did as he requested and saw the inscription inside. It read:

> *May all the days ahead,*
> *Hold you in them.*
> *Love Frank*

"I gave it to her on her birthday, six months after we met."

"I'm sorry, Frank."

"All that matters now is that we have the fucker."

"Yes, we do."

At that moment, a car pulled into the driveway. Justin Logan saw several F.B.I. agents near his busted down front door. He practically jumped out of his vehicle and yelled, "What the fuck is going on?"

Frank heard Logan's voice and before Beth or Rich had a chance to react, he was by them. He moved lightning fast toward the front of the house, looking like a lion ready to attack.

Beth cried out, "Don't let Frank get near Logan!"

Luckily two agents were near the door and blocked Frank's way as he rammed into them. Although they were built like Olympic wrestlers, they were practically knocked off their feet. Justin Logan suddenly backed up when he saw the rage in the eyes of the athletic looking man struggling to break free of the scrum that had developed at his doorstep. He didn't know what was happening, but his survival instinct prayed the man get no closer. A third man had just joined the fray, wrapping his arms around the individual seemingly intent on killing him. Logan got back into his car and locked the door. Agent Tucker, who was the last man to enter the melee, was unsure if they could hold back Sorello. All three agents were using every last ounce of strength to keep a grip on their adrenaline fueled team member.

Beth quickly ran in front of the group and yelled, "Frank, we're not vigilantes. Please stop! Logan is going to get what he deserves, but through our legal system. He'll never see the light of day again."

Frank still fought, but with a little less intensity. He appeared torn as what to do.

"You said Juliette always respected you for upholding the law. Frank, honor that memory."

With that, the fire drained from Sorello.

"Beth, I'm sorry. I just lost it. Thanks."

She signaled for the men to relax their grip on Frank and they did so warily. All the while, Justin Logan sat in his vehicle wondering what in the hell was happening. He knew something was clearly wrong, but at that very moment, he was just glad to be alive. After watching the fury dissipate in the eyes of the man still looking his way, the fear inside of Logan began to subside. Seconds later, the woman who intervened approached him in the car, along with several other F.B.I. agents.

Logan nervously lowered his window, "Can you please tell me what this is all about?"

"Mr. Logan, can you please step out of the car?"

"Only if you tell me what's going on."

"You are under arrest for the suspicion of murder. You have the right to remain silent; anything you say can and will be used against you in a court of law. You have the right to speak to an attorney. If you cannot afford an attorney, one will be appointed for you. Do you understand these rights as they have been read to you?"

"This must be a mistake, I haven't done anything wrong."

"Mr. Logan, I'll ask you again, please step out of the car."

"Alright, but somebody is going to be losing their jobs. I can fucking promise you that!"

Upon exiting his vehicle, Logan was immediately handcuffed and taken into custody. From that moment on, all the way through his trial he professed his innocence. He claimed to have been framed and threatened to sue everyone involved. It all fell on deaf ears, as a jury of his peers was unanimous in their verdict. Justin Logan was found guilty of eleven counts of premeditated murder and sentenced to life in a federal penitentiary, without the possibility for parole.

Beth and members of the task force were given meritorious achievement awards for their roles in catching the notorious serial killer. The media also heaped praise on the Bureau, but Frank Sorello was its focal point. The story of his legendary career played on for weeks, highlighting the new twist of having caught his wife's killer.

Rob Sullivan offered Frank his old position, but the former agent turned him down. He said he just wanted to move on with his life and not look back. Yet for some reason, the ability to actually do so, still escaped him. Frank's hope of finding peace, after The Magician's capture, went unrequited. Instead, his anxiety only heightened after Justin Logan was convicted.

Frank told everyone in his closest circle, "I'm just not sure if we got the right guy."

Beth, Rob and especially Sarah were troubled by his response. They thought he was refusing to let go of his past. This strange reaction given the almost insurmountable evidence against Justin Logan seemed to be a form of denial. Sarah was saddened in the belief that he couldn't shake the trauma of his past. As far as she was concerned, Frank was still showing signs of its after effect; by being hyper vigilant to the danger lurking somewhere in the shadows.

CHAPTER 43

"January 2014 – James"

JAMES CAREFULLY OBSERVED THE SURROUNDING AREA BEFORE stepping out of his car. He kept his head down in the event there were any hidden cameras and made sure to avoid any people in the area. James knew that there was no reason for anyone to pay attention to him, so he acted as unassuming as possible. All the adjacent businesses were closed as he approached the door with the lawyer's name on it. A light was on, so he entered without knocking.

"Hello, I'm Gary Jones."

"It's a pleasure to meet you. Would you like to take a seat and we can figure out whether or not I can handle your needs."

"Sure, but first I'd like to thank you for going out of your way to help me deal with my affliction."

"It was nothing, don't worry about it. Why don't you tell me what I can do for you?"

"I've written a novel and am looking for an attorney that can help me bring it to market. I need someone that can keep me out of the spotlight, which is why I've avoided contacting more well known representation. Besides, I want someone that's hungry. Fame or money isn't important to me. Obviously given my situation, I'm not comfortable being in the public eye...but since I have no family, I'd like to leave a legacy in the form of my work."

"That's not something I can promise to deliver."

"I understand that completely, but I do believe this novel has the

213

potential to be a bestseller. I may be delusional in that regard, but I want to utilize every means possible to increase the opportunity of it being read. I'll leave the reviews to the critics, but even if this book impacts even one single reader, I'll be happy...and I don't want to sound pompous, but I believe it will."

"I can't guarantee your novel will be published, but if it is, I certainly can handle the contractual agreements."

"It will be, one way or another, even if I have to self publish. But I'm hoping to avoid that necessity by getting Jill Santos to become my literary agent. She has a reputation for turning unknown authors into household names."

"Why not go directly to her yourself?"

"Because she is too public in her persona and it would be far more difficult for me to handle. I hope you understand that if you get this done for me, you will handle all of my legal affairs.

"I can have it delivered, but once again, I can't promise she'd meet with me."

"Mr. Kimmel, I'll make it worth her while to meet with you. I'm a one percenter and I know that money helps get things done. Find out what price it'll take for her to meet with you. Once she agrees, I'll want the assurance that she reads the first fifty pages directly in front of you. If after that, she doesn't want to be my literary agent, then I'll find someone else that will. I'm prepared to pay a sum up to fifty thousand dollars, for that specific request. Whatever amount she settles on, you can keep the rest. That should be a pretty nice payday for an hour or two of work."

Fred Kimmel was ripe with excitement and James sensed it. The attorney's greed was visibly obvious as he fought to maintain an appearance of calm and squash the grin widening across his face.

"I'll do the best I can. If she agrees, what do you want in the contract?"

"We'll discuss that after she agrees to represent me."

"When can I have the manuscript?"

"I have it with me. The novel's already been registered and copyrighted, but I want you to know that no one else is to see this beyond you or Miss Santos, until otherwise instructed. I would like you to quickly draft an agreement that we can sign verifying that particular fact. If I find out that you breached this agreement, you'll immediately cease to be my attorney and of course, be sued."

After both parties signed the contract, Kimmel promised to contact James the moment that Jill Santos gave him an answer. He thought that his client was eccentric, but that was none of his concern. Fred figured the book would be nothing more than a deluded piece of crap. All that mattered was that his prayers had been answered. So it surprised him, when later that night he was unable to put the book down. It was brilliant.

James stayed at the Waldorf that night and slept soundly. If everything went according to plan, Frank Sorello would once again be drawn into the darkness.

Two days later, Fred Kimmel informed him that he had arranged a meeting with the literary agent for the following afternoon. He hadn't spoken of the cash agreement, but by the sound of his voice, the attorney was happy. The subsequent evening, Kimmel was brimming with joy. Jill Santos loved the novel and wanted nothing more than to be a part of it. The lawyer called "Gary" and told him the good news. They agreed to meet once again at 11:00 p.m. the following evening.

It was here that James laid out the rest of his plan. He informed Kimmel that the other great passion he had in life beyond writing was helping others in need. James stated that he always made his charitable efforts anonymously and liked to personally select individuals in need of assistance. He gave the attorney very specific instructions detailing what he wanted done with any income derived from the book. All the proceeds from his novel would be shared among four people that he had selected. James told the attorney that his identity needed to be completely shielded. He had Kimmel set up a bank account so that any money from the publishing house would be paid into and then directly wired into four separate accounts. These would be the personal accounts of Tim Richardson, Eric Duritz, Nolan Russeck and Justin Logan. James implicitly stated that all of this information be covered in confidentiality agreements protecting the source, i.e. "Gary Jones."

Each "recipient of his charity" had been carefully chosen. Everyone served a purpose. Just as James had done extensive hacking to find the right attorney for his nefarious efforts, he did the same to find these individuals. Although far more time and planning had been covered in this search; nothing was ignored. Birth, employment, tax and criminal records, along with anything else that aided his vetting process were evaluated. James had been patient in finding the right pieces for the intricate puzzle he was putting together.

Eric Duritz and Nolan Russeck had been the most recent selections in James' process. Since they were less critical to his vision, their requirements were less involved. They only had to have backgrounds that would intrigue those hunting him. It was Russeck's background as a writer and the places he lived and visited, that drew James' interest. Duritz, on the other hand, was selected because he would present himself as having no real red flags. James figured that this fact alone might in itself, create suspicion.

Everything needed to fit and Tim Richardson was perfect. James selected him around the time he began his first novel. He had been delving through New Jersey State criminal databases attempting to find someone arrested shortly after the killing of Frank's wife. The other criterion would be that he live in the Shore area and currently be out of prison. James knew this would make him a prime suspect because of the timing.

But no person was more important than Justin Logan. He had been James' first selection and this choice had been made prior to his murder spree. This had been his opening strategy, to build his crimes around the movements of someone else. James saw the brilliance in this plan and built upon the idea. It would be far more incriminating if the person had unique travel patterns that were more spread out, because the average person didn't move about as much. This concept is what led James to look into airline pilots. He immediately filtered out anyone that didn't currently fly into the Wisconsin area because of his plan to leave a clue as to his past. James' foster father and his emulation of Harry Houdini, indirectly led to Justin Logan playing the fall guy. There were many pilots that flew this route, but Logan bounced around. He filled in for other pilots quite often and therefore his schedule was often quite varied, sometimes with longer layovers. The thing that sealed his fate, was when James discovered Logan suffered from Post Traumatic Stress Disorder. James imagined how a prosecutor would utilize this to his advantage, building the image of a man snapping because of past trauma.

It then became a simple matter for James to track Logan's flight schedule and pick times and locations based upon the length of layovers. If the pilot had ample time between flights, James would kill during that timeframe. After the rabbi was murdered he looked to establish a discernible pattern. Juliette would be the killing that would seemingly end the sequence.

The only person that would not be part of that repetitive design was Fred Kimmel. He was needed to set things in motion, first by getting Jill Santos to become his literary agent and to lay his background story. Then he would be needed to handle the contracts, set up a bank account for Gary Jones and how and when that money would be wired out to his four pawns.

Since that was now all done, James was going to pay him a visit.

CHAPTER 44

"Present Day"

SIX MONTHS HAD PASSED SINCE JUSTIN LOGAN WAS INCARCERATED and Frank Sorello was starting to accept the idea that perhaps everyone was right. It wasn't easy to overcome his instinctive sense that kept telling him to be careful. Sarah had convinced him to see one of her colleagues, a well respected psychologist in nearby Wall Township. The doctor helped open Frank's mind up to the possibility that the world around him presented little risk of danger. The evidence against Logan had been overwhelming and to question it, was more irrational than rational. Without the fear of "The Magician" returning, then life at the Jersey Shore was pretty much paradise for Sorello. He lived in a wealthy oceanfront community, with almost no crime and was once again retired from active law enforcement.

He wanted to begin his new life with Sarah and knew that it was important to break free from old habits and the residual effects of his former existence, to really be happy. Frank forced himself to stop worrying about what he couldn't control and to focus on what stood right before him. The woman that he loved deserved as much, she had been carefree and positive from the moment he met her. Aside from her beauty and intelligence, those personality traits were like a magnet to him and he didn't want to jeopardize that in any way. After all, there was a time long ago when he acted the same way. Frank wanted to regain that feeling.

Sarah brought back his happiness and provided him with a

true companion. She possessed all the qualities he admired and her spirit for life was contagious. Therefore, he was committed to giving her all he felt she deserved, which was everything he had.

Frank looked directly into the salesman's eyes and said, "I'll take that one."

"She is going to be one very happy woman," the man replied, while placing the flawless 2.5 karat ring back in its box.

"I hope so. That's all I want in the world."

"Wow, she really is a lucky girl."

"No, I'm the lucky one, I've been given another chance at happiness and I'm not going to blow it."

"Good for you."

Later that day, Frank picked up Sarah and the two of them headed over to Asbury Park. It was the weekend and they made plans to go to Stella Marina. Since it was a perfect summer evening, they agreed it would be nice to dine at the oceanfront restaurant. Frank had called earlier and made reservations. Although the establishment didn't do this for their open air deck, the hostess agreed to make an exception because of the special plans. She made sure that the best table in the house was available when they arrived. It was right at the edge of the upper level patio with a picture perfect view of the Atlantic Ocean.

Upon their arrival, they gave their name to the hostess. She said it might be a little while, so they had a drink at the bar. Frank gave her a heads up during their phone call to make everything seem as normal as possible. About twenty minutes later, they were shown to their table.

"How lucky can you get, this has the best view in the place."

"I disagree, I'd say that I do."

She smiled and said, "You just might be getting even luckier when we get back to my place."

Frank pulled out her chair and smiled back. The two of them sat down and took in the view. A million stars lit up the crystal clear sky, and shone down on the waves crashing along the beach. The ocean breeze and salt filled air created a tropical feel. It could have been the setting for a Jimmy Buffett song, with people strolling along the boardwalk, while others stared out at the boats at sea.

Frank and Sarah were lost in the moment, when the waiter came over to take their order.

"I'll have the Pasta Bolognese with the Escarole Salad."

"Excellent choice, and for you sir?"

"I'll have the same."

"Wonderful. May I refresh your drinks?"

"Not just yet, how about you Sarah."

"I'm good for now, but thank you."

As the waiter walked away, Sarah added, "I don't want you to feel like you're taking advantage of me later."

"How do you know I'm that easy?"

"Because you're a man."

The two of them laughed and then continued to tell each other stories about their past. The only time they stopped talking was while eating their delicious meal. After ordering dessert, Frank got out of his chair and kneeled down before Sarah. Her eyes opened wide, in a state of blissful excitement.

"Sarah...will you please do me the honor of making me the happiest man alive and marry me?"

She jumped up and said out loud, "Yes!"

Then seconds later they were kissing as the crowd of people both in the restaurant and down on the boardwalk, stood and clapped.

CHAPTER 45

"February 2016 – James"

FOR THE PAST TWO YEARS, JAMES HAD BEEN METICULOUSLY PLANNING his return. He didn't want to release *The Taking* until he was sure everything was in order. The sequel had been completed for quite some time, but James never rushed things. He incessantly prepared for the unexpected by anticipating problems before they occurred. As far as he was concerned people that made mistakes were simply careless, stupid and deserved to suffer the consequences. James' methodology had proven itself time and again.

As predicted, his first novel, *The Blood Hunt* was now a huge bestseller. Amazingly, even with the success of the book, he managed to remain in the shadows. Choosing Fred Kimmel to be his middle man had worked out perfectly, as had the selection of a pedestrian pseudonym. Yes, Gary Jones was now a well known author, but James Carlson remained anonymous. The pen name was only one example of his true genius. Everything he did served a purpose. By donating one hundred percent of his book sales, under the guise of charity, he laid the foundation for his first master illusion. In the eyes of the world, Justin Logan was now perceived to be "The Magician."

That deception laid the groundwork for what was yet to come. While everyone scrambled around him, his focus never wavered. James always kept his prey in sight. Most of the time he watched from a distance, but on occasion he got closer by blending in with the crowd. He never lingered, knowing this might draw attention.

On these scouting trips, he noticed Sarah and began tracking her as well, all the while visualizing her role in his end game.

By tracing an e-mail correspondence from Frank's computer, he ultimately hacked her system and electronically implanted himself into her life. This provided James with a personal vantage point into her inner thoughts, and afforded him invaluable insight. She was a psychologist, but more importantly she was Frank Sorello's lover. Therefore, seeing inside of her mind was like peering into that of his adversary's. Although James read all of their messages, the real window into Sorello's soul was opened, when Sarah communicated with her sister. Those messages contained a treasure trove of feelings, in which she conveyed her thoughts on Frank's psychological struggle and recovery. Learning of his enemy's perceived breakdown, following the release of *The Blood Hunt,* acted like an adrenaline rush for James. It stoked the belief his machination would be successful.

However, the real source of his confidence was rooted in his exhaustive hacking efforts, and all of the highly detailed information it provided. James had planted imperceptible Trojan horses, within various governmental databases, including the F.B.I. All of this, along with having complete control over Frank's laptop, was feeding his sense of God-Like superiority. The list of people that were frighteningly unaware of his omniscient presence was staggering. Their ignorance would eventually become painfully obvious, but not until after the release of his long awaited sequel, *The Taking.*

The unveiling was coming soon, and although James was anxious to commence with his work, he wanted to be sure there were no loose ends. As always, before proceeding forward, he replayed every step already taken. By thoroughly reviewing the past, it heightened his anticipation of what to expect as he moved onward. Since he was currently residing in his New York City residence, he lingered over the last time he was here and what had happened.

James' photographic memory replayed the day as if it were occurring that very moment. It was a winter's day, frigid with a storm coming. His first novel had been released to both, public and critical acclaim and he had been patiently waiting for his "charity" to be established. So after a brief phone call to his lawyer, he learned that contractually everything was ready to go and this pleased James. He was looking forward to rewarding the attorney for his efforts.

So before ending their conversation, James had asked Kimmel to go out and celebrate the impending release of his new novel. He told the lawyer that all his hard work was greatly appreciated and that a surprise awaited him. So plans were arranged and as per their usual custom, they were to meet late Friday evening at the attorney's office.

Kimmel wondered what the night held in store, perhaps a large bonus. His greed was all consuming and the oddity of the request was never considered. "Gary" was agoraphobic and the idea of going out to celebrate was completely out of character.

All week he obsessed over what James planned to give him, imagining everything from a Rolex, to the amount of zeroes on a cashier's check. So on the night of their scheduled meeting, Fred became anxious, when his client didn't arrive on time. It was almost midnight when James finally walked into the office.

"Hey, Fred, sorry I'm not on time. I should've called, but something came up that took longer than I thought it would."

"No problem, is everything alright?"

"Yeah, I just needed to talk with my therapist."

"And I thought I was the only one on twenty-four hour call," the attorney said jokingly, "So what have you got planned?"

"Originally, my shrink suggested I take the opportunity to do something we've been working on, let people into my life, celebrate and not fear the world...but outside of my private brownstone. I know she wants me to start knocking down all the barriers that I've constructed around me. I've been making real progress, but I guess this was just too big of a step."

"That's cool. I understand."

"No, I still want this to be a night to remember. I had a room reserved at Sparks, over on forty-sixth for us and a few friends. Of course, I had to make some calls to rearrange plans. I asked everyone to meet up at my place. Believe me, this is still really difficult, but I want to keep moving forward and beat this goddamn thing."

"Good for you, Gary."

"I told everyone to meet there in an hour, because I wanted to have time to...give you your bonus in private. I really do appreciate how you've dealt with my bullshit."

"It's no big deal."

"Have you told anyone about our night out, because this might be a late one? I don't want you getting in trouble. If you do, my only request is to keep my name private. Old habits are hard to break."

"I know better than that, I've always kept our relationship confidential. No one knows anything about you, other than Jill Santos...and all she knows is that you're my client."

"Fred, that's why I'm so happy to give you the surprise I have waiting for you at my place."

Kimmel started to think that his gift was going to be extraordinary, suddenly imagining a Ferrari or a Bentley. Why else, he thought to himself, would it need to be delivered at "Gary's" residence. His office was as private as anywhere else. The attorney couldn't wait to see what his client had in store for him.

"Well, I have to say I'm excited. Shall we head out?"

"I'm going to need to make one more call, in private, so why don't I go grab my car and I'll pick you up, in let's say, ten minutes?"

"Great."

James walked outside and over to the parking garage. He felt the risk would be too great in having Kimmel accompany him and therefore, used the excuse of needing to make a private call. As he drove up to the attendant, he looked away as he paid the fee, careful to not make eye contact.

Since no one was out on the street in front of Kimmel's office, he made a quick call from his BMW and told the attorney he was right outside. Fred came out and jumped in the car, noticing it was a top of the line, jet black, seven series. James wanted the attorney to admire the display of wealth and feed the man's sense of greed. It would prevent raising any suspicions as to his cover story and help to lower the man's defenses. James realized that in Manhattan, the car wouldn't draw any undue attention, which perfectly fit his needs. Even in the event someone noticed the lawyer get into the vehicle, the plates had been temporarily switched and with the tinted windows, no one would be able to identify the passengers within.

"Beautiful ride."

"Thanks, it's actually my favorite car. I have several exotics, but I really only drive those at my countryside residence, and only on the property. I hope if I keep making strides with my illness… that I'll be able to enjoy them elsewhere. They just draw too much attention."

Kimmel was practically salivating, thinking that maybe his guess was correct. At the same time, James knew the attorney was ripe to be taken, which fueled his own desires. As they pulled into the two car garage of the multimillion dollar brownstone, the lawyer let out an audible gasp. Parked on the other side, was the identical car in white, with a bow wrapped around it.

"Hope you like it."

"It's unbelievably generous. Thank you."

As they got out of the car, James pulled out of his pocket, a set of keys and handed them to the attorney. Kimmel stared at them for a moment and took them.

"Want to take it for a quick spin?"

"Do I have time? I know your guests are about to arrive."

"Sure, you have plenty of time."

"Alright, I'd love too."

As Kimmel turned his back on James, the younger man suddenly struck the man with a pair of brass knuckles. The lawyer collapsed to the ground. James picked up the keys that had fallen beside him and then proceeded to bind and gag the attorney.

When the lawyer awoke, he thought he was having a horrible nightmare. Seconds later, panic set in for real. He screamed over and over, to no avail. He was tied up in utter darkness, unable to move. It felt hot, which only added to his extreme sense of claustrophobia. The screams turned quickly to sobs, as his breathing became labored. Oxygen was in short supply.

At that very moment, James was driving back to Manhattan from his ski chalet in the Poconos. He was satisfied that everything played out exactly the way he had mentally rehearsed it. It was almost daylight and Fred Kimmel lie buried alive inside of a wooden coffin. He had given up trying to struggle, movement was totally constricted. His clothing felt damp from sweat, his mouth parched and his throat was sore from yelling for help that never came. This casket had been the real surprise Gary Jones had held in store for him. It had been built by James on the very day that he purchased the cabin. Now here on this wooded lot, Fred Kimmel would be its last visitor.

James smiled; it had been satisfying to kill again. Although he hadn't been able to watch the life drain from his victim's eyes, he visualized Kimmel's cries for help. It had been a last second decision to remove the man's gag while he was still unconscious. James knew that it would allow the man to cry for help, but no one would be able to hear him and that would be torturous. Screams would drain his oxygen supply faster and the realization of hopelessness would quickly set in, leading to thoughts of the inevitable.

James' delusions became stronger than ever after this kill. His thoughts were wrapped up entirely in how to make the world suffer. The long dormancy was now over, and it had only served to fuel his insanity, since he viewed this as his resurrection. The godlike control he felt was overwhelming; holding the power between life and death, came flooding back to him. In those moments, it was the only point in which he felt alive.

As he pulled back into the garage of his brownstone, his thoughts drifted toward New Jersey and his next move. "The Magician" would eventually return with a grand re-entrance. That day had been the precursor to what was now upon him.

Approximately sixty miles south, Frank Sorello was just waking in his Spring Lake home, preparing for his daily run. He had begun the process of recovery by taking the advice of his running partner and new friend. Sarah was teaching Frank to start anew and let go of the past. So each day now revolved around living in the moment. Unfortunately for Sorello history was soon to rear its ugly head.

If only Frank could have seen north toward the city, and the man sitting in a catatonic state, he would know there was unfinished business at hand. James' eyes stared eerily blank at the wall in front of him. The framed painting hanging upon it was that of Dante's Inferno, but he looked far beyond the work of art. He was lost in his own madness, for everything was about to change.

The battle between good and evil was about to recommence and the gates of hell were about to be opened.

CHAPTER 46

"Present Day – September 2017"

JAMES WAS EXHILARATED TO START UP THE GAME ONCE AGAIN. HE watched the beautiful woman leave the coffee shop and head in his direction. Her long dark hair, accentuated the sexuality she exuded, carrying the confidence of an athlete. Even walking, she moved like a gazelle, with her long runner's legs covering ground rapidly. James smiled as she walked directly past him and toward her Mercedes. He wasn't fearful of drawing attention, since the woman was used to men gawking. Half the men in the area had already undressed her with their eyes and he just blended in with the rest of the crowd.

James waited for a few minutes after she left before heading to his own car. He didn't need to follow her. She had been dressed in yoga pants and if she followed her usual pattern, was likely headed to the gym for a class. Normally, she would return home in about ninety minutes, to quickly shower and change, before heading over to her office. This had been her daily routine, with one important difference. James knew that she would be alone today.

The past few weeks had been spent following her movements, but today had been circled on his mental calendar. James collected details like a scientist formulating a hypothesis and left no stone unturned. When he wasn't physically watching her movements, his energy was redirected online. Tracking her through the digital universe presented him with this opportunity. James realized he needed to take advantage of the moment, since it would be far easier to accomplish his task without possible interference. Killing with someone else in the house would be far more difficult and created too many uncertainties.

That was why James had chosen this particular day. The woman's significant other wouldn't be a threat because he was scheduled to be in New York City, meeting with their accountant. Since it was an early morning appointment, he knew the house would be empty, which would provide him the time he needed. James wanted to create his art without fearing the unexpected and to match the picture he was painting.

Everything was accounted for in advance, knowing full well that preparation was critical to a smooth execution. Access wouldn't be a problem, because James already knew where they kept their spare key. It had been so easy to find. One week earlier, in the middle of the night he had gone to their home. Within five minutes of checking the usual hiding spots, he found it under a flower pot, near their back door. James always found it amusing that so many people followed such similar habits, allowing thieves or worse, direct entry into what should be their most protected space.

He parked about a mile away, in a predetermined area. James wanted to be invisible and this location would help achieve that purpose. It was a large park and was therefore the perfect place to begin his ruse. After checking to see if anyone was around, and noticing no one, James got out of his vehicle. He was dressed in a loose fitting jogging suit and began running toward his destination. Nobody would pay much attention to him, since he would appear to be just another exercise fiend, striving to stay fit. James knew how to be a chameleon. As he approached the home with its naturally hedged walls, he casually slowed down as if finishing his run. James stopped and bent over as if catching his breath. Seeing that there were no prying eyes he quickly made his way down the driveway. The red Porsche that was usually there was gone, as he had expected. Before grabbing the hidden key, he glanced inside the windowed garage to make sure it was empty. Once satisfied, he entered the house.

Like a cat he slipped inside, tuned to any sounds, fully prepared to deal with the unexpected. He flicked off the safety catch on his gun, which was hidden inside of his running jacket, moving quietly from room to room. When he realized there weren't any unforeseen visitors, he put the semi- automatic away.

James headed back to the kitchen and opened several drawers, until he located a knife with a serrated edge. He then walked into the attached garage and grabbed a pair of needle nose pliers. Once he had the necessary tools of his trade, James made his way to the bedroom. He looked at the picture on the nightstand and knew there would be no more photographs taken in the future of this happy couple. He entered the walk in closet and closed the door behind him. James sat down and gazed outward through the louvered door. He patiently waited in silence, hyper alert to the slightest sound.

It was actually only a little over an hour later, when he heard a door slam shut downstairs. James took the gun back out and readied himself if the door were to suddenly open. He knew the element of surprise would provide an added edge, if this did occur. The sound of footsteps moved closer and he slowed his breathing in anticipation. There was movement in the bedroom and then it shifted in the direction of the master bath. Seconds later, he heard the shower door open and then water cascading downward.

James waited for a minute, before exiting the closet, with the chloroform rag in hand. He walked quietly to the edge of the bathroom, where he saw her clothing laying on the floor. James decided he would surprise her when she re-entered the bedroom. He stood behind the open door, out of any clear sight line. Next, James focused all of his attention on the sound of the water and when it stopped, the tension in his body rose. He had waited for this moment for years, burying the need and now it was merely seconds before it would be resurrected.

Wrapped only in a towel, the runway model made her way into her final resting place, oblivious to the grim reaper waiting to take her. He lunged and for the briefest instant, recognition flashed, but far too late. She tried to react but instead started to collapse. Her last memory was that she couldn't quite process why the handsome guy outside of Starbucks was suddenly in her room and that her family and friends would never see her again.

CHAPTER 47

FRANK AND SARAH WERE ENJOYING THE SOLITUDE OF THE BOARDWALK. The summer season was over and gone along with it, the tourist onslaught. They'd just finished their morning run and were taking the time to enjoy the ocean's beauty. Its large waves were majestic, as white caps danced their way ashore.

A large Nor'easter was approaching, stirring the surf with its swirling winds. Yet unlike five years ago, when Hurricane Sandy left Frank in ruins, he was happy. Sarah had healed his wounded heart and with their wedding date only a few months away, she was all he thought about.

They walked hand in hand, so lost in each other that Sarah had to nudge him as his cell rang. He wasn't going to answer it, but when he looked at the number on display, Frank slipped his fingers from hers. He wondered why Rob Sullivan was calling at such an early hour. After all, he'd made it clear that he planned on staying retired. It reminded him of that day he'd woken Rob after reading about Juliette's death. He felt uneasy, but tried to control the feeling.

"Hi, Rob, you'd better not be calling to turn down our invitation."

"Frank, nothing would stop me from being there. But I do have some bad news, we either have a copycat or you were right."

"What happened?" Frank said in an alarmed tone.

Sarah noticed his reaction and immediately became worried.

"I'm sure you'll be seeing it on the news, but late last night there was a murder that fits the profile. Serrated knife, lacerations up and down the extremities and the fingernails were missing. Crime scene was clean as usual. No witnesses."

"Rob, tell me, did it happen in Jersey?"

"Yeah, but what made you ask that?"

"The pattern Rob, it's back in play. 2-1-2."

"Holy shit, you're right. The murders were so long ago, I'd forgotten about it. Also to be honest with you, I was thinking copycat all the way. The evidence against Logan was overwhelming."

"He could be communicating with someone on the outside. We need to look at his visitation log."

"I know this isn't what you wanted, but does this mean I should put you back on as a consultant."

"You might as well just reinstate me...for now."

"Okay, it's settled, you're back. I'm going to put you in charge. Do you still want the same team as last time?"

"Yes. They're all excellent agents, but I would like one request... Beth, should be co-team leader. I'm not in this for the long term, Rob."

"It's up to you, Frank. I'm sure she'll appreciate it."

"Don't tell her it was my idea, she should just think that's how you wanted it. Do you want me to head back to D.C.?"

"No, Beth and some of the team are already headed to the site. It'd make more sense for you to go directly there. The victim was a single female living in Bernardsville. She was murdered in her home; I'll text you the address and let Beth know you'll be meeting her there."

"Alright, I'll let you know my thoughts after I see the crime scene."

"I'm sorry about this, Frank. I know this isn't what you wanted right before your wedding, but I just felt you'd want to know."

It's not your fault and I'm glad you called. The only way I'll sleep is if I know "The Magician" is dead or behind bars. I hope it's a copycat, but my gut told me otherwise after meeting Logan. I didn't see the empty eyes, Rob. These types of killers always have flat eyes and this guy just didn't have them."

"Call me after you check it all out."

"Okay, Rob, I'm going to get moving. Bye."

"Take it easy, Frank."

Sarah tried to hide her concern.

She took a deep breath and said, "Go get the bastard. I don't want you to worry about us or the wedding. Do what you have to do, because I know everything is going to be alright."

"Thanks, honey, I appreciate the support. I'll be back hopefully later tonight."

Frank gave Sarah a hug, before running back to their house. He didn't even change out of his running gear, as he immediately jumped into his car and headed to the murder site. The entire ride over he hoped that this was just some other maniac, not the man he had been hunting...because that man, truly scared him. It had been the only time Frank had ever been afraid, not so much for himself, but for Sarah.

He thought to himself, "How do I catch a ghost?"

CHAPTER 48

BETH HAD JUST FINISHED HER PRELIMINARY ANALYSIS OF THE CRIME scene and was waiting anxiously for Frank to show up. She was just beginning to get her emotions under control. At the time of her arrival, the lead detective on the case had provided her with a basic rundown of the murder. She literally stifled a gasp. The detective had noticed the atypical reaction and this stirred his own curiosity. After all, Beth was a task force leader for the F.B.I.'s ViCap Unit and had seen it all. But once she began to explain the reason for her unusual response, he understood. Beth expected that Frank would be deeply troubled.

Neighbors of the murder victim were milling about outside. Their morbid curiosity was being stoked by the abundance of flashing lights. The picturesque, affluent community was normally impervious to such a disturbance. Now these residents behaved like zombies, as they aimlessly stared at the yellow tape, strewn around the household. Wealth's protective cocoon had been breached and the community was unprepared for the numbing aftermath.

Inside of the residence, the forensics unit still worked feverishly. Law enforcement personnel were taking photographs, dusting for prints, studying blood spatter and compiling trace evidence. No time had been wasted searching for a weapon, since a bloodied knife and pliers, were left right next to the body. James knew he couldn't be linked to them, since he'd worn gloves from the minute he'd entered the home. The crime scene would be essentially like all the others, fruitless.

Beth just took it all in, fully aware that a media shit storm was about to descend upon this well heeled town. A serial killer had visited the community and that always guaranteed a circus. So when a swarm of photographers rushed toward the large man exiting his car, she knew the main attraction was here. Beth watched as the lion tamer made his way up the driveway, fighting through the throng nipping at his heels.

Frank ignored the multitude of reporters hoping to catch a sound bite, as he made his way toward the front of the house. Beth stood at the entrance, realizing this case would shape the rest of her career.

"So what are we looking at?" Frank asked.

"Let's just say I don't think you're going to like what you see," Beth replied.

"Alright, where's the body?"

"Upstairs, in the master bedroom. Oh and one more thing... she's a model."

Frank stopped and stared, the hint of recognition apparent, before heading up the stairs. He walked past the forensics team and noticed the arterial spray, which had become so familiar. The naked body on the bed displayed all the tell tale lacerations. This wasn't what held Frank's gaze, but rather the twelve inch steel rope that was wrapped around the deceased model's wrists. A message was being sent by the killer.

This was the type of binding Harry Houdini used in his "Siberian Chain Escape," and was clearly the work of "The Magician" or a copycat. Frank felt uncomfortable. He began to think his initial instinct had been right. Justin Logan might have been unjustly imprisoned and with that thought, came a corresponding adrenaline rush. He recognized what Beth had already discovered. This was a living reenactment of the second murder, in Gary Jones' novel, *The Taking*.

Beth observed Frank's face and knew they were on the same page. The book had found its way back into the investigation.

"I don't think, either of us, was anticipating this."

"Beth, with this guy we need to expect, the unexpected. That's why Logan bothered me. Something was gnawing at me and telling me it wasn't right."

"We should have listened to you. You've been right ever since Gary Jones' first book."

"I wish I wasn't."

"That means you don't believe this is a copycat."

"No. I think the wrong guy's behind bars."

"Rob won't be happy; it'll make us all look bad."

"That doesn't matter."

"Maybe, but we can't discount the fact that the evidence was overwhelming. What if Logan's communicating with someone on the outside? Until we prove otherwise, he stays in prison."

"Well, that means we have to get our shit together."

The two task force leaders discussed everything on their way back to D.C. and formulated an agenda. First, they needed to fill Rob in on the homicide in Bernardsville. So upon their arrival in Washington, they had a long sit down with the director. He was on board with their plan, but as expected he wasn't thrilled. Both of his subordinates felt the Bureau had very possibly arrested an innocent man.

After their sit down with the director, Beth and Frank made arrangements for the entire team to convene the following morning. Everyone needed to be brought up to speed. Things were about to get hectic.

Frank planned on going over every aspect of the original murders with the task force. He wanted to leave nothing to chance. He knew most of the team would subscribe to the copycat theory and that was fine by him. He just didn't want anyone to discount the alternative.

"The Magician" was still out there, making them chase a mirage.

CHAPTER 49

James was lying down in a dentist chair about to have his annual x-rays taken. He smiled up at the pretty dental assistant, just before she was about to begin a full mouth series. Although she had a boyfriend, she was unable to resist flashing her own flirtatious smile. She didn't feel guilty because all the women in the office were similarly affected. They behaved like giddy school girls whenever he was around.

It had been like this ever since he became a patient, almost two years earlier. During his visits, it was like a celebrity was in the office. All the girls seemed to find a reason to enter the room to which he was assigned. They all found him irresistible. Besides being incredibly attractive, James was always so charming, polite and unpretentious.

After completing her task and just before the dentist came in the room, James made eye contact and said, "Thanks, Natalie. You make coming to the dentist something I enjoy."

"Me too," she said with a touch of embarrassment, and quickly added, "I mean...I like having you in my chair."

"Hmm, I like the sound of that," as he smiled once again.

Natalie walked out to get the Doctor and fantasized about the man she barely knew, unable to shake the dirty thoughts running rampant in her mind. Her face was still red with excitement as she informed the dentist that his patient was ready to be seen.

"Natalie, are you okay? Your face is flushed."

"No, I'm okay. Maybe I've been moving around too fast."

"Well then, take it easy."

"Thanks, Doc, but I'm alright."

A few seconds later, the doctor walked in and took a look at the x-rays. This was followed by a basic exam. All during that time, Natalie stood just outside the room. She wondered if the flirtation between the two of them had been real.

Just before leaving the office, he scheduled his next appointment for six months out. James knew the allotted time slot would come and go without his presence. He had no plans to return.

Nothing James did was without purpose. The Federal Bureau of Investigation was not far from where he now stood.

CHAPTER 50

FRANK STOOD IN FRONT OF THE TASK FORCE, ALONGSIDE BETH. THIS time though it was in an official capacity. He was no longer acting as merely a consultant. Everyone was seated and waiting for the meeting to begin.

"Good morning. As you've all probably figured out by now, we've reopened the case. However, this time I'm back as one of you."

"Does that mean we can't complain about our boss?"

Everyone laughed and followed it with applause.

"All kidding aside, welcome back to the fold, Frank."

"Thanks. Since that's out of the way, let's get down to business. Beth and I will be operating as co-task force leaders, but we want everyone to realize this is a team. That means everybody should feel comfortable sharing their ideas. Understand, the guy we're after, truly is a magician...in that he's been remarkably adept, at getting our rapt attention and then vanishing without a trace. We need to explore everything, we can't ignore even the slightest possibility, and no suggestion will go ignored. If we do this, our chance to succeed is infinitely greater."

Beth interjected, "I support that belief and with that in mind, I want everyone's undivided attention. Even though you've all read the case files, it doesn't mean we haven't missed something. Frank's going to give a briefing on the recent murder and how it may link to the very beginning of our killer's murder spree. So listen up, sometimes it's the smallest thing that can swing the investigation in our favor."

Beth nodded in Frank's direction, signifying he should proceed.

"As everyone knows, we just had a murder fitting the profile of

'The Magician.' This homicide mimics the second murder in Gary Jones' novel, *The Taking*. So the book now takes on a new relevance. Is the killer going to follow through on what's written in the rest of the book? I want all of you to read it cover to cover. If this is going to be a blueprint, then we need to know it inside and out."

"So we have a new nutcase, turning fiction into reality and imitating Justin Logan's work," chimed in Agent Bucko.

"There are two lines of thinking on that matter, John. First, a copycat is at work and somehow communicating with Logan."

"Why do you say that?" asked Agent Thorn.

"The novel described the laceration patterns, but not the removal of nails. That's always been kept classified."

"And for some reason Gary Jones or should I say Logan, left that detail out as well."

"Maybe he felt that would've been too much to explain, knowing every confidential fact of the murders...by omitting it from the novel, it leaves a greater level of doubt as to him being the killer. It'd be easier for him to deflect scrutiny by saying that he pieced things together from rumors or the occasional off the record comment. It's just a thought."

"Have the nails turned up? What about his trademark? His signature, the letter 'M' marked on the outside of a plastic bag."

"Not yet, but we're expecting they'll arrive. The deceased had her fingernails removed and they weren't left at the scene," Beth responded.

"Sick, fucking bastard."

Everyone in the room agreed with the sentiment and it served to heighten everyone's focus. They all felt this had gone on too long.

"The second theory," Frank continued, "is that we got the wrong guy. Logan is innocent."

"Frank, the evidence was enormous. Even if it was somehow planted, the odds of two separate people being at the locations of every murder site at the same time would be astronomical," said Agent Tucker.

"That's true, Rich. It's also why we have to explore how that might have happened. I know that doesn't sound like the logical line of thinking and might be a waste of time and resources, but I want someone looking into it. You might think I'm crazy, but I'm a proponent of theory number two."

"Frank, you said you wanted everyone to speak their mind. So I have to say that seems like a long shot," responded Agent Thorn.

"Julia, anytime I've ignored my gut instinct, it's cost me dearly. I'm not saying I'm right. I'm sure most of you will continue to operate with the copycat line of thinking. That's okay. It gives us a well rounded perspective. Just don't ignore, what might seem at the time, to be unlikely. It'll make you a better investigator in the long run."

"I appreciate that piece of advice."

Frank nodded his head in acknowledgment. He then walked over to an overhead projector.

"Can someone please turn out the lights?"

"I got it, Frank," called out Agent Carson.

When the lights went out, Frank turned on the projector and a diagram lit up the screen.

"The next thing I want to address is the 2-1-2 pattern."

Everyone looked up at the diagram. It looked as follows:

Homicide Date	Victim	Location	
October 31, 2011	Rabbi Goldberg	Wisconsin	
November 12, 2011	Bob Roland	Wisconsin	= 2
December 17, 2011	Brooke Sanders	Arizona	= 1
February 3, 2012	Heidi Torgston	Maryland	
February 26, 2012	Alison Colton	Maryland	= 2
May 10, 2012	Mandy Vernon	South Carolina	
May 19, 2012	Richard Kettle	South Carolina	= 2
June 3, 2012	Saul Porter	Maine	= 1
July 29, 2012	Matthew Braille	Montana	
August 27, 2012	Cassie Wilpon	Montana	= 2
October 30, 2012	Juliette Sorello	New Jersey	
September 5, 2017	Megan Starr	New Jersey	= 2
?	?	?	= 1
?	?	?	
?	?	?	= 2

2-1-2 PATTERN

"Based upon the pattern you're proposing, we could assume the next murder isn't happening in New Jersey," said Agent Thorn.

"That's true...if this continues to follow suit," Beth responded.

"Since this is the beginning of another 2-1-2 sequence and the states seem to be different each time around...that leaves forty-three open, more than eighty percent of the country. Not exactly helpful," Bucko replied.

"The numbers obviously mean something. That's the key to catching him," Frank interjected.

"The most obvious thing is the Manhattan area code," said Rich Tucker, "maybe that's where he's from?"

"Or something significant could have happened there... triggering the murders? But who the fuck knows how this psycho's mind works," Agent Newton said clearly frustrated.

"What if the city's the next target site?" Thorn continued with the suppositions.

"It's possible, but I don't think that's it. The pattern's on its third cycle and if he's delivering us a message, that wouldn't be clear enough. We have no idea when he plans to stop. Therefore, New York could come at any time. That's too random. He's testing us... showing us he's superior," Frank stated with confidence.

"Frank, how many murders are there in Gary Jones' novel, *The Taking*? asked Agent Tucker.

"Good question, Rich. The answer's four. The first two already occurred, which leaves two more. Assuming the pattern holds true and the middle gets completed, the end part of the cycle would be left incomplete, in essence, 2-1-1."

"Just like before. I'm sorry for having to mention it. But when Juliette was killed, the pattern was left incomplete for five years, 2-1-2, 2-1-2, 1. The model in New Jersey re-established the cycle and connected it back to your wife. The '1' became '2' and completed the front half of the pattern," Rich answered back.

"No need to apologize. The past is the past and nothing's going to bring back my wife. The only thing I care about is stopping this guy from killing, so nice observation. I've been playing around with that exact scenario from the moment the murders started up again. I think he plans to go dormant again, but only after following through with the two remaining murders in the book. That means we have to catch him before he does."

"Do the murders in either of his novels correlate location wise to the actual states? Does fact follow fiction?" Asked Bucko.

"The first novel, *The Blood Hunt* has no relevance to reality. The murders in it aren't tied to any real killings…location or otherwise, it was basically just fiction," Frank answered.

Sorello felt a twinge of discomfort upon answering Agent Bucko, knowing how *The Blood Hunt* impacted him during the most vulnerable point in his life. Binge drinking, anger and depression had clouded his judgment, but the novel still struck a nerve. He knew the fictional murders had no basis in truth, but something had bothered him. Frank thought to himself he might need to re-visit Gary Jones' first novel at some point. Sorello was pulled from his brief introspection with the next question.

"What about *The Taking*?"

"His second novel seems to be more of a roadmap to what's actually happening. It described Juliette's murder, accurately as to location and detail. The next murder in the book described what happened to our model in Bernardsville, but left out a specific location, as do the remaining two murders in the novel."

"So all we'll learn from the book is a broad sketch of whose next, said Thorn.

"Yeah, but maybe this puts us inside his head" responded Beth, "and with this pattern, leads somewhere…to something tangible."

"I can't see how this can help without more information. Just like Frank said, we don't know when this guy's going to stop killing. All we have is a sketchy 2-1-2 hypothesis," said Joe Gelaszus.

With that statement, Frank suddenly started scribbling on a piece of paper, extending the 2-1-2 sequence. He drew a line between every fifth digit and realized it created three possible, five number, repetitive patterns.

21221/22122/12212/21221/22122/12212

"Zip codes! They're only three possibilities!" Frank shouted out loud.

"What are you talking about?" asked Beth.

"Can someone please tell me if there's a zip for 12212?" Sorello asked energetically.

Rich Tucker checked the web browser on his phone and said, "Albany, New York."

"How about 22122?"

"Newington, Virginia."

"And finally 21221?"

"Essex, Maryland."

"Fuck me! Did you say, Essex, Maryland?" Frank exclaimed.

"Yes," Rich replied.

Frank turned and pointed at the diagram still lit up from the overhead projector. He poked his fingers directly next to a name.

"Heidi Torgston. She was murdered by 'The Magician' in Essex, fucking Maryland. She was the front half of a 2-1-2 sequence."

Beth immediately said, "We have to relook at everything concerning Miss Torgston. Maybe there's a personal connection to our killer? We also need to find out if there were other murders in Essex, Newington or Albany that might fit the profile? Maybe something wasn't logged into the Law Enforcement Online database. Could someone check 'LEO' and talk to the police chiefs in those areas?"

"I'll handle it," said Agent Gelaszus.

"Thanks, Joe."

"I'll begin looking into Torgston," replied Thorn.

"I'll help you with that," added Bucko.

Frank said, "I'm guessing that you won't find anymore murders in those locales, but there might be something relevant regarding Heidi."

"What makes you say that?" asked Gelaszus.

"I think that 'The Magician' sees himself as untouchable, almost god-like and believes we can't stop him. It's all a game to him. Eventually a murder's going to match another of the two remaining zip codes. I'm betting it'll be in the midpoint of the 2-1-2 cycle. Then at some point later on we're going to see the final zip code fall into place, at the end point of the pattern. He's leading us there, I fucking know it!"

"In the meantime, everyone find a job to do, whether it's looking into Torgston or checking the other zip codes for homicides, both past and present. Also, continue your work with the Bernardsville Police Department regarding the recent murder," Beth ordered.

"Don't forget to read *The Taking* and see if it helps point somewhere, especially given our recent breakthrough," Frank added.

"One final thing, I want everyone to stay current with law enforcement networking...NLETS, ViCap Alerts, NCAVC and LEO," Beth added.

"Geez, anything else? Can I please sign out of this class?" joked Rich Tucker.

"Too late, you already missed the deadline," Frank responded.

The task force meeting ended with a degree of levity, masking the palpable tension everyone felt. A serial killer was at large and was playing a game of cat and mouse.

Unfortunately, no one involved, knew exactly who was the cat or who was the mouse.

CHAPTER 51

Bud Kavanaugh reached up and pulled the Buffalo Bills knit cap down over his ears. He didn't break stride as he attempted to ignore the swirling wind and frigid air. Dark grey clouds circled overhead as the steely sky threatened to storm. Any vestige of warmth quickly evaporated, as the last light of day began to fade away. The desolation of the Albany Pine Bush was all encompassing. No sane person chose to be here, but Bud took advantage of the solitude.

He had injured his ACL, the previous year, playing basketball and was distraught because during that time he was training for the Boston Marathon. It had been a self appointed milestone and nothing would stop him from attaining it. The middle aged man was a highly driven investment banker and didn't believe in failure. Therefore, taking a break from training wasn't an option. The cutting winter air only added to his resolve.

Bud viewed the Pine Barrens as the perfect place to challenge his willpower. Its utter isolation simulated the vision he had of the marathon. The physical strain would be immense, but Bud knew that his mind would be his greatest opponent. He imagined the other runners would cease to exist during the grueling race.

Yet, Bud couldn't project what trailed behind him on this heavily wooded path, out near Rensselaer Lake. It was something far deadlier than the weather or the demands of a twenty-six mile race.

James began to pick up the pace, in order to close the distance separating himself from his objective. The man came into his sights and Bud was shocked to hear the footfall of another runner approaching from behind. He glanced back and saw a tall, athletic man running at a pace that even during his youth he could never have maintained.

James swallowed up the ground like a cheetah chasing a gazelle. He was preparing to reenact the third murder from *The Taking*, knowing only one more murder followed in the book. From the inception of his plan he had foreseen the final act and the thrill was mounting as he got ever closer. Frank Sorello would be coming soon and the battle for supremacy would anoint a victor.

It was all falling into place. The unsuspecting runner up ahead was chosen before James ever set words on to a page. And now, as foretold, Bud's fate was about to be sealed. The illusion that was being created needed to be complete, in order to take all eyes off of the magician.

Two months prior to writing his second novel, James had found Kavanaugh through a random Internet search. The wealthy financier made the mistake of posting pictures on his Facebook page, detailing his secluded runs with captions underneath. Shortly thereafter, James began to follow him. It wasn't long before he knew this man's routine and the manner in which his victim would die.

The Albany Pine Bush created an ominous setting and its dreary seclusion set the scene for both fact and fiction. James let his imagination run wild and those images were about to become reality. Bud Kavanaugh was a creature of habit, which was perfect for a serial killer choosing prey and a novelist acting out his prose.

Approximately one hour ago, he'd left work at the usual time. James watched him climb into his Porsche, already dressed for his daily run. It was going to be all too easy. Bud hadn't noticed being followed from the parking lot of his investment banking firm. James needed to only track him as far as the pine barren access road. At that point he knew where the man was headed from previous scouting efforts. James then drove ahead and entered the wooded trail from a different location. There he waited among the trees until the man ran past. A few minutes afterwards, he began the chase. James didn't want to be seen exiting the tree line. The delayed pursuit caused him no concern and after a fast initial pace, he soon had the man back in his sightline. As he got within earshot, he noticed the runner's head turn in surprise.

James wondered what the man might be feeling...certainly not the intense craving he felt, as the distance between them continued to shrink. In actuality, Bud Kavanaugh was shocked to see another runner along the secluded path. During this time of year and especially at dusk, he'd never encountered another person on the trail. Bud's curiosity perked up and although the man approaching from behind looked like an Olympic athlete, not a man intent on slaughter, his body's internal warning system flashed. Cortisol and adrenaline started pumping and his muscles tightened with anticipation. Bud's heart pumped faster and so did the pace of his running. His fight or flight mechanism was kicking in and although Kavanaugh reasoned the fear was irrational, it still felt very real to him. Logic told him that it was just coincidence...another runner looking for an undistracted workout in the pines. Yet like an animal in the wilderness, innate instinct kicked in and Bud ran ever faster.

James noticed the ground between them suddenly increase...he smiled. The hunter felt an adrenaline rush and instead of picking up the pace, deliberately began to match strides with Bud. His quarry was exhibiting fear, which fed his own satisfaction, and in order to prolong the sensation, chose to extend the chase.

For he knew that all alone in the woods, there'd be no escape. James' physical reserves were far from being pushed. He'd wait until lactic acid coursed through the legs of the older man, causing corresponding muscle fatigue. Plus, there would be less of a fight when he overtook him.

A mile later, Bud's breathing became more labored and he once again looked back. He knew that it would be impossible to out run his opponent and tried to calm down, by addressing the apparent silliness of the situation. Bud kept telling himself, "It's just another runner," hoping that the red flags waving were simply false signals. Kavanaugh's wish would be met with unforgiving violence.

James left the Pine Barrens an hour later, still sated by the acrid smell of blood in his nostrils, which he etched into his flawless memory.

CHAPTER 52

EARLIER THAT SAME DAY, WHILE JAMES WAS IN UPSTATE NEW YORK, A small package arrived at F.B.I. Headquarters. It had been ten days since the model in Bernardsville had been killed. Today, her missing fingernails arrived, along with a note addressed to Frank Sorello. It had been the first message delivered by "The Magician," since the pawn broker in Norristown.

2 down and 1, 2 go
During my magic show
A copycat on full display
A killer that got away
2 down and 1, 2 go

Sorello stared blankly at the note addressed to him. He focused on the difference in style from the original communication. That had been the only other note, but there still had been thirteen identically marked bags and the futility of it all felt paralyzing.

"What is it you're trying to tell me? C'mon think. What the fuck am I missing?" Sorello yelled out loud in frustration, as he kicked over a chair.

"Frank, it's not all on you," Beth said while placing her hand on his shoulder.

"It sure feels like it. He's so sure of himself and it makes me feel helpless. The 2-1-2 reference is pure arrogance."

"That could lead to him slipping up."

"Maybe...but I think he's too smart to just make a mistake on his own. Everything is on his terms and that needs to change. I can play the game too and feed his narcissism. It's like he's leaving me a trail, just to show that I can't follow it. I'll feed that belief."

"How?" Beth asked.

"Through the media, when we're interviewed we let him think we're getting nowhere."

"That's not going to help our public image."

"I couldn't give a rat's ass about that!"

"Frank, I'm arranging for the entire task force to meet this afternoon. I want us to go over everything once again. If you're right, maybe he is creating a trail. Do you think he'd really put himself at risk?"

"Let me ask you this, Beth...if I viewed myself as a God, what worries would I have from mere mortals?"

"Let's all meet at 3:00 in the conference room."

"I have some stuff to take care of, I'll see you then."

Frank left Beth's office and made a quick call to Sarah. He hadn't been home in a week and wanted to hear her voice. So he decided he'd take the opportunity to call.

Sarah answered, "Frank, we must be on the same wavelength. I was just about to give you a call."

"I'm sorry that I've been M.I.A., but until it's over...you know what...let's forget about that for a little while. How are you?"

"Busy, but that hasn't stopped me from missing you. Is it possible you can get home for a few days?"

"I have a meeting in a few hours, but after that I'll check what flights are available. Hopefully I'll be home later tonight. Things have hit a little standstill, so I think it'll be alright for a day or two."

"Should I wait up?"

"No, sweetheart, but I'll make sure to wake you."

"Lucky me."

"And to think you're going to be Mrs. Sorello in six weeks."

"Thirty-eight days...but I'm not counting."

Frank broke into a huge smile and said, "I love you."

"Tonight, you can show me how much."

After their conversation, Frank called the airlines and booked a flight home. He really wanted to see Sarah and although the visit was going to be brief, it didn't matter as long as he got to see her.

The remaining time he spent going through e-mails and catching up on other business. Just before the scheduled conference, Frank double checked the flight confirmation that had been sent to his laptop. He was excited by the thought of seeing Sarah and wanted to reconfirm its details. When he was done he headed over to the conference room and waited for everyone to arrive.

Frank was grateful that the meeting was going to start on time. He understood its purpose, but truthfully didn't expect any new revelations to surface. He'd already run through everything in his mind a thousand times and was more focused on not missing his flight home. It was good to have everyone on the task force constantly briefed. Yet Frank felt until something else happened, there wasn't much more that could be accomplished. His mind wandered back to Sarah while Beth stood up to get things underway.

"I called this meeting so that the entire team can share what they've learned since our last gathering. It's possible we might have missed something. So why don't we start with you, Julia. Have we found anything else about Heidi Torgston?"

"I've been in frequent contact with the lead homicide detective in Essex and he believes the murder was strictly serial in nature. Family members, boyfriends, co-workers...virtually everyone with a personal tie to her had no motive. She was well liked and there were no red flags anywhere. The people closest to her all had solid alibis. Nothing of merit surfaced on the forensic side. The medical examiner feels the wounds are consistent with the other victims. Additionally, there were no other homicides in Essex that fit our profile. It was basically one and done."

"John, you were following up there too. Do you have anything else to add?"

"Unfortunately, Julia, pretty much summed it up. There's not much to go on."

"Let's move along then. Joe, what about 'LEO,' and our criminal databases?"

"I've contacted the local P.D.'s in Albany, Essex and Newington, along with the State Police. Torgston's the only current case fitting our profile. Everyone's been alerted to contact us, if anything even remotely fits the profile we've established. In the meantime,

I have Tony Hillmann working around the clock. He's been cross referencing every database known to mankind, hoping to find something we might have missed. Nothing's turned up."

Beth replied, "We just have to keep at it. Sooner or later something will go our way. What about you, Frank?"

"Logan once again passed his lie detector test and extensive handwriting analysis. The two notes appear to be written by the same person...but our experts agree it's not his. They used various methods designed to draw out his innate style. Logan wrote his name, 50 times in rapid succession and then without any notice was dictated passages to write down, which would highlight certain traits inherent to whoever wrote those notes. He came up clean. Additionally, any signatures on file...loans, bank statements, you name it...all were compared to the messages. Everything indicated it wasn't his handwriting. Logan's attorney is filing for another trial. "

"It didn't help him the first time."

"That was before a second note was written while he's incarcerated. There's also no prison record that he sent out any mail. That would have been recorded."

"Maybe he has an accomplice that's been working with him the whole time. It doesn't have to be a copycat that just started communicating with him?"

"I considered that possibility, but I think it's unlikely. The wound patterns would indicate the same killer. There's also a fixation with me. Somehow I'm personally significant, which lessens the odds as far as I'm concerned."

"Why?"

"Two separate people, both brilliant and psychotic. If I'm that smart I'm not working with an idiot. I just don't buy it. That doesn't mean I'm discounting the theory completely, which is why I had Logan agree to certain stipulations while in jail. He'll do anything to help prove his innocence. From this point on he's agreed to remain in solitary confinement. The guards will be his only human contact and they've been instructed to not deliver any messages to anyone. This eliminates the possibility of messages reaching someone on the outside."

"That won't prove anything. An accomplice could have been given instructions in advance."

"You're right, if someone had been part of this from the beginning, he might be following through with their plan. But I still believe Logan has nothing to do with this and is innocent, he doesn't strike me as a mastermind."

"What if Logan was the accomplice and got set up to take the fall?"

"That would be the more likely scenario, if you believed two men were operating together."

"But you still don't believe it?"

"No I don't. In working with someone less intelligent you take on added risk and our killer has been too careful, overly meticulous with every detail. I think Logan was targeted at the start of this to be the fall guy."

Agent Thorn interjected, "Frank, I have a question?"

"What is it, Julia?"

"If it's not a copycat...then what viable explanation do we have as to how he pulled this off? The physical evidence at the house could've been planted, but Logan was at the site of every single murder location...in multiple states. Frank, that's pretty strong evidence. I know we touched on this before, but no one ever answered it. So what's your working theory?"

"Someone gained access to Logan's flight schedule in order to create a unique fingerprint, a very specific and identifiable kill pattern. It's really ingenious if you think about it. Now, imagine for a moment that I'm a talented author...able to weave together a story. I establish a complicated money trail with numerous potential suspects. Then I watch and wait until an arrest is made. Later when I begin killing it's blamed on a copycat."

"That would require immense forethought, Frank."

"It certainly would, but then factor in the patterns and the deception. We're talking about a certifiable genius, a crazy one, but still a genius. It was my wife that he murdered, followed by books and notes directed at me. I know I'm right, this is a single individual on a psychotic crusade."

"I'm becoming more convinced," Julia replied, "but it would have required constant monitoring of Logan's whereabouts."

"The person could be affiliated with the airlines, someone privy to those details. Maybe he's a very skilled hacker. In either case, he'd also need a flexible schedule and have the means to travel all over the country."

"Plus a fair amount of luck to avoid detection during all of this."

"That means time to scout and prepare. He leads us one way and then another. Everything seems to have a purpose. He's created a puzzle to solve, filled with intricate patterns. His first note gave the impression of being uneducated, a lack of schooling. Why?" Beth asked.

Frank paused for a few seconds and then answered the question, "Misdirection. By constantly changing things up, he remains one step ahead. He wags his tail and we follow. But there's two dogs in this hunt and I have his scent."

Beth replied, "Okay. Let's start checking the airlines to find out who might have access to that information. Also, we'll want to access their databases and cross check passenger manifestos. Search for anyone that parallels Logan's travel schedule."

"I'll work on a warrant," Rich Carson said.

Beth continued, "Could you also get Tony working on the hacker angle. If anyone can find a 'black hat,' it's him."

Frank added, "We'll need to check the hotels and motels in those areas too. Any links we can establish to Logan the better."

"It finally feels like we're closing some ground," Beth said hopefully.

"One last thing, any new insight on Jones' book?"

"Nothing that I could find, Frank."

Beth said, "The two remaining murders in *The Taking* haven't happened yet and unfortunately all we know from the novel is that the next intended target is going to be a wealthy male out on his daily run. The final murder will be a married couple on vacation, assuming the book is being copied to its end."

"Yeah, since there weren't any details as to when or where they might occur...that doesn't amount to very much," replied Tucker.

"If the final murder happens the way it did in the book, then we might have something more to evaluate. All the killings are similar in the novel to The Magician's handiwork. The lacerations up and down the extremities are consistent with what we've seen, except the fingernails aren't removed in the novel. The couple match that too, but the male suffered a much more brutal ending. Maybe that person is significant in some way to our killer."

"I was thinking about that too, Beth."

"Let's not forget that if the pattern continues, then the next murder will happen in a virgin state. The front half of the 2-1-2 cycle was completed in New Jersey."

"That's completely unmanageable, Frank. Most of the country has been untouched and even if we knew what state to focus on we'd still be searching for a needle in a haystack."

"The haystack would be a lot smaller if we knew what town. It can't hurt to inform local police in Albany and Newington. At some point those zip codes are going to come into play. Maybe we'll get lucky."

"Alright. Well notify those police departments to be extra watchful on known running trails. I'm not sure how long they'll stay on it though without something more tangible to go on."

"I'm heading home for a day or two. I have a flight to catch, so I'm heading to the airport. If you need me, just call."

"I will. Say hi to Sarah."

When Frank arrived at his terminal he had some time to kill. He turned on his laptop and opened his e-mail. There was a message from Sarah. It was just a quick note telling him that she was thrilled he was coming home. Frank replied and let her know he was at the airport waiting to catch his flight home.

An hour later, James shut down his own laptop and said aloud, "Enjoy your visit, Frank. I'll be seeing you soon."

CHAPTER 53

WHEN FRANK ARRIVED HOME ALL THE LIGHTS WERE OUT IN THE house. He entered through the front door, careful to not make a sound. He decided that if Sarah was fast asleep he wouldn't disturb her. It was close to midnight and normally she'd be out cold by this time of night. Frank knew how hard she'd been working lately and didn't want to selfishly wake her. He thought to himself they'd have the entire day to themselves tomorrow.

So he slipped his shoes off and made his way up the stairs. For such a large man he was light on his feet and barely made a sound. The door to the bedroom was slightly ajar and Frank peeked inside. He could see that she was wrapped in the covers. Her long flowing hair was draped across the pillow as her back was to him. Frank stopped to take in the moment and picture her face. He was truly in love and something as simple as watching her sleep, gave him a sense of peace. It had been a long time since he felt this way and suddenly, Frank pictured her walking down the aisle. Their marriage was right around the corner and he couldn't wait for the day to arrive. She made him feel young again, when the world felt trouble free and safe.

Sarah was the only thing capable of taking his focus away from the manhunt he was immersed in. She helped transport him away from the scary place that occupied most of his thoughts when he worked. Frank loved her with his heart and soul and when he walked over to the side of the bed he gently kissed her on the forehead. Sarah's eyes opened and she reached out for him. He climbed into bed and held her tight. She fell right back to sleep. The cool ocean breeze came through the partially opened window and quickly Frank followed her into the land of dreams.

In the morning they woke up and made love. Afterwards, they headed down to the boardwalk for their morning ritual. During the long run together they talked about everything from Frank's case to their wedding plans. When they got back home, Sarah made them breakfast. As Frank was drinking his morning coffee and reading the sports section the phone rang. The smell of bacon and eggs made him not want to answer it because he sensed his day wasn't going to go as planned.

Forty minutes later Frank kissed Sarah goodbye.

CHAPTER 54

AS THE SPECIAL BULLETIN WAS BEING BROADCAST, JAMES WAS HEADED toward his next destination. Meanwhile, Frank was on his way to where he was being led, Albany. Years earlier, a similar situation had unfolded as Juliette died while her husband was far away. The irony of this wasn't lost on James because he wrote the story and now the characters were just playing their parts.

James drove south with the intent of creating a grand denouement. The stage had been set and the final act was about to begin. He knew that his latest victim would soon be found. Respected members of the community didn't disappear without attracting attention.

A missing person's report got the ball rolling. Bud Kavanaugh had been unreachable for nearly three days and eventually the police had been contacted. A few hours later, a patrol car came across a Porsche parked just inside the Albany Pine Bush. The officer ran the plates and found out the car belonged to the man gone missing. A large search party was organized and eventually his body was discovered at the edge of a running trail. The detectives on the scene immediately called the F.B.I. upon noticing the killer's trademark lacerations. Their captain had already alerted everyone on the force about the possibility of a serial killer being on the loose in the area. A memorandum had been circulated weeks earlier detailing his methodology and that runners were potentially at risk. It had been taken seriously, but the Albany Pine Bush went virtually unpatrolled. During winter it was basically deserted and therefore drew little attention. Resources were concentrated in more populated locations.

When Sorello arrived at the scene, along with Beth, they were approached by the lead detective. He gave them a rundown of the pertinent information, but they both already knew this was the work of the man they were chasing. The third murder of the novel was now complete and they both felt a pang of disappointment. They realized this was the closest they'd ever been to anticipating what "The Magician" was to about to do. Beth regretted not allocating Bureau personnel to the area.

It was like Frank read her mind, "Even if we'd stationed men up here it wouldn't have helped. This is the middle of nowhere and impossible to have anticipated. The good news, Beth, is we're finally on to something tangible."

"You're right, I need to remain positive. I'm going to station agents in Newington. Sooner or later, he'll turn up there. It's the final zip code in the pattern."

"Can't hurt, but it might be a waste of resources right now."

"What do you mean, Frank? Your 2-1-2 theory is playing itself out."

"It is, but we don't know if the next set of murders will happen in Virginia. That's why I think we can wait on deploying our men there. He's laying out a map. The final zip code won't be the first in the sequence, it'll be second."

"Why"

"He's going to want to put on a majestic performance. He's placing the spotlight right on himself, so he can vanish with all eyes upon him. That's why I believe when he actually does kill in the state of Virginia, it'll be in another city. Newington will come second and complete the back end of his 2-1-2 pattern. It's what I'd do if I was showing my dominance. Here's where I am...try and stop me, because it won't make a damn bit of difference!"

"Wow, Frank, your head's a scary place."

"I don't disagree. It's like over the years I've learned to think like them. Being able to see inside the mind of a psychopath isn't something I recommend."

"I guess that's the price to be a legend. I always wanted to be like you, now I'm not so sure."

"It's that very ability to emotionally connect, Beth, which can lead you there. If you let your mind wander into dark places and remain there long enough, a toll gets paid. Unfortunately, my wife paid with her life."

"Frank,...you've based your whole life on making the world a safer place. That's the definition of a hero and a noble path for anyone."

"Is it? Sometimes I wonder did I do enough. The bodies never seem to stop turning up."

"Maybe you couldn't save them all, but you've saved untold lives. Never forget that."

"I won't and thanks for the pep talk. I guess we both needed a pick me up."

"Anytime, Frank...anytime."

The two task force leaders didn't head back to Washington until all of the crime scene analysis was completed and they had the time to properly coordinate their operation with local and state police. As always there seemed to be little in the way of forensic evidence, but this time they felt more hopeful.

It was just before 8:00 p.m. when they landed at Dulles. Beth said she needed to use the ladies room, so Frank took the spare time to call Sarah.

"Hi honey, I can't talk now I'm about to go into session."

"You're working late."

"Yeah, it's a new patient and this seemed to be the only time that worked for both of us. I should be done here around nine thirty. Can you call me tonight at home?"

"Sure. Love you."

"I love you too. Talk to you later."

Sarah hung up and went out to the waiting area to see if her client had arrived. There was no one there and she frowned. She normally hated scheduling someone this late. Being an early riser she liked downtime in the evening. Her previous patient left almost an hour and a half earlier leaving her waiting alone. Her frustration was compounded by the fact she had recently purchased the new building in which her office was situated. Currently there were no tenants in the other offices and because of the high mortgage on the commercial property she felt stressed. The anxiety is what led to her agreeing to a session at this hour. Sarah hadn't wanted her new patient to go elsewhere. He'd explained that he worked long hours in the city and couldn't get here any earlier.

It looked like her efforts were going to be unrewarded as fifteen more minutes passed. Just as she was about to lock up, she heard the outer door open and smiled. The night wasn't going to be wasted after all. Sarah quickly walked back into her office not wanting to seem as if she were waiting impatiently. When she heard the door to her waiting area open from the outer hallway, Sarah walked back out.

"Hi, you must be Adam."

"Dr. Shepherd, it's a pleasure to meet you."

"No need to be so formal, you can call me Sarah. Why don't we head back to my office, Adam."

The young man followed Sarah into her office and took a seat on the couch. She then asked him to fill out some paperwork while going over the Hippa Laws. When Adam was done, he handed the documents back to her.

"Now that's out of the way, can you tell me what brings you here?"

"I've been feeling really depressed for the last several months. It's like I'm having a tough time making it through the day and that's not like me. I can't shake it and it's scaring me."

"Has anything happened recently that may have played a part in what you're feeling?"

"Not really. I think I'm just lonely. My girlfriend and I broke up almost two years ago and I can't seem to meet anyone?"

"Have you been trying to meet someone?"

"Initially no, but I'd say after a few months I started going out again with my friends...kind of going through the motions. Yet now I don't even think about her and I can't figure out what's wrong."

"What makes you say something's wrong?"

"Every woman I'm attracted to seems to want no part of me."

Sarah paused for a moment. The man sitting across from her

looked like a model or a movie star. His blond hair and striking blue eyes were captivating. He was tall and athletic in appearance. The way he moved when he entered her office was in stark contrast to what he was describing. His demeanor had been both confident and relaxed. She knew that just because his affect wasn't matching his words, didn't necessarily mean it wasn't true. Sarah felt perhaps he was trying to mask his inner turmoil.

"Can you tell me more about that?"

"Anybody I get close to sooner or later disappears."

"It always hurts when we lose someone that we love. But that can also open a door for something better. Do you think that's true?"

"Sort of like, what doesn't kill us...makes us stronger."

Sarah noticed the subtle inflection when he said the word kill and wondered if there was something he was hiding or unable to discuss. She also felt a sense of palpable anger in that instant.

"Yes, I'd say that's a good comparison. Adam, have any of these losses left you feeling bitter or angry?"

The question almost seemed to knock him off balance. He sat immobile looking lost somewhere in the past. The two of them sat silent for almost a minute and then he focused his gaze directly at Sarah.

"You're good Doctor. I'd say you hit the nail on the head," he said in a completely flat tone. Then Adam smiled with totally vacant eyes.

Sarah suddenly felt unnerved and wished she hadn't taken the session. A chill ran straight through her. Sarah felt vulnerable and thought to herself, "Could this be him?" She tried to shake it off and remain calm because it was likely paranoia, but she'd never had this type of reaction to a patient.

"Did I say something to upset you? You look like you've seen a ghost."

Sarah was even more taken aback by the question. Her training taught her to hide displaying outward signs of aversion or potentially harmful emotional reactions. She thought she'd given no perceptible indication of what she was feeling. This raised her guard even more.

"Not at all, why do you ask?"

"Because I've seen what fear looks like," as James moved off the couch like a tiger.

Before Sarah even had time to scream, he was upon her holding a rag over her face. She briefly attempted to struggle, but seconds later her eyes closed.

CHAPTER 55

FRANK WAS EXHAUSTED FROM THE INCREDIBLY LONG DAY. IT HADN'T turned out anything like he'd planned. His vision of relaxing the hours away with Sarah never materialized. Most of the day was spent in Albany dealing with more horror and now he was ready to collapse on an empty hotel bed, in Washington, D.C.

As he began to undress his thoughts drifted to Sarah. Their wedding was approaching and he wanted it to be worry free. Frank realized how close they were to "The Magician" and imagined with some luck, maybe they'd apprehend him before their big date. Sarah was the center of his universe and he wanted to remove the threat to their world as soon as possible. She deserved nothing less because she had been a godsend, taking him out of the darkness and into the light. But earlier this morning the embodiment of his nightmares resurfaced, dragging him away from the Jersey Shore and his wife to be.

Now as his head wearily hit the pillow, he began to drift off and within minutes was asleep. In his dream, Sarah and he danced underneath a moonlit sky in Waikiki. Bob Marley was serenading them with "Is This Love" just as the ground began to vibrate. Frank quickly threw his arms around his bride and lifted her up, the way she had when he'd fallen. He ran carrying her toward shelter, but it seemed they were trapped in an earthquake, as the tremors became stronger.

Frank woke up from the dead of sleep momentarily displaced. He looked around and noticed his cell phone glowing on the nightstand. It had been placed on vibrate and the humming snapped him out of his dream. He figured it was too late for Sarah to be calling, so Frank thought something must have happened on the case. He expected to see Beth's name lit up on the phone's display, but was surprised to see Sarah's instead. It was almost 1:00 in the morning and Frank wondered what was wrong. It was unlike her to call at this hour since she knew he had trouble sleeping. She had witnessed the countless nightmares that left Frank tossing and turning in bed. Most of his nights had been restless since Juliette's death.

He reached for the phone and saw a text message had been delivered. When Frank read it, he momentarily stopped breathing.

Remain calm and follow my instructions or Sarah's life will be over. Do you really want to lose wife number 2? (1) Wait for my call, it will come soon. (2) Do not involve anyone else. Do not attempt a trace. That would be breaking the rules. If you do not comply, you will hear her die. I promise. I was going to add another order but it would have ruined the symmetry and besides, Sarah is looking forward to speaking with you.

Time seemed to stop for Frank as he waited, sitting paralyzed at the edge of his bed. The seconds began to feel like hours while his heart pounded incessantly. He desperately needed to regain his composure and settle down. The only way he could concentrate was to block out his fear. He was Sarah's only chance to survive.

A half hour later, his cell phone rang. The display listed it as a private caller. Frank answered and his hand began to tremble the very moment he heard Sarah speak.

"Frank, I love you. Please, no matter what happens remember that," as her voice broke.

"Sarah, has he hurt you?"

"No. He hasn't touched me."

"I'm going to get you out of this, I promise."

Frank was unprepared to hear a male voice respond, "I like your confidence."

"If you harm her, I'll fucking tear you apart."

"Like you did after Juliette. When it's come to me you've always fallen just short...always a bit too late. Hopefully, for Sarah's sake that'll change this time."

"Let her go and you can have me. No tricks, I swear."

"Frank, I give you my word I'll release her as good as new, if you meet my deadline. What fun would there be in me just taking you?"

"What do you want me to do?"

"To play the game and to take me very seriously. You must also, follow my rules, exactly. If you contact anyone about what has happened, then it's over before it even starts. Make no mistake; Sarah will suffer if you do. This is our battle alone. Let's see how smart you are, Frank. I've written two books and two notes and now you have one last chance. Funny how those numbers keep turning up, 2-1-2. It's 1:36 a.m. I'll give you two days and the clock starts now."

"How do I know you'll keep your word?"

"You don't, but I honor my promises. The question is will you do the same? I'll have Sarah call once a day from a different number, each time. She won't be on long, so don't get any foolish ideas. I have to go now. I'm currently in transit and heading south. That should be obvious, shouldn't it?"

"Is there anything else I should know?"

"I liked the chess set in your library. It's a shame, I haven't seen it in such a long time. I guess I'll just have to force you to play. Will anymore queens be sacrificed this time around? Remember, every ending once had a beginning. It's your move. Don't be late, it's vital to be on time."

Frank heard the dial tone and tried not to panic. He looked at his watch and realized he didn't have a minute to waste. To help deal with his anxiety, Frank told himself all promises made would be honored. This perception allowed him the capacity to function. If the clues were laid out, then he would find them and in turn, Sarah. There would be no other acceptable option.

He took several slow deep breaths and calmed his nerves. Frank closed his eyes and began to think analytically. If what he were told was true, then the answer was attainable. To save Sarah he would have to find her and the obvious choice would be in Newington. Virginia was south of New Jersey and that was where Sarah had been abducted. The Magician had taunted him with that information.

Frank walked into the bathroom and splashed his face with cold water. He got dressed and headed downstairs to the garage of the hotel. Within minutes he was on the road headed toward the only zip code in the pattern that was left untouched. As he drove, his mind continued to process the facts at hand. He replayed the conversation over and over in his head. The man stressed their connection to one another and the dialogue had an almost bitter tone. It was personal, "our battle alone" had been his words. Frank inferred that he failed the man in some capacity. But how, he wondered? The man had twice mentioned to Frank about being late. Was it just a reference to not catching him or something else? He then focused on another allusion...being inside of his home. Juliette...sacrificing queens again, did the man lose a woman he loved? Frank felt that was somehow important and concentrated. He tied it to the words, "every ending once had a beginning." He was certain the roadmap would be in that message. This was in some way all about revenge. There were too many cases over the years to narrow down exactly who might have been spared, if he'd been "on time." The man had given him a finite deadline and the time allotted wouldn't be enough to research that possibility. Therefore, Frank's deductive reasoning led him to believe the information already given was sufficient. He would find Sarah.

Less than a half hour later, Frank turned off of I-95 South and merged onto VA-286. Minutes later he was looking for a place to stay in Newington. Although Frank was filled with adrenaline he knew that sleep would keep his mind clear and that was essential. He recognized that he had a two day deadline and couldn't lose his mental edge. While driving along Loisdale Road he pulled into the Hilton Springfield. He went straight to the front desk and booked a room. Before heading up, he asked the clerk for a 7:00 a.m. wake up call. Once inside, he knew the only way he'd fall asleep was by taking a sleeping pill. A little while later, his little pharmaceutical aid knocked him out.

Around that same time, James drove his van across Virginia state lines. Sarah's body lay still in the back.

CHAPTER 56

It was still dark when James drove his van up the long tree lined driveway. Everything stood in stark contrast to the picture perfect surroundings. The night kept hidden the terrified passenger bound in the back of the vehicle. No lights could be seen anywhere on the rolling acres of land and the blackness of the starless sky enhanced the irony of the situation. The normally idyllic setting was about to become a living Hell.

James' estate on the Potomac River looked like a plantation depicted in "Gone With The Wind". During the spring and summer months, its rustic beauty was bountiful. The green lawn was endless with lush colorful flower gardens everywhere. Large columns lined the front of the home like soldiers guarding the Old South. The cold of winter created a stark contrast to those seasons now past. The barren landscape fit the night's coming horror and like Sherman marching through at the end of the Civil War, destruction was at hand.

James turned his head and looked at the guest house sitting about an acre away from the main house. He planned on visiting there very soon, but first he needed to take care of Sarah. James reached for the chloroform rag in his pocket and climbed into the back of the parked van. As he approached Sarah, she squirmed and reflexively tried to pull away. The shackles she was attached to on the van's floor kept her from being able to move more than a few inches. James calmly placed the rag over her face and she passed out. He removed her from the bindings and carried her toward the house, as easily as he might a bag of groceries.

Once James was in the house, he took Sarah down into the fully finished basement. It was like another complete living quarters. Aside from its large bed and bath rooms, there was a huge centralized game room and wine cellar. James took her to the bedroom and placed her on the king size bed. After tying her securely to the bed posts, he walked back upstairs.

Knowing that he only had a few hours until daylight, he headed back outside. When he reached the guest house, its front door was locked. Reaching into his pocket, he took out a key. Careful not to make a sound, he opened the door slowly. James didn't want to awaken his guests. It had been a long time since they'd seen one another and he hoped to surprise them. James' anticipation was palpable.

He slipped off his shoes and quietly approached the master bedroom. There was a noise and James instantly stopped moving. He listened for a few seconds and realized it was the sound of snoring.

James thought, "It's finally time to cure that problem."

The door to the bedroom was slightly ajar, so he peeked inside. His visitors were dead to the world. James reached inside his jacket and like a shadow drifted across the floor. Just as the cloth in his hand was being placed over his foster mother's face, her eyes opened.

A look of confusion quickly spread across Karen's face. She wondered if she was actually awake or in the middle of a bad dream. Seconds later, the chloroform did its job and she was back asleep. James kept his eyes focused on Paul the entire time, watching like a hawk for any signs of movement. But he never budged and as James moved closer, the smell of alcohol was apparent.

"Old habits die hard."

He placed the same rag over his foster father's face. The booze probably would have kept him comatose, but James figured it was better to be cautious. As he held the cloth down, he fought the urge to suffocate the man right then and there. James didn't cave in to the impulse. This was the person he most wanted to suffer and nothing would get in the way of that objective.

It was like a dream coming true for James. He had planned this day for a very long time. Everything had gone as expected. Paul and Karen had accepted his invitation not out of love, but from greed. It was the only emotion that truly motivated them both.

Ever since he bought them their house in New Jersey, James methodically led them to this moment, by feeding their insatiable avarice. They in turn showed the requisite amount of love and gratitude for the gifts they received. James knew it was all an act, because he recognized a chameleon when he saw one.

Once he began to condition them to the idea that his money was almost gone, their need to perform disappeared with it. The con artists happily disengaged themselves from his life.

During his initial time at Princeton, they called for a few weeks, speculating he might have had more to offer. But James squelched their hopes. He indicated the house and the cash that immediately followed, drained away the majority of his inheritance. So when Paul and Karen felt the well had dried up, their contact with him became nonexistent. They stopped calling and consequently so did James. That had been his objective from the moment his friendship with Marty blossomed. After falling in love with Maria he stopped thinking about them altogether. His love of life during that time period temporarily erased them from his memory.

They contacted him once more after they noticed he was all over the news for being a potential Heisman Trophy candidate. It had nothing to do with them being proud of their foster son. Paul fished around to see if James was considering pro football as a career path. He saw visions of more dollar signs, but James shot down that notion. He told Paul he played college ball for the fun of it and nothing more.

Later on, when he was getting married, no invitation was offered. Communication had been completely severed. After all, they had been largely responsible for causing the cavernous hole in James' heart. Yet with Maria, Marty and Grace, it was healed and he didn't care. James just wanted to be surrounded by goodness.

It had been the only happy period of his life. Evil was simply forgotten. His foster parents had been part of the purging. Their true wickedness was never more apparent than in the very event which brought them back "home."

After the news of James being the lone survivor of a horrible triple homicide, in which, he lost his wife and friends, Karen and Paul never even called to offer their condolences.

The moment his wife died, this day was set in stone. James need for retribution resurfaced a hundred fold. From that point forward, all things led to this death trap on the Potomac River.

James waited until every last detail was in place and made contact. He'd left a message on their answering machine.

"Mom, dad...this is James. I know it's been a long time and we've lost touch with one another. I don't blame you because I know I stopped being receptive to your calls. It was just that I felt you only wanted my money and it made me bitter. Maybe that hurt you too. But I've learned family is the only thing that matters. I've been working as a hedge fund manager and even with all the money in the world...I'm still lost. I miss you both and hope you feel the same way. I have some vacation time built up and I'd love for you to stay in my guest house on the Potomac River. If you'd like to take a vacation with me, call. I'll have my limo driver come pick you up. Life's too short, so please, say yes to my invitation. My cell number is still the same."

Later, that same day, Paul called back. He took on the role of an emotionally wounded parent and expressed regret for not having fought through his own pride. He said he blamed himself for being too stubborn and the only thing that mattered was for him to have his son back. To top off his performance, he said "mom" was crying tears of joy.

The ensuing conversation led to arrangements for their current visit. James informed Paul he'd be returning home from business on the day they were scheduled to arrive. Before the conversation ended, Karen got on the phone briefly to say she loved James. He asked her to please tell Paul that his flight wouldn't get him home until the middle of the night, so neither of them should wait up. Finally, he told her the guest house was fully stocked with food and beverages and to make themselves at home. The limousine driver was going to provide them with a key.

The bait had been irresistible and now that they were reeled in, it was time to gut the fish.

When Paul and Karen opened their eyes they were strapped to chairs which had been placed directly across from Sarah. They had no idea who she was and vice versa. She was still tied to the bed posts, but now had an extra pillow propped under her head. James placed it there to give her a better view of the coming show. His foster parents attempted to free themselves from the bindings, but soon realized it was pointless. Their fear was rising by the second.

In the center of the bedroom, James had set up a table. It separated the strangers from each other. The scene was surreal. A woman bound to a bed on one side and a couple on the other sitting tied to matching armchairs. The table between them was dressed with a pure white table cloth. Sitting on the artisanal, hand woven material was a singular place setting and a bottle of Dom Perignon.

James poured half a glass into his crystal flute. Before drinking it, he raised it up to make a toast. However, nobody could focus on anything else but the table's utensils. A large serrated knife and a pair of pliers were sitting on a folded, blood red linen napkin.

"Thank you all for coming...although not everyone is going to be leaving," and then he paused again, "I'm sorry for my poor manners. I haven't allowed anyone else to speak."

He casually picked up the knife and walked directly in front of Karen. Tears were now running down her face, as he took the flat edge of the blade and slid it up under the cloth gag that was tied to her face. He held it there for a few seconds and violently pulled the knife back toward him. The sharp serrated edge sliced the rag away and it fell to the floor.

Karen screamed instinctively, expecting her blood to flow from an imaginary wound. The blade hadn't cut her at all. She then began yelling for help. James watched without a reaction until she stopped and just began to cry.

"As you may have already figured out, no help is coming. My neighbors aren't close enough to hear you and besides, my basement has been soundproofed. I don't like being disturbed. So when I remove your gags, I'd like us all to behave like adults and have a polite conversation. If you misbehave, you'll be punished. Nod if you understand."

Sarah and Paul both shook their heads up and down.

"What about you, Karen. You didn't acknowledge my rule. Do you understand?"

She remained sobbing and ignored the question. James reached out and picked up the pliers.

"Karen, I said I would punish anyone that misbehaves. When I ask you something, I expect a response."

James then placed the pliers onto her thumbnail and ripped it out. She shrieked in pain and the terror of the audience was apparent. Karen, Paul and Sarah all felt the same primal fear. They were trapped by a predator with no chance of escape.

"I'm going to remove the gags from your mouths. I'm requesting your obedience. If I don't get it, I'll be very unhappy. I don't believe you'll want to test me again."

First, James removed the cloth stuffed in Sarah's mouth. She remained silent, as the tears flowed uncontrollably down her face. There was no good way to control the situation. All the years of study in psychology would likely prove to be useless in this moment. Her captor was clearly beyond rational reasoning and worse yet, perhaps a true sociopath. If that were the case, attempting to humanize herself would fall on deaf ears. The lack of an emotional spectrum would mean he would possess no empathy. Sarah reasoned logic was the only tool that could be used, if the possibility existed to gain a semblance of control. She had to find out what was making him tick. Even if he were operating under some psychotic delusion, she might be able to work with that and find a way to diffuse the situation. At the very least, buy time.

"Sarah, you seem upset."

Quickly she processed the statement and decided it would be best to answer, as honestly as possible. He was testing her and she didn't want a non-response to result in the same reaction that had befallen the woman in the chair. She knew his calm affect was in stark contrast to the rage beneath the surface.

"Yes, that's because I'm afraid. I'm not sure why you've chosen to bring us here. I suspect in some way, it has to do with you having been severely hurt by someone or something. I've been lucky in my own life. My family and friends have always been loving and supportive. I've never had to deal with anything terrible until now...

273

so that scares me. If you've been scarred by something tragic, I'm sorry. I can't imagine what that must feel like."

"I can see why you're so successful in what you do, a perfect text book response. You didn't ignore my question, because you accurately deduced that might have upset me. At the same time, you tried to establish a connection with me. Sarah, unfortunately it's much too late for therapy. You're right though, I have seen my share of horror."

"Why's it too late?"

"Because nobody can erase the past, Sarah."

"That's true, but people can and do recover from traumatic losses."

"There's no healthy way to address my life!"

The forcefulness of his response told her she shouldn't push that line of questioning. It obviously struck a raw nerve. She moved in another direction.

"You mentioned earlier about us having a polite conversation. I'd like to do that, but since you know my name...may I ask yours?"

James appreciated intellectually the psychology she was employing. She was desperately attempting to develop a rapport and he would play along. Divulging his name wouldn't matter, his identity would be known soon enough.

He paused and acted as if he were deliberating, whether or not to answer. Sarah waited through the silence.

"I'm sure Frank has called me a few things...'The Magician,' 'Gary Jones,' a fucking psychopath. I guess it really doesn't matter anymore. My name is James."

Sarah felt good about engaging him. She also felt a shiver run down her spine. She inferred everything was already a foregone conclusion; he planned on killing them all. Yet, his tone carried with it a sense of resigned sadness.

A stream of consciousness flowed through Sarah's head. Was he potentially suicidal? Did he care if he lived or died? She heard him say to Frank that he kept his promises. He'd also said he would free her, if Frank arrived before the deadline. Maybe that was true. Was this solely about Frank? Kill or be killed? That it was all going to end here between them?

Sarah knew of his fixation with Frank. She began to reason. Maybe his fixation always led to that eventuality? She hoped she was right. At least then, Frank might end up the victor. There was a chance to survive.

He stood looking into her eyes, but didn't interrupt her silence. She recognized the longer she held his conversation the better it was for everyone.

"James, what makes you say it doesn't matter anymore?"

"Sarah, I'm going to ask something of you. I'd like you to stop analyzing me. If you're worried about being one of the people that I implied wouldn't be leaving my home, don't fret. You at least have a chance. I will honor my promise that I made to your future husband. That's if he makes it here on time, otherwise you'll die his fiancée. I'm sorry for being rude and cutting you off, but I need to focus my attention elsewhere. I have a limited amount of time to take care of what's most important to me. If Frank is as resourceful as I expect him to be, you'll be okay. Do you understand?"

"Yes."

James walked back toward the woman who was still bleeding profusely and pulled the gag from her mouth.

"James, please stop this. I'm sorry. I thought you wanted us to be a family again," Karen said barely above a whisper.

As the woman tied to the chair wept, Sarah processed what she'd just heard. Was this his mother and father? She knew now that he'd been truthful with his name. The woman had called him James.

"When were we ever a family?" James said as he ran the blade's edge down one arm and then the other.

Karen screamed at the top of her lungs, as Paul started shaking. His reaction had more to do with his own panic, than it did with his wife's wounds. She bled profusely and all he could think of was his own safety. Meanwhile, Sarah felt genuine empathy and tears ran rampantly down her cheeks. She knew the woman was likely to die and there wasn't anything she could do to stop it. Yet, she had to try. Even though James had warned her to be quiet, she looked past her fear.

"James, this isn't going to erase your pain. Your rage is controlling you. It's only fueling the hurt inside of you."

Just as he began to make another cut down his foster mother's thigh, he stopped. James turned and looked at her with crazed malice. With the knife still in his hand, he rose up and walked in her direction. Sarah began to pray out loud.

"Our father, who art in heaven..."

"God isn't going to save you, Sarah."

CHAPTER 57

AT THE EXACT SAME INSTANT, IN WHICH SARAH BEGAN TO PRAY FOR her life, Frank's alarm sounded. He practically vaulted out of bed, impervious to the exhaustion gripping his body. The few hours of sleep helped him to cope physically, but did little for his mental stress.

Minutes later, Frank was driving up and down the streets of Newington. He was on a time clock that was attached to Sarah's life and he didn't know where to begin. The thought of losing her was too much to bear. Sarah had made his life worth living again and without her it would be meaningless. He wished he knew where to look because without a specific destination, he felt like he was driving blind. It was maddening.

The town of Newington was very small, roughly seven square miles. However, Frank still felt helpless as he glanced at his watch. He'd been driving around for hours. So far, he'd found absolutely nothing. Every store, every home that Frank drove by elevated his blood pressure. He kept thinking maybe she's inside there and I have no way of knowing it. He scrutinized every piece of property, analyzing store fronts, reading graffiti written on walls...looking for anything that might contain a message.

Frank subconsciously tapped his steering wheel. He was oblivious to the road itself and accidentally ran a red light. A trucker slammed on his brakes and blasted his horn. If Frank had passed through the intersection five seconds later there would have been a fatal crash. The near accident actually helped him regain his focus. He knew he had to get his head back in the game.

"You'll find her, Frank. You'll find her," he repeated aloud.

He wanted to seek help from the Bureau, but couldn't take the chance. He believed the threat was real and that Sarah would die if he didn't follow the instructions verbatim. He worried that Beth would begin to wonder where he was and make an attempt to contact him. So he decided to be proactive because they couldn't interfere. If agents started looking for him and showed up in Newington, it might mean Sarah's life.

In order to buy time, he made a call to Beth and told her he was heading back home for a few days. He made up an excuse that there'd been a death in Sarah's family. Beth expressed her condolences and seemed to believe his story. However, he worried if he were gone too long she might begin to look for him. Frank wanted to ditch his cell phone because of the GPS tracking chip, but it was also his only means of contact with "The Magician." Besides, he figured if she was serious in her search it wouldn't matter. Phone records would show his cell pinging off towers in the area and he knew if that happened, the troops would show up in full force.

Frank was glad he didn't toss it away. Because a short while later his phone rang. The number displayed was listed as unknown. He immediately pulled over and answered.

Just before speaking, James made a calculated guess that Frank wouldn't have risked being noncompliant to his orders. He was certain the fear of losing Sarah would keep him in line. So he decided to take advantage of that fact. He'd make it seem like he was aware of everything that was happening. James would appear omniscient.

"Hi, Frank. I appreciate you not contacting anyone. That would have left us with one less piece in play. I'm sure you wouldn't want that."

"You don't have to worry. It's just you and me."

"I never worry. If you know what's going to happen before it does, you get to choose your path."

"I've done as you've asked. May I speak to Sarah?"

"First, I'd like to ask you a few questions."

"Go ahead. What do you want to know?"

"Can you tell me where you are at the moment?"

"Newington, Virginia."

"Excellent. At least I'm not dealing with a novice. That would make the game far less interesting."

"Okay, I answered your question. So can I please, speak to Sarah?"

"You're going to need to be a better listener, Frank. I said questions. That would imply more than one query. If Sarah is to survive, you'll have to do a much better job. Where's your deductive reasoning?"

"What else would you like to know?"

"Since time is ticking away, how are you feeling?"

"Not so great. I've been playing your game and it's led me to Newington. Now I'm at a bit of a loss. You haven't left me anything since I've gotten here. "

"Maybe your reputation is hugely overrated. Those intuitive skills of yours definitely need to be further honed. You can find me and it really shouldn't take long. Then again, maybe your legendary intellect is nothing more than a media creation. How very disappointing it would be if you weren't the great savior you've been depicted as."

Frank took a chance and said the only thing that came to mind, "If I don't hear her voice right now, this conversation's over!"

Frank's demand was met with complete silence. A full minute went by and there was nothing. The quiet became uncomfortable. Frank worried that he overplayed his hand and swore that if she died, he would never forgive himself.

"Frank," Sarah said while crying, "I'm..."

Then her voice disappeared.

"I told you I honor my promises. She's alive...but won't be the next time you give me an order. I hope you understand this isn't under debate."

"Understood."

"For Sarah's sake, I do hope so."

"Listen, I'll do anything you want. Let me trade places with her. You can kill me, if that's what you want. I don't care. Just let her go."

"What you ask requires trust."

"How many times have you said you'll honor your word? I have to accept that without reservation. You seem to know something about me. Then you should know that under the circumstances I'll keep my word."

"You certainly have a point. Frank, if I was planning to kill her, why is she still alive?"

"That's easy. You love to play your little game. You just want to toy with me. Once you have me, you'll kill us both."

"I've already won the game. You just said you're giving up. That doesn't sound fun or honorable. Frank, have you ever played someone in a contest that's vastly inferior to you? Would you take any satisfaction in winning?"

"No."

"That's my sentiment exactly. As a result, I'm going to deny your offer of resignation. I want to see if you're a worthy opponent. I've never met my match and if you haven't already surmised...this game is extremely personal."

"Then just tell me, what is it you want? I'll do it."

"To finish this game. You're back on the clock. Tick tock."

"I'll hear from Sarah, tomorrow?"

"As always, Frank, once a day...until the sand runs out."

CHAPTER 58

SARAH HAD NEVER BEEN MUCH OF A CHURCHGOER, BUT NOW wondered if prayer had kept her alive. She couldn't shake the thought that maybe her autonomic response to quote the "Lord's Prayer" somehow led to survival. In that moment she'd expected to die, but James let her live. She never thought she'd have the opportunity to speak to Frank ever again. Yet she had. It had only been for a split second, but she did get to call out his name while on the phone. James had ripped it away, before she could say anymore.

This provided some comfort because she knew the man she loved had heard her voice. Her faith desperately wanted to believe God did too. After all, she was still breathing.

Sarah contemplated her situation. She knew she needed to stay mentally sharp to have any chance of being saved by Frank. The longer she could prolong things, the better. She searched her mind for a weakness in James, one in which she could exploit. So she began to reflect back on what had happened a few hours earlier. During that moment, in which, she thought death was imminent, he'd whispered in her ear.

"The only one that can save you is Frank."

She remembered closing her eyes as he knelt down in front of her. Sarah hadn't begged. She knew it would only stir his desire. She believed that her life was about to end right then and there. The tip of the blade had grazed the nape of her neck. Her thoughts had gone to Frank, hoping he would somehow recover from another traumatic loss.

Sarah began to hyperventilate as she began to relive the

memory. It was as if the past was being replayed. It was all real again, a flashback.

Sarah could feel his breath upon her, "I appreciate your faith in God and because of it...I'll show you mercy. At least more than my foster father will receive. There will be no God in where he's headed."

James got up and without warning walked over to Karen. He plunged the knife straight into her heart. The urine spread across Paul's pants as he watched his wife die before his very eyes. He surmised his fate would be far worse.

Sarah closed her eyes and then reopened them. She wished she hadn't. Blood was everywhere. Then she watched as James removed the gag in Paul's mouth.

"Please, don't hurt me. It was all her fault. I was the one who talked her into letting you out of the basement. Blame that bitch, not me!"

James dropped the knife from his hand and Paul suddenly felt a tinge of hope. A second later, James threw a punch, adrenaline enhanced, directly into Paul's stomach. His foster father threw up and began to gasp for air.

"You idolized Houdini, so let's give you a taste of how he died, sucker punched by a college kid," then James struck Paul several more times, "and it wasn't just once. You read his autobiography, 'dad'. Houdini claimed he could take any punch to the abdomen and not be affected. Then again, that was if he was prepared for the blow. Sorry, just wanted to be consistent."

James paused as Paul began to whimper for mercy.

"You know dad, old 'Harry' had an undetected case of appendicitis at the time. He didn't cry like a baby...he actually performed a show in utter agony. Of course, he died shortly thereafter. I'll make sure you follow in his footsteps."

"Please, I'm so sorry."

"Really? You're only contrite because you know that you're not going to escape. Maybe, if you were a better magician like Houdini, you could pull it off. Instead, you chose to have your wife shake her tits. That's what drew in your crowd. You're not a fucking magician, you're a fucking monster!"

"Just give me a chance, James, please…I'll change," he said while crying.

"So you want forgiveness, that's funny," he smirked and then continued, "I have something planned for you that Mr. Houdini survived. Maybe, you will too…and then you'll have your opportunity for redemption."

James pulled out the chloroform drenched cloth from his pocket and held it over Paul's face. When his foster father blacked out, he walked back to Sarah. James knelt down and put his face an inch from hers.

"Sarah, I'm going to spare you the indignity of taking out the trash. It's going to be a bit messy. I'll be back soon enough."

Through tear drenched eyes, she watched James turn and walk away. Next, he bent over to pick up Paul.

Taking the pliers and blood soaked knife with him.

As Sarah broke out of her flashback in a cold sweat, she felt reliving those horrible images was beneficial. She knew that her captor's inner turmoil was tied to his past, but more importantly she now had some direct insight as to its origin. Maybe, she had found something to actually exploit.

CHAPTER 59

Immediately after his conversation ended with Sarah's abductor, Frank went straight back to his hotel. Somewhere there was a message to be found. He quickly accessed the notes and decided there was nothing there that could help locate Sarah. Frank also decided to dismiss the *The Taking*. He had already read it cover to cover, three times in the last month and was certain the information didn't lie there. He'd done so, in order to stay ahead of the killings being mimicked in the novel. Time was ticking down and therefore, couldn't be wasted.

Deductively, Frank assumed it was hidden somewhere in the first novel, *The Blood Hunt*. His first go round with the book was during a bout of heavy drinking and that allowed for mistakes in memory. Afterwards, his professional associates refuted his claims it was connected to his case. They said everything written in it was pure fiction.

Although Frank read it a second time, on a more cursory level, he agreed nothing fit an actual homicide. It had bothered him initially and that is why he'd re-read it, albeit superficially. The sequel hadn't yet been released.

When *The Taking* finally was published, the focus was on preventing additional homicides. That novel was the killer's current focus and therefore, became the Bureau's also. *The Blood Hunt* was effectively ignored based on its lack of reality connected facts.

However, this time, Frank would read it with an investigative edge. He wouldn't skip over a single word, assuming it to be filler. No details would be considered superfluous. So he sat down with a cup of coffee and began to read.

Chapter after chapter produced that same feeling of discomfort he'd felt years earlier. Again though, there was nothing he could find which bore a significant reflection to reality. But the more he read, he realized what it was that caused that uneasiness. Images like the color of a wall or the layout of a house were highly descriptive. The details themselves didn't fit a specific crime scene, but were more or less juxtaposed with another. It was such a subtle touch, but now Frank could see it clearly. Viewed as a whole, the jumbled picture took shape. It was unnerving.

It was early evening and Frank was nearing the end of the novel. Even though he'd recognized "The Magician's" hand in the prose, the clue he searched for continued to prove itself elusive. He was beginning to feel it was all futile. Only a few chapters remained and Frank's sense of despair was rising as he neared the finish. Tomorrow, Sarah would die. Then he read the next two lines of the book.

"Her husband rushed off to the unveiling of the hospital's new wing. He didn't want to be late."

Frank knew it wasn't much, but the hairs on his arm were standing on edge. He understood why he could have glossed over this previously. It was innocuous information for the average reader, but not for someone with intimate details regarding a serial killer. This wasn't there by coincidence. The author had placed it there with intent. The zip code 22122 was Newington's. Everything was tied to the pattern.

Frank broke the name of the town down into syllables and said aloud, "New wing, Newington," and then continued, "plus, you kept emphasizing me being late. Okay, I've fucking found something. I just need more!"

Frank kept reading, deciphering every word, every letter. But as the pages slipped away, his hope did too. There were only two pages left and if there was nothing else, he wouldn't find Sarah. Was this meant to be a cruel irony? Frank pondered if the pattern was designed to offer the hope of salvation, but instead, turn out to be nothing more than a false prophecy. It wasn't. The last sentence of the novel told him where he needed to go. It read:

"She never got to mail her letter."

CHAPTER 60

Sarah sat alone for hours. She hoped against hope that Frank would arrive before James returned. Her fear was growing once again. Graphic images intrusively bombarded her thoughts. They centered on the message whispered just prior to when James carried his "dad" away. After witnessing what he'd done to his "mother", she knew that man's destiny would be far worse. She felt sick to her stomach and tried to block it all out.

Thankfully, she couldn't see what James was doing or her nausea would have been exacerbated. Paul was currently inside of a bronze coffin. His foster son had placed him there still alive, just as he had done with his former attorney. However, the symmetry of the situation ended there.

James had promised he'd let Paul attempt one of Harry Houdini's great escapes. The famed magician was once lowered into a hotel swimming pool in a bronze coffin and survived. Now, Paul would have the same opportunity. James began to lower him into the pool that was in his backyard. He thought it would be both, fitting and ironic.

Paul had always fawned over Houdini memorabilia and now he would die inside a similar casket. After Harry's death, he was shipped for burial in the same bronze coffin that had been used in his former act. Further connecting the two magicians during their demise were their badly damaged internal organs. Yet in this case, Paul would finally best Houdini.

As he lay gasping for air, in an ever growing pool of blood, his pain was excruciating. James had administered the blows and cuts with expert precision. The damage was designed to produce a slow death. James wondered whether Paul would die from asphyxiation or the trademark cuts expertly carved into his arms and legs. He was wrong on both counts. Paul died of a heart attack. The sheer terror of his situation produced a massive coronary.

As James walked away from the swimming pool, he carried with him his knife and pliers. Both were now bloodied, as all twenty of Paul's nails had been removed, prior to him being placed inside the coffin. James' fury had never been greater.

He walked inside of his home.

In his study, he opened a drawer. He took from it two plastic bags and a black sharpie. He placed the nails inside and wrote with indelible blank ink, the letter "M." He repeated the procedure on the other bag, but it only contained a single nail. Karen was lucky that James' hatred for Paul had held most of his attention. He never bothered to go back and remove the other nails from her hands. James made up for it, by taking Paul's toenails.

He left them right next to a pile of mail, which sat directly on his filing cabinet. There would be no need to deliver them because he knew this place would eventually be combed over by the local and state police, along with the Federal Bureau of Investigation.

It was now dark outside and James went back down into the basement. Sarah could hear the footsteps coming down the stairs and tried not to cry.

As James came into view, she asked, "May I please go to the bathroom?"

"Of course, I'm sorry if I left you feeling uncomfortable. Where are my manners?"

Before he untied her, he stared once again directly into her eyes. The message was delivered as if spoken aloud...be careful because I'll be watching. When he released her from the bindings, Sarah rose from the bed and thought for a moment to run. She was fast, but he looked like a natural athlete and thought the better of it. James put out his hand and Sarah shivered, as she took it in her own.

He then led her to the bathroom. James allowed her to step inside and didn't follow. She shut the door and quickly surveyed the room. There were no windows that she could climb out from and escape. Sarah surveyed everything inside the room. There was a toothbrush on the sink and nothing was in the medicine cabinet. She considered breaking the mirror and using a piece of glass as a weapon. She quickly ruled out that option, knowing that it would cause a loud noise. James would hear it and be prepared to react. Sarah knew she would lose in that type of confrontation. Finally, she glanced inside of the shower stall. There was only soap and a bottle of shampoo. The razor she hoped to find wasn't there. Without a weapon she resigned herself to what she had needed to do in the first place. Sarah relieved herself.

As she sat on the toilet and urinated, she realized she wanted more time…free of bondage and to continue living. She fought the urge to cry, thinking the wedding she dreamed about, would sadly, never happen.

Sarah called out, "Would it be okay if I took a shower?"

"Absolutely. I'm in no rush."

"Thank you," she replied subserviently.

The hot water felt good beating down on her skin. She took the brief moment of respite to clear her head. Sarah reasoned if she showed no sign of rebelliousness, then perhaps he'd grant her more freedom. Since she had no keys to open doors, the downstairs was effectively a controlled space. Perhaps, he'd allow her to move about in the rooms that provided no exit point. This would allow her to search for something that might come in handy.

Fifteen minutes later, she walked back outside and demurely stretched out her arms, with her hands, palms up…touching one another. She wanted to display a total lack of defiance. By indicating she was ready to be tied up again, it provided the appearance of submission. James pointed toward a chair and she sat down.

"Would you like a glass of wine? I'd like to chat."

"If that's what you want, James, sure. Thank you for the shower."

He walked away and used a key to enter into another room, leaving the door open. Every ounce of her being was crying out to run, but she knew it was a test. Less than a minute later, he walked back in holding two glasses and a bottle of Merlot. James filled her glass and then his own. It was like they were old friends. His demeanor was so unthreatening. It made the moment all the more chilling, given what she'd already witnessed. His ability to transform, shifting from hospitable host to a monster, was what made it so terrifying.

James handed her the glass and Sarah waited for him to take a sip. He smiled and drank.

"Don't worry, it won't kill you. L'Apparita is from a small estate in Tuscany. It's really quite delicious, even if you're not a fan of Merlot."

She took a sip, and although the wine was considered by connoisseurs to be fantastic, it was like her taste buds had been removed. But Sarah followed his lead and played her role.

"It's wonderful. So what would you like to talk about?"

"Frank?"

"What about him would you like to know?"

"Tell me how you met?" James asked, even though he knew the answer.

"I was getting ready for my morning run and he was there on the boardwalk. One thing led to another and that was it."

"Was it long after his wife died?"

The question was designed to shake up her confidence and it had. James knew the reference to Juliette would highlight her own peril. He enjoyed testing Sarah, to see what Frank had found so enticing.

Sarah managed to reply calmly, "A little bit before your second novel, *The Taking.*"

"Touché. I admire your ability to parry. I'm beginning to root for your paramour, Sarah, for your sake, of course...not his."

"What exactly, do you mean, James?"

"That I will honor my commitment and let you live. I've made no such promise to Frank."

"How has he harmed you? Why do you hate him so much?"

"It's complicated."

"As you said earlier, I'm in no rush."

James laughed.

"You really are charming. I can understand why he fell in love with you. I felt that way once. Anyhow, I'll try to give you a condensed answer. He's received a lot of undue adulation. I'm sure you've seen the movie making him out to be a hero. Let's just say that he's consistently fallen short, at least, as far as I'm concerned. I have been given gifts to allow me to unmask the fraudulence. My history, as painful as it might have seemed at the time, was perhaps...necessary. You might say that the *Master Magician* is destined to reveal the smoke and mirrors. Destined to reveal Frank Sorello for what he really is."

His cold blue eyes seemed to look right through Sarah. She observed the faraway look, recognizing he was momentarily lost in his thoughts and wanted to keep him engaged.

"What is he really, James?"

He seemed to come back to her, looking directly into her eyes, and said "I can tell you, but I won't. But it will give you something to look forward to, no matter how this plays out. I'm sure when all is said and done, everything will be abundantly clear. I realize I've painted myself into a corner, in which, there's really no escape."

"Why now? You've avoided detection for so long. What's making you do this?"

"Sarah, you're extremely bright. Haven't you guessed? I've already given him a taste of the pain he left me with because of his incompetence. I've killed his wife...successfully sullied his storied reputation by having him arrest the wrong man. I've also quite recently restored some long standing karmic imbalance...Paul, Karen...I believe you've met. Well, they've completed the circle of life. Now I have very little in which I can look forward to. So I've created another challenge. Frank can redeem himself or be further destroyed. The only way I lose...is if he kills me. That's not going to happen. If he fails to get here on time, I'm sad to say you'll die. If he manages to save you, I'll have him alone, without the help of his cronies. I believe that's all the advantage I'll need."

"But that means you'll end up in jail. You've exposed yourself and it'll only be a matter of time till you're caught," Sarah paused briefly, "I assume that means, I'm to die either way. So I won't lead Frank here! I refuse to let him hear my voice again on the phone. He'll think I'm dead."

"Sarah, he'll come either way. Do you really think he'll leave it alone? I have no intention of killing you, if he arrives. If all I wanted to do was kill Frank, I could have done that a thousand times. He never had a clue as to my identity. I've watched over him like a dark angel or the grim reaper. I could have snuffed out his life at any time. However, doing it this way creates a grander story, a bigger stage to annihilate everything about him! If I spend my life in prison, I'll be the subject of a million stories. Interviewed to see what makes me tick. I'll make sure the great Frank Sorello will be a laughing stock. The public will realize he's a fraud. I know he failed me, time and time again. People will stop worshipping demigods. That gives me all I need."

Sarah listened to his diatribe and knew James was right. Frank would never give up. Besides, she realized that either one of them could have been killed while he was in essence, invisible. So perhaps, his delusion would help save them both. If Frank arrived, there was always a chance that he might kill James. She wanted to test James' promise, because it would further strengthen her belief that he wasn't lying. If what he rambled on about was tied to this public spectacle, maybe they'd come out of this alive.

"Can I ask you one more thing?"

"Yes."

"Why let me live?"

"Let's just say, you remind me of someone from long ago."

"If you kill Frank, you've taken my life with him."

"You'll get over it."

"You haven't."

"That's not quite true, I did recover. Once. But twice, I think we'd both agree that's too much to ask."

CHAPTER 61

Frank was waiting outside the Newington Post Office at 8:55 in the morning. Five minutes later, when the doors opened, he rushed inside. He approached the postmaster and pulled out his badge.

"Excuse me, but I'm a federal agent and would like to know if you have a post office box in the name of Gary Jones?"

The postmaster asked to inspect the badge and then asked for further identification. Frank provided it.

After taking a closer look, he replied, "I'll check. This post office is for delivery points within the post office itself and that means we don't send trucks out to mailboxes. Residents come here to pick up their mail and I've gotten to know most of them over the years. That doesn't mean there isn't one in his name. But I just want to let you know I can't grant you access without a warrant."

"Any way around that?"

"Not unless you're listed as an authorized person to access the box."

The postmaster walked away from the desk and was gone for a few minutes. Frank felt encouraged knowing that someone other than the person who opened the P.O. Box could pick up the mail. He felt certain he'd be listed.

The man returned and said, "I'm sorry, but we haven't anything listed under that name."

Frank suddenly felt nauseous. He couldn't believe he was wrong. He turned away with a look of defeat and despair. He looked like a beaten man as he headed toward the exit of the post office. Just before reaching the door he stopped and turned.

He called out to the postmaster, "Would it be possible to tell me the name associated with box 212?"

"I'll be damned. Did you say P.O. Box 212?"

"Yes, why do you ask?"

"I'd forgotten all about it, until you just jogged my memory. A few years back a guy called the post office and asked for that specific box. It was already rented. Now here's the funny part, he asked if I'd write out a note and put it inside. He said he'd pay me for my time. I told him that was unnecessary...I'd do it out of courtesy. So I wrote down what he wanted. He offered to pay the person renting the box ten thousand dollars if he'd give it up. He claimed he was superstitious. I just thought he was crazy. Hey, but folks can do what they want with their money. Obviously, the customer gave up his P.O. Box for another. Anyway, I think the guy's name was James. I can't remember his last name, but I'll check."

Frank was bursting with anticipation. The postmaster returned with an even more perplexed look on his face.

"This just keeps getting stranger and stranger. Agent Sorello, you're listed as an authorized person with access to the box. Here's the key."

Frank ran over and opened it up. There was a letter inside. It had a recent postmark, dated one week earlier. He ripped it open and began to read.

Call me at this number. If you're not too late, I'll give you instructions as to where you'll find Sarah. Best of luck.

Yours truly,

James Carlson

CHAPTER 62

JAMES HAD JUST FINISHED EATING HIS BREAKFAST AND WAS PREPARING to head back down into the basement. It was 9:45 in the morning and he began to wonder if he would need to implement his secondary plan. Today was Frank's deadline and if Sorello didn't find the note, before 5:00 p.m., the Newington Post Office would close. Then it would be too late. This would force James into deviating from his current course of action. He hated the thought, because it would require several months of additional preparation. He had worked very long for this day to happen.

James began to evaluate the clarity of his previous actions and assessed the potential likelihood of Frank failing. He kept coming to the same conclusion. He wouldn't be disappointed. James believed he'd leaked out just enough information, so that Frank would figure out where to look.

He knew without additional pieces of the puzzle falling into place, it would have been nearly impossible for anyone to put it all together...unless their genius was unsurpassed, like his own. But by highlighting the trail, it would be easier for the hunter to follow.

James felt satisfied, as he approached his live bait.

"Hello, Sarah. I see you're awake. I've brought you a bagel and a cup of coffee."

"Morning," she replied.

"It seems I've forgotten my manners, again. Let me untie you and then you can enjoy your breakfast. I sincerely hope it won't be your last."

Sarah was aware she had less than twenty-four hours and what that meant. James held the serrated knife in his hand, almost as a visual reminder. Everything with him had a purpose.

Sarah wouldn't give him the satisfaction of showing fear. She began to eat the bagel and then James' cell phone rang. She noticed how quickly the smile formed on her captor's lips.

"It seems your dashing hero has found his golden ticket. Good for you, Sarah. It appears…this won't be your last meal after all."

A rush of adrenaline coursed through Sarah's veins. The excitement of knowing Frank had made it this far, provided her with hope. At the same time, her trained listening skills achieved the opposite effect. Her body was in a state of chemical crossfire. Cortisol was secreted by her adrenal glands, all because her body's stress hormone reacted to one word…"appears." Sarah intellectually reasoned, if James were really planning to release her, he wouldn't have used that particular word. Its meaning carried with it a degree of ambiguity. James' intelligence was seemingly off the charts and everything he said was carefully chosen. Sarah thought he should've simply said, "This won't be your last meal after all." She hoped her logic was just an overreaction and listened to the ensuing conversation.

"Congratulations, Frank. I'd hoped you'd be a worthy opponent."

"I made my deadline, James," he responded with an edge, "May I speak to Sarah?"

"Patience, my friend, you still have to get here. I've waited a long, long time and now so should you. You'll get to speak with Sarah soon. Afterwards, I'll provide you with directions as to my location, but with a non-negotiable arrival time. By the way, I'm glad you finally know my name. I was beginning to think you didn't care."

"Your wife and friends deserved better. I'm sorry I couldn't have saved them. But as I've said before…if you need to blame me for that, fine. I'll do whatever it takes, including giving you my life…if that's what you need. But only, if I'm assured Sarah will be let go."

"Are you implying that I might be dishonorable?"

"I just can't come up with a scenario, where you'll let us walk away. Once I have Sarah safe, what's to stop me from calling every asset I have at my disposal, to prevent you from escaping? I'm sure you've considered that possibility. If I remember correctly from the news, you're a Princeton graduate."

"Nice memory, Frank. But before I answer your question, I'd like to thank you. I appreciate your heartfelt sympathy for my loss. However, I must say I'm still a little upset. You didn't extend a condolence to my parents."

Frank was momentarily caught off guard. When he'd seen the name, James Carlson, on the letter at the post office, it all began making sense. It triggered memories of media stories, regarding the quarterback of Princeton University, being the lone survivor of a robbery with multiple fatalities. This had been Frank's case and apparently was at the center of James' personal vendetta. But now Frank realized there was more to it. He tried to reference what James was talking about, but was at a loss.

"How easily you've forgotten? Every ending, once had a beginning, mine started as a little boy in Hollywood."

It was like a bolt of lightning struck Frank. He shuddered; James was the eight year old boy that survived "The Tinseltown Strangler." It gave him the answer to a question that had always bothered him. Why had Juliette been the only person strangled by "The Magician"? Apparently James had wanted to personalize her murder because of his own loss. Frank hoped he could use this new piece of information to help negotiate Sarah's release.

"There was nothing I could have done. I wasn't even involved on the case at the time of your parent's murder. You've killed my first wife. You get me next. We're even. As long as you let Sarah go. Game over. Isn't that enough?"

"Yes it is, but apparently you still don't trust that I'll live up to my end of the bargain. Maybe this will allay the concerns you expressed earlier, as to a scenario, where I'd let her go. I've prepared a contingency to prevent you from foolishly calling in the cavalry."

"What if this is just another trap?"

"In any well played chess game, there are always traps. I assume with your intellect, you fancy yourself an advanced player. I've already played my opening, the first set of murders. During my mid-game, I released my novels for your reading pleasure. The end game began when I chose to resurface. So let me answer your question with another. Tell me Frank, what usually happens when two highly skilled players engage in a confrontation? Tell me what pieces usually come out to play? Come on Frank, what's the objective of the game?"

"To kill the other king."

"I'm looking forward to it."

"You're on! Now let me talk to Sarah."

A second later she was on the phone, but once again only briefly. Afterwards, James provided his address, further instructions and the allotted time slot to arrive. Midnight.

Frank decided he would utilize his time and prepare for the confrontation. Before heading to the wealthiest area along the Potomac River, he went to a gun shop for more ammunition and some other items. Then he stopped at a hunting store along the way and purchased outdoor, camouflage gear. He wasn't going to go down without a fight.

CHAPTER 63

JAMES BEGAN HIS OWN FINAL PREPARATIONS. HE RAISED THE KNIFE
up, and with the serrated edge he sliced into his own finger. It began
to bleed and he let the blood drip on the floor, in front of Sarah.

"I hope I have your attention."

She nodded, this time her subservience was real.

"If you obey me, I'm not going to hurt you. Do you understand?"

She nodded again, as tears flowed down her face.

"Do you need to use the bathroom? If you do, I suggest you tell
me. I'm going to tie you up until Frank arrives, but that won't be
until late this evening. That's when I've scheduled our little date."

"Yes."

Just like the day before, James led her to the bathroom. When
she was finished, she followed all his instructions. Once she was
tied to the chair, he walked away. He was gone for a few minutes
and then returned, holding some type of bulky jacket. When she
noticed the wires on it, her fear multiplied.

"What's that for?" She cried out.

"It's my insurance, Sarah. I need to make sure Frank follows my
every order. It's a bomb, which will blow you to pieces if he doesn't
comply. I have a remote detonator and any attempt to remove it
will be very detrimental to your health. Unless Frank was ever on
the bomb squad, you won't have much of a chance to survive if he
tries to disarm it. There's a host of trip wires and if the jacket's
removed once I turn the bomb on..." his voice trailed off, smirking
he raised up his hands, leaving the rest to her imagination.

"I thought you said you were honorable. How is there honor, in not giving someone a chance?"

"Who said I'm not giving you both a chance. If Frank follows my rules of engagement, you'll live...and contrary to what you might believe, I'm giving him a chance, too. I'm going to ask him to follow me onto the field of battle. Of course, I'll have the advantage of fighting on my own turf. If he's better than me, then that won't matter. After all, the North defeated the South here. That's certainly honorable. Wouldn't you agree?"

Sarah sat silent as James placed the jacket upon her. Without saying anything more, he walked to a door that he'd never used in her presence. He took out a key and opened it. A second later he was gone.

James walked down the hallway and headed directly to the stairway. He picked up the rifle with the night vision scope that was leaning against the wall. It was time for target practice as he headed outside. His property was large enough that he wouldn't break the state's gun laws, by firing across a road or right of way. Besides, on all the acres of land that his home sat on, no one would even hear it. The woods would muffle most of the noise.

With his innate hand and eye coordination, James was a natural with a rifle. He'd also spent many hours practicing and had the expertise of a military sniper. He surveyed the land for the hundredth time, looking at the expanse of his property. Carefully he studied the tree lines and the areas that provided cover. He noted the open and exposed sections as well, while walking down toward his boat house. It served as a trial run in his mind. He imagined how he would lead Frank to him and bring this chapter of his life to a close. Destiny was about to show up at his doorstep.

When James got down to his private dock, he placed the rifle down next to a tree. He walked inside the boat house and climbed into his forty-six foot, 1300 horsepower, cigarette boat. He fired up the twin-turbocharged engines and the loud thrush of the speed boat sounded. It was capable of speeds in excess of a hundred miles an hour. James took it out of its protective environment and instead of racing it down the river, he parked it just outside the boat house doors. That was the location of the fuel pump. Once he topped it off with gasoline, James left the eight hundred thousand dollar boat outside. He wanted everything ready for tonight, so he walked over to the various blasting agents he'd set up. They were a mixture of Ammonium Nitrate and Fuel Oil (ANFO). James added potassium chlorate to sensitize the explosive, making the mixture susceptible to detonation with a supersonic bullet.

He walked back over to the tree where he'd placed the rifle and picked it up. He got into his shooting position and lined up the targets he'd left on his lawn. James fired a round and a can placed fifty yards away, danced off into the distance. The next several shots hit targets that were progressively further away. The last one was approximately one hundred fifty yards from where James was perched. There was a tiny sonic boom, as the rifle recoiled. James felt satisfied and walked back in the direction of the house. He stopped a few feet from his last target and then approached the damaged 16" x 20" photograph. Frank Sorello had a hole in the middle of his forehead.

James went back inside and prepared lunch.

CHAPTER 64

ABOUT TEN MINUTES BEFORE HIS SCHEDULED ARRIVAL, FRANK SAT parked outside the gates to the massive property. Large bushes obscured the giant stone wall running its entire length. But they might as well have been invisible, because Frank wouldn't dare risk Sarah's life. James had instructed him to wait and the maniac had proven he should be taken very seriously. Frank wondered, would he be able to save the woman he loved? Never in his life had he faced someone that truly scared him, until now. His body shuddered. This psychopath had stayed one step ahead from the very beginning. He killed Juliette and now Sarah faced the same fate. It was up to him to prevent it, but doubts ran rampant. James Carlson was a pure genius, intent on making him suffer. So far he had succeeded.

Frank stared at the camera next to the intercom button. Any minute he'd be hearing his tormentor's voice. Sorello fought the urge to climb the barrier and enter James' lair. But he'd been warned about the high level security system. Without a full team assigned to disable it, sneaking onto the property wasn't an option.

As Sorello sat paralyzed outside, James crouched down next to Sarah. She couldn't even make eye contact and found it hard to breathe. Her fear was all encompassing.

"I'll be going soon. Remember everything I've told you. This game involves only Frank and me. Goodbye, Sarah."

Without saying another word, he left. Tears streamed down her face, thinking that "Evil" had just left the room. Trembling, Sarah began praying to God...hoping he was listening.

At exactly midnight, James' voice came over the intercom. He stood at the base of the stairs to the rear entrance of his property.

"It's time, Frank. Remember to follow your instructions and you'll find Sarah. She'll tell you what to do next, although she did seem to have trouble concentrating. I wish you good luck."

The gates swung open and Frank raced down the winding driveway. He saw a large house and suddenly braked. But even before his car stopped, he hit the gas pedal and nearly spun out. Frank realized it was only a large guest cottage. His eyes had caught sight of the huge mansion sitting atop the crest of a rolling hill. The few lights that were on operated as a beacon to the woman he knew was inside.

Frank leapt from the car and sprinted into the house. Hopefully Sarah was still alive. He ran through the grand foyer, turning left into an expansive hallway. After passing numerous rooms he saw the floor to ceiling window of the huge den. The stairs leading to the basement were located in this room. He raced down the steps and saw her.

She was alive, but Frank felt utter panic. Sarah was strapped to an armchair. A vest with straps and wires surrounded her. She was a living bomb.

He wanted to rip it off her, but knew that would be a mistake.

"Sarah, I'm going to get you out of this. He wants me. Otherwise, you'd already be dead right now."

Frank saw the terror on her face. She tried to speak, but no words came out. Sarah just kept shaking. Frank put his arms gingerly around her, careful not to dislodge any trip wires. He had to get her to speak. James made it clear that he was to follow whatever instructions he'd passed on to Sarah. It was their only chance.

Frank spoke slowly, "Look me in the eyes. We're going to be alright. I promise I'll kill him, but I need your help. Sarah, what did he say?"

She struggled to speak and started hyperventilating.

"You can do it. I'm right here."

"He's waiting outside to kill you," she said barely above a whisper.

"That's not going to happen. Tell me what he wants."

"He said he has a remote detonator and you need to get it before the deadline."

Frank glanced at his watch. It was 12:07 a.m. He had eighty-nine minutes.

"Is that all of it?"

"Yes."

"Which way did he go?"

Sarah tilted her head in the direction that James had exited, "Through the door over there."

"I will be back for you," as he looked her in the eyes and said emphatically, "believe me, Sarah."

Frank kissed her and then ran toward the door with his gun drawn. As soon as he entered the hallway he felt the cool breeze of the night. The door at the top of the stairwell, directly up ahead had been left open. When Frank was at the edge of the doorway, he cautiously glanced outside, leaving his body sheltered inside. The night sky was pitch black and Frank felt lucky. Since James had the advantage of knowing the property, the darkness Frank surmised would help mitigate the advantage. He needed to be silent to not give up his position.

The man waiting for him was a crazed genius. Frank knew that James could have killed Sarah or him by just detonating the bomb. He inferred from their conversations that this was all some deadly game and James was forcing him to play. The constant chess references indicated the board had now been set and it was his opening move. The time had come.

Frank turned out the light switch near the top of the staircase. He waited until his own eyes had the opportunity to adjust to the blackness outside. After a minute, he scanned the immediate area. There were no noises to be heard and nothing was in sight but a grouping of trees a few feet away.

Frank thought, "It's now or never."

He took a deep breath and then ran for the first tree. The dry leaves crackled underneath his feet and Frank cursed internally. If James were nearby, his position would have been exposed. Frank backed up against the tree. When he felt the bullet proof vest touch the bark he paused and listened again. He thought he'd heard a noise off in the distance and moved slowly among the other trees, heading in that direction. Frank took cover all along the way. He was glad he wore his camouflage gear, because he further blended in with his surroundings.

James sat watching down near the boat house through the night scope of his high powered rifle. His eyes weren't focused on Frank. Instead, they were trained on the large oak tree that had been the focal point of his long range shooting. The photograph that formerly hung on it had been removed. Its crumpled remains were on the desktop in his study, right next to the plastic bags containing his foster parents' nails.

James knew Frank would eventually make his way to that location. Once he exited the tree grouping near the house, there was at least thirty yards of open field. The old and massive oak tree was the next obvious cover point. James had played it all out beforehand, every move had been anticipated. Frank would certainly head there, all the while being led to the boat house.

Frank held cover behind the last tree in the grouping and glanced at his watch. It was now 12:26 a.m. He still had seventy minutes left. Frank waited, listening for a sound. He decided he would have to make a run for it soon. There was a fairly large open area; he needed to cross, if he were to advance. It would be dangerous, but he saw no other option. This had been the direction of the only noise he'd heard. He still had time, but it was limited and every second counted.

When he heard another faint noise further off in the distance he made up his mind. It seemed to come from far beyond the tree he was set on reaching. Sensing he was being led into a kill zone, Frank briefly hesitated. But his hesitation was short lived. He knew the only chance at saving Sarah was to move forward.

"Here goes," he said to himself.

Frank sprinted across the open field and just as he approached the tree, there was the report of a large caliber rifle. He felt the painful sting, as blood oozed from the wound on his leg. James could have killed him, but wanted to drag out the game. Another shot rang out, as Frank saw the trace fire, narrowly pass by his face. He dove toward the base of the tree, while firing his own gun blindly in the direction of the muzzle flash.

Frank crouched down with his back against the oak tree. He glanced at the blood that was flowing profusely from his right thigh. He reached into his jacket and took out his medic pack. He had been prepared for the possibility of being shot. Frank didn't want to bleed out or lose consciousness. He had to stay alert to save Sarah, because nothing else mattered. Frank applied the clotting agent to the wound and then wrapped the compression bandage tightly around his leg to stem the blood loss.

Satisfied, he began to assess his situation. Frank made the assumption he was dealing with an expert marksman and worse yet, that man had a night scope. The advantage of darkness had actually shifted to James. Frank wished he had similar rifle skills, because he would have come equipped. Instead, all he had was his handgun and two full magazines. He had incorrectly anticipated any shooting was likely to come in closed quarters. The flash bang he carried would be of no real use, unless he got up close to James. There had been no basis to expect for James to have the skills of a sniper, because every victim had been killed with a knife. Yet, Frank always prepared for the unexpected. He had learned over the years that predictability in a fight could be a death sentence.

Frank sat and thought, "Time to unleash my own surprise, motherfucker."

He reached into the inner pockets of his jacket and pulled out the flares. The bright light would neutralize his opponent's edge and temporarily blind him from using his night vision equipment, unless it was Gen III. If that was the case, then it would be all over because the auto dim feature would override a sudden exposure to bright light.

Frank snuck a quick look out from behind the tree. He needed to cross another large open area, before he could reach the next cover point. There were several smaller trees off to his right. It wasn't a direct line to where he needed to go, but it was more important to be smart in his movements. Frank calculated that was the area he was expected to move towards. Acting rashly, would surely get him killed.

He remembered what James had said to him, "there are always traps in a good chess game."

Frank figured this was it. He was in the middle of two open areas. There was nothing but field, both ahead and behind. Time was ticking on Sarah's life. So far, at least James had honored his promise. She was thankfully still alive.

Frank estimated that his chance of making it to cover was very slim, but he would die trying. He had no fear, just steeled determination. He was prepared to do whatever it took and he assumed that would mean, being shot again. He just had to make sure it wasn't a kill shot, by doing the unexpected.

Frank had a basic idea of where the gunfire had originated. While sprinting toward the tree that he now hid behind, he'd noticed the outline of a smaller structure near where he saw the muzzle flash. It was somewhere down near the waterline, near what appeared to be a much larger group of trees. Frank made the assumption it was some type of boat house. He couldn't be sure because of the sheer darkness of the night. There were no stars to be seen and storm clouds shaded the moonlight. The threat of a bullet also made for hasty observations.

Yet, the more Frank thought about it, he was certain it was a boat house. In the event of being trapped, James would have a method to escape. If the police were called in to establish a blockade, the river would be more difficult to contain. Especially, if James had a fast boat and based upon his obvious wealth; Frank was sure that would turn out to be the case. James probably had a planned escape route, with a car waiting somewhere across the river. Frank thought that would make the most sense.

Again, he glanced at his watch. The time had come for him to execute his own plan. Frank decided he would shoot the flare in the general area of where he'd seen the muzzle flash. Then he would begin firing rounds in the direction of where the gunfire originated, the very second he left shelter. The open field ahead was almost fifty yards and a near certain death trap. He wouldn't stop shooting until he reached the trees or found himself dead in the process.

While Frank had taken cover, James had dropped further back into the forest that lay directly behind him. When he found the bipod he'd set up earlier in the day, he stopped and assumed a sniper position. There was only one real sightline, but it was perfect. James looked through the Mil-Dot of his telescopic sighting and adjusted his sight angle one MOA. The wind had picked up slightly.

He'd anticipated what Frank was planning based upon the man's current predicament. The coming gunfire would be concentrated into the area that he'd just vacated. James visualized exactly how it was all going to play out.

At the moment of engagement his muzzle flash would appear to be coming from the same area. Under the hail of gunfire and with the distance separating them, pinpointing his location would be extremely difficult. James waited.

It was everything he'd dreamed about for so long. Killing his foster parents had allowed some of his rage to boil over and now the one man that had become a symbol of his hatred was here. Frank Sorello, as far as he was concerned, was responsible for the murders of everyone he loved. His inability to prevent their deaths was the same as doing it himself. The man was revered for his skills at stopping monsters, so he'd put it to a test. James felt calm, confident in knowing that Sorello was not his equal. He began to visualize how he would prolong the man's suffering, incapacitating Frank by shooting his kneecaps and then his arms, leaving him defenseless. Once that was accomplished he would walk over and remove the most prized finger nails of all. James knew he wouldn't send these to the Bureau in a baggie. They would be kept as a trophy to remember the battle, commemorating the conquest over his long time foe.

Suddenly, it began but not how James had anticipated. While he was looking through the night scope, a flare blinded him and impacted his ability to see. Gunfire sounded and James was temporarily disoriented. Frank broke his cover, moving as quickly as possible.

The chess game had reached its end point. King was taking on king. All the other pieces had fulfilled their roles. Frank ran in a crouch, firing relentlessly. Shot after shot rang out in the night, as he desperately ran straight ahead.

Although, James had lost sight of Frank, he fired several shots in the area where he'd expected the man to run, to the right toward the cover of trees. Sorello dove to the ground upon hearing the rifle's report. He immediately got back up and resumed firing. Bullets were ringing about all around James. For the first time ever he felt a moment of panic, feeling that the tables had somehow turned. It all seemed incomprehensible. No one had ever bested him in anything and he couldn't think clearly.

With bullets flying all about, James made the decision to fight another day. He couldn't fathom the possibility of losing. Sorello was too dangerous to allow any closer. Originally, he was going to wait for Frank to enter his kill zone, down near the boathouse, but that was when he had him under control, in his rifle sights. Now the man he'd underestimated was getting too close for comfort. James knew it would take too long to get him back within his night scope, every second mattered, so he took quick aim and fired.

Suddenly, there was an ear deafening explosion. Flames shot upward and lit up the field. Frank could see the boat house was on fire. The smoke started to make it difficult to see. Although he wasn't sure what had just happened, he decided this was his best opportunity. Instead of continuing toward his immediate cover, Frank sprinted directly toward the heat of the explosion. As he got closer, he could see the docks aflame and then another series of explosions followed. A large speed boat disintegrated as it blew apart.

The inferno made it impossible to get closer. If James were in there it would be impossible to reach him. He needed to get that detonator. So he stood in plain sight, hoping to draw another round of gunfire. He'd likely die, but needed to find his assailant. Perhaps the hazy smoke would cause his adversary to miss hitting a vital organ. The shot never came.

Frank looked at his watch. He had less than ten minutes to go before the deadline. He sprinted back toward the main house and Sarah.

He thought, "I won't let her die alone."

He raced back down the stairs and into the room where she was bound. Sarah turned her head, as she heard the footsteps.

"Oh my God, Frank...it's you," she cried out.

"I love you, Sarah," as he knelt down beside her.

"Did you kill him? I heard a huge explosion. What happened?"

Frank shook his head, with a look of desperation, tears formed in his eyes.

"I couldn't find him. I don't have the detonator. I'm so sorry."

They both glanced down at the jacket, it was still armed. Sarah tried to force a smile.

"It's going to be okay," although she didn't believe it.

It was 1:31 a.m. Five minutes remained.

Sarah pleaded, "Please go, honey. You did all you could do. Please..." She began to weep.

Frank sat resolute, ignoring her plea. Another minute passed. They looked into each other's eyes and conveyed the same unspoken message.

CHAPTER 65

THE SOUND OF FIRE TRUCKS AND SIRENS GOT CLOSER. THE FEROCITY of the multiple explosions had woken the only neighbors within earshot. They lived at least a half a mile away on the other side of the riverbank. The billowing smoke was the only thing they could see from the balcony of their bedroom. They'd placed a call immediately.

A procession of flashing lights rushed up the long driveway. The fireman onboard could see that the fire was off in the distance, far away from the mansion on the hillside. They attempted to gain closer access to the fire, but were thwarted by nature's obstacles. Firemen began jumping from the vehicle. They ran toward the blaze to check if any people were in danger.

Inside of the house, Frank was talking on the phone with the bomb squad. The deadline had come and gone without fanfare. It was 1:45 in the morning, but until the bomb was diffused, Sarah's life remained in peril.

Several minutes later, he heard police race into the house.

Frank called out, "Federal Agent...downstairs," holding his badge in plain sight.

The police came into the room with their guns drawn. Even though they'd been informed of the situation by their commander, the officers asked Frank to raise his hands in the air. After checking his identification, they let him know the bomb squad was minutes away. After Frank filled them in on the details of what occurred, the officer in charge, made some phone calls. Quickly, a dragnet was established. Until James' body could be found, everyone operated under the presumption that he was still alive. In calculating the elapsed time since the explosion, they felt their search attempts might be futile. Regardless, roadblocks were established in the area, blocking off all major exit points within a twenty-five mile radius.

The bomb squad arrived, and had everyone clear the area. Frank tried resisting, but officers dragged him away. The explosives expert dressed in protective gear carefully approached Sarah. After a few minutes of inspecting the device he determined it was a "dummy." He cut her free and removed the jacket. Sarah tried to stand and nearly fell. The officer reached out and steadied her. The stress had taken its toll on her body.

As she walked through the door leading outside, Frank ran over. He wrapped his arms around her and she wept while her body began to tremor. Somehow they had survived.

CHAPTER 66

THE FOLLOWING DAY, AFTER THE FIRE WAS PUT OUT, A BODY WAS discovered in the ashes. The inferno had left the body charred beyond all recognition. A wedding ring was removed from the corpse. The remains were taken to the coroner's office for an autopsy, along with the bodies of Paul and Karen Cortland.

A preliminary analysis of the crime scene helped to formulate a basic working theory of what had gone down the night before. After analyzing the remains of the ANFO blasting devices it was assumed that a stray bullet had struck one and this led to the blasts. When they found the rifle setup on the bipod in the woods and determined its sightline, they deduced James decided to escape when Frank hadn't gone into that area to the right. They figured he'd been blinded by the flare, effectively losing sight of Sorrello and made his way toward the speed boat. After all, the body had been found on the ground a few feet away. The blasting devices were seen as a last line of defense to help in an escape, which they felt ironically backfired.

A few days later, a determination was made. It was the body of James Carlson.

Dental records confirmed it was him. The coroner also corroborated that the sex, age and height of the deceased was consistent with what was on record. Finally, a photograph from James' wedding had been found. The wedding ring taken from the body matched the one in the picture.

Official statements were taken from both Frank and Sarah. Shortly after, they left for Hawaii. The planned ceremony and reception were cancelled. There were no set plans to return, but when they did they would celebrate with those they loved. For now, they just wanted to be alone with one another. Far away from the painful memories left behind on the Potomac.

Law enforcement agencies continued collecting evidence. Mortgages, deeds and anything tied to Mr. Carlson were analyzed. This resulted in the discovery of another victim. The body of Paul Kimmel, his former attorney, was found buried in the Poconos. It was located on a formerly owned property of the serial killer.

Forensic teams scoured through the mounds of evidence. The final two plastic baggies containing nails from his foster parents were taken from James' study. The filing cabinet it sat upon provided the link to the most critical evidence. Amid the numerous folders were bank records, legal documents and paid bills. Several receipts showed work done at a local dentist's office. It was there that they compared dental records to the skeletal remains.

In a locked storage closet, there was a vault. Inside of it was the story of another life, before a serial killer was born. Princeton memorabilia was scattered about. A framed photograph showed the face of a smiling little boy. He was in the arms of Amy and Sam Carlson, his biological parents.

There were no photos of his foster parents.

Pictures of Marty and Grace had been carefully placed in the shrine. There was another photograph showing James smiling proudly after defeating Giovanni Luca, the chess grandmaster.

However, one thing stood out above it all. Maria's wedding ring was encased in a crystalline glass. It sat upon their wedding album wrapped in her veil.

CHAPTER 67

SEVERAL WEEKS LATER, BETH DECIDED TO GIVE FRANK A CALL. SHE planned on making it brief, because she didn't want to disturb his prolonged honeymoon. He hadn't yet returned from the island of Oahu with his bride.

He didn't pick up and she figured just as well. She left a message.

"Frank, I hope you and Sarah are laying on a beach somewhere soaking up the sun. You both deserve it. I just wanted to say the case is officially closed and most importantly...Justin Logan has been released from prison and cleared of all charges. You saved him...and a lot of others," and she hung up.

CHAPTER 68

JILL SANTOS WAS SITTING IN HER OFFICE WHEN HER ASSISTANT knocked on her door.

"Come in."

"Jill, a manuscript arrived today in a box. It had no return address. The note attached implied there was some relationship to you and the author."

Curiously, Jill took the box from her assistant.

"Thanks, Allie."

She glanced at the note first. It was addressed to her pet nickname, "Vegas Girl." Very few people knew that information because the story behind it was quite personal. One night over drinks she'd shared the lurid details with her assistant. The only other information on it was, "I think you'll enjoy this."

The title of the novel was "The Resurrection."

EPILOGUE

SEVERAL MONTHS LATER, FRANK AND SARAH RETURNED HOME TO Spring Lake. They both felt ready to begin moving forward with life. It was time to let go of the past and look to the future. So once they were settled in, they decided to have their long delayed wedding celebration. Sarah picked a date and sent out invitations.

On the day of the bash, Frank and Sarah partied as if there wasn't a care in the world. All the guests stayed until the wee hours, letting go of their responsibilities and just having fun.

The following morning a U.P.S. driver rang their doorbell and left a package outside. Frank took it inside, figuring it was another gift.

Sarah walked over and said, "Ooh, what's that?"

"Let's find out."

Inside was a beautifully handcrafted chess set with a note attached.

Sorry, I couldn't have been part of your celebration. I hope you enjoyed your vacation and my gift. Our first game was played to a draw, kudos. Maybe, our next will have an actual winner. Till next time.

It was signed, J.C.

(aka "The Magician")

The End

CPSIA information can be obtained
at www.ICGtesting.com
Printed in the USA
FFOW04n0848171014
8137FF